PRETTY MONSTER

JILL SOMERS

D1444051

ISBN: 9781980540892

DEDICATION

To my family. You are my superpower.

PROLOGUE

It was late—much later than a girl her age was supposed to be awake. She had intended to keep running, miles and miles farther, away from that strange city and that strange state, back to her little bed in her little trailer in her little town in New Jersey. But it was cold, and she was tired, and she didn't live in that little home any more. She didn't live anywhere.

The steps were cold and hard, but the area was well concealed by the shadowy awning above her. No one would bother her, she told herself. Not there, at the Bank of America building, in the middle of the night. Regular people got their money in the daytime.

But slowly, and then all at once, they emerged. Raised voices, then yelling, then screaming.

Did you see it?

Is it true?

Where do we go?

What do we do?

And then, the alarms. Piercing. Deafening. *Emergency. Evacuate. Leave everything behind.*

This is not a drill.

She tried to be as still as a statue as they came past her. Most of them paid her no heed, far too intent on their own survival. But the few who did frightened her the most.

So she pulled out her fuzzy pink blanket, the last thing her mother had given her, wrapped herself in it, and hid from the world.

Minutes passed. Maybe hours. The temperature grew colder. The screams grew louder. The people near her became the people *on* her, and she was being trampled, kicked. She stayed still, frozen, firmly wrapped up in her blanket, not even her face exposed.

And then, a voice.

"Hey."

Her eyes widened beneath the blanket, and she clutched it even tighter, her breath hot as it had nowhere to escape.

"Hey," the voice said again. It was a male voice. Soft, serene. Almost mystical; unlike anything she had ever heard. "Please don't be afraid of me."

She *was* afraid; she was afraid of everything. But the trampling had stopped, and in that moment somehow things were better, and she couldn't help but hope that it was because of him.

She peeked out from the blanket, just enough to make out his face.

His face... What was he? He was young, but still a man—or was he a man at all? Far too beautiful... His eyes seemed to emit an entire light of their own, a golden one, flickering like fire.... His bright, translucent skin was equally vibrant, contrasting sharply with his thick, golden-brown mane of hair. He was inhuman; he was something else entirely.

"You can trust me," he whispered, and he held out his hand.

She hesitated. She had a feeling she would always hesitate. In the eight years she had lived, everyone and everything around her had taught her to.

But then she took it.

And as the bright light came and swallowed up the city, at least she was not alone.

1. CROWLEY

Quinn knew from the moment she walked into Crowley Enterprises that she didn't have much time. There were three different receptionists at three different help desks, and they all looked up at her as soon as she walked in. One look at her long, raven-colored hair, vibrant, silvery eyes, and translucent skin was all it took to know exactly who she was and what she was there for.

She could tell from his heavy breathing that Kurt Rhodes, the sixteen-year-old, hundred-pound boy next to her, was thinking the same thing.

But it wasn't the first time she had been recognized, and it wouldn't be the last. *I've survived this long,* she mused, pressing forward.

Two females at the desks, one male. The choice was clear.

"Keep an eye on the other two," she murmured to Kurt. "Any phones or silent alarms, come tell me. Immediately."

Kurt gave a meek nod, baby-blond hair falling into his cloudy blue eyes, and took a single step toward the women. Taking a slow, deep breath, Quinn made her way toward the man.

Sizing him up, she decided he wasn't unlike Kurt. An easy enough target. Skinny; nerdy. Glasses that needed to be pushed an inch up his nose bridge. Nearly drooling at the sight of her.

"Hello," she said to the young man, and his eyes bulged.

"You're… you're…" He lifted a finger and pointed behind her, and she didn't have to look to know why: her face was all over the flat screens in the lobby. Good Morning America.

They really didn't have much time.

"I need to meet with Mr. Crowley," she said, voice even and level. Direct eye contact. When her eyes were on them, they never stood a chance.

"Mr. Crowley? But he's—you would need—weeks in advance—"

"It's urgent business," she interrupted, starting to lose her cool. Kurt was heading toward her, and she knew why. "He'll make time for me." She glued her eyes to his on the final line, silvery gaze as electrifying as it always was. She knew the answer before he gave it to her.

"Of course. Come with me."

She glanced backwards at Kurt, nodding at him to come with her. He shuffled into step behind her, following her and the young man toward the elevators, sweat dripping down his temple.

"They know," Kurt whispered, glancing back toward the other two receptionists. "They were pulling out their phones. We should turn back."

"I don't care," she said sharply, not bothering to keep her voice down. "Let them come. It'll be me against them, and I always win."

Kurt swallowed. She knew what he was thinking. She stepped behind the young man onto the elevator and turned back to face Kurt, locking eyes with him. But it meant something different with him. She didn't want to manipulate Kurt. She only wanted to help him.

"If I win, you win. I would never let anything happen to you."

She could tell from the look in his eyes that her words meant more to him than she had intended, and it was with a heavy heart that she looked away from him, not wanting to tease ideas back into his head that she had been trying to put to rest for months. She focused her energy back toward the young man, who had punched the button for the top floor and was looking nervously over at her.

A sense of guilt washed over her as the floors ticked by and she listened to the overwhelmingly rapid heartbeat of the poor young man she had only just met. He was no doubt some mixture of terrified and enraptured, as if he were about to begin a game of Russian roulette.

"Hey," she said softly to him, meeting his gaze one last time. "You're going to be okay."

Somehow, he seemed to believe her.

The *ding* of the elevator snapped her out of her daze, and she refocused her attention to the floor in front of her: Cole Crowley's executive suite.

She knew instantly that something was wrong.

For starters, both the receptionist at the front desk and the security guard standing next to her were females. This wasn't terrible news for Quinn, whose compulsion ability, though stronger on those attracted to women, worked on anyone. But it was a sign—a sign that someone had been expecting her.

You're just paranoid, she told herself. How many times had she suspected conspiracies against her? How many times had she refused to trust the people around her—even Kurt? *You're fine.*

"Miss Harper," said the receptionist, smiling politely at her. Quinn could tell by the receptionist's shaky smile that the calmness in her voice was an act. She knew who Quinn was.

But how does she know my real name?

"Mr. Crowley has been expecting you," the receptionist continued, standing up. "Right this way."

Quinn stiffened, turning to look at Kurt with wide eyes. There was no reason for Crowley to know they were coming. Had the word gotten up that quickly from downstairs? Had Kurt joined the ranks of the dozens of people in her life who had betrayed her?

Why would he betray you? she asked herself urgently. *You're doing this for him.*

"Quinn," Kurt whispered to her, sounding terrified. He hadn't betrayed her; she hated herself for even thinking it. "This is bad. We should turn back."

"It's too late." She did her best to give him a reassuring smile. "Come on."

Crowley's enormous office building had always disgusted Quinn. It stuck out like a sore thumb, climbing higher and higher into the Manhattan skyline as everything around it decayed. But Crowley's personal office—the room the receptionist led them to—was something else entirely. It was nauseatingly ornate, from the sculpted glass and marble to the floor-to-ceiling window overlooking the forgotten city below it.

Everything was white, she noticed; even Crowley himself was wearing white.

As was the bodyguard next to him. Male.

"I couldn't resist," Crowley said to her, gesturing to the massive television behind him, which was showing the same news story that had been playing downstairs. "They were running a Siren special." He smiled a coy smile, flashing too-white teeth. Everything about him was too much: his shiny, silver hair; his fit, trim physique; his sharp, birdlike black eyes. She instantly felt shivers run down her spine.

"That's alright," she said, forcing her voice to feign collection. "I was having a good hair day."

Crowley laughed out loud, and it shook her. He was too comfortable. Too unafraid. What was he thinking? Hadn't he read the articles, seen the segments? Didn't he know what she was capable of?

"Do you like the place?" he asked her, gesturing to his office. "We've got our work cut out for us, but we've certainly made some improvements these last few years."

"Interesting, isn't it?" she asked him through gritted teeth. "How the rest of the country has barely begun to recover from the worst depression in its history, and yet here you are, basking in your billions?"

He smirked. Not ashamed in the slightest. "I'm a businessman, my dear. Timing is everything. Besides, it's not as if I *caused* the depression. Was it not a resistance of deviants who caused the terror and devastation that led to it?"

She wanted to defend the resistance, a movement she had been too young to be a part of, led by a woman they called Blackout—the one deviant more famous than her. But Blackout was dead, and the resistance had all but been forgotten. Quinn wasn't there to defend its lost cause. The last thing she was going to do was let him stall; it was only a matter of time before whatever made this man as comfortable as he was revealed itself.

"I'm here for the money you stole from Jeff Rhodes," she said, deciding not to waste another second. "Clearly you know who I am and what I can do. Give me the money and you'll never hear from me again."

"I know why you're here. Why do you think I stole the money in the first place?"

Her heart began to pound in a way it hadn't in a very long time.

The building began to shake and rumble, and the thick smell of smoke began to overtake the room. Her doing, of course. But still, Crowley didn't look afraid.

"I could kill you," she hissed at him. "Right here. Right now."

"You probably could. But you won't."

She glared at him, taking a step toward him, and another. Just because she hadn't killed before didn't mean she wouldn't. Especially when it came to someone like him.

"I could make you do whatever I want," she said, locking her eyes onto his, hating every second of it. "I could make you give me the money... right... *now*."

She waited. Waited for him to obey. Waited for him to call up one of his employees to fetch the money from some safe somewhere down below.

But he didn't. He didn't even blink.

"Miss Harper, might I have the pleasure of introducing you to my associate? His real name is Parker Harris, but around here we like to call him Shield."

Quinn's eyes slowly made their way back to the bodyguard, who was smirking at her with eyes almost as hateful as Crowley's. *Shield...*

"Normally," Crowley continued, "I am passionately against the allowance of deviants to coexist in our community, even when they are properly tamed. Shield, of course, is my one exception."

She swallowed. Tried to keep her breathing even. Flames began to lick at the edges of the room. Somehow, Kurt was the only one who seemed to notice them.

How was this possible? How did Crowley have a deviant employee? Sure, he was rich and powerful, but *deviants*, in his control? He was a CEO, not a king.

"He's not stopping me from using all of my abilities," she warned him. "Or hadn't you noticed?"

"Your physical abilities, no." He tapped a finger to his temple. "But you're not getting in here, are you, Miss Harper?"

And before she could send the flames where she really wanted, the elevator gave another jovial *ding* and in came a horde of men and women in the red windbreakers that she recognized all too well: DCA. Deviant Collection Agency.

There was only one place you went once the DCA had you, she mused grimly.

Devil's Island.

That, or Hell.

And that was when she realized it—the reason Crowley was able to have a deviant as a pet—the reason he had lured her here. Crowley wasn't just a CEO. He was the director of the DCA—the man who had led the hunt against her for years.

He may as well have been a king.

How was this possible? How had the leaders of the free world agreed to put a Fortune 500 CEO in charge of hundreds of peoples' lives?

She didn't have to linger on that question long; she already knew the answer. They weren't 'people.' Not to regulars. They were just weapons—weapons that needed to be collected and stowed away. Or, in Shield's case, used to their advantage.

"Kurt," Quinn whispered, her voice reverberating in an entirely unnatural way. She reached for her dear friend and pushed him sharply behind her. She backed slowly toward the wall opposite Crowley, silver eyes flickering from him to the officers and back.

"Quinn," Kurt whispered back, and his voice was so truly human, so soft, that she almost couldn't hear him. "We don't need the money. We should just—"

But she didn't give him the chance to finish. She was afraid, certainly, but giving up? Running away? After all Crowley had taken from Kurt's family? Not a chance.

"You call me the criminal," she spat at Crowley. "Gather the whole militia up against me. But you're the one who's committed the crime here. We're just asking for what you owe Kurt's father. Give us the money, and we'll leave you all in peace."

She found herself hoping, praying, that someone in that room, someone who had just gotten off that elevator, even the deranged deviant bodyguard in front of her, would sympathize with this statement. Maybe they would wonder, *is her story true? Did he steal from the boy?* Would it really surprise any of them? She found it hard to believe anyone could respect or trust a man like Crowley.

"I'm sure you would," Crowley said, crooked smile spreading. "But surely you must realize by now that that's the last thing I want."

Her voice was even when she responded, but her eyes were sad. She had already put together the pieces; she already knew Crowley's plan. Still, the part of her clinging to some semblance of hope asked. "Then what do you want?"

"You."

Kurt reached out, gripping Quinn's arm with all of his strength.

"You're not the one with the bargaining power here," Quinn growled at Crowley. "You think their bullets can hurt me? You think I can't kill them all, with or without your Shield? You think I'm afraid right now?"

"No—I suppose you aren't."

She put it together the rest of his plan without him having to say a word. This time, she didn't ask.

It suddenly became so cold, she could see her short, uneven breaths in front of her. The flames did not subside.

Crowley lifted a hand, and all the guns were pointed. Toward Quinn, but not at her... At Kurt.

"Sure, you're protecting him," Crowley said to Quinn. "Even if I have all fifteen of these officers shoot, you'll probably take every last bullet for him. But what about when you leave? What about when you get home, use the bathroom, hop in the shower, run out to the supermarket? What about a few months from now when he gets sick of the chase and goes out to Hunts Point for some action on the streets? You think you'll always be there, at his side, to take the bullets for him? One hundred percent of the time?"

"He's not a deviant," she told him, voice more full of hatred than it ever had been. "He's innocent."

"He's joined forces with the Siren—the number one most wanted deviant in the world and the biggest threat to humanity since the resistance. No one would bat an eyelash."

The flames were stronger now, the smoke more overpowering, the fire fighting its way through the cold and creating a stinging, icy-hot sensation everywhere. And yet no one seemed afraid, and to her, that was the scariest thing. They knew she wouldn't kill them. They knew she would give in.

"What do I have to do?" she whispered.

Crowley gestured for one of the armed men to step forward. He did, pulling out a syringe full of a strange, glowing liquid she recognized as some sort of enhanced tranquilizer—one that had come out after the event. The man approached her, not waiting for a final word.

Well, that just wouldn't do.

She might have lost this battle, but she would be damned if she lost every last inch of her pride along with it.

She froze him in place, adding a layer of pain that sent him writhing. She almost felt bad about it. Almost.

She turned back to Crowley.

"Will it kill me?"

"Kill you?" he repeated, and laughed. "Six years ago, I probably would have gone for it. But things are different now. Regulations, limitations. Your own country might be okay with me killing you, but the UNCODA would never let me hear the end of it. I think it will be enough for me to be known as man who captured the Siren and sent her to Devil's Island. Wouldn't you agree?"

Quinn was surprised by his comments about the UNCODA—the United Nations Council of Deviant Affairs, the newest and most aggressive branch of the United Nations. She and the deviants she had encountered growing up had all thought of the UNCODA as an international version of the DCA, charged with capturing the deviants who had fled the States to seek refuge in foreign territory. It provided some small comfort for her, knowing that even if that were true, they were still keeping the DCA in check.

But none of that mattered in that moment. All that mattered was her final question for Crowley.

"And Kurt? He's left alone? As if none of this ever happened?"

"As if none of this ever happened. I might even throw a chunk of his old man's money his way, if I'm feeling generous."

It was amazing to her, how they all seemed to know her decision before she made it. Despite her reputation as the media's favorite super villain, it was so easy for them to look at her and just know.

And, of course, they were right. Kurt mattered more. More than herself. More than anything.

She unfroze the man with the syringe, closed her eyes, and waited.

The injection came quickly; the effects, less so.

For seconds, even minutes, she stood perfectly upright, eyes just as bright as they ever were, still darting from person to person. There was a trace of amusement in her eyes, almost playfulness; she was pleased with herself for not succumbing.

But then that brightness began to dull; her vision became hazy; she started to sway. And they all learned then that she was not flawless, that she was not invincible.

She looked over toward Kurt, a sad, loving expression in her eyes: a look that clearly said, *I'll never regret saving you.*

And then it happened.

"Kill him*."*

Their guns raised instantaneously, the whole lot of them, aiming straight for Kurt, and not a second passed before every single one opened fire.

She dove in front of him, focusing all of her thoughts and all of her abilities on stopping the bullets. But it didn't matter, because her abilities were gone; her sight was gone; her reality was gone.

She crashed to the ground at the same time Kurt did, but her screams were louder.

And then she was completely silent.

2. SILOH

When she woke up, the first thing she noticed was that she was in the air. Not of her own accord—flight was one of the few abilities she still struggled with—but on some sort of aircraft.

The second thing she noticed was that there was someone touching her.

"I'm telling you, it's a waste of your time," someone was saying, probably to the person with the clammy hands pawing at her stomach with some kind of gauze. "She's a healer. She would have fully healed already if not for the sedatives."

"If she dies, it's our asses on the line, not yours, Ridley," the clammy-handed man snapped back. "Just shut up and let me—"

But the alcohol he attempted to pour into her open bullet wounds burned deep into her like fire, and she shot up so fast, she knocked him backwards.

"*Never touch me again!*" she screamed at the man, disgusted by his pudgy, lumbering appearance and even more so by his DCA uniform. She spun around, eyes wide and bright, full strength suddenly returning to her as she scanned the helicopter. She tried to break the handcuffs off her wrists, which normally would be a small feat, but struggled. She didn't like to think about the kind of technology awaiting her at Devil's Island if even their handcuffs negated her abilities. Her heart began to pound, and the helicopter began to shake.

There were three people besides her on the helicopter, she assessed as her eyes darted around the rocky aircraft. Two were members of the DCA. The third was a visibly affected deviant—a monster, as they had been so affectionately nicknamed by the general public.

He had a surprisingly friendly face, despite the fact that it was covered in scales, and he was the only one looking at her with any sympathy. The other two were looking at her in utter terror.

Probably because she had half a mind to kill them all—that, and because she was bringing the helicopter down.

"Quinn," the reptile man said. She recognized his voice as Ridley, the one who had advised the pudgy man not to touch her. "I need you to stay calm. You're going to crash the helicopter, and we haven't reached our destination yet."

"Maybe that's the idea," she snarled, glaring fiercely at him. "Did you think I'd stroll willingly into Devil's Island? Hold hands with the men who killed my best friend?"

He took a step towards her—*bold move*—but he still didn't seem threatening. If anything, his presence seemed to calm her. "I understand," he said. "But there are things you don't understand. These men weren't there when you were captured. And the island isn't what you think. Give it a chance."

She could hardly believe her ears. Who cared if the men were there when Kurt was killed or not? They were still DCA agents. They still worked for Cole Crowley. And give Devil's Island a chance? The place where deviants were sent to be locked up and waste away?

The helicopter was spiraling out of Quinn's control at that point—not enough to send her into a panic, but enough that the two members of the DCA dropped to the ground, clinging to the seats, whimpering.

She had to admit, she was impressed by how well Ridley was doing. He kept one hand rooted to the handhold and his eyes rooted on her.

"If you want me to trust you," she asked him, "why am I still in handcuffs?"

Ridley glanced at the two men as if debating whether to break the rules in front of them. They shook their heads desperately, urging him not to do it. His muscles tensed as he gripped the handhold tighter, deciding. Finally, he pulled a key out of his pocket and came toward her. She waited unflinchingly as he popped the key into her handcuffs and unlocked them. The DCA men's whimpers became louder.

"I need you to listen to me," Ridley said to her in a collected, rational voice, ignoring the men. "We're a mile from the island. If we crash here, these men will drown. Can you keep the helicopter up? For one more mile?"

Even if she wanted to help any of these people—the last people on Earth she would want to help—she couldn't. Her telekinetic abilities weren't strong enough to singlehandedly control a helicopter; its downfall was the result of her more emotionally charged, elemental abilities. Wind, fire, water, electricity. She could probably subdue the elements enough to buy them a few minutes, but she couldn't land the aircraft safely.

But she wouldn't admit that to anyone, especially someone so closely connected with the DCA. He wasn't wearing the uniform, but he was still traveling with them, so she gave him the short answer. "No," she told him, fierce gaze unwavering. "I won't help you. Any of you."

"Look," Ridley said, impatience starting to rise. He seemed to understand that what she really meant was she *couldn't* help them, but he didn't seem ready to accept that. They were running out of time. "Forget about saving the helicopter. Once we hit the water, we'll have to swim to the shore. These men won't make it on their own. I can probably take one of them with me. I need you to take the other."

"I said *no!* They're lucky I haven't killed them already. Why the hell would I do anything to help the people who captured me and killed my best friend? Why would I help *you*?"

"I told you, they weren't there. I wasn't, either."

But it wasn't enough for her. Not now, with it still so raw. Not when she could still see Kurt's body clattering to the ground, shot repeatedly by men in the same uniforms these men were wearing.

"And because you're not who they say you are," Ridley finished, voice softer, but just as desperate. "You're not going to let them die."

She swallowed, holding his gaze for several seconds, deciding in those seconds who she wanted to be from that point forward. She could break away from the helicopter and attempt to fly or swim or whatever she could come up with to make it back to the mainland. Start over. Keep running. There was nothing left for her; she didn't even *want* to go back. And yet, what was her other option? Go to Devil's Island? 'Give it a chance?'

Why did she actually want to take his advice?

And the men… the DCA agents. Why should she help them? Maybe Ridley was right—maybe she wasn't the type to let them die. But *shouldn't* she be? Why not change? Why not become the same as Crowley, the same as all the wicked people who had done so many unforgivable things to her? Surely Crowley never had to feel half the pain that she did.

But then the helicopter hit the water, and the brainstorming went away, and all that was left were her instincts.

The first thing her instincts did was soften the impact—an impact which, she realized as they were all thrown up against the ceiling, glass shattering around them, otherwise would have killed them instantly.

Ridley grabbed the pudgy man, and she grabbed the other, destroying what was left of the glass to make way for their escape.

Quinn practiced flying often, but she had never gotten comfortable with it. Hovering a foot or two in the air was easy enough, but anything beyond that was more of a challenge. The higher she went, the harder it got—like the home stretch of a marathon run—hard to breathe, hard to see, hard to focus. She could only assume that it would be twice as hard carrying a body.

She considered swimming. That was Ridley's approach, and it would probably be easier. But it would be slow. She could see the island on the horizon, but it was far—farther than she'd ever swam before. Her bullet wounds had almost fully healed, but she was still recovering from her takedown of the helicopter, and she was in no mood to spend the next ten to fifteen minutes gasping for air and dragging a man she despised through cold, choppy water.

So she flew.

It wasn't too hard at first. She stayed slow and close to the water, saving her strength. But then she caught the thickening flames of the helicopter debris in her periphery and glanced over at Ridley in the water, having the same thought as him: *explosion.* And they both increased their speed.

It was easier for her than for him, and before long she knew that he wasn't going to make it. She could see the exhaustion in every stroke he took, the silent panic on his face. She doubled back, grabbed Ridley and the man he was carrying, and pulled them all into the air.

She was exhausted within seconds; a dozen later, she was so dizzy, she could barely see. But she was closer now. The island was upon her, and even though all she could see was the massive, stone wall stretching around its perimeter, she knew she was going to make it. She just needed to push.

"Let me go," Ridley urged her. "I've got this."

But not a second after the words escaped his lips, the remains of the helicopter exploded, their farthest reaches gusting toward the group and launching them even further toward the island. By the time the momentum from the explosion mixed with the blast of water had finished propelling them, they landed in the water just meters from the shore of the island. The DCA men immediately began to sink.

"Disgusting," she muttered as she spit water and smoke from her lungs, reaching down into the water to grab the pudgy man as Ridley grabbed the other. "Can't even swim and they're licensed to carry assault rifles and 'collect' people."

Ridley said nothing as he swam alongside her, grasping for sand and grass as they reached the shore. He coughed up even more water than she had, crawling to the dry land, chest heaving. She rose to her feet as soon as the pudgy man was safely ashore, trying to pass off the entire ordeal as a non-event despite the fact that her own chest was heaving quite a bit.

Here she was.

She couldn't see much, but even the wall itself didn't seem quite as daunting as she had imagined. Despite how high it stretched, it was almost inviting; old, simple stone, carved and crafted here and there, vines crawling up and down it. The vines came to an end where the stone turned to wood: at the gates. The gates that would open for them when the time came. And then, up above…

Faces.

People.

Not guards. Not prisoners. Just… people. Young, old, monsters, makers. All sorts of people, gathered at the top of the wall, peering down at her. Wide-eyed and eager.

How could that be?

She glanced over at Ridley, who was climbing to his feet, but he didn't look like he was going to give her any answers. Instead, he began to walk towards the gates, gesturing for her to follow.

She glanced back at the two DCA agents, curious what their fates might be, but she cared even less now than she had minutes before; they were safe from immediate danger, and whatever befell them next, they probably deserved. So she followed Ridley until they were face-to-face with the gates.

Without a word from anyone on the other side, the gates opened.

She tried to remain calm, but no part of her felt up for the challenge. Her heart was pounding, her breathing uneven, her skin hot with sweat. Those faces up above weren't the only ones staring at her. There were people on the other side of the gates. The same kinds of people. Deviants.

Except… They weren't in chains. They weren't in cells. And the expressions on their faces were… eager. Innocent.

Why weren't they trying to escape?

Her confusion didn't lessen when she saw the island itself.

It was beautiful. Rich, green, flowered. Full of bright whites and deep browns, wood and brick, picket fences, small cottage homes. Off in the distance, she could see a few taller buildings—three stories high, maybe more. Around them, fields. Trees. Some sort of cell tower. If she wasn't mistaken, she even saw a horse stable atop one of the hills.

What *was* this place? Had she really left a destitute New England for a flourishing Devil's Island?

"I told you," Ridley whispered from her side, sneaking her a small, supportive grin. "Give it a chance."

She didn't return his grin or his gaze, but she found herself unable to ignore his advice. What could she do but walk in? She had no desire to go back to the world she'd come from. And, really, this place was already a thousand times better than she had ever imagined.

All these faces staring at her… if they were deviants, too, how bad could this place be?

She began to walk, even though she wasn't sure where she was going. She had never been much of a follower, and had no intentions of following Ridley anywhere. She might like him by nature, but he was still more or less her captor.

Most of her audience made way for her as she walked, but some were bolder.

A little girl, probably not more than twelve years old, ran right up to her, blue eyes wide and eager. "You're the Siren!" she exclaimed, jumping up and down at the sight of her. "I'm your biggest fan! I thought they'd never catch you!"

Quinn ignored her entirely, not in any mood to make new friends, but it didn't end there. Her next fan was closer to her age, maybe even a hair older. Male. Good-looking in the traditional sense, though by no means a 'pretty monster' like herself. He seemed almost as eager as the little girl, though he was trying harder to hide it.

"If it isn't the Siren. I have to say, I'm a little disappointed to see you here. But only a little." And he winked at her.

She threw him backwards several feet using only a flick of her wrist and continued to walk.

She made her way past the extravagant entrance fountain and over to a huge building that read *Town Hall* before finally stopping to glance at Ridley, who had been following just behind her the whole time. But before she could ask him where exactly she was supposed to be going, someone stopped her.

She seemed to appear out of nowhere, though on second thought Quinn saw a revolving door to the town hall swiveling to a stop behind her. She was older than anyone who had approached Quinn thus far, probably in her fifties. She had a regal look about her, though not a magical one. She was dressed professionally, conservatively—almost like a politician.

"Ah," the woman said. "Quinn Harper. I'm Savannah Collins. We've been expecting you."

So far, everyone had called Quinn by her media name—the Siren. That, she was comfortable with; everyone knew that name. But this woman knowing her first and last name? That could only mean one thing.

"Did Crowley tell you about me?"

"We have many things to discuss, Miss Harper. Mr. Crowley is one of them. But not here. If you hadn't noticed, you've drummed up quite the audience, and I'd much prefer to have this conversation in private." She took a step back, gesturing to the revolving door she had just come from.

There was nothing about this woman that Quinn liked, but she was hungry for answers. Besides, the woman didn't seem particularly threatening. So Quinn followed her through the door, glancing back at Ridley and almost giving him a nod goodbye until she caught herself. Utterly confused, she turned to face the foyer.

"This is what we call the town hall," Savannah told her as they walked, "though really it is more of a Capitol. It is the only governmental building on the island. I am the only regular on the island. I work here—as do my sons." She gestured to two desks in opposite corners of the room. One was cluttered and currently unoccupied; the other was organized and occupied by a man about five or ten years older than Quinn. He had softer, gentler features than his mother's. Brown eyes, brown hair. Handsome in an unassuming way. He glanced up at them, offering a friendly smile.

"Miss Harper," Savannah said, "this is Reese, my eldest. Reese is responsible for most of the lawmaking, as well as law enforcement, on the island."

Reese chuckled, reaching out to offer a hand to Quinn. She hesitated, but shook back, adding a light electric zap just to see how he would react. He seemed amused.

"She says 'enforcement' as if we've had a single issue in the eight years this place has been around," he joked. "Don't worry, Quinn. We all get along around here."

"Reese will show you around when our meeting is finished," Savannah told Quinn. "But for now, let's go into my office. We have things to discuss."

Quinn followed Savannah into her office, which was nearly the size of the entire lobby. It was a beautiful office, filled with rich mahoganies and thick marble. It was the office of someone important—someone in charge.

"You can think of me as the president of Siloh," Savannah explained.

"Siloh?"

"That's our name for this little home of ours. Or did you really think we call it Devil's Island?"

Quinn said nothing. It certainly didn't *look* like a place called Devil's Island. But why the cover-up?

"Humanity sleeps better," Savannah explained, as if reading her mind, "thinking that people like you are locked away, tortured, confined to cells and darkness and isolation. It comforts them. The worst of them, anyway. Which are often the ones in power."

Quinn couldn't disagree with her there. But it only led her to the same thought she had before—the man whose name alone made her want to send everything around her up in flames. "Crowley."

"Yes, yes—quite possibly the worst of the lot. I know that, Quinn. We all know that. Believe me, no one here is a fan of Cole Crowley. But he has power, and he has influence. As I'm sure you've started to realize."

"Does he know? What this place really is?"

"No, my dear. No one knows."

Quinn couldn't always sense when someone was lying, but she could tell that Savannah was. "I doubt that. What about Tweedle-Dee and Tweedle-Dum on the helicopter with me? What about pilots who fly over this area? Satellite imaging? The fine-toothed comb both the DCA and UNCODA keep on the entire deviant community?"

"I suppose you're right; I misspoke. The UNCODA—it's easy to keep them in the dark. This island is American property and falls under its legal and governmental jurisdiction. But you are right—everyone involved in the DCA knows that it isn't truly a prison. Still, it has a wall, and it has security. And an escape rate of zero. That's all they care about. They don't know about the school. They don't know about the jobs. They just think it's a place of isolation—a place to hide you all. They don't understand the extent we go to in order to keep everyone here happy."

Quinn still didn't buy it. They had to know more than that. No one with a healthy dose of fear would knowingly turn a blind eye when it came to the world's most powerful threat—especially not so soon after the resistance. And Crowley? Why would he dedicate so much time and attention to their collection, and so little to the conditions of their imprisonment?

But she knew better than to argue with the alleged 'president' of her new homeland quite so quickly. "So, you're not his friend," she said carefully. "You had nothing to do with Kurt."

"Friend?" Savannah laughed. "My dear, I live on an island full of deviants. Two of them are my own sons. I'm not friends with anyone back in the real world, especially not someone whose job it is to rid the world of anything to do with your kind. As far as he is concerned, I'm just another deviant, brought here with my sons many years ago. Just another prisoner."

Again, highly doubtful, Quinn thought. If Crowley thought Savannah was just a prisoner, but understood that everyone on the island was adhering to some sort of limited freedom arrangement, who did he think was in charge? Who did he communicate with?

She decided that all that really mattered to her was whether or not Savannah had been involved in Kurt's death. If she was twisted, if she was corrupt, fine. But if she had had anything to do with Kurt, even mere knowledge of the plan...

Quinn would kill her with her bare hands.

"And Kurt?" she asked, eyes rooted to Savannah's, searching for any sign of recognition or admittance. Just saying his name out loud sent Quinn's mind into a frenzy of rage all over again. She breathed slowly, knowing better than to start another elemental disaster in the middle of the town hall.

"I don't know who Kurt is, but I can see in your eyes how much he meant to you. If I know Mr. Crowley, I know that he took him away from you. I'm sorry for that, Quinn. I am. I don't have the power to fight someone like him—none of us do. The best we can do is protect ourselves, out here—far away from him."

Quinn hated that. She hated the thought of all the people he had wronged hiding out in fear. But she was beginning to understand it.

She decided that she believed Savannah—not her whole story, but that she knew nothing about Kurt.

"Enough about that wretched man," Savannah said. "I've brought you here to tell you about your new home—what we offer you, and what we expect of you in return."

Of course. The catch.

"First of all, you are required to go to school. I know you're eighteen. I'm sure you think you're too old for school. I don't care. You'll be in school until your teachers feel you've gotten the proper level of education you deserve."

"You must be joking. I haven't set foot in a school in years. There's no way I'm going to now."

"I'm afraid it's not up for discussion. You having not been to school is exactly why I must insist. We are a self-sustaining society, Quinn. Everyone here must learn so that everyone here can support each other. When your teachers clear you, you are free to leave school. All but power practice, of course."

"Power practice?"

"Technically, it's called power stabilization. That's my other son's job. He works with many of the residents, particularly the ones your age. Helps them gain control over the ties between their emotions and their abilities."

A class where she was encouraged to use her abilities, after a lifetime of hiding them? *That* class, Quinn wouldn't mind attending.

"Until you've been cleared by your teachers," Savannah continued, "you will be receiving a monthly stipend of money. Consider it your allowance. Once you leave school, you will be expected to get a job and work for a living, like the other adults here. If you cannot find a job, we will place you in a security position similar to your new friend Ridley's."

Quinn found it bitterly unsurprising that Ridley had a hard time finding a job. Apparently prejudice even existed on an island full of deviants.

And how did Savannah already know that Quinn and Ridley had gotten along?

'Gotten along' was a generous term, she supposed—but she hadn't hated him like she hated just about everyone else.

"As far as living and dining goes," Savannah said, "until you are cleared, you will live in the dormitories. You will have a roommate." She ignored Quinn's instant groan. "And you will eat in the community cafe."

Community cafe? This place was starting to sound more and more like a cult to Quinn.

"As far as what's expected of you, and what you need to know, that's about it. Follow the rules, and you won't have a problem. But there is one thing I must ask you, and I must insist that you answer it honestly."

Quinn shrugged a shoulder. She had no reason to lie to this woman, that she could think of. Not yet.

"We have deviants of many types here. Monsters. Makers. *Pretty monsters,* as the media was so fond of calling you. What we don't have, though, to the best of our knowledge, is a seer."

Quinn watched Savannah, not blinking, not wavering. But her breathing slowed.

"If you're not sure what a seer is," Savannah said, "it is someone who was affected with psychic abilities."

"Like how I can make people do what I want?" Quinn asked, deciding to play dumb for now. She knew what Savannah wanted; she had known the moment she said the word. Savannah wanted a fortune teller.

And even though Savannah said she wasn't friends with Crowley, even though she said she spent her time on the island and not in the outside world, Quinn wasn't quick to trust anyone, least of all this woman. She knew how valuable fortune telling was to just about everyone, all around the world.

"No, my dear. That is a nice parlor trick, but that is not what I mean. I mean the ability to see the future."

Quinn tried her best not to let her laugh sound forced; it wasn't easy when the last time she had laughed was with Kurt. Her eyes burned at the memory. "Are you suggesting there's someone out there who *can*?"

"Miss Harper, we live in a world full of superpowers. You're a smart enough girl. Is it really so hard to imagine?"

"I'm sorry," Quinn said, ready to be anywhere but there. "I guess I'm just a little surprised you thought I might even be capable. I mean, sure, the media likes to talk me up, but—"

"That's enough," Savannah said sharply, and for the first time in their entire meeting, Quinn actually felt threatened by her. Savannah was clearly angry, and Quinn had a feeling this wasn't someone she should piss off.

"I understand what you are telling me," Savannah said. "I would like *you* to understand that if I find out that for any reason you have lied to me, or that you in the coming weeks or months experience a premonition and do not report it to me, I will make your experience here at Siloh very different than the one I have just described to you. Very different indeed."

Quinn's reflex for sarcastic comments tried to kick in, but for the first time in a long time, she knew better than to utter a word.

"Are we clear?" Savannah asked.

Quinn forced a shaky, hateful smile. "Clear as a crystal ball."

"Very well. You can go."

Quinn rose, starting to make her way to the door, but stopped when she heard Savannah's final words.

"This isn't Devil's Island, Miss Harper. But it could be."

3. DASH AND REESE

Quinn couldn't leave Savannah's office fast enough. The woman was bad news, she told herself as she stepped back into the lobby. Clearly lying; clearly delusional. She must be in direct contact with the mainland; that was the only explanation for her desperation to find a seer. She worked for Crowley. She worked for someone worse than Crowley. That, or...

Or she was worried about her own fate on the island.

Quinn shook her thoughts away and bee-lined for the door, not really even sure where she was headed, only stopping when a voice reminded her that she wasn't the only one in the lobby.

"I'm still open to showing you around," Reese told her, rising from his desk. "Unless she scared you so much you're already contemplating your first jailbreak."

She laughed in spite of herself, appreciating any semblance of humor regarding Savannah. Then again, she had to remind herself, the woman was his mother. If Quinn didn't trust Savannah, she probably shouldn't trust Reese, either.

"Jailbreak," Quinn repeated. "From this place that people keep trying to assure me isn't jail?"

"It was a figure of speech. Look, if there's any advice I can give you, let it be to ignore my mother. You'll interact with her maybe once a year from here on out, if that."

A part of her wanted to say more—ask him a question or two about his mother—how he could possibly be related to someone who looked and acted so different from him. He seemed so much warmer, so much more familiar than she did. Quinn almost liked him instinctively, just as she had with Ridley... something that didn't happen often.

But she didn't dare say more so close to his mother's office, so instead she said, "Lovely as this little White House is, I'd like to get the hell out of here. What exactly were you planning on showing me?"

He grinned, gesturing for her to follow as he made his way outside. "There's lots for me to show you, but something tells me the first thing we need to do is get some food in you."

She hadn't thought about it since waking up on the helicopter, but his words made her realize how famished she was. How long had it been since she'd eaten? Judging from the tropical temperatures and vast ocean surrounding them, she could only guess her helicopter ride had followed an extensive plane ride.

But then she remembered the last time she had eaten—Big John's Pizza, Kurt's favorite spot in all of New Jersey. It had been a staple in their relationship for some time—she ordered the pizza, Kurt picked it up, they chowed down with his father in his cozy little trailer, all laughter and warmth. But not that night—the night before Crowley's. Kurt's father had been out at his new night job, working road construction, and Kurt had been quiet the whole time. Afraid.

She hated remembering him that way. She hated what she had done to him.

Nausea and self-loathing replaced her hunger.

"Quinn?" Reese asked, stopping and turning to face her. He seemed to sense that she had gone to a very different place. "Are you okay?"

Was she okay? What a ridiculous question. She wanted to hate him for even thinking he could ask her that. But for some reason, she didn't. For some reason, she found it strangely comforting.

"No. And I'm not hungry. But I should eat. So, as long as you're not going to tell me the community slaughters its pigs and cooks them by a campfire holding hands and singing kum-ba-yah, let's go."

Reese laughed out loud. "I know certain things about this place can make it seem like some sort of cult or freak show, but it really is as close to the real world as a place like this can be. It was modeled after New York—upstate, outside of the city, of course—since that's where most of its inhabitants came from."

Quinn hadn't spent much time in New York, despite the landmarks in her life that had occurred there, but she found it hard to believe that this place had much in common with it.

They began to walk again, deeper into the island, away from the fountain and the gates and toward what seemed to be the center of the island. She wondered whether he would go full tour mode and point things out as they walked, but he didn't, and she appreciated that. If she was really going to live on this island for the rest of her life, she'd have plenty of time to figure all of that out. She had other questions that she wanted answered, and while she still didn't feel particularly social, she'd rather ask someone like him than someone like Savannah.

"You talk about the island's history and origins like you had a hand in their creation," she told him. "But how old could you have been when this place came to be? Eleven? Twelve?"

"I'm flattered, but I was nineteen when my mother, brother, and I came to the island. Eight years ago—two years after the event. And I didn't have much of a hand in any of this, to be honest. My little brother had more of a hand, and he was only seventeen at the time. But Savannah always trusted him so much, even then. I was more of the black sheep."

"How did you get this law enforcement gig, then? If you were such a black sheep?"

"After a few years, she decided she could trust me. It took time for all of us to get into the groove. All the island had when we got here was the wall. As the residents began to trickle in, they each brought something new to the table. Money, experience, abilities… Different things. The more of them there were, the more need there was for things like law enforcement and power stabilization."

"And school," she added, voice dripping with disdain at the very word.

He laughed. "And school. Look, I know you're not thrilled at the prospect of going—no one is at first. But you'll be thankful one day. That's what's great about this place—despite all its bullshit, all its attempts to be something it's not—there are things it can give people like us that we never would have gotten otherwise. Education is one of the biggest."

She knew he was right. She couldn't count the number of times growing up she had wanted to set foot into schools, just to try, just to see if anyone would kick her out. Not for the education, but for the experience. For being with other kids her own age.

That was years ago, of course. She had long since said goodbye to that kind of wishful thinking.

"Anyway," he said, gesturing to a large, one-story building labeled *Community Café, "w*e're here."

Her nausea seeped away as the smell of food overtook her.

Despite its casual 'café' title, it seemed to be the dining hall for the entire island; there were easily two hundred seats in the room, if not more, about half of which were currently occupied. Naturally, the moment she and Reese stepped in, all eyes turned to her and all conversation silenced.

Reese, clearly trying to make the situation lighter, whispered to her, "This how it always is for you?"

It wasn't his fault, but his joke wasn't funny. It wasn't funny because it *was* how it always was for her, and yet, in every other circumstance she had been in, a hundred eyes on her meant she had to either run or fight. She wasn't going to forget that feeling any time soon.

She stepped up to the counter without answering him.

She scanned the menu, deliberately avoiding eye contact with the poor attendant who seemed completely star-struck. Quinn had never been great at reading; it was probably some combination of dyslexia and a lack of formal education. But she could make out her options: chicken, steak, salad, pasta.

"I'll have the steak," she said shortly to the attendant. She glanced back at Reese, not sure whether she'd be expected to pay or not. But when she turned, she caught sight of something else—some*one* else.

Someone she had spent the last ten years convincing herself was a figment of her imagination.

Like clockwork, the temperature in the room dropped about forty degrees. The lights began to flicker. The door to the building slammed shut on whatever poor soul was attempting to open it. Whatever few eyes had stopped staring at her all started again. Everyone knew it was her doing.

But it was *him*... and nothing else mattered.

She stepped past Reese, who was looking at her like she had completely lost her mind, past a table of twenty-somethings looking at her like she had never had her sanity to begin with, and past a table of ten-year-olds who looked ready for her to act even crazier. But she didn't pay attention to any of them. She paid attention to one person, and one person only.

The man from that night.

It was him. There was no denying it. He had those same flickering, fiery eyes, bright like embers, emitting a light of their own… The same bright, translucent skin that at the time had mirrored nothing she had ever seen before, and now somehow mirrored her own…

He was exactly the same.

She had reached him. He was staring right back at her.

"You haven't aged a day," she whispered, and even though it was a whisper, it echoed a thousand times into the dead silence that surrounded them, and she knew everyone was listening. "How is that possible?"

The man stared coldly into her eyes—*coldly;* how was that possible with those eyes?—and responded, "I don't know what you mean."

"It was me," she whispered, the loudest whisper she had ever uttered, and yet the most afraid. "The little girl. That night, outside of the bank. You stayed with me."

He shook his head. There was no recognition in his eyes. No understanding. Nothing.

She found herself completely unwilling to accept this response. How was this possible? After all this time—after thinking she had gone crazy that night, seen an angel, seen a ghost—how could he stand right in front of her and deny that it had ever happened?

"I was alone," she urged, her voice desperate, pleading. "You told me not to be afraid of you… You told me to trust you."

Still, there was nothing in his eyes. She felt the room growing even colder, everything getting darker. Her heart growing weaker.

A tear slid down her cheek, and it felt like it was burning, and she hated that tear, and suddenly she felt hot despite the cold, and everything hurt.

"I had a pink blanket. Don't you remember?"

In a voice as cold as the ice that was starting to freeze over the windows, he told her, "No."

· · ·

She ran out after that. She left him behind. She left Reese behind. She had no idea where she was going. She didn't care. So much for her front. So much for convincing everyone that she had no feelings and not a care in the world. She'd been on the island for one hour, and they had already seen her tears.

She hated him. She hated him almost as much as she hated Crowley. How could he do that to her? How could he look into her eyes, the same eyes that stared up at him when she was a child, and deny ever having helped her?

Unless...

Was it possible that he wasn't just denying? Was it possible that he really hadn't been there? That who she had seen really had been a figment of her imagination?

But how could they look so *similar*?

She forced herself to shake her thoughts away before she walked into a part of the island she wasn't meant to be in. She wasn't even sure that such a place existed, but she certainly didn't want to find out the hard way. Deciding that she had fled far enough away from that wretched dining hall, she stopped to gather her thoughts and surroundings.

Despite how much of the island there was to explore, her exhaustion and metal state got the better of her and she decided to find the dormitories. Given how many students she had seen in the dining hall, she assumed it would be a large building. She scanned the buildings around her, eyes settling on a three-story brick building about a block away.

She started walking again, glancing back to see if anyone had followed her from the lunch room. To her relief, she saw that Reese hadn't; she wasn't ready to start answering questions about what had happened. A part of her hoped she'd see Ridley behind her, the one person she might be willing to talk to, but she didn't.

She didn't see anyone.

She kept walking until she reached the front of the building, which, sure enough, read *Dormitories* just above the door. She stepped inside, entering another lobby. This one was much cozier than Savannah's. Sitting at the front desk was what could only be described as a vampire.

He smiled pleasantly at her when she walked in, revealing piercing canines. "Hi! I'm Drax. You must be the new girl."

Still dazed and reeling from the café, it took her a second to register what she was seeing and hearing. "Drax," she repeated. "Drax the vampire."

He rolled his eyes, but he didn't seem to take it personally. He flattened his slick, black hair before responding, "And you're Siren the seductress. Don't tell me you think yours is any better."

She wiped the remnants of tears from her eyelids, forcing herself out of her delirium and coming over to the front desk. "Touché. But I didn't give myself that nickname. And I don't go by it." She extended a hand—first time she had done so on the island. She liked his spunk. "I'm Quinn."

"Nice to meet you, Quinn." He shook her hand. She noticed with amusement that his was cold as ice. "My real name is Stuart, but I prefer Drax. If I had a name as cute as yours, maybe I'd feel differently."

Her normal red flag alert didn't go off at this compliment, which usually meant the person played for the other team. Normally learning this about men disappointed her, since it meant her compulsion wouldn't work as well on them, but in this case, she didn't mind.

"Maybe you could help me," she said. "I'm supposed to live here and have a roommate. Could you could tell me where my room is and whether I'll need you to conveniently suck the blood out of my roommate before I make an appearance?"

"As much as I'd like to help, I'm all monster and no maker. Good, in that I don't melt in the sun… Bad in that I don't have any 'vampire' abilities, including sucking people's blood."

"Not sure that's really an ability," she pointed out with a tiny grin. "Think any old Joe Blow could do that."

He laughed. "Regardless, I know your roommate, and there won't be any need to resort to such things. Haley is an absolute delight, and if you don't like her, there's just no hope for you."

Quinn considered pointing out that there hadn't been any hope for her in a long time, but she decided to keep the mood light. She waited as he pulled a key out from his desk and led her to the elevators.

"You'll be on the third floor," he told her. "With the rest of the Young Adults. Myself included."

"Young Adults? Like the bad tween romance books?"

"I know, it's a stupid name. Not sure where it comes from initially. But it's a good group of people. We're the oldest students on the island. Think the youngest of us is about fifteen, oldest is about nineteen."

"And you? I thought none of us had to work until we're 'cleared' by our teachers."

"I'm eighteen, and I'm close to getting cleared. I'm terrified of going into security, which is typically where monsters end up—the makers get all the good jobs. I convinced the last person who worked the front desk to recommend me when she left for a better gig. Figured if I started early, at least I'd know I've got this job when I get kicked out—I mean, cleared."

He spoke optimistically enough, but his words made her sad. Again, it was so evident that prejudice existed here on the island just as it did in the outside world.

But she said nothing. Instead, she watched the floor numbers tick up until they reached the third floor and the elevator doors opened.

"You're room 307," Drax told her, leading her down the hall. "Most of your floormates are still at lunch. Did you get something to eat already?"

Her stomach chose that moment to groan. She had never grabbed her food from the order window; she had run out before she got the chance. But there was no way she was going back now.

"I'm good," she said, waiting pointedly next to the door.

He took the hint, unlocking the handle and handing her the key. "Well, get some rest. Haley will be here soon, and you can make your introductions. I'm at the front desk between classes and from six to nine every evening, if you ever have any questions. And I'm sure I'll see you in class tomorrow."

She smiled politely, but the sight of a waiting bed was all she could think about, and she couldn't help but shut the door in his face without so much as a thank you. She collapsed into bed, falling immediately to sleep.

• • •

"Guys, she's probably sleeping. Why don't you just come back in a few hours?"

"She probably won't be here in a few hours. I'm surprised she isn't already gone. Come on, what's the worst that can happen?"

"The worst that can happen is, she blows us all up. The whole dorm, even. The whole island, even! But I still want to meet her."

Quinn stuffed a pillow over her head, cringing at the noise from the other side of the door. Clearly the Young Adult brigade was back from lunch.

"Fine, but five minutes, and then I want you both to clear out of here. I'm going to be living with her for the foreseeable future. I'd at least like a few minutes to get to know her before she writes me off for being friends with you two weirdos."

"Five minutes. I solemnly swear."

Quinn tried to lie as still as humanly possible as the key turned in the lock and the door opened, but it didn't make a difference.

"It's her, it's her!" exclaimed one of the three voices, jumping onto Quinn's bed and bouncing around. The person was a child, judging from her high-pitched voice and ability to jump on the bed and not break it.

"Rory, she's sleeping!" the first voice chastised—the same voice that had warned the others not to stay longer than five minutes. Quinn's new roommate. As annoyed as she was at the lot of them, she did appreciate on some level that this girl was attempting to give Quinn some peace.

"No, she's not," Rory said as Quinn pulled the pillow away from her head, glaring up at the girl. "See?"

Quinn squinted as she scanned the three bodies in front of her. Two of them, she realized, she had already met. The girl was the one she had passed shortly after arriving on the island—the one who had said she was surprised Quinn had been caught. The third person, the man, was the one she had passed just after the girl—

the one who had attempted to flirt with her.

"Hey," he said in that same, flirtatious tone. She imagined it probably seemed charming to most girls. Not to her. "I'm Trent."

She ignored him again, turning to face the girl she had gathered was her roommate. "You must be Haley."

Haley's expression brightened; Quinn's small courtesy seemed to be more than she had expected. Haley was pretty, Quinn observed, with creamy, caramel skin, large, hazel eyes, and thick, curly hair. There was a smattering of freckles across her cheeks. She was a bit shorter and stockier than Quinn. She looked pleasant. Friendly.

Not Quinn's usual type.

"I am Haley. Haley Mylar. I'm afraid I really only know you as the Siren, though. Is that the name you prefer to go by?"

Quinn had never introduced herself as the Siren or been called it by anyone she remotely cared about. "I'm Quinn," she said, extending a hand for the second time that day. She didn't extend the courtesy to the other two, to their dismay. "Quinn Harper."

"It's nice to meet you," Haley said, shaking Quinn's hand and then reaching into her bag. "I brought you some food—I hope that's okay. I asked Reese and he said you had started to order the steak, so—"

Quinn's eyes lit up at the sight of the box, snatching it so quickly, she inadvertently used her abilities. "Thanks," she mumbled as she dug in.

"You're welcome," Haley said, smiling softly. "Reese was a little worried about you. He was going to bring you this, but I offered to go instead. Told him I was going to be your new roommate."

A part of Quinn wished it had been Reese and not Haley, but she knew better than to linger on it. Haley seemed perfectly nice; maybe it was time Quinn had a female friend for a change.

"What happened in there?" asked Rory. "How do you know Dash?"

"Dash?" Quinn repeated, assuming that she was referring to the man from the dining hall. "That's his name?"

"So, you don't know him," Trent inferred. "Why the meltdown, then?"

She glared at him. "None of your business, One Direction. What are you even doing here?"

He laughed out loud at the insult. "I'm not even British, but I appreciate the spunk of the attempt nonetheless. I'm here to say hello. If you couldn't tell, Rory and I are your biggest fans."

Rory shoved Trent with one of her tiny hands, which barely made it to his abdomen, he was so much taller than her. "*I'm* your biggest fan," she told Quinn. "He just thinks you're pretty."

Trent grinned. "Well, she's not wrong about that."

Quinn retained her straight face, but was starting to find the two of them amusing. She wasn't sure who was more pathetic. At least the girl was cute.

"Well, you're both insane," she told them as she chewed. "Go listen to some music, watch some films. Find better celebrities than me to fuss over."

"We can't," Rory insisted. "They're not like us."

That was when Quinn realized why her fame within the wall was different from her fame outside of it. To the outside world, she was awe-inspiring, fear-inspiring, but not simply *inspiring.* Here, to these people…

She was like them.

There wasn't much of her heart left to be warmed, but what was left was warming. She decided she liked this little girl—at least, the part of the girl she didn't find tirelessly annoying.

"Okay, okay," Haley said, "time's up. Both of you, out."

"But, Haley," Rory whined.

"No buts," Haley said, pushing Rory and Trent towards the door. "We don't know what sort of day this poor girl has had getting here."

"Actually, we more or less do," Trent said. "Crowley Enterprises, DCA raid, helicopters, airplanes—"

"Okay, well, those of us that don't stalk her don't know. Either way, she clearly had a long day."

"Fair enough. Quinn, it was a pleasure finally meeting you. You're only escaping me for now. I'll see you in class tomorrow."

Quinn said nothing, nodding a short goodbye to both him and Rory. Finally, they left Quinn and Haley in peace.

"Sorry about them," Haley said, shaking her head. "They mean well. They're just excited."

"Them, I can handle."

Haley nodded. "Is there anything you want to ask me? I know you hardly know me. But if you do have questions, about Dash or—just about anything…"

Quinn did have questions. Haley clearly knew Dash, the mysterious man who had shot Quinn down in front of a hundred people. Quinn did want to know more about him. But with thoughts of Kurt, Crowley, and night of the event lingering in her mind, all she was up for was finishing her food and going back to bed.

"Thanks," she said, trying to be as sincere as possible. "I probably will have questions eventually. But for now…"

"Of course. Get some rest. Here's your new phone—everyone gets one when they arrive here. Reese gave me yours. I went ahead and programmed my number into it. I think Reese's is in there as well, along with Siloh's emergency hotline. Don't worry—there are never emergencies."

Quinn accepted the phone, wary that anything given to her for free on the island might be watched by Savannah. Not that she planned on having any particularly juicy phone calls in the near future.

"Thanks," she said, placing the phone on the bedside table. It wasn't her first phone, though it was probably the first one she'd have for more than a few weeks. She had always cycled through them quickly on the run.

"No problem," Haley said warmly. "I'm going to go finish my classes for the day. Make sure you get enough rest to make it to class tomorrow morning. Our schedules are the same, so I can show you the ropes."

Quinn nodded, but she dozed off again before Haley even left the room.

• • •

Quinn would have been happy to sleep for the rest of the afternoon and all through the night, if not for one small problem.

Her stomach.

She should have known better, she thought as she sat with her head in the toilet, vomiting up the bulk of the food she had eaten. She was in a foreign place, hadn't had a decent meal in weeks, and a steak dinner had been her first choice?

She tried to get back to sleep in between bouts of vomiting, but her queasy stomach repeatedly woke her up, and it became more and more difficult to fall back asleep. The only silver lining was that Haley didn't return to the room until Quinn had gotten it all out of her system, so she was able to fake sleep and avoid an unwanted conversation.

An hour or two after Haley returned, Quinn finally drifted off for real. She actually managed to get a decent rest, until Haley's obnoxiously shrill alarm clock woke her up the next morning.

She tried covering her head with a pillow again, but it didn't make much of a difference. Haley turned the alarm clock off, switched the light on, and came straight for Quinn.

"I know you don't want to hear it, but you really should come to class with me. Trust me, it's not worth the Savannah headache to skip."

Quinn inferred that she wasn't the only student Savannah liked to threaten and chastise. Maybe Savannah had given the same speech about seers to all of them, she supposed. Maybe it was just standard practice, and didn't have anything to do with Quinn specifically. She made a mental note to ask Haley when she felt more comfortable around her.

Bottom line, she knew Haley was right. Savannah had made it clear that missing class was not an option. Quinn had enough enemies in the real world without forming them here, too. She removed the pillow from her head, groggily stood up, and looked down at herself.

Same tight, snagged, frayed, all-black clothes as the day before. And probably the day before that. And, quite possibly, the day before that, too. She still had no idea how much time had elapsed while she was under.

"I guess we should have taken you shopping yesterday, huh?" Haley giggled, eyeing Quinn's rags. "Don't worry. I've got plenty of things you can borrow. Do you want to shower?"

Quinn had always been a night showerer—with a beer, preferably—but she could make an exception just this once. She knew she smelled even worse than she looked. "Yeah, that's probably a good idea. Whatever throwaway clothes you hate the most are fine, honestly."

Haley chuckled, rifling through her dresser and pulling out a casual, blue-green dress. It was the farthest thing from Quinn's normal wardrobe. "I know it's not as fabulous as the things you always wore on TV, but…"

Quinn, who had been a bit of a master thief in the real world, always preferred to steal from big, designer stores rather than small, family-owned places, but it didn't have to do with her taste in fashion as much as who she wanted to take from. "This will be just fine," she assured Haley before stepping into the bathroom.

For the few months leading up to her capture, Quinn had been sleeping on the couch in Kurt's trailer in New Jersey. She always had other options—before that, she had stayed at the mansion of a wealthy artist who bragged far too much to his friends about her—but smaller homes were familiar and comfortable to her. She felt too far removed from her own skin in mansions.

That being said, the bathroom of the dorm was a whole lot nicer than the one in Kurt's trailer, and the heat and pressure of the water felt incredible as it pounded down on her. She closed her eyes and thought of nothing but the clarity and steam sinking deep into her chest.

At least, until she saw Kurt's sweet face in her head. And then she could think of nothing but that.

She tried to tell herself her tears were just drops from the shower head, but she knew better.

She shut off the water, dried herself, and pulled on Haley's dress, staring at her reflection in disbelief. She wasn't sure she had ever worn something so innocent and conservative. It came almost down to her knees, hanging loosely around her body and masking her normally prevalent curves. It was… simple.

Quinn had never really done simple. The girl staring back at her looked like a stranger.

Haley had the same reaction when Quinn stepped out of the bathroom.

"Wow. You look like a different person."

"Yeah," Quinn managed, pulling at the dress's fabric awkwardly. "I really need to go shopping."

She could tell Haley's feelings were hurt by the implication that she hated the dress, but Haley didn't say anything, and neither did Quinn. They weren't friends. Not yet, at least.

"So," Quinn said. "Breakfast?"

Haley frowned, glancing over at the clock. "You spent longer than I anticipated in the shower," she admitted carefully. "We could probably swing by the café on our way…"

Sensing that they were already late and Haley was just trying to be nice, Quinn said, against her better judgment, "No, no. It's fine." She could hear her stomach screaming at her, but she ignored it. "Let's just go."

Haley beamed. "Great. Follow me."

They headed into the hallway, where they spotted another girl walking in the same direction. She was of Asian descent, petite and athletic with long, silky black hair and a collected countenance similar to Haley's. She smiled in a friendly way when she saw the girls, not losing her mind as everyone else seemed to when they met Quinn. Quinn appreciated that.

"Hey, Pence," Haley said as they made their way to the elevator. "This is Quinn Harper. Our newest recruit."

Pence nodded at Quinn, not offering a hand. Quinn didn't mind; she had had quite enough handshakes for one week, anyway. "Nice to meet you. According to the rumors, you might be one of the last recruits, eh?"

Quinn shrugged, punching the button for the elevator. "So they say, but I don't know if I buy it. Maybe all the monsters have made their way here, but makers? In control of their abilities? Not such a hard thing to hide, is it?"

"You'd be surprised," Haley said as they filed into the elevator. She glanced at Pence. "Correct me if I'm wrong, but slip-ups are almost guaranteed to happen. For me, they happened just about every time I walked outside."

Pence grinned. "Absolutely. Everyone at my school knew about my abilities within a month. My family tried moving, but it didn't make a difference. Water was, like, drawn to me. Literally. I'd pass a water fountain, a sink… the whole flow of the thing found its way to me."

"Exactly," Haley said. "Leaves, dirt, plants—it all just started uprooting around me. Like it was saying, *at your service, Haley.*"

Quinn was impressed; she was heading to class with a manipulator of water and a manipulator of earth. Of course, she could manipulate both, but probably not as well as them. She had never taken the time to focus on either of those attributes. Fire was generally her go-to. Fire and compulsion.

They exited the elevator, passing the front desk of the dormitory on their way out. Quinn glanced at it, hoping to spot Drax, but realized he was probably on his way to class, too.

"What class are we going to, anyway?" Quinn asked the girls. "And what classes do we take here?"

"We're on our way to math," Haley explained. Seeing Quinn's panicked look, she added, "Don't worry—it's not crafted the same way as classes you'd be used to. Everyone is split into groups based on how much education they received in the real world. The teacher, Zerrick, is very good. He gives every student the time and focus they need, especially at first."

Quinn could feel her heart sinking with dread. She didn't know what she had been expecting, but not math. She knew next to nothing about math.

"We take all the general subjects," Pence told her. "Math, science, social studies, English. None of them are specified further until your teacher learns what you need personally. They're pretty cool about that. All the teachers are very good. Although…" She glanced at Haley, hesitating.

Quinn looked from Pence to Haley. "What?"

"Well," Haley said carefully, "one of the teachers—you'll have him later today—well, can be a bit difficult to get along with." She swallowed. "Maybe particularly for you."

Quinn froze. She couldn't mean *him*? The man from the dining hall?

"It's Dash," Haley said. "And I know you're still probably not ready to talk about him. But judging from the look on your face… you didn't know he was one of the teachers."

Quinn had assumed, based on Dash's appearance, that he was a little old to be a student, but she hadn't even considered that he might be a teacher. He certainly didn't *look* like one.

"Whatever," she grumbled. "I don't want to talk about it."

They had reached the school. Quinn smiled a forced smile as Pence grabbed the door for them, leading them inside. This building, like the dorm, was cozier than the dining and town halls. There were students scattered about the lobby, which was filled with bookshelves, tables, toys, and a front desk. Past the lobby was a hallway, where there were elevators and several doors to classrooms. Haley and Pence led her to an elevator, which they took to the third floor again. Everyone remained silent in the elevator.

When the doors opened, they stepped into the classroom across the hall. Quinn was surprised to see that they were the last to enter. In fact, the teacher was already standing at the front of the room, braced to speak.

"Ah," he said, glancing pointedly at his watch. "Right in the nick of time."

"Sorry, Zerrick," Haley said. "My fault."

Quinn appreciated the cover-up, not wanting any more attention drawn to her than there already was. She scanned the room with mild interest, recognizing both Trent and Drax from the day before. The rest of the students staring at her included a pretty, fair-haired girl with giant, white wings like an angel; a thin, dark-skinned, friendly-faced boy with big hair puffing out from under his baseball cap; a dark-haired, pale-skinned, sullen-looking young man in the back; and a few others she didn't quite get to scan before the teacher, Zerrick, began speaking.

"No problem, Haley." He nodded to Quinn. "You must be Quinn."

"That's me."

Zerrick waited a second, as if giving her a chance to redeem herself, before continuing. "Why don't you have a seat next to Angel for now?"

He gestured to an empty seat next to the white-winged girl.

"Angel the angel," Quinn quipped, unable to resist. "That's even worse than Drax the vampire."

Angel didn't take the joke nearly as well as Drax had. "And *you're* even worse than the over-hyped Siren the media forced down our throats," she fired back, not a lick of humor to her tone. "At least her, I didn't have to share an island with."

"Angel!" Zerrick scolded. "That will be quite enough. What have we said

41

about letting our anger get the better of us?"

Angel crossed her arms, glare subsiding to a pout. Quinn took her seat, floored by the girl's hostility.

"Welcome to today's math class," Zerrick said to the room. "Those of you who have been working on calculus, go ahead and group back up and crack open the textbooks. I'll be with you in a few minutes."

Quinn glanced around curiously as a handful of students rose from their seats to gather. Of those she had already met, the only one in the calculus group was Haley. Not a huge surprise to Quinn. The other two in the group were the friendly-looking boy with the baseball hat and the pale, sullen boy.

"Right," Zerrick said, turning to face the rest of the class. He had an interesting face, Quinn decided. Rich, dark skin; warm eyes; sharp cheekbones. He looked to Quinn like he could have been a movie or music producer in the real world.

"Trent, Pence," he said, "I know you two just finished up trig. I think we should try advanced algebra next. Why don't you go grab two Algebra 3 books from the back and start taking a look? I'll be with you shortly."

Trent and Pence rose and headed for the bookshelves in the back. Quinn had to admit she was a little impressed to see that Mr. Boy Band was one of the better-educated people in the room.

"The rest of you, pull out yesterday's homework, and I'll make the rounds. Quinn, why don't you come on up to my desk? Bring your chair."

Quinn bit her lip, glancing around to see how many eyes were still on her. Most of them had looked away by then, though her biggest fan over in Algebra 3 world was still watching. She grabbed her chair, lifted it like a paperweight, and made her way up to Zerrick's desk.

"Have a seat," he said, taking a seat at his own chair across from her. He smiled encouragingly at her. "Tell me about yourself."

She frowned. "What do you want to know?"

"Well, where are you from?"

"All over."

"Okay." He didn't seem to be growing frustrated, though she wasn't sure how. "Where were you born?"

"New York."

He nodded. This couldn't be much of a surprise to him. Everyone in that room had spent at least a little time in New York.

"Did you ever attend school in New York?"

She shook her head.

"Okay." He lowered his voice slightly. He seemed to be choosing his next words carefully. "Did you ever attend school anywhere?"

She had known this question was coming, but that didn't make her hate it any less. "Do I have to answer that?"

"No, but I think it might save us a little bit of time."

She sighed, knowing he was right. Might as well get it over with and admit how little education she had now, rather than let them all learn the hard way. "I made it to second grade or so. Then off and on, a little bit, til maybe fifth. And by off and on, I mean... mostly off."

He nodded, scribbling something down on the notepad in front of them.

"Is there any way you can, like... tip this off to my other teachers?" she asked. "The only thing worse than having this conversation would be having this conversation seven times."

"I would be happy to," he told her. "Though I have specific questions regarding my own subject, and I imagine they will, as well."

"I'll tell you right now, I know almost nothing about math. Basic addition and subtraction. I might know how to set up a multiplication problem, if my memory is on my side in the moment."

"I understand," he said gently. "Quinn, I know you might think you're alone in this, but you're truly not. When Pence got here a few years ago, she was in a similar situation to you. It wasn't easy for her, but she's been doing incredibly well. Drax, Angel... Being visibly affected is always the hardest on education. You can't attend school when you look the way they do."

"Yeah. I learned that the hard way."

She had attended school on and off for a few years after the event, but the older she got, the more her enhanced features began to stand out; before long, her teachers were calling the authorities on her. It was always easy for her to escape before things got bad, but the red flags were still raised.

Still, she couldn't imagine not even being able to set foot inside a school. With her, it always took people a moment to register that there was something different, and even then, they weren't sure. But Drax and Angel... They must have had to live in complete hiding.

"Anyway," Zerrick said, rifling through a binder, "start with this." He pulled out a small packet and a mechanical pencil. "It's technically a test, but don't think of it that way. It won't be graded. It'll just give me a better sense of what I can teach you. It should be about your level."

She felt grateful that this was being handled as discretely as it was, and decided that she might just like Zerrick, just as she had started to like so many of the other people on the island. Zerrick, Pence, Haley, Reese, Ridley... She couldn't remember the last time she had liked this many people in such a short span of time.

She took the packet back to her desk and began to work on it, but she had an incredibly hard time focusing on it. In fact, she found it hard to focus on anything... hard to even *see* anything...

She dropped her pencil, tried to pick it back up, couldn't. Her stomach began to cramp up in such incredible pain, she was sure she was about to snap in half. The lights in the room began to flicker, which was never a good sign... Everyone began to stare again, which was also never a good sign...

Luckily, she didn't have to deal with their stares much longer.

She fainted.

4. STABILIZATION

"It's dehydration, isn't it? Sounds like dehydration."

"I'm telling you, it's starvation. Pence told me she could hear her through the wall the night she got here, vomiting for hours. And none of us saw her at dinner that night—or breakfast yesterday."

"It's my fault she didn't make it to breakfast. I wish she would have told me she threw up all of that food. I would have woken her up earlier, or gotten her to eat some toast, at least."

"I just can't believe how long she's been out. Do you think it's something else? Something that has to do with her abilities?"

"Both of you, stop talking, would you? She's waking up."

Quinn's eyes fluttered, looking around in confusion. There was a mask over her nose and mouth and a needle in her arm. Hovering over her were Haley and the baseball cap boy from class. A little further back was an older woman wearing scrubs and writing what seemed to be a small novel on a chart. Quinn realized she was in some sort of hospital room and that the woman was probably her doctor.

"Quinn!" Haley exclaimed, breathing a sigh of relief. "I'm so glad you're okay. I'm such a bad roommate for not noticing you were sick that night. Dr. Donovan's been shooting you up with some good nutrients, and Reese is going to go get some nice, tame food in you after this."

Quinn glanced over toward the doorway and saw that there was a fifth person in the room: Reese. He smiled at her when they made eye contact, and she lingered a beat too long on it before turning her attention back to the boy in the baseball cap.

"Who are you?" she asked him bluntly.

He laughed. "My name's Charlie. I'm in your class. This is Dr. Donovan, my mom. I helped Haley get you here yesterday, and I've tried to come help my mom between shifts. We don't get a lot of emergencies around here, so she tends to be short-staffed when we do."

Quinn wondered whether he and his mother were both deviants, or whether she had come to the island just for him, as Savannah had for her sons.

"Charlie is Pence's boyfriend," Haley told Quinn. "She came and checked on you a few times, but she had to go to class and get our assignments for us since we've been mostly here."

"So, it's been, what, a full day since I passed out?" Quinn asked, trying to catch up. "Is that normal?"

She tried not to notice Reese's concerned expression; he seemed to have the same question.

"It's been just under 24 hours," Dr. Donovan said, coming over to Quinn. "Miss Harper, this isn't just a matter of you not eating enough food—though it certainly didn't help. I'm told that in the past few days alone, you've been shot multiple times, caused—and survived—a helicopter crash, and flew yourself and three others nearly a mile to the shore."

Quinn crossed her arms, irritated. Obviously, Ridley had recounted his experiences with her to at least this person, if not more. It was just another example of everyone on the island knowing everything about her.

"Look," she said. "I'm a self-healer. Do you see any bullet wounds?"

"I see that your surface wounds have healed. That's not where my concern lies. Quinn, you've been exerting your abilities at an astronomical rate—one that would put anyone here in a coma. You need to be careful."

"Careful?" Quinn repeated. "What would you have had me do, Doc? Run faster from the bad guys shooting at me? Not attempt to bring down the helicopter that, to my knowledge, was leading me to my permanent imprisonment? Not that I was necessarily wrong about that…"

Haley and Charlie glanced at each other, clearly stifling a mixture of laughter and shock. The doctor didn't look amused.

"Quinn, I understand the situation you were in. But you have to understand that you aren't a victim of those circumstances any more. I'm sure you spent a long time not being able to take good care of yourself, but now you're in a position where you can. And you even have help doing so. It's not the rest of the world that's hurting you here. It's you."

Quinn understood what she was being told, but that didn't mean she had to like hearing it. "I've been taking care of myself my entire life. I don't need anyone to help me now."

The woman sighed, looking over at Reese. "She's cleared on my end. Take her to get some food. Try reasoning with her where I can't."

Reese nodded, saying nothing.

"And you two," the doctor said to Haley and Charlie. "Back to class."

Haley and Charlie both rose, pouting. Haley made a move to give Quinn a hug, then thought better of it. "Good luck. I'll see you at home."

Home. The word sounded so wrong, and yet just a little bit right.

· · ·

"What you told Dr. Donovan," Reese said to her over bread and soup a few minutes later. "Was that true? Do you really think you don't need help from anyone?"

Quinn glanced around the café, frowning. Breakfast rush was over, and most everyone was either at school or work. But she didn't feel much more comfortable then than she had the last time she was there.

"I guess it's not that I don't *need* it," she admitted, nibbling on her bread. "I just don't think it's worth the risk."

"The risk," Reese repeated. "What do you mean by that?"

She crossed her arms, dodging the question. "Don't you have law to be enforcing? Why were you there, anyway?"

"The criminals aren't awake yet," he joked. "Haley was a little worried that you might not be in a good way when you woke up, so she came to me for backup. She mentioned that she thought you had taken to me." Seeing Quinn's alarmed face, he added quickly, "I think she just meant I'm one of the few people you don't hate. You know—unlike my brother."

"Your brother?"

"Yeah—Dash. Which, by the way, I've been meaning to ask you about."

She gasped, coughing and sputtering soup at him in a less-than-graceful way. *"He's your brother?"*

"Yes," he said, seeming almost as confused as her. "I thought you must have known that. You seemed like you knew him pretty well…"

"But… Haley said he was one of the teachers. I thought your brother worked with you and your mom."

"Right—when he's not out in the field doing power stabilization. I think she mentioned that…"

Power stabilization? That was the 'class' he taught?

"He also teaches special seminars, here and there," Reese said. "He likes showing off his very random, specific knowledge." He rolled his eyes.

Quinn could hardly believe her ears. How could Reese, someone so unassuming, easygoing, and gentle, be directly related to Dash, the most striking, alluring… *cold* person she had ever met?

"Sorry," Reese said; "would have told you if I'd known you didn't know. Like I said, the whole thing was on my list of questions to ask you."

She shook her head, floored. "Well, what else were you going to ask?"

"I guess, just… what happened between you two. I've seen powers tied to emotions before, but never like that. I thought you were going to bring the whole building down."

If he were anyone else, she would have snapped at him, *None of your business.* But she wasn't bothered in this instance. If he wanted to get to know her, it was valid for him to wonder what had happened between her and his brother.

"It's stupid, honestly," she said. "I'm just an idiot. He probably hates me, huh?"

"I wouldn't know. We aren't exactly on speaking terms, my brother and I."

She raised her eyebrows, interest piquing. Now that she thought about it, Reese had mentioned being the black sheep of the family… What did that make Dash, then? Savannah's right hand?

The thought made her want to vomit all over again.

"What happened?" she asked him.

"I asked first."

She sighed. "The night of the event, I was alone. Seven years old. Scared shitless. This guy came over to me, stayed with me, told me everything was going to be okay. When I woke up, he was gone. I never saw him again. When I saw your brother…"

"You thought it was him."

She nodded. "Which, really, doesn't make any sense at all. He would have aged ten years since then. He'd be in his thirties at least. Besides, I saw the guy for ten minutes of my life ten years ago. I don't know how I could possibly have thought I still had an image of him crisp in my mind."

"All true. But you seem like the type of person whose instincts are rarely wrong. I can see how that could have gotten to you."

She smiled a small smile. "Thanks."

He straightened, clearing his throat. "Dash and I have been estranged for a long time. I mean, we exchange pleasantries in the office on the days he comes in, but I wouldn't say we've really talked since before the event. Long as I can remember, he's been on her side. Savannah's. Wanted to be just like her when he grew up. Political. Wealthy. Influential."

All of the things she hated in people.

"He's gotten better, I think, since we came here," Reese continued. "Working with students, and the public, it's helped him. But he's never been good with people. Most of the students would agree with me, I think. His mind just never really worked the same way as everyone else's."

It was hard for her to judge anyone for that; her own mind also worked differently from everyone else's. But not like Reese was describing.

"Anyway," Reese said, "enough about my little brother. How are you feeling?"

"I'm alright. I could use some rest, though. Are you going to force me to go straight to class on your mother's behalf?"

He chuckled. "I'm sure she'd like me to, but I think you deserve a free pass, just this once. Our little secret."

· · ·

When she got back to her room, Quinn realized she wasn't sleepy at all. In fact, for the first time in a long time, she felt well-rested and, thanks to her outing with Reese, well-fed. Still, she didn't intend to return to class. Not when she had a free pass from the man in charge of the law.

She pulled open the cell phone Haley had given her. It was a standard smartphone, complete with all the apps and games that they had back on the mainland. There were even social media apps, though she was sure there was some sort of Siloh web bubble that kept the rest of the world out. But Quinn had never had much interest in any of that.

She glanced around the room, taking in the details for the first time. If she hadn't already known Haley was smart, she would have deduced it from the decorations. Maps, globes, diagrams, statistics. Photographs, some of her traveling the world, some of her with family. Quinn wondered what had happened to Haley's family—where they were now.

Finally, her eyes settled on the bookcase. She couldn't remember the last time she had read a real book.

She skipped over all of the classics, the authors with an initial or two followed by a too-long, made-up sounding last name, the textbooks, the dictionaries. She would have to start small, she knew. Her gaze found its way to a smaller, simpler book. It was bright blue; hardcover. An electric yellow title embedded in the spine. *STARGIRL.*

This was the book she chose.

She wasn't sure what speed she was reading at or how much time was passing. She became absorbed in the book so completely, everything else seemed to disappear. She wasn't sure if she was supposed to be hungry, or thirsty, or anywhere, or nowhere. She wasn't sure of anything at except that she was finally doing something normal—something other kids got to do whenever they liked.

She probably would have read well into the night if not for the knock at her door that tore her from her trance.

She glanced over at Haley's alarm clock. 4:47P. Classes were probably just about over, but Haley had a key. Who else would be knocking?

She rose and stepped over to the door, peering through the peep-hole. It was Ridley.

She reached for the handle, but hesitated. Her instincts had liked his personality from the beginning, but that didn't change the fact that he had been on the helicopter that brought her there—a helicopter that had also carried two men from the DCA. Didn't that have to mean he was in on the capturing of deviants? Didn't that mean she should hate him?

Looking around the room, she had to remind herself that even if he was, maybe it wasn't the worst thing. In a strange way, her life had improved since she her arrival at Siloh two days earlier. She wasn't *free,* something she wasn't bound to forget any time soon. But for the first time in ten years, no one was hunting her.

She decided to open the door.

"Hey," Ridley said, offering her a kind smile. "I hope you don't mind that I came by. I visited you once in the medical wing, but you were still out cold. I heard you were discharged and I just wanted to make sure you were okay."

"That's nice of you," she said, smiling guardedly. Everything in his words seemed genuine; there didn't seem to be a drop of ill will in him. She backed up to let him in. "Come in."

He seemed surprised by the invitation, and glanced around as if unsure whether to accept. But, after a moment's hesitation, he stepped in. She closed the door, taking a seat on her bed and gesturing for him to do the same.

He shifted awkwardly from one foot to the other. "I'm okay standing."

She shrugged. "Suit yourself."

"So... you're okay?"

"Yeah. Just forgot to eat, I guess. Exerted myself a little too hard. Wasn't really sure how long it was that I was, you know, drugged up and stuff. Do you know? How long I was on that helicopter? And whether I was on a plane before that?"

"Oh, yeah." He sounded amused. "We were on the helicopter for about two hours, but you had twenty hours of flights before that. Do you even know what part of the world we're in?"

"I guess I hadn't given it much thought."

"We're north of Australia—east of Papa New Guinea and Indonesia. About as far from New York City as it gets."

"Good riddance," she muttered. *No love lost there.*

He chuckled.

Both of them fell silent, and she hesitated before asking her next question, but decided she had to. "Look. You seem like you want to help me for some reason. You seem like a good person. But I've been proven wrong before, and I keep coming back to the same question... Why were you on that helicopter?"

He didn't seem surprised; if anything, he looked relieved that the ice had been broken. "I'm sure it's confusing for you. As you probably know, I work in security for Siloh. To me, my boss is Savannah, and I'm here to protect everyone inside our wall. But to the DCA, I'm here to protect *them* and everyone outside. It's one of those lies we have to go along with to keep everyone out there in the dark."

This made some degree of sense, she supposed.

"When we've worked in security long enough," Ridley explained, "we rotate being members of what we call the 'greeting party.' None of us are allowed in the States, or anywhere close. But we are allowed, with special permission, to go to Fiji and meet the airplane that brings newcomers in. They usually ease the sedatives when they switch the newcomer from the plane to the helicopter, and use people like me to keep them calm when they wake up. Probably not the best idea in your case."

She grinned slightly at that, but she was surprised what had happened with her didn't happen more often. Sure, Ridley's friendly face might have calmed her in some subconscious way, but her mind had been reeling with a thousand other thoughts at the time.

"Do people not usually panic the way I did?" she asked him. "Does that panic not usually... cause problems?"

"Well, for one thing, the average deviant isn't quite as powerful as you. But I will say your abilities seem particularly tied to your emotions. You'll really benefit from Dash's—" He saw her wince at the name, and he seemed to know why. "I heard about that. I didn't want to ask."

"There's really not that much to say," she assured him, not wanting to repeat the story all over again. "But from what I hear, he's a pretty loathsome guy to more than just me."

"Don't believe everything you hear. A lot of the students will grumble about him, sure. He doesn't exactly have a way with people. I'm sure you can relate to that."

She frowned.

"But Dash is very good at what he does," he continued. "And he cares. It's evident from how hard he works to help people. I know he would have a lot to offer you. Were you planning on going to his class this evening?"

She glanced at the clock, surprised that classes were still going on. It explained why Haley wasn't there. "What time is his class?"

"Five o'clock, every day."

It was 4:56. She'd never make it in time. "I don't know. Reese told me I was off the hook for classes today. And there's no way I'd make it there by five—I don't even know where it is."

"I'm sure Reese knows what he's talking about," he said in a somewhat disingenuous way, "but if you're feeling up for it, I say you try to make it. I can take you there, if you'd like. I can say something to Dash so he doesn't give you a hard time. I know the guy very well—he trusts me."

Quinn was surprised to learn that Ridley and Dash were, from what she was gathering, friends. She wasn't sure whether it made her like Ridley less or Dash more. But she was pretty sure she liked Ridley, and she was curious about this mysterious power stabilization class. Besides, she would be forced to take it every day for the rest of her life. She might as well start now.

"Okay," she said. "Let's go."

• • •

It was a farther walk to Dash's class than to anywhere else she had traveled on the island. It was deeper than the school and the dorms, back toward the smattering of forests and river, not far from the horse stable.

"Hey," she said to Ridley as they walked, reaching into her pocket and surfacing her cell phone. She handed it to him. "You should put your number in here. In case I'd ever like to see you again. You know, other than in a security setting."

He put his number in, looking genuinely surprised. She wasn't totally thrown by his surprise, but it did make her a little sad. It reminded her of Kurt, who always used to ask her, *Why do you even talk to me?*

Because you're one of the few good ones left in the world, she would tell him. And, looking up at Ridley, she had a feeling it was true of him, too.

They reached a large clearing about the size of a football field. Scattered about the clearing were various pieces of what could only be described as training equipment. Obstacles, balance beams, even weapons. The YA were gathered around Dash in the center of the clearing, listening to him give some sort of speech.

Dash stopped speaking the moment he saw her and Ridley. As usual, everyone turned to look at her. As usual, all fell silent.

Dash's initial expression was the same glare he had worn when he encountered her the day she had arrived. When he saw Ridley next to her, though, his expression softened, and he came over to them.

"Everything okay?" he asked Ridley, not looking her in the eye.

"Quinn's had a rough start here," Ridley explained. "I'm sure you heard about her stint in the medical wing and why she missed class yesterday. She was discharged this morning. Reese told her she could take the rest of the day off, but she wanted to give your class a try. She got lost on the way and I helped her find the place."

Quinn appreciated the lie he had tagged onto the end on her behalf, but she wished he could have avoided the 'wanted to give your class a try' bit. She had already led Dash to believe she had an inexplicable fixation with him; she didn't need any icing added to that cake.

Dash glanced from Ridley to Quinn, this time making eye contact. He held her gaze for a moment, and as much as she wanted to look away, she refused to. Finally, he nodded, breaking contact.

"Okay," he said. "Thanks, Ridley. I'll take it from here."

Ridley nodded, turning to Quinn and offering her a parting smile. "You gonna be okay?"

"Yeah," she said, and, before she could stop herself, she hugged him.

She wasn't sure who on the field was the most surprised. They were both beet red as they pulled away. Ridley gave her an awkward wave before leaving.

Dash stared at her for a second, curiosity clouding his eyes, before clearing his throat. "Electricity. Fire. Ice. Light. Am I missing anything?"

She crossed her arms. "Sorry?"

"Your abilities. The ones I had the pleasure of witnessing, at least. What other abilities do you know of?"

She glanced behind him toward the rest of the class, all of whom were standing impatiently several meters away from them, watching.

"Don't worry about them," he told her. "Answer the question."

"I'm a seer," she snapped at him. "Is that what you'd like me to say? So you can run and tell Mommy?"

Any semblance of kindness he might have had towards her for arriving with Ridley was gone now. He glanced back at the rest of his class for a second, then, with no warning whatsoever, attacked.

A barrage of fire and ice hurtled towards her, slamming her to the ground so hard, the wind was knocked out of her.

But her passionate hatred for the man quickly brought her back to her feet, and she hit him right back with a taste of his own medicine.

Her ice melted before it hit him, and her fire subsided to smoke.

He was powerful.

His turn.

The earth beneath her began to shake, the dirt disappearing like quicksand. But before she could force herself into the air, he was doing it for her: the wind around her turned into a tornado, spinning and jarring her until she was suspended fifteen feet in the air.

Shrieking fiercely, she projected a blast of electricity so intense, the students across the way doubled over in pain. The shock distracted him from his tornado, and the wind slowed, allowing her to drop back down to the ground. Before he could conjure up his next attack, she was on to her next: She walked up to him, looked him into the eyes, and hissed, "*Kneel.*"

He did not.

He glared down at her, eyes blazing, and that was when she felt it. Something unlike anything she had felt before. Complete, utter captivity. All she could think, all she could want, was to do exactly what he said.

"*Kneel,*" he commanded.

She did.

He turned away from her, looking back toward the rest of the class and allowing her to rise to her feet. Several members of the class burst into cheers. Angel's, Quinn noticed in annoyance, were the loudest. The rest of the class looked at her with a mixture of surprise and sympathy.

How was this possible? How could he have all of the abilities she had— probably more? How could he, of all people, be the only person she had ever met who was so much like her?

She *hated* him.

"The lesson to be learned here," Dash told the class, "is not that I am more powerful than she is. You have all seen what she can do. The entire world has." He didn't say this with any admiration. "The lesson to be learned is that I have spent the last ten years separating my abilities from my emotions, and she has spent the last ten years operating off pure emotion."

She stared at her classmates' faces, disgusted even more by their excited and inspired looks than by the idiocy of what he was saying.

"We'll break into the regular pairs," he said, apparently done with that train of thought. "Angel, Drax. Pence, Haley. Trent, Charlie. Izzo, Tommy. And Shade, it looks like you finally have a partner other than me."

The pale-skinned, elusive young man Quinn had noticed several times, but not met, looked over at Quinn without a hint of curiosity or excitement. In fact, she couldn't read a single thought he was having.

"Shade," Dash said, "when she is ready, I'd like you to introduce Quinn to one of your illusions. When she says stop, I would like you to stop."

Illusions?

"I'm sorry," Quinn said, staring at Dash in disbelief. "This is your idea of power stabilization? Pitting people against each other in a free-for-all?"

"Free-for-all? This isn't a free-for-all. You are not free to return fire on Shade here. He unleashes on you, then, once you've surrendered, you'll have your chance with him."

"Who says I'll surrender?"

"Everyone surrenders. Just remember: use your abilities against him before his time is up, and you lose. Automatically."

She groaned. "Let's just get this over with."

Shade looked over at her, still not revealing a hint of emotion. "Does that mean you're ready?"

"*Yes,* dead eyes," she snapped, "I'm ready."

Shade placed his hands together, closed his eyes, and breathed. For several seconds, nothing changed. Quinn stared at him, poised, waiting.

All of a sudden, everything became black—not dark; not shadowy—a true, endless black unlike anything she had ever experienced.

Her heart nearly stopped in fear, but she refused to show it. She wouldn't let him win. Not after letting Dash win.

"Nice trick," she teased. "So, if I don't surrender, do I just stand here in the dark until class is over?"

But he said nothing, and neither did Dash. In fact, come to think of it, she couldn't *hear* anything, either. Was that possible? Was Shade so good that he could affect not only what she saw, but what she heard, too?

Or was no one saying anything because no one cared?

A spinning sensation was next. First, tiny white lights began to appear, almost like dim stars. Not bright enough to light her way, but bright enough to catch her eye—and, as they began to spin and swirl around her, enough to make her dizzy.

The gravitational forces around her began to make her dizzy, too—as if she was floating. This, combined with the moving stars, almost made her feel like she was falling through outer space. It was simultaneously one of the most beautiful things she had ever seen and one of the most frightening.

"Very cool," she told him, hearing the tremble in her own voice but ignoring it. "Think they offer something similar at Disney World."

And, suddenly, the spinning stopped. And the lights went away. And she was left with the darkness. Just the darkness. And...

Her sharp intake of air was so loud, she was sure it echoed for miles around. Her hand flew to her lips, a sea of tears flying to her eyes.

"Kurt?" she whispered.

She knew it wasn't true, knew it couldn't be him, knew he was dead, knew ghosts weren't real, but *there he was,* standing in front of her. He was a ghostly, glowing, frightening version of Kurt, but those were his sweet, sad eyes, and that was his small, goofy smile, and—

And suddenly he was being shot—over and over again—so many times, his thin, gangly body was being shredded to pieces. She reached out to touch him, to hold him, to protect him, but the closer she got to him, the farther he was, like some terrible, taunting mind game—which was exactly what it *was,* and she knew that, and yet...

She screamed, punching at the air, knowing perfectly well how it looked and not caring. Hating everything and everyone around her, everywhere.

"*You sick fuck,*" she screamed, not at Kurt but at Shade, at the terrible, cruel man hidden somewhere before her, "*you do not get to see him, you do not get to know of him, you do not get—*"

And, suddenly, everything disappeared. And she was back in the real world.

She looked from Shade over to Dash, and back to Shade, then over at the students, all of whom had stopped to watch her. For several seconds, no one said a word.

Then Shade asked her, in utter confusion, "Can you see us?"

She stared back at him, just as confused. He hadn't ended the illusion? He hadn't heard her screams and freed her from the spell?

"Yes, I can see you," she said, her voice still shaking. "Did you not mean to stop?"

Shade looked down at his own hands as if questioning everything about them. "No. This has never happened before."

Quinn let that sink in for a second, but it didn't take long. She turned back to Dash. "Who did you say he was training with before I came along?" she asked him pointedly, knowing the answer perfectly well. If anything could make up for Dash defeating her in combat, it was her breaking away from an illusion that he couldn't.

"Impressive," he admitted. "But your stopping Shade was a result of pure emotion, not conscious control. Your rage may have gotten you this far, but it exhausts you. Last time, it landed you in a 24-hour coma. If you don't learn how to harness it, it could get you killed."

She was in no mood for a lecture. The images of Kurt were still burning in her head; all she wanted was to retaliate against Shade. "Is it my turn yet?"

He sighed, gesturing for her to begin.

She turned to face Shade. One look at the cold, dark eyes that had made her see such terrible things was all she needed to decide what to do next. It was something she only reserved for the very worst people—the people who had done unspeakable things to her.

Showing her Kurt's death—making her relive her own inability to prevent it— to her, that was the most unspeakable.

"When you're ready," she told him, voice simultaneously silky-smooth and stinging. She could see the effect it had on his nerves instantly.

"I'm ready," he said, looking just the opposite.

She took a step toward him, then another, until she was inches from his face. She gazed into his dark, emotionless eyes, knowing the effect her gaze had on him before the words escaped her lips.

"*Immeasurable pain.*"

He screamed ten times louder than she had.

It was only a few seconds before he begged her to stop, and she did, just before Dash reached her to force her to. Once she stopped, she looked down at Shade. He was little more than a curled-up ball of a boy, still whimpering.

She turned back to Dash, daring him to challenge her.

And, of course, he did.

"That was heartless," he told her, voice thick with disgust. "Cruel."

She didn't blink, didn't back down, not even for a second. He didn't get to judge her. Not then. Not after what had just happened to her.

When she spoke, her voice was laced with an honest sadness that she hadn't intended to reveal. But it didn't matter. She didn't owe him any explanations.

"You don't know what he made me see."

• • •

She and Shade were both excused at that point, leaving early as Dash turned his attention to the rest of the students. She didn't care. She couldn't believe Ridley had recommended the class to her. She couldn't believe such a class was allowed to exist, even at a place like this.

She considered calling Ridley, giving him a piece of her mind, letting off some steam. She considered calling Reese, too. She was sure he wouldn't mind hearing her complain about his little brother—not after the earful he had given her on the same subject.

But in the end, she didn't do either of those things, heading instead to the dining hall for a nice, quiet meal before the dinner rush hit.

Or so she hoped.

"*Quinn*!" exclaimed Rory from her spot alone at one of the tables. She jumped away from her food, running over to hug Quinn at the counter. Quinn stiffened on instinct, surprised that the girl thought they were anywhere near hugging terms, but didn't bother pushing her away.

"Hi," Quinn managed, awkwardly patting the girl on the head. "Uh… Rory, right?"

"Yep! It's so nice to see you again. I'm so glad you're feeling better! You'll sit with me, won't you?"

Quinn considered ordering her food to go, but didn't have the heart to do that to the doe-eyed girl staring up at her. She tried to force a smile. "Sure."

Rory cheered, running back over to her plate and staring anxiously back at Quinn as she ordered her food. By the time Quinn made it to the table, Rory was already finished eating. But Quinn had a feeling she wasn't going anywhere.

"Rory," Quinn said, scanning the room, which seemed to have five or ten occupants about Rory's age. "Can I ask you a question?"

"You can ask me anything you'd like," Rory said eagerly.

"Okay... Why aren't you sitting with the other kids your own age?"

"Oh." Rory visibly deflated. Quinn instantly felt guilty for asking, but knew it was too late to take it back. "Well... I don't know. They all think I'm weird. They're just jealous, I think. I'm really powerful, you know. Not like you, but..."

Quinn laughed. "Really. And what, may I ask, are your abilities?"

"Well, electricity, thanks for asking! I can do really big bursts of it, too. If you wanted me to, I could shock everybody in this room with a big blast, right now!"

Quinn grinned. "Maybe another time. But I'm certainly impressed."

"Thanks," Rory said fondly. "I know you have some electric powers, too. I've seen you use them on TV a lot."

"It's one of my favorites," Quinn said, thinking back to the giant shockwave she'd thrown at Dash earlier. She'd almost had him at that point, she marveled. Maybe she should kick her electric practice up a notch.

Quinn chewed on her chicken, watching Rory observe everyone in the room. She was very perceptive for her age, Quinn noticed.

"Can I ask you another question?" Quinn asked.

Rory nodded.

"Do you take the power stabilization class with Dash, too?"

"Not with Dash. He doesn't work with the kids. We have another teacher who's not nearly as good as him."

Quinn raised her eyebrows. "What makes you say that?"

"We barely even use our abilities in class! It's all about what she calls 'suppression.' All we really do is use them a tiny bit and then practice not using them any more."

"That sounds pretty pointless, doesn't it? You go through years with a teacher who tells you not to use your abilities, and then you graduate to a teacher who runs a Gladiator-style tournament every day? And our uptight President Savannah is okay with that?"

Rory's eyes widened. "Be careful how loud you say that stuff," she whispered. "And I don't know. Savannah comes to our classes all the time, but I never see her and Dash together. Maybe he's ignoring her rules?"

That certainly threw Quinn for a loop. *Dash* was the one ignoring Savannah's rules? Sure, it would surprise her if Savannah encouraged him to push people's abilities to their limits, given that she was all about rules and regulations, but Reese had told her that Dash and Savannah were birds of a feather. So why would Dash do something so openly rebellious? There had to be more to the story; she just couldn't quite figure out what it was.

"I can tell you don't like him," Rory said. "But I do. I don't think he cares what his mom wants him to do. I think he cares about us. Letting us get strong in a healthy way." She grinned. "Well, mostly healthy."

Quinn found Rory more and more fascinating by the minute. She might not agree with her assessment of Dash, but she couldn't deny the girl's smarts. "You're pretty damn bright for a kid. You know that?"

"I know. But I don't mind hearing it from my favorite person in the world."

You won't think that for long, Quinn wanted to tell her. *Just wait until you get to know me. You'll run for the hills.*

It was her automatic response to the kinds of statements Rory had made, ingrained into her for years. It was the response she would have given Haley, Ridley, or even Reese if any of them had dared telling her that she was their favorite person in the world.

But something about the way Rory said it made Quinn stop herself. Something about the way Rory was looking at her made her actually want to be the heroine the girl thought she was.

What were these people doing to her?

5. ROOFTOPS

Quinn wasn't sure what to expect when she said her goodbyes to Rory and made her way back to the dorms. Sure, Dash had given her a hard time after she had put Shade in immeasurable pain, but she hadn't stopped to see what everyone else thought. It would certainly make her living situation more tense if Haley was now afraid of her.

Quinn could tell before opening the door that Haley was there. She could hear the hushed whispers and concerned voices on the other side.

"…got to figure out what happened with her and Dash." Male voice. Deep. If she had to guess, she'd say Trent. "I mean, sure, the dude's a prick, but I've never seen him act *that* harsh."

She smiled to herself, satisfied with both legs of that statement. Other students thought Dash was a prick, too. And they understood that she had been singled out and inappropriately treated. Right?

"Yeah," said another voice, female—not Haley's, but still familiar. "But whatever happened with her and Dash has nothing to do with what she did to Shade. I mean… that was borderline cruel."

Why didn't anyone understand that what Shade had done to her was worse? Simply because they couldn't see it themselves?

"We should stop talking about her and wait for her to get here so we can ask her ourselves," said a third voice. This one was Haley's. "Which brings us back to… where *is* she?"

Quinn took that as her cue, turning the knob and stepping inside. They looked panicked, which gave her a bit of satisfaction. Haley, Trent, Pence, and Charlie, she assessed. Pence must have been the one criticizing her.

"Quinn," Haley said, standing up. Trent stood, as well; the other two remained seated. "We were worried."

"About me? Let me give you a piece of advice: never worry about me. It'll drive you mad and I'll always be fine in the end."

She felt Trent's eyes on her as she spoke, and she snuck him a small, teasing grin. She didn't know why she did it, exactly. Manipulating boys like Trent had always been so easy for her—so familiar. How many Trents had she met in the real world? Crashed with when she had nowhere else to go? Conned into doing things they wouldn't normally do? Dozens, if not more. They were typically the more harmless of the bunch. Sure, they only wanted one thing, but at least she always knew what that one thing was.

"Not just you," Pence said to her. "We were worried about Shade, too."

Quinn had to give her credit for saying the same thing to her face she had been saying behind her back.

"Oh," she said, edging up to the challenge, "you mean because of the three seconds of pain that I put him in? You're right. My own *teacher* unleashes the flames of hell and a death barrage of ice on me, not to mention sticking me in a tornado. Then your precious little Shade puts images in my head I won't be able to erase for the rest of my life. But let's all worry about the *three seconds* of pain I put him in instead, right?"

Everyone fell silent. Pence looked guilty.

"I thought it was a *training* class," Quinn continued, shaking her head. "Ask me the last time the pain I went through was *only* three seconds. When I got shot at by a firing squad of DCA agents just a few days ago? When they tried releasing a mixture of smoke and laughing gas into my house while I was sleeping a few months before that?" She stopped herself at that, not wanting to go into any more detail with these people.

"Quinn," Haley said carefully. "I understand how hard it must have been, seeing whatever he made you see. But you have to understand... Shade isn't a mind-reader. He's an illusionist with the rare ability to make you see your darkest thoughts, actualized. He doesn't hand-pick or manipulate them. He doesn't even see those thoughts, himself. He did to you what he's done to all of us; your darkest thoughts were probably just... a lot darker."

She had to admit, knowing that changed things. His attack on her hadn't been intentionally cruel; it had just been his strongest ability, unleashed.

But if that was his strongest ability, why shouldn't she unleash hers?

"Look," she finally said. "Sure, it helps, knowing that. And maybe it means I overreacted. But you have to remember something. This might not be Devil's Island, but the way you're all acting, it's like you've been living at a five-star resort. We're *monsters*—I don't care if we're visibly affected or not, we're still monsters— and I for one would rather know how to take a few punches, because I know this isn't the end of the line for us. The rest of the world finds out how good we've got it, there goes how good we've got it."

Everyone remained silent. Pence and Charlie glanced at each other as if considering telling her something.

"You're right," Charlie said to Quinn. "We talk about it a lot. What will happen when the word gets out about what it's really like here. When legislation changes. When the UNCODA stops trusting the DCA and starts monitoring us themselves. Or even... whether there's more to our situation here that we don't fully understand. We think about it every day."

"That's why we push Dash to *train* us, like you said," Pence added, "rather than just teach us stabilization, like he's technically supposed to. We don't even call the class 'power stabilization' like they do, because it's about more than that. To us, it's power tech."

Quinn lingered on the words *like he's technically supposed to.* It was like Rory had said: Savannah didn't want the students using their abilities to the extent that Dash was having them do. Who was wrong? Reese, or Rory and Pence?

"We were just surprised, is all," Haley told her. "For your first time, someone you didn't know. I think it was really your use of the word *immeasurable*... Maybe avoid that word from now on?"

Quinn heaved an overdramatic sigh. "Fine. Just measurable pain from here on out."

"I've got an idea," Charlie said. "No one's really welcomed you to the island

65

yet, have they, Quinn? No sort of celebration, or anything like that."

Quinn snorted. "You throw me a celebration, you'll be the next one feeling immeasurable pain."

"I'm serious! Maybe if we actually get you to have some fun, you'll stop wanting to put us in pain. It won't be cheesy. You know that big, stone building toward the east side of the island? The tallest one—four stories?"

Quinn shrugged a shoulder, familiar with the building but not sure what he was getting at.

"My parents own it," he explained. "We call it the tower. The top floor—it's a penthouse suite. Bar, patio, dance floor. It's where we throw parties. Sanctioned ones and… unsanctioned ones."

"And your parents just leave you a key to the place?" she asked doubtfully.

"Actually, they do," Pence said. "Charlie's parents trust him. They know how important it is to keep friends close here. If they were to ask him why he threw this party, and he were to tell them you needed to get to know your classmates…"

"They'd understand," Charlie finished. "Then again… Best we keep it between ourselves, just in case. You know, let them find out the hard way."

Quinn sighed. "There's no chance you're going to let this go, is there?"

He grinned and shook his head.

"Fine," she said, admitting defeat. "I never was one to turn down a party."

• • •

They agreed to throw the party the following Saturday, which left Charlie and the gang three days to prepare. Quinn did her best to lay low over the next few days, but it wasn't easy. As promised, Zerrick had shared her education experience with her other teachers, but they still had dozens of questions apiece for her. Her new science teacher, Lydia, was the worst of the lot. Quinn spent a good fifteen minutes moaning her way through Lydia's questions before finally the teacher handed Quinn a textbook on geology and told her to get to work.

As bad as Lydia was, she was nothing compared to Dash, who hadn't forgiven her as readily as her new friends. He continued to pair her with Shade every day, encouraging him to try different illusions on her. Shade, undoubtedly terrified of being subjected to the pain Quinn had subjected him to before, toned it down several notches. He put her under illusions of darkness or dizziness, but never memories; she returned the favor by putting him in very mild pain for a matter of seconds before accepting his surrender. Shade still seemed to resent her for the embarrassment, but not nearly as much as Dash, who could barely look at her.

"This is an opportunity for you," Dash urged Shade the first day of the subdued illusion. "This is the first time someone has had the ability to negate your illusions. Don't you want to push it farther? Push her to negate them, then push yourself to keep them going?"

But Shade's expression remained as dark and dull as ever as he responded simply, "No."

"And that's fine with you?" Dash asked Quinn, turning to glare at her. "You don't want him to challenge himself? To challenge you?"

"It's not my fault he won't challenge me," she responded evenly, and he gave up on them both, moving on to the next pair.

The pattern continued for the rest of the week. Every day, Dash was even more disappointed in her than the last. Every day, she did her best not to care.

Finally, it was Saturday, and Quinn made it her mission to do nothing but lie in bed and sleep on and off the entire day.

At least, until Trent barged in to remind them all what day it was.

"We know what day it is, Trent," Haley said when he stepped into their room, already fully dressed for the party. Quinn glanced groggily over at the alarm clock. It was just past two in the afternoon.

"What are you still doing asleep?" Trent asked Quinn, eyes wide and genuinely confused. "Don't you have to, I don't know, do girl things? Style your hair? Put on makeup?"

"Trent," Haley said, laughing out loud. "The party starts in, like, five hours. How long do you think it takes us to get ready?"

"I don't know, but I'm happy to be an observer of the process."

"Trent," Quinn said, chiming in for the first time as she shoved her covers off and rose to look at him, tank top strap dangling tauntingly off her shoulder. She cocked her head to the side in a deliberately irresistible way.

"Yes, Quinn?" Trent asked her, cocking his head to mirror hers. He was clearly trying to be cute, and in a way, it was working. But it was nothing she hadn't seen before.

So she said, voice sweet and smooth as butter, "Get the hell out."

As usual, he didn't look discouraged by her abrasiveness. He stood up, smiled charmingly, and said, "You'll miss me."

And he left.

Quinn rolled her eyes as she grabbed a towel and started to head for the bathroom. Seeing Haley staring after the door Trent had exited, she joked, "He's really the worst, isn't he?"

"What? Oh—yeah." Haley laughed a distracted laugh. "Totally."

Quinn raised her eyebrows and said nothing. She thought about that look on Haley's face as she stepped into the shower. Was it... *wistfulness* she had seen? Lust? As if... Haley *wanted* Trent?

She hoped not. Haley could do so much better.

When she returned to the bedroom, Quinn was amused to see that despite making fun of Trent for being ready so early, Haley was already laying out clothing options for both of them. Quinn had intended to go shopping that weekend, but she hadn't been given the mysterious 'allowance' yet, so she appreciated Haley's loaners.

"I keep looking over everything I've got to see if there's anything you would actually wear in the real world," Haley told her. "But I doubt it."

Quinn laughed, scanning the clothes herself. They weren't bad; it wasn't as if Haley had all frills or florals. Everything was just... basic. And not in the black-on-black way that Quinn was used to.

"What about this?" Quinn asked, something out of the ordinary catching the corner of her eye. It was fire engine red, hiding between something navy and something gray. She reached to pull it out and gasped.

"Haley!" she exclaimed. She would recognize the knockout Armani dress anywhere; she'd worn one exactly like it to a DCA fundraising event a year earlier. Of course, after sneaking into the event, she had proceeded to burn the place to the ground. The dress had been for the cameras; she had pulled quite the audience that night for her anti-DCA demonstration.

"Oh," Haley said, blushing. "I didn't think I still had that."

"I wore something just like this once. How did you get this?"

Haley hugged herself uncomfortably. "It's embarrassing. When you caused that scene at the DCA fundraiser that night, we were all watching. I admired you so much for it. The way you looked fearlessly into those cameras, wearing that bold, red dress—the way you caused utter mayhem while deliberately not taking any lives—I couldn't stop talking about it. When my birthday came around a few weeks later, Charlie and Pence pulled some strings with Charlie's parents to get the same one ordered for me. I never wore it—never had the guts. But it was sweet of them, all the same."

Quinn didn't know what to say. She had known that Trent and Rory had been fans of hers before her arrival, but not Haley. And how did Haley know that Quinn had deliberately avoided taking lives that night? The majority of the press coverage had suggested just the opposite. They had called it a terrorist attack, saying that it was a miracle no lives had been lost.

"I just knew," Haley said softly, as if reading Quinn's thoughts. "I could see it in your eyes."

Quinn stared at Haley, utterly floored. She could feel her eyes tearing up, but she pushed the waterworks away, determined to have a good time that night. "Well, one of us is going to have to wear it tonight. You've got first dibs, but seeing as you've had it for a year and not worn it…"

"No way. All you."

Quinn didn't need to be told twice. In a strange way, the dress gave her a sense of home that didn't even fully understand.

She popped into the bathroom, hung her towel up to dry, stepped into her underwear, and pulled on the dress. It didn't fit quite as well as the one she had stolen from Bergdorfs, but it certainly did the trick.

She finally recognized herself again, she thought as she looked in the mirror. She hadn't regained all of the spirit and fire she had lost since losing Kurt, but it helped. A little curl to her hair, a little red to her lips, and she could almost fully fake it.

She glanced down at her phone, considering who was in her contacts—who she might see that night. Reese? The man in charge of law enforcement, attending an underage party? Doubtful. Ridley? The security guard who had graduated from the school system with no prospects? Also doubtful.

She sighed, tapping her finger against her lip. What was the point of going if two of her favorite people on the island wouldn't be there?

She was wearing the red dress, she reminded herself. She could make things happen.

• • •

"*Ridley*?" Haley asked in an uncharacteristically high-pitched voice as Ridley joined them in the dormitory courtyard. "*He's* your last-minute date?"

Trent, who had insisted on escorting Haley to the party after being turned down by Quinn, groaned. "Shot down for a lizard. Low blow."

Quinn smirked, pleased with the reaction her decision was having already. "Hi, Ridley," she said to her friend as he took her arm.

"Hey," he replied, smiling gently. "You look great."

Quinn appreciated his tone and what it meant for both of them. There wasn't lust or flirtation in his voice; just fondness and gratitude. Ridley wasn't any more infatuated with Quinn than she was with him. He just liked her company, as she did his.

"Thanks," she said. "You, too."

She could tell from his expression that he didn't buy it, but she didn't care. She meant it. With his charcoal-gray, dragonlike scales, bright, piercing eyes, and understated-classy outfit, he looked far more interesting than Trent or probably any other guy at the party they were headed to.

Quinn usually followed Haley's lead when it came to navigating the island, but tonight she knew where she was going. There was only one multi-story office building with a penthouse suite; it had to be Charlie's parents'.

Charlie's parents'... She made a mental note to ask someone how owning things worked on the island. Really just economics in general.

"So, who's going to this thing, anyway?" she asked as they walked. "Everyone in the YA, I'm sure. But who else? Younger people? Adults?"

"Not younger people," Haley said. "They won't be let in. Underage drinking with our lot is one thing, but any younger and we'd just be asking for Savannah to give us a hard time."

Quinn would have guessed even underage drinking with their lot would risk Savannah's wrath, but apparently that wasn't the case.

"As for the older crowd," Trent added, "a smattering of people, here and there. But barely. Everyone older than us is just so *boring.* They all settled in. Got jobs. Forgot how to live life on the edge." He grinned over at Ridley. "Excluding you, of course, Rid."

Ridley laughed. "I agree. Then again, even when my class was still in school, we weren't nearly as exciting as yours. The whole community has a lot to say about your class."

Haley giggled. "I choose to take that as a compliment."

"It *is* a compliment," Trent assured her. "Mainly because we're by far the most powerful."

Quinn had to admit, as a whole, the YA *did* seem surprisingly powerful. Haley's earth abilities; Pence's water abilities; Shade's powers of illusion…

She realized that she didn't know what Trent's abilities were.

"Trent," she said. His eyes, of course, lit up at the sound of her voice uttering his name. "What's your deal, anyway? What can you do?"

"I must say, even the girls who *aren't* interested in me normally ask that question within a few minutes of meeting me. Is it a lack of curiosity in general, or just regarding me?"

"I learned Haley and Pence's abilities pretty quickly. Must just be you."

She didn't mean it; ever since she had arrived, she had been so absorbed in confusion and curiosity surrounding this island, the normal questions had completely escaped her. The only reason she had learned about Haley and Pence's abilities was because they had talked about them.

But she would never turn down a chance to tease someone like Trent.

"Consider me your everyday Superman," Trent explained cheerfully. "Minus, you know, the x-ray vision, flight, bulletproof skin, and all that. Oh, and the super-speed—that's Charlie."

"So, basically just the super-strength?"

"Sure, but that's the best one, isn't it?" he asked with another wink.

She laughed, not dismissing him for his singular ability. Super-strength was no small ability, nor was super-speed, which was apparently Charlie's. They really were an exceptionally gifted class.

But she didn't give Trent the satisfaction of further attention, because they had reached the tower.

All of the lights were out inside, but Haley and Trent continued through the glass doors, at least one of which was unlocked. Quinn glanced at Ridley, wondering if he was as used to this near-breaking-and-entering as the others. He did seem a little uncomfortable, she noticed. She wondered whether her bringing one of the island's security personnel on a rule-breaking party bender was the best idea, but decided not to worry about it.

She and Ridley followed Trent and Haley to the elevators against the far wall—elevators that nearly rivaled Crowley Enterprises' in elegance. The doors opened immediately, and the group stepped in. Haley punched the button for the fourth floor, and up they went.

"Remind me," Quinn said as the floors ticked up, "to have one of you explain to me at some point how economics work on this island."

Trent laughed. "That's a conversation for several drinks in."

And the doors opened.

It couldn't have been past nine o'clock, but the party was in full swing. Quinn recognized just about everyone in the YA along with at least a dozen people she didn't know. Virtually everyone had a drink in hand.

"I see a spot for myself at the bar," she told Ridley, glancing over at him. "Want me to grab you a drink?"

"I'm okay. I'm probably going to pop over and say hello to Drax and Angel. Catch up a little later on?"

Quinn nodded, a little irked at the thought of her new friend spending time with Angel, who so far was one of her least favorite people in the YA. But, glancing over at Angel and Drax in the corner, she knew better than to stop Ridley. Being a monster in the way that those three were was something she and the others couldn't even begin to understand.

So she headed to the bar, rolling her eyes as Trent took the barstool directly next to hers.

The bartender, she noticed, was another monster. He resembled Ridley slightly: grayish skin, not scaly, but almost slimy, like a dolphin's. He had a bald head like Ridley, but his face was even less humanlike: slits for nostrils, lips so thin, they were almost nonexistent. She felt her heart go out to him just as it had for Ridley, and yet, as usual, she refused to show it. So, when he came over, she had different words for him.

"Whiskey on the rocks. Single barrel, if you've got it. And a pack of Parliaments."

The poor man's expression was of utter shock. She might as well have just told him she had killed a man. Trent laughed out loud.

"I don't think Hank here is used to such bold orders," he said. "Best to start with something simple."

Hank glared at Trent, turning quickly to Quinn. "Ignore him. I can get you the whiskey. I just—I'm not sure we have any cigarettes…"

Quinn had never had a serious addiction to smoking, but with alcohol in the mix, she always wanted a cigarette or two. The level of stress this place was putting her under didn't help, either.

"You didn't even think to ask me," Trent said to her, pulling a pack of Marlboro Reds out of his pocket. "I'm a little hurt."

"I'm a little surprised," she admitted as Hank began rummaging around for her whiskey. "You strike me more as a quarterback than a bad boy."

"I'm a little of everything." He waved the pack tauntingly. "What'll it get me?"

All it took was a snap of her fingers, and the pack flew into her hand. "Points," she said as she slid the pack into her bra. "For future reference."

The move was so smooth, he didn't even seem mad about the theft; he just turned back to Hank, who handed her the whiskey, and said, "I'll take whatever you're willing to make me."

Hank gave him a dirty look that indicated he would be getting bottom shelf. Quinn enjoyed the exchange.

"So, Hank," she said as Hank worked on Trent's concoction. "How old are you?"

"I'm 36," Hank said, a hint of embarrassment in his voice. "Why?"

"Just curious. What do you do when you're not bartending?"

"I'm in security." It wasn't a surprise, but it made her sad. "I work with Ridley a lot. Saw you come in with him."

"Yeah. I like Ridley."

He said nothing, but she could see the appreciation in his downward-cast gaze.

"But," she continued, "this 'security' thing. Kind of a dull job, huh? Doesn't really seem fair. Is there something else you'd rather do?"

He poured the shaken drink he had prepared for Trent into a glass and handed it to him before answering her. "If you'd asked Ridley, I'm sure he'd say yeah. But not me. Getting on those helicopters, meeting the new recruits, walking the perimeter of the island… It's the closest someone like me can get to the real world. The most someone like me can really see."

His answer made her heart ache; she did what she could not to show it.

"Well," she said, "I'm glad you're happy."

"So," Trent interjected, leaning in close to her ear. "Where are you planning on smoking that? Someplace nice, quiet, private?"

She turned to face him so that her lips were quite nearly touching his, eyes locking onto his so certainly that she knew she could control him with a single word. But she didn't give him that word. Instead, she gave him two.

"Dream on."

And she rose, deciding to find someplace nice, quiet, private.

•　•　•

She settled on the roof.

It was just so *crowded* in the penthouse. Ridley was still talking with Angel and Drax; she thought about going to say hello to Drax, at the very least, but Angel's death glare kept her away. Haley made her way over to Trent at the bar, and Pence and Charlie were off cuddling in la-la-land. Quinn *did* have that handy pack of cigarettes she had stolen from Trent, so why not?

She didn't need to look for the stairs. She opened the first window she found, opened it, and flew up to the roof. She didn't really even have to fly; it was more of a jump.

It felt incredible up there. The wind was stronger than it was on the ground level, the temperature a bit lower, though still fitting into the warm tropics pattern of the rest of the island. It was more serene than it had ever been on any of the rooftops in the cities she used to jump to and from. She could hear the ocean all around her. She could *see* the ocean, just on the outskirts of the island. She was high enough to see over the wall.

She didn't need a lighter for her cigarette; she could start a fire that small in her sleep. Once she took her first drag, she closed her eyes and dreamed. Dreamed of smoking on the roof of Kurt's trailer. Dreamed of being back there with him. Even before him. Even with... family.

Not that she could even picture her mother's face any more.

Dash's voice woke her from her muddled daydream. She wasn't even sure how she knew it was his voice; he only ever spoke a few words at a time to her in class. But she knew.

"Sorry," he said. She opened her eyes reluctantly, glancing over at him. "Didn't think anyone would be up here."

"Free country." She grinned in spite of herself at the irony of her comment. "Well... supposedly."

He didn't laugh, but she thought she caught a hint of amusement in his eyes. He hesitated, as if debating whether to continue toward her. But he did.

"Wouldn't have expected to see you here," she told him, taking another drag of her cigarette. "Didn't exactly peg you for the party type."

"I'm not," he said, coming to stand next to her, looking out at the same world that she was. There was no drink in his hands, no lowered inhibitions in his eyes.

"I come here for them."

"Them?" she repeated, taking a sip of her whiskey. She loved the burn. Always had. "Your students?"

"I guess that's what you'd call them. They're certainly the first class I've had with access to a place like this. The most... trouble I've had."

"My kind of class."

He didn't look amused. In fact, whatever brief civility had just existed between them seemed to disappear instantly. "Well, there you have it. I'm here because of people like you."

As quickly as his distaste for her returned, so did hers for him. What was wrong with him? Why was he so quick to judge? What did he know about her?

"'People like me,'" she repeated. "As if you know me. As if you know anything about me."

"We all know about you. We've all seen the stories."

"The stories?" Her voice rose along with the temperature around them. However hot she was making it, she felt ten times hotter. Straight whiskey was no joke; it had been too long since she'd had it. "You're referring to the stories regulars concocted out of fear and loathing towards me, a pretty monster living amongst them who they couldn't predict or control? And you choose to believe *their* stories?"

He was silenced by that, at least for a moment, and she was glad. She could see the self-doubt in his eyes. But she could also see a persistence that she couldn't understand. Why did he hate her so much?

"That's a vulgar term," he said quietly. "'Pretty monster.' You should learn to use other verbiage here."

"And what about just 'monster'? Don't like that one either?"

"No, actually. I don't."

"I'm not surprised," she snapped, stomping out her cigarette and lighting the next. "I'm sure your beloved mother doesn't, either. Kind of like racists avoiding saying 'black;' it's okay if they say African American, isn't it? Makes all the other problems go away."

His glare went from hateful to confused. "What are you getting at?"

"The *obvious problem* that exists on this island. Monsters going into 'security' because there's nothing else for them. Drax having to work while being in school just to secure some other line of work for himself. Hank only being welcome at a party when he's agreed to bartend."

To say that he looked surprised would have been an understatement. Surprised, and somehow, still confused. "I know that it's a problem, Quinn. I'm just surprised *you* do."

She wasn't sure what to say to that.

"Is it true?" he asked her, looking into her eyes. She didn't feel captivated, the way he had forced her to on the field before commanding her to kneel. But she'd be lying if she said she didn't feel captivated in a different way. Were her cheeks red? She had to stop drinking the whiskey…

She finished the whiskey.

"I saw you come in with him," Dash said. "With Ridley. I've never seen him at a party like this before in my life. And then you asking Hank all those questions?"

She stared at him, not following. "What are you asking me?"

"Did you really bring him here? Ridley. As your date."

"Oh. Yeah, I guess. I mean, as friends. I'm not looking to get into his pants, if that's what you're asking. Not that it's any of your business."

He squinted at her, not seeming satisfied with her answer. "And what does *he* think? What are you leading him to believe?"

She took a long drag of her cigarette before tossing it sharply to the ground. "Look, asshole. Ridley is a friend. Just because no one else in this godforsaken place chooses to be friends with him doesn't mean I shouldn't. Just because everyone else in this godforsaken place wants to get into my pants doesn't mean he does. And just because I brought him here doesn't mean I'm leading him on. What is wrong with you? How can you possibly make so many judgments about someone you know so little about?"

He held her gaze for a long time. His brain was firing on all cylinders; that much was clear. She had him rethinking things. Wondering things. Admitting things to himself for what might be the first time in a long time.

"Tell me this," he said, leaning against the post next to them, turning his back to the beautiful view and facing her directly. For the first time that night, she felt like she had his full attention. "Why do you smoke? Knowing perfectly well that it will kill you. Why do you do it?"

She stared back at him, not blinking, not missing a beat. "Not that I owe you any kind of answer, for any kind of question, but—if I give you this one—will you promise to shred whatever nasty opinions you've made of me, and wipe the slate clean?"

He held her gaze, breathing slowly, carefully. "If you'll do the same for me."

"I never had any opinion of you but a positive one. Until you forced me to feel otherwise."

"Regardless," he said, seeming to take her point. "If you'll do the same for me."

"Fine," she said, mind racing. "Because I know. I know what fate has in store for me. I know I'll be lucky to last another decade."

He stared at her, nothing in his eyes but fascination. Intrigue.

This look, she was used to.

"If cigarettes are my downfall…" She laughed dryly. "It'll be a fucking miracle. And I'll have lived a longer life than I ever would have thought possible."

And then, deciding that she owed him nothing more, she headed back down to the party.

• • •

Quinn spent another hour or two at the party, but she found herself unable to focus—and not just because of the whiskies. She couldn't shake Dash's eyes from her head—eyes that made no further appearances at the party. Eyes that she knew she had gotten to… eyes that she knew had gotten to her.

Drax and Pence, an unlikely pair she hadn't even realized were friends, caught her in her trance.

"Quinn," Pence said as they approached her at the bar, where she was staring dazedly down at the pattern on the counter. "You okay?"

Quinn glanced up at her, blushing slightly. "Yeah. Weird night, is all. Think

I'm still getting used to this place."

Drax smiled sympathetically. "I've been here for almost as long as this place has been around, and I'm still getting used to it. It's always changing, too. But some things stay the same. Like your friends."

It was cheesy, but she appreciated it. She glanced up at Pence, who seemed to have grown pensive. "What about you? You been here long?"

"Just a few years. Like I said before… It was hard for me to keep my abilities a secret. But since I looked normal, we tried for a long time. Moved around a lot. My parents tried so hard to protect me. But the DCA caught me eventually. My parents are still out there somewhere. Worried sick about me, I'm sure. Wondering whether I'm alive or dead. Assuming if I *am* alive, I'm in a place much worse than this."

Sadness washed over Quinn for Pence. She wondered how many others on the island had been separated from their families. Everyone in the YA had been small children during the event. Had they all been alone in the city? Had their parents been the lucky few that weren't affected?

Or had they been killed, rather than affected?

"Don't feel bad for me," Pence said, waving a hand. "At least I get to know that my parents love me. Some people, like Tommy and Izzo—their parents were afraid of them. Just about handed them over to the DCA. And then there's people like Shade, whose parents died in the event."

Quinn wondered what Haley's story was—where her parents were. She had a sinking feeling she already knew the answer.

She had never considered herself lucky before, but in that moment, she did. She might have had a shit father, but she'd had an incredible mother when she was alive—one who would never have turned her own daughter into the DCA.

Her somber thoughts must have come across as exhaustion, because Ridley came over to her at that point, politely interrupting to offer to walk her home. She considered staying, but decided she had enough to process for one night already, accepting his offer.

"You disappeared for a good bit there," he said as they headed back to the dorms. "Everything okay?"

"I went up to the roof for a smoke. Dash was up there, for some reason. We talked a little bit."

"Well, I'm not surprised he was hiding out on the roof. What'd you guys talk about?"

She considered this. So much, and yet so little. They still knew virtually nothing about each other, and yet in a strange way, she felt as if she had spilled all of her secrets.

"You, for one," she said. "He seemed totally confused by our friendship. Almost… protective."

He nodded. "Dash is very protective of me. That doesn't surprise me. He doesn't need to worry, though. Neither do you."

"What do you mean?"

"I'm sure he saw you in that dress and assumed the rest. It's undoubtedly very hard for him and any other guy to take his eyes off you in it. I'm sure he assumed I felt the same way."

Had Dash been right? Had she been leading him on all of this time? She usually had good instincts about this kind of thing, but if she was wrong, it would completely change her dynamic with Ridley.

"And?" she asked. "Is it so hard for you?"

"I'd be lying if I said I wasn't looking. But that's not what it's about for me, Quinn. It's about the fact that when I look, I see. I see in you the same thing that I see in myself. Being a monster, even a monster as beautiful as you… It's ruined your life."

She held his gaze, unable to breathe, he was so spot-on.

"I like you because you understand," he continued. "I like you because I can trust you. Because I can be your friend. Because you know what it's like to be judged the moment eyes are laid upon you."

She *did* understand. But more importantly, she had found someone who understood *her.*

"Dash doesn't need to worry about me or for me," he told her. "And neither do you. Don't worry, Quinn—he'll come around. He just didn't spend long enough in the real world to know what you and I know."

"And what's that?" she asked, already knowing the answer.

"It doesn't matter that you're pretty," he said, "and it doesn't matter that you're powerful. It only matters that you're different. They know you're different, they eat you alive."

6. RIVER AND SKY

Quinn spent the following day nursing a painful hangover.

Whiskey had always given Quinn hangovers. She always tried to conveniently forget that fact, just as she spent the days after trying to conveniently forget the ignorant decisions it influenced her to make. But it always came back to remind her. As delicious as it was, it was still poison.

Haley, she learned with amusement, was right there with her. They helped get each other through the day, watching old movies in their sweats and trading off getting boxed meals for each other.

"I have to say," Quinn told Haley between films, "I'm a little impressed. Wouldn't have pegged you for the drink-until-dawn type."

"I'm not, really, but Trent tends to bring out the worst in me."

Quinn tried to laugh, but it felt forced. She liked Trent in his own way, but she *really* liked Haley, and she knew Haley could do so much better than him. She just wished Haley knew.

Sunday evening came sooner than Quinn would have liked, and she actually managed to get a decent night's rest. By the time she woke up Monday morning, she felt halfway decent.

English was first up that morning. Quinn had met the English teacher, Simon, the previous week, and didn't mind him. He, like Lydia and Zerrick, had asked her a few uncomfortable questions, but he had been pretty easy on her, setting her up with a textbook on grammar that she had thumbed through with moderate ease.

Today, though, she was in for a surprise: it wasn't Simon waiting at the front of the room when she and Haley entered.

It was Dash.

She froze, suddenly becoming hyper-aware of her post-hangover appearance, from her oily, unkempt sea of hair to her second-hand sweats from Haley's drawer. The only thing that annoyed her more than what she was wearing was how much she cared what he thought.

That, and how well-dressed and hygienic he looked.

His eyes met hers almost immediately. She tried to gauge what he was thinking, but she found it difficult. It was a new expression. Not the loathsome one he usually glared at her with, but, perhaps… The clean slate they had agreed upon?

"That's weird," Haley whispered as they took their seats. "Dash usually only teaches special seminars. Simon must be sick today."

Quinn said nothing, attempting to comb a hand through her hornet's nest of hair.

"Good afternoon, everyone," Dash said, voice surprisingly warm. Had her perception of him changed, or was he in a better mood than usual? "Simon asked me to fill in for him today. Let's start with your assigned readings. I'll come around and you'll give me your brief thoughts on your chapters from the weekend. Those of you who were out partying and not reading… I have assignments in mind for you."

The class full of exhausted teens managed awkward laughs at that, and Dash began to make his rounds.

"Did you see him at the party?" Pence whispered to Haley and Quinn from behind them. "Charlie said he was there, but I didn't see him once."

"I didn't see him," Haley said. "Not exactly his scene, is it?"

"I saw him," Quinn said, instantly regretting it when she saw their wide eyes. She shrugged nonchalantly. "Just for a few minutes. When I went up to the roof for a smoke."

Both of them looked like they had more questions, but neither of them dared ask at that moment, as Dash made his way over to chat with Drax in the seat in front of Quinn's.

She tried not to eavesdrop, color rushing to her face as he and Drax discussed a lengthy French book she had never heard of. Was he going to ask her if she'd done the reading? Simon hadn't assigned her anything yet.

Finally, he rose from Drax's desk, coming over to kneel at hers. She braced herself for a conversation that would undoubtedly be embarrassing for her on many levels.

"Hi," he said to her, eyes making his way to hers almost...

Nervously?

"Hi," she replied, confused.

"Has Simon given you any reading yet?"

"He, uh… he kinda just had me reading some textbooks on grammar."

He nodded, eyes not leaving hers. "We'll have to fix that. Simon's a great teacher, but I think you would have a better time learning grammar by seeing it in action. What kinds of books do you enjoy reading?"

"Um," she said, shifting her weight uncomfortably. "I don't know. I never exactly had a lot of time to read when I was on the run."

He nodded, seeming to understand. "Why don't you tell me about your interests in general, then. Comedy? Drama? Fantasy?"

Comedy? She wasn't sure she had the ability to laugh at anything a regular from the real world had to say. Drama? She wasn't sure she could take any regular's problems very seriously. Fantasy?

What even *was* fantasy those days?

"Look," she said. "I don't know. I read this book of Haley's called *Stargirl* the other day. I liked it. It was probably at a fourth-grade reading level. I couldn't even tell you what genre it was. Why don't you just assign me your favorite book and we'll see how I do?"

He smiled softly. "I know *Stargirl.* That's a very good book."

Quinn said nothing, mainly because she couldn't. He was being… *nice.* How was that even possible?

"Why don't you take this," he said, pulling out a small book that had been stowed away in his back pocket. "It's one of my favorites."

She looked down at the book, which was worn and tattered by time and attention. *Salvage the Bones.*

"What's it about?" she asked.

"It's about a teenage girl who comes from nothing—*has* nothing—yet tries relentlessly to protect and provide for herself and her brothers. She's sensitive, but tough; impulsive, but intelligent. She grew up in a world full of men, and it hardened her. Gave her this unique, almost poetic understanding of the world. It's set in coastal Mississippi during Hurricane Katrina... a story of survival."

He had heard her, she realized. He was finally starting to understand.

"I'll give it a try."

. . .

Math class was next. Quinn felt embarrassed and guilty, as usual, about how much of Zerrick's time and attention she took away from the rest of the class, but Zerrick was as patient and kind about it as always. After math came lunch break, but with power tech up next, and the knowledge that she would be spending another hour or two with Dash, Quinn found herself unable to eat, or even focus, on anything but the book.

He had clearly read it many times. She could see his notes in the margins. Some of them made sense. Some of them were the same thoughts and questions she had while reading. Some of them made less sense—more or less jibberish. And then there were things so provocative, so well-thought-out, they would have never even occurred to her; and yet, they were so spot-on, they made her see things in ways she would never have seen them before.

She read at the fountain for a while, enjoying the warm sunlight and gentle breeze. Then, not wanting to be late to power tech but having left her cell phone (and only source of time-telling) in the room, she headed straight for the training grounds. There, seeing she was early and alone, she took a seat on a bench and continued to read.

She didn't even notice Dash until he sat down directly next to her.

"Glad to see you're actually reading it," he told her. She started to set the book down, but shook his head. "Don't stop on my account."

"It's okay." She laughed. "I think I needed to be brought out of my trance a few minutes ahead of training."

He smiled a small, careful smile, saying nothing.

"I'm not sure what's more interesting," she said, taking note of the page she was on and closing the book. "The book, or your notes in the margins."

"The book, I'm sure. But it's always interesting to see someone else's perspective on things."

She held his gaze, sure that he was referring to more than just the margins. But he didn't admit it, and she didn't ask.

"It's a little… beyond me," she admitted. "A lot of the words…"

"Don't make sense," he finished for her, understanding. "I know. Zerrick talked to me, a little, after your first class."

Had Zerrick really needed to share that information with Dash, of all people?

"Great," she said, hanging her head in shame. "Is there anyone who doesn't know?"

"Quinn, there's nothing to be ashamed of. I like that book for so much more than the author's vocabulary. And I knew you'd be able to understand it in spite of that. I could have given you a much more elementary book, but you didn't need it. English isn't like math or science. Sometimes your understanding of the subject is more about life experience."

"Well, I've got plenty of that."

He laughed softly, and she found herself captivated by that laugh. What was wrong with her? Why was she suddenly so smitten with the man who not long ago had disgusted her so much?

Whatever the reason, she needed to be careful.

"Hate to interrupt," said a voice from behind them, "but I was here for the five o'clock power tech… Unless this is a private session?"

Quinn didn't need to turn around to know that this ornery voice belonged to Trent. She virtually dismissed it, unconcerned that someone had walked in on her and Dash having a moment, but she noticed that Dash did seem a little embarrassed.

"Very funny, Trent," Dash said, standing up. "Glad to see you on time for a change."

Trent said nothing to Dash, glancing instead at Quinn. "You're looking better than you did yesterday. Staying hydrated?"

It was hard for her to read his tone, but it almost seemed intentionally hurtful. Was it possible Trent had actually given up on pursuing her and started resenting her instead?

She cared, but only minimally.

Haley and Pence arrived next, and everyone else soon after.

"I've been giving it some thought," Dash told the group, "and I think it's time for a change of pace. We're all a little too comfortable with the current pairings. So today, we're going to try this: Shade, you'll be with Pence. Charlie, Tommy. Trent, Haley. Angel, Drax, you'll stay together, for obvious reasons… Izzo, you'll join up with them. Two against one."

These pairings didn't make as much sense to Quinn as the original pairings, but maybe that was the point. If Pence was as skilled as she was smart, she was probably a fair match for Shade; besides, she seemed to have a more level head than Quinn, which would help when it came to tolerating visions. Quinn wasn't sure what Tommy's abilities were, but Charlie's super-speed could use a fresh foe. Trent and Haley was a match Quinn certainly wouldn't want to miss. Earth and strength didn't have much in common, but she wasn't sure who she would put her money on. As for Izzo, Quinn was pretty sure she had seen her turn into an animal before. Could Angel and Drax, two monsters with no abilities, take her on?

Depends what kind of animals she can turn into, Quinn mused.

She realized she didn't have a partner for herself.

"Quinn," Dash said, "I think we'll have you pair with me for a little while."

The class broke off into groups at that. Quinn strolled up to Dash, head cocked to the side, genuinely curious. "Is this because you think I could benefit from this pairing, or because Shade finally refused to work with me and everyone else is scared of me?"

"A little of both," he told her gently. "I'm sure you can't blame them."

"Oh, I don't. I'm very used to people being afraid of me."

She had meant it in good fun, but she could see from his expression that he took her comment all too seriously. He said nothing.

"Well, come on, then," she said, trying to lighten the mood. "Aren't you going to unleash some kind of turbulent force on me like last time?"

"You didn't seem to have any difficulty handling that one." He took a step closer to her. "Nor did you have any difficulty retaliating. It seemed to me the one thing you couldn't get a handle on was your mind control."

"I'd hardly call it mind control," she said, making a point to avoid any connection to his mother's seer-related questions. If Reese was right, Dash was still close to his mother, despite how he ran his power tech class. She didn't need him reporting back to her. "More like a light influence."

"You and I both know that's an understatement."

"Look," she said. "Compulsion is my most advanced ability. I have never, *ever* had an issue with it. Except for the time I got captured. But that was for a very specific reason. If I can't control *your* mind, it's not a problem with my abilities. It's just you."

"Right," he said pointedly. "It's me keeping you out."

"What's your point?"

"My point is, I'm winning. Are you going to let that stand?"

He was good. *Very* good. He knew what made her tick and what drove her crazy. He knew she couldn't stand to lose.

"After all," he said, "*I* was able to control *your* mind."

She took a step closer to him, gaze competitive, challenging. Locked on.

What was it about him that kept her out? Some sort of resistance. What to? Her sexuality? Her appeal? What was it that he didn't see in her, that everyone else did?

She thought back to their previous encounters. What had made him finally open up to her? What had made him stop hating her? It was her honesty. It was her fondness for Ridley and Hank. It was…

Her being *real*.

She stopped focusing on seduction and focused on whatever vulnerability she could muster.

It wasn't much. She wasn't ready to be vulnerable to anyone, especially someone like Dash who already made her so unsettled.

But it did seem to throw him off.

"How am I doing?" she asked him softly. "Feeling hooked?"

"Not particularly," he told her, holding her gaze. "You?"

Yes. She felt absolutely, positively hooked.

It was a catch-22, really. If she admitted it, she could probably hook him back. If she lied, as was her instinct, he would win. He knew when she was lying. And that knowledge kept her from influencing him.

She decided to change the subject entirely. "Do you think it's wrong? What we're practicing? What I did to so many people? Compelling them to do what I want?"

"Yes. I do think it's wrong. I think the most basic human right is to have control over your own mind."

She waited, knowing there was more.

"But what I'm starting to understand about you is that there were reasons behind everything you did. Maybe you shouldn't have compelled so many people. Maybe you shouldn't have stolen from so many people. But as wrong as it is that we have this ability, it's something we have no say in. It's who we are now. And those people, out there? The ones that forced us here, kicked us out of our own country, our own homes? They did have a choice."

The honesty pouring out of him only compelled her more; at that point, every ounce of her was at his bidding; she knew that he could get her to do anything he wanted.

She was completely entranced.

"You're still winning," she whispered.

"I wouldn't be so sure."

They stared at each other, dead silent, each waiting for the other to test the theory, see who was compelling whom. But neither did.

"Go ahead," he said softly. "Try."

The words were on the tip of her tongue. Commands. Suggestions. But in that moment of pure honesty—in that locked-in, deep connection—it just felt wrong. Wrong, on every level.

She shook her head, breaking eye contact, looking away from him. Releasing both of them from their mutual holds on each other.

She could tell he wondered why, but she wouldn't have an answer for him if he asked. And he didn't. All he said, in a low volume, directed only towards her, was: "Class dismissed."

• • •

The rest of the week went so smoothly, Quinn almost stopped remembering to act miserable. She liked the majority of the students in the YA. She liked the majority of her teachers. She liked the majority of *everyone*.

Dash continued to pair up with her all week. They worked on things besides compulsion. He didn't suggest trying it again, and she appreciated it. It wasn't that she couldn't do it; it was that she didn't want to. He seemed to understand that.

By the time Quinn reached the dorms that Friday night, she was exhausted—but in a very good mood. In fact, when she spotted Reese out in front of the building waiting for her, she realized it was showing on her face.

"Wow," he teased. "Is that an actual smile I'm seeing?"

She rolled her eyes, smile lingering. She was glad to see him. "Must have been something I ate. What are you doing in my neck of the woods?"

"I came to show you something, if you're interested. I heard you've been behaving yourself, getting along with everyone, attending classes. Things that I know don't come naturally or easily for you."

"Thanks," she said, genuinely meaning it. His understanding meant more to her than he probably knew. "What did you want to show me?"

He extended both of his hands out to her. "Do you trust me?"

She eyed his hands skeptically. She didn't trust him; she didn't trust anyone. It was her number one rule. But what did she have to lose?

"No," she said, putting her hands in his. "But, as usual, I'm up for anything."

Apparently that was all he needed to hear, because the next thing she knew, they were airborne.

Quinn was no expert on deviants, but even she knew that the ability of flight was a rare one. And Reese was *good*. Within seconds, they were higher than she had ever flown. Within a minute, she could see the entire perimeter of the island's wall below her, and the ocean around it. His power was not only keeping him in the air, but her, too; their connected hands acted more as a transfer of power than a means for him to hold her up.

She glanced up at him, wonder written on her face. How had she never thought to ask Reese about his abilities? How had she not known how incredible they were? Dash might be the more powerful brother, but this... This was something else entirely.

"You sure this is allowed?" she joked, releasing one hand from his and turning shoulder-to-shoulder with him to look down at the island. "Chief of law enforcement on the island, breaking free so easily?"

"Don't you see? It's no prison break. There's no one stopping us. Even the wall—it's just for show. The outside world is at our fingertips. If you wanted to leave, right now, I wouldn't stop you. Hell, I'd take you. But I'd come back. And that would be no one's choice but my own."

She knew he was right. There was nothing left for her out there. Not without Kurt. Not without her mother.

Her thoughts flashed briefly to her father, but it hurt too much to even think about him. Then she thought of Crowley. There might not be any positive incentives to go back, but there were still incentives. She had to consider it. She was who she was. She wanted vengeance. She wanted freedom. She didn't want to be stuck here, to be caged... To lose.

"Staying here," she said. "Staying away. Giving them what they want. It doesn't make sense to me. We could take them. Us against them? We'd win."

"That's a discussion Savannah and I and the rest of Siloh have all had repeatedly. The thing is, Quinn, I don't think we would win. I don't think we could. And it's not because of power or numbers. It's because of people like him—people like Cole Crowley. People who know everything about every single one of us. Every weakness. They use cruelty as their weapon—cruelty we can't even imagine."

She held his gaze, suddenly feeling incredibly sad. "You know?" she asked him. "What he did? How he got me?"

"It was in your report," he explained, sympathy in his eyes. "Savannah and I have to read the reports when new recruits come... We're the only ones, though.

And neither of us would ever share that information. I'm so sorry, Quinn. I'm sorry he did that to you."

"Then you must understand, right? Why I should leave—why I should find him? I have to get justice for Kurt."

"I understand the urge. But you're smarter than that. That's why you haven't left already. You understand how well protected he is. How he'd probably kill you. How your best shot is staying with us, here—getting stronger. Getting ready."

"Getting ready," she repeated, looking down at the quiet, beautiful island. "So there is a greater plan."

"I don't know about a 'greater plan.' But I think we'd be fools to not prepare ourselves for the future."

He was right. She would be 'getting ready' to exact her revenge on Cole Crowley no matter where she was—no matter how long it took. But it was a comforting thought that perhaps if she stayed, she wouldn't have to do it alone. "Right. The Joe Strummer question. Should I stay or should I go?"

He watched her, silently awaiting her decision. And without another word, she dropped his other hand and swan-dove head first back to the very island she had fought being dragged to for most of her life.

• • •

The weekend was uneventful. She spotted Reese in the dining hall a few times and considered going over to him, but decided against it. There was something she liked about the privacy of their friendship. And, catching his eye briefly from across the room, she had a feeling he felt the same way.

She had most of her meals with Rory instead, pity returning for the girl with no friends her own age. Besides, the girl's enthusiasm was so unrelenting, Quinn was beginning to admire it.

Quinn didn't see much of Dash that weekend, and when she did, she couldn't get a read on him. He almost seemed to be avoiding her, but the moment she thought it, she shook the thought away. What could he possibly have to be upset with her about? They were finally getting along.

When she got to power tech that Monday evening, Quinn was equal parts excited and nervous. A small part of her wanted to suggest that they work on compulsion again. She had a feeling the results would be the same as the last time, but that was okay with her. In fact, as much as it scared her, she almost looked forward to it.

But she could tell from the moment she saw Dash that it wouldn't be so simple. He avoided eye contact with her, deliberately starting a conversation with Tommy and Izzo the moment she came toward him. Her suspicions over the weekend had been correct, she decided. He was upset with her.

How was this possible? How had he turned from hot to cold, again, so quickly? How were they back to square one?

She approached him guardedly. He was done talking to Tommy and Izzo, but he still didn't look up at her.

"Hi," she said uncertainly.

He finally looked up, eyes dark. "You'll be with Haley today."

"Oh," she said, crossing her arms. "Okay. Something wrong?"

"Nope."

"Right." Her confusion was rapidly becoming frustration. "I'm sorry. Either one of your seventy abilities is to have the PMS of a teenage girl, or something happened between Friday and today that I don't know about. Did I do something to offend you?"

"Look, Quinn, I saw you the other night. With Reese. You want to go on moonlight flights with him, be my guest. But I make a point not to spend time with people who spend time with him. If I'd known you two were so chummy, I would've made that point sooner."

"Seriously?" she demanded. "*That's* why you're pissed? Get over yourself. It's a small island. And last I checked, he's your brother."

"Are you really going to tell me you've never had a family member you wanted nothing to do with?"

Her mind flashed to her father—the man who had turned her away the night of the event, sending her wandering, lost and confused, until she curled up into that little ball at the Bank of America building. The man who had looked upon her tiny face, slammed the door on her, and never looked back.

Well, that wasn't entirely true, she reminded herself. She had seen him a few times since then. None of those meetings had gone well, either.

Maybe his point was valid. He didn't have to get along with his brother. But why didn't he want to? What was so bad about Reese?

"Reese has been kind to me," she told him. "Ever since I got here. He's helped me. Been nothing but decent. What would you have me do? Choose which brother to get along with?"

"No. I'll choose for you."

And with that, he turned to the rest of the class.

"New partners," he announced, and he began to rattle them off. She didn't process a word of what he was saying, she was so livid.

"That's us," Haley whispered when Dash called off their names. Her breath tickled Quinn's ear, startling her so much, she sent an accidental blast of electricity straight at Haley, who shrieked on impact.

Dash glared over at them, snapping something about practice starting when he said it started. Quinn said nothing, heart still pounding. Finally, Dash told them to begin, and she tried to focus her attention on Haley.

"Are you okay?" Haley asked, eyes wide and concerned. "We can do this however you want, Quinn. Whatever you want to practice on me, and if there's anything you'd rather I do or not do—"

"No," Quinn said quickly. "Please. Give it your all."

Haley frowned, glancing down at her hands and making a pushing motion. The ground below Quinn began to vibrate and crumble—something that might have caused a regular to trip and fall, at the most. Quinn took a simple step to the side, not even needing to utilize her abilities.

"Come on," Quinn said, rolling her eyes. "That was not your all. That wasn't even your ten percent."

Haley sighed, fingers coming together to form a snapping noise. Quinn heard the sounds of branches snapping and leaves breaking, and she glanced up to see long, skinny pieces of wood shooting down at her. For a moment, she was impressed, thinking the wood pieces were going to come down and impale her.

Instead the pieces rooted themselves around her wrists and ankles, forming binds. She sighed, breaking them with ease.

"You're not listening," she said, anger towards Dash getting the better of her. She took a step toward Haley. She could feel Dash's eyes on hers. She felt an urge to do something that would make him angry. She wanted to make him as angry as he had made her.

"I said," Quinn urged, eyes locking onto Haley's, feeling her power of compulsion flowing as strong as it could get, "*give it your all.*"

Before any of them knew what to do, Haley sent them all flying.

Quinn had only experienced one earthquake before. It had been rated a 5 on the Richter scale, and she'd experienced it during her brief stint in California while on the run. She remembered it scaring her—something she, who could control just about everything, couldn't control. But, ultimately, she had been fine.

If that had been a 5, this was at least a 10.

It wasn't just the earth shaking, though that was enough to send the equipment and obstacles around them crashing down. It was everything around them, from the leaves to the dirt to the grass, gathering together, magnetizing, smashing into lightning-fast torpedoes that began to tornado all around them. Even the trees began to break apart and uproot themselves from the earth, crashing to the ground along the perimeter of the field, sending everyone running, screaming, terrified.

And it wasn't just earth this time—it was so much more. Streaks of light shot down at them from the sky, nearly blinding them; fierce gusts of wind zipped past them, so sharp they could slice skin; even the sounds around them intensified.

Quinn stood there, dazed, watching the calamity of power that Haley had been sitting on destroy the group of people she had started to befriend.

She hadn't intended for Haley's powers to hurt anyone else—only herself. She knew she should stop her before something terrible happened. But then she saw Dash running over to them, trying to get to Haley, to stop her. He was having to fight his way through the debris, the chaos. She knew she could so easily stop Haley herself. But she wanted to make him do it. She wanted to watch him struggle, dodging all of the obstacles Quinn had created through Haley, as Quinn stood there, protected by some sheer force of will, some self-created shield.

Her anger had always made her more powerful. Today was no different.

But before Dash reached Haley, before Quinn got her satisfaction, a crashing tree hit a member of the group who couldn't protect himself. In fact, he had no physical abilities whatsoever. Drax let out a painful scream before being silenced completely, the weight of the giant tree overtaking him.

Dash finally reached Haley, eyes locking onto hers, ending it all with one simple, desperate word: "*Stop!*"

Trent was already lifting the tree off of Drax; Charlie was already grabbing him, carrying him at breakneck speed to the medical wing. But it didn't matter. She had done it again.

Whatever progress she had made here, whatever delusions about her good character she had led herself to believe, this was who she really was. This was who she would always be.

So she ran.

• • •

As she ran, she jumped. She flew. She tried to fly high, high enough to reach above the wall, high enough to fly away. But every time she got close, she came crashing back down. The third time, she landed in the river—a river that was flowing out toward the ocean, toward the wall. She let the current carry her, swimming along with it, pushing harder and faster than she ever had. She didn't come up for air. She didn't particularly care if she drowned in that moment. Where the river met the ocean, she would somehow get beneath the wall. That was where she would escape. She had to.

She tried to erase her thoughts of Drax as she swam, but she couldn't. Each time his face flashed in her mind, so did Kurt's. How many? How many innocent people's deaths would she be responsible for before someone took her own life?

The current was getting stronger, and it was carrying her at this point; her strokes were doing nothing; she was smashing against the rocks, falling, drowning, but it felt *right;* it felt like the punishment she deserved. She embraced every ounce of pain. She was so close to the ocean, she could almost taste it, and—

She felt a hand on her ankle, pulling, yanking, and she didn't know what was happening, but the water was everywhere, in her lungs, in her eyes, and she couldn't see, and she couldn't breathe, and then she was being thrown onto some sort of grass, and her eyes shot open, and she *could* see, she could see Dash leaning over her, shouting things at her, but she couldn't hear him, and she still couldn't breathe.

His hands found her chest, and he was pushing down on her, hard, performing CPR, or perhaps trying to kill her—really she wasn't sure which—and then, before she knew it, his lips were on hers, and he was breathing into her mouth, in and out, in and—

She shot away from him, sputtering water, sand, and dirt from her lungs and scrambling so far back that she very nearly fell back into the river.

She looked around, chest heaving, face streaked with tears, dirt, and water. She hadn't reached the ocean, she realized. She had crashed down a waterfall.

"He's not dead," Dash told her, eyeing her carefully. "Drax. I could hear his heart beating when they took him away."

She stared at him, desperate to believe it, but wary.

"But that tree," she whispered. "It... crushed him."

"Drax may not have abilities like you or me, but he's not unlike Ridley. His skin is almost like skin of stone. It's very strong."

She exhaled, heartbeat finally starting to slow. She was glad to hear it, and yet it wasn't enough; Drax could still die from the repercussions. And the point was the same. Haley could have killed any one of them, and it would have been Quinn's fault.

"It was stupid," he told her. "It was. But it was a mistake. And you didn't mean to hurt anyone."

She shook her head, attempting to stand up and walk away. Feeling dizzy and lightheaded, she sat right back down. "You don't know anything about me," she grumbled.

He sighed. "So we're back to this."

"Well, what did you expect? You told me you made the choice for me, didn't you? Decided to cut me out? So what are you even doing here? Why not just let me drown?"

He groaned. "Quinn, I would never let you drown. I probably couldn't even leave you alone for more than a few days, as much as I would like to. Look, I'm sorry about how I acted. I know if I hadn't, we wouldn't be here."

"I don't know if I'd give you *that* much credit."

He gave her a sarcastic look.

"Well, what do you want me to say?" she demanded. "That I've changed my mind; that I'll stop talking to Reese? I won't. That I understand where you were coming from? How could I? You've told me nothing. And he's told me nothing of you. Other than that you're the momma's boy."

He laughed out loud. "That *I'm* the momma's boy? Oh, that's rich."

She raised her eyebrows. "Really."

"Come on. You've met my mother. Clean-cut. Polite. Regal. All about manners and politics. Which son do you think she prefers?"

Quinn had to admit, when he put it like that, Reese was clearly the son to take pride in. Well-behaved, friendly, accommodating. Dash was pretty much a nightmare. But why would Reese lie about that?

"How did you even know?" she asked him. "That we went flying. Were you watching me? Were you watching him?"

"I make my rounds at the top of the wall almost every night. I talk people down a lot. Usually kids, new recruits. People who have decided they can't fit in here, that they'd rather roll the dice back in the real world. To me, it's almost like talking people out of suicide. I know they're safe here. I consider it my job to protect them." He shook his head. "Meanwhile, he's up there, telling you to leave."

"That's not what he said. He just told me I had a choice."

"You already *knew* that—you didn't need him to tell you," Dash said, frustration rising. "And he *knows* that, which is why it's so absurdly brilliant. Can't you see that he's trying too hard to get you to trust him? Can't you see that he's trying to manipulate you?"

"No. I can't. But that's fine, because I don't trust him, and it's not because of what you're telling me, Dash. It's because I don't trust anyone. I haven't in years. So, if that's what you're worried about, don't."

He watched her, a mixture of confusion and understanding clouding his eyes.

"Just…" He sighed. "Just be careful."

"I could tell you I will," she said, holding his gaze. "But I've found myself doing this strange thing lately where I'm honest with you."

And they stared at each other, silent.

Finally, he spoke, changing the subject.

"How about we go for a swim?"

She glanced down at the river, where minutes ago she'd had near-death experience. The thought came with the dark reminder of the Drax-Haley event that had led to it. "I should go check on Drax," she said hesitantly. "I should… see if there's anything I can do."

"There's nothing you can do," he told her gently. "Drax will be fine. Dr. Donovan is a miracle worker—and his skin already worked the real miracle."

She bit her lip. It did help, hearing that. But she still wasn't convinced.

"It's okay," he said, grin playing at the corners of his lips. "Probably wasn't a good idea, anyway. I did just finish giving you mouth-to-mouth after your last attempt at swimming…"

"I would have been fine," she said, unable to conceal her own matching grin. "You just knew it was the only chance you'd ever get to ever kiss me."

He laughed, but from the silence that followed, it was obvious that neither of them believed that. She could even feel her lips tingling at the thought of—

Lips tingling? She stopped her train of thought before she wanted to slap herself.

"Oh, come on, then," she said, standing up and stripping off her soaked clothes, leaving only her underwear on. She set her clothes in the sun on a nearby tree branch, grinning coyly at him as he watched her. "Unless one of the many rules on this island is not to have any fun."

He peeled off his own shirt, revealing an impressively sculpted chest underneath. She knew from her own experience that his perfect body had more to do with his visible affectations and less to do with how much he worked out. But she still enjoyed the view.

She jumped in first, foregoing a swan dive in such rocky rapids and opting instead for a nice cannon ball. He followed suit, landing quite nearly on top of her;

99

she shrieked and laughed out loud, shoving him off her. Their combined powers had the water splashing and waving at more accelerated rates than usual; it was like they were creating their own water ride.

When the waves settled, they turned to face each other, contented expressions on both of their faces. Dash was the first to speak.

"Since you think I'm incapable of having fun, might I make a suggestion?"

"You can try."

"Have you ever played the game 'I Never?'"

"As in the high school drinking game? I guess I played it a few times. Is that your suggestion?"

"You're clearly a woman of mystery. I'm guessing you might feel the same way about me."

"Don't flatter yourself," she said automatically, even though he was right.

He clearly didn't buy it. "What do you say?"

"I say there's no drink in either of our hands. Isn't that the penalty in the game? Drink if you've done it?"

"I have a better penalty. Go all the way underwater if you've done it. Stay up if you haven't."

She was enjoying seeing this side of him, she had to admit.

"Fine," she said. "You first."

He kicked his feet up and leaned back, treading water easily with his arms as he considered his statement. Finally, he returned to an upright position, deciding. "I never had a pet."

"Really," she said, surprised by this. Even *she* had had a pet, and she hadn't exactly had a white-picket-fence upbringing. She closed her eyes, sank into the water, completely submerged herself, and resurfaced.

"What kind of pet?" he asked her.

"A dog. Just for a few years. I didn't buy him or adopt him or anything. He just started following me around one day, and we stuck together for a while. He was a scruffy thing, scarred from head to toe. I think someone had tried and failed to turn him into a fighting dog. I called him Dumpster Dog—never really had a real name for him." She regretted not giving the poor creature a better name. She realized she was surprised by the memory, and by how much of it she was sharing with Dash.

He watched her—nothing but her. "What happened to him?"

She bit her lip, a pang of pain hitting her. "I don't know," she admitted. "One day I woke up and he was gone. Might have died. Might have run away. Might have decided he'd run from one too many gunshots with me."

He didn't say anything, but in his eyes was the same sadness that she felt at the story. She missed that dog. It had hurt, losing him. It had hurt more than losing any of the men she'd lost—until Kurt.

"Your turn," he said, probably sensing that it was time to change the subject.

He had played it safe, but the end result had still been personal for her. It was only fair she play it less safe. But what had she not done that he had?

There was only one thing that came to mind.

"I never fell in love."

His eyebrows twitched at this, doubt shadowing his eyes. But he didn't say anything. He simply dropped down into the water, submerged himself completely, and came back up.

He shook the water out of his hair awkwardly, almost like a wet dog. She tried not to notice how cute the gesture was.

"What was her name?" she asked him.

"Charlotte. You remind me of her, sometimes. She was fearless, like you. Headstrong. Wanted to take on the whole world. Make it better."

So, he had been in love... with someone like *her?* When she had first met him, he had loathed everything about her. Was it some kind of twisted grudge he held against this Charlotte girl?

"But she was different than you, too," he continued. "Less concerned with what people thought of her. More trusting. She tended to see the good in people. I think you tend to see the bad."

Quinn tried not to be offended by this; it was undeniably true. But it still hurt. "What happened to her?" she asked. "This better version of me?"

"She was killed. Many years ago. And I think that's about all I can say about that for now."

She watched him, just as he had watched her during her story, utterly transfixed. This girl had clearly been the love of his life; she could see it in his eyes. What had happened to her? Had she made it to Siloh with him? Had she been killed there, or out in the real world? Who had done it?

And had Dash gotten his revenge?

"Your turn," she said quietly.

"Okay," he said without hesitating. "I never knew my father."

She had wondered about this. There hadn't been any extra desks or offices in the 'capital' building Savannah had shown her. Neither Reese nor Dash had ever mentioned their father. But she wondered what the story was.

She dropped down into the water, stopping just before the water reached her eyes.

And she rose.

"Halfway," he observed as she came back up. "What does that mean?"

"I never really *knew* mine, either. But I had the unfortunate experience of meeting him a handful of times. Each more painful than the last."

He nodded, watching her. He was waiting for more, she knew. But that was all he was going to get, for now.

"I never hated my own mother," she said, not missing a beat.

He dropped down all the way without a moment's hesitation.

Why would Reese lie, she wondered? She didn't sense dishonesty from Dash. She felt fairly confident that she and Dash could tell when the other was lying. It seemed to be tied to their powers of compulsion.

"There are things you don't know about this place," he told her. "Things you don't know about her. Things you don't know about Reese. But they aren't things I can just tell you… They aren't things I can just tell anyone."

"Why?" she asked impatiently. How was she supposed to trust him—not that she *would*, but if that was really what he wanted—if he couldn't even tell her the truth about his own family? About *himself*?

"If the things I know were to spread to the wrong people, it would dangerous for a lot of the *right* people," he said. "It's about protection. It's about safety. Just give it time, Quinn. You'll learn."

She wanted more, sooner, but she knew she wasn't going to get it. Besides, she understood what he was saying, on some level. It was the same reason they weren't sharing all of their secrets with each other.

And that was when he said it. The thing she knew he had been wondering for a long time. The likeliest reason that he had been so cold to her upon meeting her.

"I never killed anyone."

She stood, feet plastered to the mucky, rocky base of the river, eyes riveted on his. It wasn't a glare, exactly, that she was staring him down with. But it was fierce. Daring him to not believe her. Daring him to keep thinking he knew things about her that he didn't.

Her turn.

"I never wanted to kill anyone."

This time, they sank together. Eyes never leaving each other's. Dropping down into the cloudy water, hair spidering out around each of them, rays of light catching the rippling water and casting strange, magnificent glows upon each of them.

And still they stared at each other.

And then they were kissing.

It was the strangest thing, kissing beneath the water. It was an even stranger thing, kissing someone so *powerful* beneath the water. It was as if the water around them had disappeared, a strange sensation of fire and electricity replacing it. The streaks of light hitting them seemed to multiply tenfold, and everything else disappeared.

They broke apart, rose back to the surface, and stared at each other, back in a world so very different from the one just below them.

"I should go," he said, eyes straying from hers, voice tight, concerned.

She didn't mind. She had a lot to think about, and the last thing she needed was him staying there, confusing her further.

He hoisted himself out of the water, climbing onto the grass and turning back down to look at her. "Are you staying here?"

She nodded wordlessly, lifting a wet, dripping hand in a silent goodbye. She would stay there for the night.

She wasn't ready to face Haley, anyway.

7. RORY

She stayed in the water for quite some time, until her fingertips began to shrivel and her body began to shiver. When she looked up at the sky, she saw that the sun was starting to fade, and she knew she would have to get out and dry off before it went completely away. She climbed out of the water, stretched out into the tall, overgrown grass, closed her eyes, and soaked up the last rays of sunshine.

She thought of many things as she lay there—everything from Dumpster Dog to her long-lost father to her kiss with Dash. Her mind wandered to Drax, who she could only pray was alive as Dash had said, and then to Haley, who was undoubtedly furious with her. Quinn had always made a point not to use compulsion on her friends back in the real world, but on those rare occasions that she had, they had always been angry with her. They felt betrayed. She didn't blame them. What was worse than your own friend controlling your mind?

She finally drifted off into an uncomfortable sleep. Flashes of Kurt invaded her dreams. She was used to seeing his face every night, but it still hurt. She had been responsible for many people's pain over the years, but he was the only one whose death she was responsible for. *I never killed anyone...* Had she lied to Dash? Had she killed Kurt?

She wasn't the one who had commanded them to pull their triggers, she reminded herself. The man who had was the man she would kill. One day.

She woke up at the same time as the sun, but she stayed there even longer. She knew she would probably be late for class, but she didn't care. She had to get her things from her room, and she had no intention of returning to her room until she was sure that Haley was out. She hadn't decided what she would say to her new friend. She wasn't sure it would even make a difference.

She gave it about an hour, lying there, staring up at the sky all over again, thinking. Thinking about Dash. Thinking about Reese. Wondering which of them was telling the truth. Wondering whether they were both lying. In her experience, men lied, and men left. It was why she had never let herself fall in love. It was why it had never even been an option.

And yet, now, with Dash… it was something new. Something she had never felt before. Not *love;* not even close… But the unfamiliarity had her worried, and she knew it had him worried, too.

She finally rose and made her way to the dormitory, anxiously stepping through the front door and eyeing the desk where Drax usually worked. He wasn't there, of course. In his place sat Angel.

Not late enough, she mused, glancing at the clock on the wall. If Angel was still there, there was a chance that Haley was, too.

"Hi," Quinn said carefully, knowing perfectly well that Angel was not her biggest fan. "Are you covering for Drax today?"

Angel gave her a sarcastic look. "Clearly."

"Right… Any word on how he's doing?"

"He's alive. No thanks to you."

Quinn nodded. She deserved every inch of resentment Angel wanted to give her when it came to Drax; she was just glad he was alive. "Did you—erm—did you happen to notice if Haley already left for the morning?"

Angel's giant, white wings flapped in annoyance. "Yes. She looked terrible, if you were wondering. Hasn't forgiven herself for what you made her do. Probably never will."

Quinn sighed. "I'm not surprised, but it wasn't her fault. It was mine."

"I know. Everyone knows."

With that comforting knowledge, Quinn headed upstairs.

When she reached her room, she saw something waiting for her on her bed: an envelope with her name on it. She reached for it, unable to remember the last time she'd received a piece of mail, and opened it.

It was her monthly allowance. *About time.* But there was more to it than that.

Behind the allowance was an additional stack of bills, on which there was a note.

Because Savannah's cheap, and Haley's clothes have never quite fit you right.
–Reese.

She laughed to herself. The timing of Reese sending her a flirty note the morning after she had kissed his brother was bizarre, though she was fairly certain it was a coincidence. If the two brothers were as estranged as Dash had suggested, Reese would have no way of knowing about the kiss. She felt strange about him giving her money, but she wasn't about to complain. She had a whole new wardrobe to buy, and she doubted the island's monthly allowance would begin to cover it.

She put the money into her pocket and headed back out, certain at this point that she was going to be late to class. Of course, with no time to shower, she would show up in the same outfit she'd worn the day before, which couldn't smell great. But there was something almost comforting about that to her. Who had she been kidding the last two weeks, really? Getting along with everyone, showering every day, sleeping normal hours, eating normal food? Did anyone really buy it?

Maybe she should just skip class altogether.

When she opened her door, she learned that Rory had the same idea.

She didn't look like herself. She didn't look like Quinn had ever seen her. In fact, she looked like Quinn had when she had arrived on the island.

Rory's normally bright, eager eyes were dull and tired. Her bouncy curls were weighted and heavy. There was a strain—almost a mania—in her expression that Quinn had never sensed before.

"Rory?" She stooped down to her knees to look the girl in the eyes. "Are you alright?"

"I need your help," Rory said, eyes eager, desperate. "I can't control it any more."

"Control what?" Quinn asked, suddenly feeling as desperate as Rory.

"My power."

Quinn had seen it before, particularly in younger deviants—the magnitude of their abilities becoming too much for them. But she hadn't experienced it personally. It tended to happen to people who hid or ignored their abilities; she had never done much of either.

Quinn and Rory had become fairly close over the past few weeks, but Quinn still found it hard to believe she was the girl's go-to in a situation like this. Was there really no one else who could help her?

"What can I do?" she finally asked.

"I need Dash. I've tried to ask him, but he's always so busy. He tells me he will teach me in good time. Which is true. Once you guys graduate, and the class below you does, eventually he'll teach me. But not for years. And I need his help, Quinn. I need it before I do something bad."

Quinn put her hands on Rory's shoulders, doing what she could to calm her. "It's going to be okay, Rory. But I need you to tell me. What exactly happened that scared you so much?"

"I just keep… losing control. Hurting people without meaning to. Scaring my classmates, my roommate. I feel like I'm going crazy, and my teachers won't help me; they just tell me to stay calm, to 'focus.' Won't you talk to Dash for me? Or even just help me yourself? Please?"

Quinn sighed, pulling the girl into a hug. She considered helping Rory herself, not in any mood to talk to Dash or anyone else at the moment. She liked Rory; she wanted to help her. But Quinn was no teacher. "I'll talk to Dash," she promised.

Rory smiled slightly, but it wasn't the kind of smile she usually wore, and it was hard for Quinn to see. Until then, Rory had been one of the happiest people she knew.

Quinn knew she should talk to Dash sooner than later, but she couldn't bear to leave Rory in such poor spirits. "How about the two of us blow off first period and do a little shopping?" she suggested. "I finally got my first allowance, and I could use a little help picking out some clothes."

She had expected Rory to jump at the opportunity, but the girl's expression barely changed. Quinn had to give her credit for that; like Quinn, it meant her emotions weren't easily manipulated. She felt how she felt.

Despite her lack of enthusiasm, Rory finally nodded. "Yeah. That would be nice."

The two of them headed out to the shops, each eyeing the other silently. Quinn's mind wandered as they walked. Who had Rory hurt? How severely? Why did none of her teachers care?

But Quinn knew that she wasn't going to get answers any time soon; Rory was far from her usual talkative self. Instead, she focused on helping Quinn pick out clothes. She seemed to have a complete understanding of Quinn's style based solely on Quinn's previous publicity; she picked out the exact blacks, leathers, reds, and combat boots that Quinn had always been fond of back in the real world. She even helped Quinn pick out a dress or two that Quinn wouldn't normally have felt comfortable choosing in front of a child. She supposed if the girl was strong enough to kill someone, she was ready to know about provocative dresses.

By the time they had finished their shopping, Quinn had made up her mind to go see Dash about Rory before doing anything else. She was probably well into missing her second class of the day, and would undoubtedly be chastised for it by Reese or Savannah—or even both—but she couldn't bring herself to care.

After thanking Rory for the company and dropping her off at her next class, Quinn ran back to her room, raced through her shower, towel-dried her mess of hair, and threw on the first thing she could find in the shopping bags—a black tank top and a pair of black jeans. Her staple.

She had to admit, it felt good to be back in the kind of clothes she used to wear.

She pulled out her cell phone, trying to recall whether she had Dash's number in it. As she scrubbed through her contacts, she realized she still had almost no numbers in her phone, Dash's included. Sighing, she weighed her other options. She didn't know where he lived. She didn't want to wait until power tech, where curious minds would surround them. Her only remaining option was to go see him at work.

She hadn't been to the town hall since the day she'd met Savannah—her first day on the island. She had no desire to speak to Savannah again. But how else would she find him?

It was worth it, she decided. It was for Rory.

They were both there when she stepped through the revolving door—both sons. She couldn't tell if Savannah was in her office; the door was closed, and the blinds were drawn. But there sat Reese in one corner of the room, and Dash in the other. Both staring right at her.

She stopped at the entrance, glancing from one brother to the other, suddenly finding her situation incredibly amusing.

Reese was the first to speak. She had a feeling Dash hadn't had nearly enough time to mull over what to say to her after their last rendezvous.

"Quinn," Reese greeted easily. "I see you've already put your allowance to good use. On a school day."

She grinned sheepishly, glad he wasn't more upset. "Whose brilliant idea was it to withhold the money for two weeks, and then give it to me on a Tuesday?" she teased. "I blame them."

"You're not wrong. Just don't do it again. And if you do, keep the twelve-year-old out of it, would you?"

She blushed. She supposed she shouldn't be surprised he knew she and Rory had been together. They hadn't exactly been subtle about it.

"Oh," he added, "and you look great."

She didn't even try to hide her glow from that compliment; it was the kind of thing Dash would have trouble saying to her, but the kind of thing she still enjoyed hearing, especially when it was being said in front of him.

"Thanks," she said, turning to look at Dash. "You hear that?"

"Yeah," Dash muttered, annoyed. "What's going on? Is everything okay?"

She appreciated that. He might still feel awkward about the previous day, but at least he was extending *some* basic courtesies. It made her next question easier to ask.

"Well, mostly. There was something I wanted to talk to you about. Could we…?" She gestured to the door, hoping this wouldn't offend Reese. It wasn't so much about keeping secrets from him as leaving him to do his job. The Rory situation didn't concern him.

Dash stood. Quinn snuck a peek back over at Reese, who was watching them. He seemed curious, but not upset. She appreciated that.

Dash and Quinn headed outside, picking up a walk without a direction in mind.

"Look," Dash said, "you should be in class. If you came here to talk about—"

"It's not about that," she said quickly. "I wouldn't… Trust me, it's not. It's actually about this kid named Rory. Do you know her?"

"I think so. The one who skipped class with you today? Electric abilities?"

"That's the one," Quinn said grimly. "She talk to you lately?"

"Yeah—just for a few seconds, though. She was so nervous, I kind of shrugged it off as a preteen crush or something. She said something about wanting my help with her abilities."

"It wasn't a preteen crush. When she came to me this morning, she looked terrible. Like she hasn't been sleeping. Like she's afraid. I took her out shopping to try to cheer her up, but it's more than her being in a bad mood. I think she does need you, Dash. Would you be able to help her?"

"Not very easily," he admitted. "I couldn't take her into my class, if that's what you're asking. Savannah would never allow it. And I couldn't help her in any kind of public place, either. There are rules about that kind of thing here. Again, all Savannah." He rolled his eyes.

"What sort of rules? Specifically?"

"Well, really they're just rules for *me,* and if I break them, I lose my job. Basically, they state that I teach who she tells me to teach, and no one else."

"And she has that kind of power?" Quinn asked, disgusted. "Just with, what, the wave of her hand?"

"She can do whatever she wants, Quinn. She's in charge around here."

Quinn sighed, frustrated. "But your classes—the way you run them. Rory says it's different from the way they run power tech for kids. She says that Savannah watches those classes. Why doesn't she watch yours?"

"It's complicated. She lets me do it my way because she expects me to report back to her about everyone's abilities. She thinks having a record of who does what is necessary for Siloh's safety, or something like that."

Quinn's mind raced. Did this mean Reese had been right all along—that Savannah and Dash really were spying on Siloh's inhabitants? "Do you *do* it? Report back to her?"

"Yes and no," he said uncomfortably. "I give her just enough... Not everything. Look, Quinn, this conversation is inevitably going to lead us to the same conversation I told you we couldn't have. I can't go there. Not yet."

She felt like she was always playing catch-up with him. Figuring him out. Waiting for him to tell her more. It was maddening, and yet consistently intriguing.

"Look," he said, stopping and turning to face her. There was encouragement and truth in his eyes for the first time that day. "Back to Rory. You don't need me. She doesn't need me. She has you."

"*Me*?" she repeated doubtfully. "What do you expect *me* to do?"

"The same thing I do. Work with her. Engage her. Test her limits. Help her find them. Help her know them. Nine times out of ten, someone struggling with controlling their abilities really just needs to *use* them more, in a safe environment."

She had a feeling he was right. And yet... *her,* teach someone?

"Give it a try," he said. "If you find you're not helping, or that she still needs more help, give me a call. I'll do what I can. Okay? Do you have my number?"

She couldn't help but grin. "No," she said, reaching for her phone, "but very smooth there, Dash. Slipped that right in."

He accepted her phone with a sarcastic look, programming his number in and handing it back to her. She pocketed it, grin fading as silence set in. The confusion that had brewed in both of their minds after the kiss was back; she could sense it.

She half expected him to turn around and leave, but he didn't. Instead, he asked, "Have you gone to see him yet? Drax?"

She shook her head. She hadn't yet worked up the guts to actually face him. "He doesn't want to see me."

"Actually, he does. He told me this morning in the medical wing."

She gaped at him, completely thrown. Drax *wanted* to see her? After what she had done to him?

"Everyone involved in the YA training understands the risks, Quinn," he told her. "Things happen. Mistakes are made."

"Usually not ones so intentional."

"You didn't intend to hurt anyone but yourself," he said, looking at her pointedly. "Which, frankly, is almost more concerning."

"There's your first mistake," she said, reverting back to the same line she had given Trent once. It was a line she had used for years, almost like a security blanket. It reminded both her and them that she needed no one but herself. "Don't waste your time being concerned for me, Dash. It'll more than likely drive you crazy."

His response was something no one had ever thought to say back to her. It was so simple, so straightforward, and yet so fearless.

"Maybe that's a risk I'm willing to take."

And before she could respond, he turned back away from her and headed for the building.

She stood there for a moment, not sure how to feel or what to think. She glanced past Dash and into the building. Through the glass she could see Reese sitting there, watching her, smiling politely. He gave her a wave. It didn't seem to be the wave of a liar. Then again, it didn't have half the passion of any exchange she'd ever had with Dash, either.

Once again, she found herself wondering which brother was lying and which was telling the truth.

• • •

Knowing that there was no chance she'd make it to any class but power tech that day, she headed for the medical wing. She sent a text message to Rory as she walked, asking whether she would be free to meet up that Saturday for some practice. Rory responded almost instantly. *Yes!*

It was easy to find Drax's room in the medical wing; it was the only one with lights on. There were several visitors surrounding him when Quinn entered, Pence and Charlie included. *Guess I'm not the only one skipping.* She thought back to her own time there, and how Charlie and Haley had been there with her, and decided that maybe they weren't as strict on attendance as Savannah and Reese had let on.

Drax was still bedridden, though he looked better than she had feared. Bruised, certainly; swollen; but there didn't seem to be anything broken.

He smiled when he saw her, which surprised her right off the bat. What was wrong with him? Who smiled at their attacker?

"Quinn," he said, lifting a hand to wave her over. He winced slightly at the move, but said nothing of it.

"Hi," she said weakly, coming to join Pence and Charlie next to his bed. Both of them smiled politely enough at her, but she had a hard time believing it was genuine. "How are you feeling?"

"I feel great, actually. I know it sounds crazy, but I mean it. Quinn, I had no idea I could withstand something like that until then. All this time, I've been thinking I'd be virtually defenseless if something happened to us. Now I'm feeling just the opposite, and it's thanks to you. Well, you and Haley."

She blinked. This certainly wasn't what she had been expecting. It made sense, in a strange way. But she still didn't deserve his kindness.

"Drax, because of me, a tree fell on you. You could be dead. Don't you at least hate me a little?"

"Nope," he said brightly, and then his expression grew more serious. "That's what you want, isn't it? For us to hate you? For us to distrust you? I could tell you were a lone wolf the moment I met you, but you're just going to have to learn to deal with people around here caring about you, because I'm pretty sure we all do."

Quinn stared at him dubiously, turning her gaze toward Pence and Charlie, who both nodded in agreement.

"*You* might be the most forgiving people in the world," she finally said, "but I doubt *everyone* feels that way about me. Not Haley. Not any more."

Pence and Charlie exchanged a look, and she inferred with a sinking heart that she was right.

"Haley was hurt," Drax said. "Hurt in a different way than me. But it's within your right to practice compulsion during power tech. She knows that."

"She does," Pence agreed. "I think more than anything she was just hurt that you avoided her afterwards. If not for Dash letting her know that you were okay, she would have thought you'd run away."

Quinn didn't mention that running away had been her intention initially.

"You should talk to her," Drax said. "Class is almost over—you could meet her in your room. Talk it out. You both deserve it, Quinn. You're good people, and you clearly care a lot for each other."

Quinn had never been good at 'talking it out,' but she knew he was right. "Okay," she said, heaving a sigh. "I'll go."

"Good. By the way… We're having another party. This weekend." He winked at her. "It's for me this time."

. . .

As Drax had predicted, Haley was already in their room when Quinn got back. She didn't say anything when Quinn walked in, but she did look up at her. Quinn recognized that sad, disappointed expression. It was the same expression she had seen written all over the faces of the people whose hearts she had broken back in the real world. *I've never been in love,* she had told Dash. But people had been in love with her. Kurt included.

"Look," Quinn said, swallowing. "I'm sorry."

She had known, of course, that it wasn't enough—wasn't what Haley was looking for—but it was hard for her. With all those boys whose hearts she had broken, she hadn't had to apologize. She hadn't had to work things out with them. She had just moved on, gone somewhere new, started over. Again and again.

Besides Kurt, of course. Kurt had always been the exception.

"It was stupid," Quinn continued. "I was angry at Dash over a conversation we'd just had. All I wanted when I compelled you was for you to attack me so I could, I don't know, prove myself. Prove that I was tougher than him. Than all of you. It was selfish and stupid. But if I had known that it would hurt Drax…" She trailed off, casting her eyes downward.

Haley gathered her thoughts for a moment. Finally, she spoke.

"What is it with you and Dash?"

This was Haley's question? Of all the things Quinn had just said, of all the pain they had caused Drax, *this* was what she wanted to know about?

"What… what do you mean?" Quinn stammered.

"I mean, we knew about you before you ever got here. How you were with men. How they couldn't shake you. Couldn't win you over. Couldn't have any effect on you whatsoever, from what we could tell. And then you came here, and our theories were confirmed. You barely blinked at Trent. But then, with Dash…"

Quinn said nothing.

"It was like your own rules flipped on you, all of a sudden," Haley said. "I

115

mean, that first day in the cafeteria, and every day since. You said you were wrong, didn't you? That you didn't really know him?"

She *had* said that. She still didn't really believe it, but she didn't believe that Dash was lying, either. Why would he? What could possibly be his motivation for telling her that he didn't remember her?

"I guess," she mumbled. "I don't know. What does it matter?"

"I like Dash. Really, I do. But between him, and his brother, and his mother… they're all just… a bit of *drama*. And for someone like you, someone who's a ticking time bomb, ready for the next thing to set her off… I just want you to be careful, Quinn."

This conversation was starting to remind Quinn of the ones she had just had with Drax and Dash. Conversations that should have been about her concerns for others turning into conversations about others' concerns for her.

People on this island really *were* too forgiving.

Quinn was faced with two options. The first was to actually put a little trust into their friendship—to open up to Haley. The second was to do what she always did and shut her out.

All of her instincts told her to shut Haley out. Her instincts had been trained ruthlessly for a decade to trust no one; they couldn't change overnight. But it was about more than that. It was about getting Haley to forgive her. And for the first time, forgiveness mattered more than instinct.

She opened up—as best she could.

"Look… I know I've been letting him get to me more than I should. But it's not what you think. I mean, yeah, I'm a little emotional when it comes to him. But the ticking time bomb thing—that's just… me. That's just my temper. The Drax thing could have happened because of something Angel said, or Trent, or whoever, if they'd picked the wrong thing to say."

She liked to think this was true, even if it wasn't.

"So, you don't have feelings for him?" Haley asked. Point-blank.

Quinn had to admire Haley's no-bullshit personality. She didn't sidle around things. She wasn't subtle. She was who she was.

"Sure, I do," Quinn managed, only because she knew Haley would know if she was lying. "But that doesn't mean I'd trust him as far as I could throw him. And it doesn't mean I'd ever let myself really fall for him. It just means..." She considered her word choice carefully. "It means I'm infatuated with him."

Haley nodded, seeming satisfied with this answer for now. "Fair enough. That's sort of how I feel about Trent, I guess."

Quinn knew for a fact that it *wasn't* how Haley felt about Trent. The way Haley looked at Trent was pure, embarrassing adoration. The look of someone who had been ignored for too long.

But, of course, she wouldn't say any of this to Haley. Besides, she stood by her initial opinion: Haley was way too good for Trent.

"Have you ever thought about finding someone else?" Quinn asked. "I mean, I know your options are kind of limited here, but maybe Tommy?"

Quinn still wasn't sure what Tommy's abilities were. She had never had a single conversation with him. But he was in the YA, and he seemed nice enough. Quiet, maybe. Certainly a more sensible option than Trent.

"I don't know," Haley said, frowning. "Tommy's a nice guy, but I don't think I could ever really be at ease, dating someone who could be invisibly spying on me at any given moment."

So *that* was Tommy's ability, Quinn realized. It made sense that she hadn't ever caught notice of it; it was the opposite of noticeable. She was impressed; she had never managed to render herself invisible.

"Just promise me you'll give it some thought," Quinn said.

"Okay. I guess this weekend would be a good opportunity for me to talk to him. Drax tell you about his party?"

Quinn had almost forgotten. As Drax had pointed out to her before she left, she had spent much of the last party—her own party—on the roof, ignoring the majority of the guests. She had a feeling that if Dash made another appearance, that was exactly where she would be again. But she didn't tell that to Haley, who was worried enough about her as it was.

"Yeah, he did," she said. "We should make it a good one, shouldn't we? 'We're Glad You're Alive' themed?"

"'We're Glad You're Alive and Sorry We Almost Killed You.' I think we should make a banner."

Quinn smiled, glad things were back to normal. "Absolutely."

. . .

As the week came to a close, things mostly went back to normal—whatever 'normal' was on an island full of deviants. Drax recovered quickly, returning for a half-day of classes Thursday and a full day Friday. Dash continued to pair Quinn and Haley together in power tech, and Quinn didn't dare attempt to compel Haley again.

Dash was back to mostly ignoring her, but he wasn't as rude as he had been when he was upset with her. If anything, he just seemed unsure—unsure of what to say, how to act, even what to make of her. Every once in a while, she would catch him watching her—whether she was reading his book, blasting Haley's tree roots with fire, or just staring off into space, thinking about Kurt. She would lock eyes with him, and for a split second that honesty would return—the feeling that, if she wanted to, she could compel him. And with that feeling, the desire to do nothing of the sort.

Finally, the weekend came, and with it, the promise she had made to Rory: that she would help her control her power. A promise that she had intended to fulfill around ten or eleven in the morning, but one that came knocking a lot closer to eight.

She groaned through Rory's loud banging, tossing off her covers and glancing at herself in the mirror. She had thrown on a tank top and pajama shorts the night before. They didn't look like daytime clothes, but she cared less and less each day about how anyone perceived her. Besides, the longer she spent focusing on her appearance, the louder Rory would knock.

She decided that her pajamas were fine, opened the door, and followed Rory out to the practice field.

She watched the girl as they walked, trying to gauge whether she looked better or worse than she had the last time they'd talked. Certainly not better, she decided. Same weathered expression, deep-set eyes, and limp hair. Her spirit still seemed subdued.

"Tell me again," Quinn said, forcing herself to engage the girl despite her own mental exhaustion. "What exactly has been happening to make you ask for help? You've been unintentionally hurting others? Yourself?"

"Not myself; not the abilities themselves, anyway. But others, sometimes. Mostly in my sleep—I'll kind of electrocute the whole room, bust it up pretty bad. They had to switch my roommates. They gave me this girl who's got this weird, rubbery skin. The electricity doesn't bother her."

"So, they know that you're having these problems, but they haven't done anything to help you? Who have you talked to besides me?"

"Well, first, my old roommate and I talked to Drax, you know, at the front desk. We both wanted to get switched. But he said he had to take it to Reese Collins, and then Reese took it to Savannah, and while I was waiting for all that to happen, I asked Dash for help, and then I got this letter, and... Here." She pulled out the letter, handing it to Quinn.

I have spoken to your power stabilization advisor, Miss Donohue. She has taken note of your struggles with your abilities and assures me that she is doing everything in her power to help you cope. It has also come to my attention that you have contacted Dash Collins regarding one-on-one training. This is strictly prohibited. In the future, any questions of a similar nature should be taken up with me initially.

No signature. No need. It was more than clear who this letter was from.

"But at least they got me a new roommate," Rory said dully.

"Wow," Quinn said, baffled. "When I talked to Dash, it was the same thing... like Savannah had some kind of problem with him working with anyone outside of the YA. I can't see why that would even matter."

"Me neither."

They had reached the practice fields, and to Quinn's relief, they were alone. She was starting to feel like she might be taking some sort of risk, working with Rory.

Not that she really cared.

"So, this power tech teacher that you have," Quinn said. "She's no good?"

"She's awful. All she does is talk to me about how to suppress my abilities—how to basically act like I don't have them at all. It doesn't help."

Of course it didn't, Quinn thought. It was like Dash said—the best technique was simply *using* abilities in a safe environment.

"Okay," Quinn said, crossing her arms. "Well, I guess there's no easy way to start, is there? Why don't you just… show me what you've got? Give me a blast of something."

"Just… a blast of something?"

"Yeah. What's the worst that can happen? You said it doesn't hurt you. Electricity is one of my go-to's, so it shouldn't hurt me. And no one else is around for, like, a mile."

Rory glanced around, considering. She looked back over at Quinn, still skeptical. "Take a few steps back, would you? I don't want to hurt you."

Quinn took a few steps back just to appease the girl. "Okay," she said. "Let's see what you've got."

Rory closed her eyes, lifted her arms, and struck.

The blast of electricity was so big and so strong, it brought Quinn to her knees. Deep-rooted, nerve-grappling shocks rippled through her so intensely, she gasped out loud.

And then, as suddenly as it had started, it was over. And Quinn felt *incredible*.

"Wow," she said, rising shakily. She looked down at her hands. Steam—or was it smoke?—was emitting from her. It was almost like Rory's electricity had juiced her up.

"Are you okay?" Rory asked, eyes wide and afraid, running over to Quinn.

"Yeah," Quinn said, touching the skin of her arm and wincing slightly as it sizzled. But she was unscathed. "Yeah, actually, I feel amazing. That was incredible, Rory."

Rory blushed. "Thanks. I've never really let myself go like that before."

"Why don't we try something a little different? This time, try to focus a little more. Rather than just letting it rip, think about a specific spot you want to shock—maybe that pole over there." She pointed to a tall, metal pole about a hundred feet from them.

But she lowered her hand when she saw someone running over to them: Ridley.

"Rory!" he shouted, chest heaving, as if he had sprinted halfway across the island to them. "Quinn! Are you guys okay?"

"Yeah," Quinn said, laughing slightly. "Relax, Ridley. We're just goofing off."

Ridley's eyes were serious—too serious. "Quinn," he said, his voice urgent. "I know you're new here, but you don't understand. This is the practice field. You might as well be holding up a giant sign asking Savannah to notice you."

Quinn had a feeling she knew what Ridley's point was, but she still didn't understand what Savannah's problem was. "So what? Last I checked, we're still allowed to use our abilities, aren't we?"

"It's not about using your abilities. It's about Rory's situation. Savannah knows she's been looking for a teacher, Quinn. And now she starts making giant electric blasts with you? After you've both already been caught skipping class? It's trouble. Trouble you don't want to get yourself into."

Quinn didn't like this side of Ridley, nor this side of the island's politics. She knew he was right—based on the note Rory had shown her, and everything Dash had said, she should have been more careful. But why did Ridley have to get involved? "If Savannah's the one who cares so much," she said, "why are you the one stopping us?"

"For your own sake. Savannah didn't see you, but that's only by sheer luck. If she had, this would be a very different conversation. Look, Quinn, I understand what you're doing. I know Rory's been having a hard time. I applaud your efforts to help her. But you're going to have to go much, much deeper into the forest."

Quinn held his gaze, the small degree of trust she allowed herself to have for him returning. She believed him. But she still didn't really understand.

"Okay," she said. "Fine. But I still don't get it. What does she think we're going to do? Have some sort of uprising? Overthrow Queen Savannah? Couldn't the YA do that, with how advanced we are? We wouldn't even need the kids' help."

"Quinn," Ridley said, sounding exhausted, "there are things you don't know yet. Things you will understand, in time. And then there are things none of us understand—maybe not even Savannah herself. For now, just know to be careful. Much more careful than you were just now."

Why did everyone keep saying that? First Dash, now Ridley? If there were so many things about the island she didn't know, why didn't someone just *tell* her? When was she going to find out the truth?

And, most importantly—how?

. . .

Quinn left Rory with a small homework assignment: creating small sparks using only snaps of her fingers whenever she was out and about. She decided the girl's best bet would be to frequently use her abilities in small bursts—the opposite of what her power tech instructor had told her.

How were there so many *idiots* on the island, she couldn't help but wonder? And so many idiotic rules? She supposed she was lucky she didn't have to interact with more of them.

Quinn started to make her way to the café for breakfast, but rerouted when she saw a text from Haley: *Banner time!*

Quinn had never been much of a party planner—kegs and handles were about all she considered necessities—but she felt like she owed it to Drax to help make his celebration all he could hope for. Besides, she was still getting back into Haley's good graces; if not for him, then for her.

She found Haley stretched out on her stomach on the floor of their bedroom, already well into the We're Glad You're Alive and Sorry We Almost Killed You banner they had discussed. Laughing out loud, Quinn popped a CD into the stereo, knelt down next to her friend, and helped.

Quinn and Haley worked on the banner for at least an hour before Pence and Charlie knocked on the door, poking their heads in.

"Hey," Pence greeted. "We heard the jams and thought you might want company. Have I mentioned how glad I am you two are back to normal?"

"We are, too," Haley said cheerfully. "Please join us! We're working on some decorations for Drax's party. Do you think you could let us into the tower early,

Charlie? Get some of this set up?"

"Yeah," Charlie said. "Actually, we were on our way there to start working on it. What do you say we get the whole YA together? Have a bonding session for the first time in weeks?"

"I'm sure it'll thrill Drax that his near-death experience brought us closer together," Pence joked.

"I think it's a great idea," Haley said, turning to Quinn. "You down?"

Quinn could think of a million things she would rather do than group bonding with a bunch of teenagers, but she knew better than to say no. She liked the three of them, and she liked Drax. The rest, she could tolerate.

So she agreed, and they all made their way to the penthouse.

Angel was the first to arrive. Despite Quinn's initial dislike for Angel, she had to admit, the winged girl seemed to care very deeply for Drax. The two had undoubtedly bonded heavily over being the only two real monsters of the group.

After Angel came Izzo, the girl who could turn into animals. She arrived in human form, to Quinn's disappointment, and didn't seem likely to be shape-shifting any time soon.

Trent was next, arriving in better spirits than the last time Quinn had seen him. He even sent her one of his trademark, cocky grins, which she took to mean everything was back to normal between the two of them.

Tommy was the last member to come, and he didn't seem particularly interested in being there. Quinn was disappointed for both Haley's sake and her own that he wasn't more talkative; she found his invisibility ability fascinating. She began to suspect that he and Izzo were outsiders to the entire group, not just to her.

Shade didn't come, which wasn't a surprise to anyone. Quinn had mostly forgiven him for the Kurt illusion once Haley explained to her that the specifics were beyond his control, but she certainly hadn't bonded with him since. In fact, she hadn't seen him bond with a single other person in all of her time at Siloh. A part of her almost felt bad for him.

"So," Haley said, "tomorrow. What sorts of things should we set up? Card games? Drinking games? Board games?"

"Drax likes board games," Angel offered. "Everything from Monopoly to

Twister."

Quinn couldn't help but roll her eyes. "If Drax spends this party playing Monopoly, we should all be ashamed."

Angel glared at her. "This isn't *your* party. It's his. Besides, what do you care what activities we do? We all know you'll be on the roof with Dash all night, anyway."

Quinn considered firing back, but she decided against it. Angel's resentment toward Quinn's relationship with Dash was news to her, but it made sense. There had to be some reason Angel had disliked her all this time. If she wasn't mistaken, there was jealousy written all over that comment.

Trent was the one to confirm her suspicions. "Jesus, Ange. Cool it, would you? Just because you can't have Captain Fireplace Eyes doesn't mean no one can."

Quinn certainly didn't need Trent of all people defending her honor, but she decided not to complain under the circumstances.

"He's our *teacher*," Angel snarled at Trent. "Not all of us would go there."

Quinn ignored her, confident that any response would be giving her what she wanted. Luckily, Haley chimed in before it got worse.

"Look, this kind of bickering—this kind of distance between us—it's exactly what Drax won't want tomorrow night. I know Shade's not here, but every single other member of the YA made it today. For Drax. That means something to me. Doesn't it mean something to you guys?"

Everyone remained silent, but no one dissented. If anything, they all looked a little guilty.

"I've got an idea," Charlie offered. "We all know Drax likes games, right? We just can't agree on one. Let's create a new one—one we all like."

Pence nodded eagerly. "It's got to be something that goes along with the flavors of drinking and socializing without actually being a *drinking* game. So that everyone can participate."

"Drax is all about learning people's secrets," Angel said, warming up to the idea. "Something about life stories would be good."

Quinn's mind flashed to the game of *I Never* she had played with Dash. She decided not to mention it. She had no intention of getting that personal with anyone in the room, with the exception of possibly Haley.

"How about," she offered, brainstorming, "strip story? The group requests a specific story they want from you. If you refuse to tell it truthfully, you remove an article of clothing."

Haley gave her a sarcastic look. "Quinn."

"What? It doesn't force people to drink."

"No," said Izzo, piping up for the first time, "just to remove their own clothing."

"Or to tell the truth," said Tommy. "I don't hate that idea."

Quinn smirked, pleased not only that he agreed with her, but also that he was finally talking.

"Strip story," Angel said, shaking her head. "Frankly, I hate it. But it does seem right up Drax's alley. I think he'll like it."

Quinn did, too.

She made a mental note to be nowhere near that game when it was played.

· · ·

With the game sorted out, the conversation dwindled. But as Quinn continued to decorate, glancing around at the people around her, she decided she wanted to get to know them better. Sure, she knew Pence, Trent, Drax, Haley, and Charlie well enough. But Angel? All Quinn knew about Angel was that she hated Quinn. And Tommy and Izzo? Pence had mentioned their parents being afraid of them, but she didn't know the details.

She snuck behind the bar, grabbed some beers, and decided to make things more interesting.

"I have to say," she said to Tommy, who was blowing up balloons next to Izzo, "I'm surprised I had you beat on last person to be captured by the DCA. I mean... if they can't see you, they can't catch you, right?"

She hadn't intended to upset him, though she supposed his upset reaction made sense. "You don't know the first thing about it," he snapped.

"I know," she said, taking a sip of her beer. "That's why I'm asking."

"Our parents turned us in," Izzo told her from her other side, taking a sip of her beer and wincing at the taste. "Waited 'til we were both asleep. Told them to be quiet so we wouldn't hear them."

"But you," Quinn said, pushing despite sensing that she was irritating both of them. "Couldn't you just change into something small and slip out of the cuffs?"

"They sedated us both before we had the chance to act. I'm sure they sedated you, too—or had you already forgotten?"

Her capture had been more complicated than her simply being sedated; still, Izzo was right: once she *was* sedated, there was no using her abilities.

"You're right," she finally said. "I understand. Sorry for pressing. I didn't realize you two knew each other, back in the real world."

"We were neighborhood friends," Izzo told her shyly. "Our parents were close…"

"Encouraged each other to turn us in," Tommy added grimly. "Told themselves it was to keep our other siblings safe. We were both from big families. Got cut loose without a second thought."

Quinn doubted that, but she could imagine how much it must have hurt, all the same. She could sense from both of them how fresh the betrayal was in their minds.

"The whole point of this game was to hear people's stories *at* the party," Angel pointed out, "in exchange for your own. Were you planning on telling them anything about yourself, or are you only saving that for Dash?"

Two comments in one night? Trent had certainly been onto something, Quinn mused.

But Trent wasn't within earshot, and Tommy and Izzo weren't about to jump to her defense after her tactless questioning about their own lives. She decided to breach the subject herself. "Angel, if something happened between you and Dash once, or if you have any sort of feelings for him—"

"I already said I wouldn't go there with a teacher. I'm frankly disgusted that *he* would go there with a *student.*"

Tommy and Izzo took their leave at that point, and Quinn couldn't blame them. Besides, maybe now that it was just the two of them in, she could actually get to the bottom of the girl's hatred for her.

"Nobody's 'gone' anywhere," she told Angel. "We just get along, is all."

"'Get along?' I *get along* with Drax. He plays for the other team, of course, so that's about all we do. You *get along* with Trent. But you and Dash…" Angel shook her head. "I see the way you look at each other. And it's fine, Quinn. It is. I just… I've known girls like you before. And I've known guys like him. He seems dark, he seems complicated. But he's a good person, deep down. Are you?"

It made sense now, Quinn realized, staring into Angel's hauntingly light eyes. Angel had probably been a heartbreaker herself once. Beautiful, certainly; she still was, in her way. Then she'd become a monster and had probably been taken quickly to the island, where Dash would have helped her for years and years before Quinn arrived. If what he had told Quinn was true about only having ever loved one girl, Charlotte, it meant he had never loved Angel back. But it made sense that she would still feel protective of him.

"I'm not," Quinn finally said, holding Angel's gaze. "I try to be, when it suits me. But no, Angel. I've done bad things. I keep doing them. And you're probably right. Dash deserves better."

Angel nodded, gaze remaining cold, hard. "Don't forget it." And she walked away.

Quinn thought about Angel's words as she finished her beer and said goodbye to the rest of the group. Somehow, despite her hostility, Quinn was starting to admire Angel, whose protectiveness towards Dash was no different than her protectiveness towards Drax. She might not have as many friends as Quinn on the island, but she cared for them much more deeply than Quinn was able to let herself.

She headed back to the room with Haley, chatting amiably with her for a bit before stepping into the shower. Standing beneath the comforting blanket of steaming water, all she really wanted to do was curl up and go to bed.

But she had a party to get to.

8. GAMES

Following the party planning meet-up, the YA hallway of the dormitory had transformed into a completely different place. As all of the teenagers got ready for the party, a strange phenomenon occurred: all of them left their doors open. All of them blasted music. All of them went from room to room, chatting, even pre-gaming for the event with each other.

Drax, who had known nothing about the meet-up, came up from the front desk with a dumbfounded expression on his face. When he stepped out of the elevator, they all cheered, offering him hugs and congratulations on his recovery despite the fact that he had returned to class two days earlier.

Quinn, who had only managed to half-zip her new little black dress and was still in the process of figuring out her hair, stepped into the hallway to offer him a similar greeting. He shook his head when he saw her, eyes wide with admiration.

"I think this is all your influence," he said, hugging her tightly. "None of these jokers were like this before you came along."

"It's true," said a voice from behind him, and she pulled away from Drax to reveal two YA outsiders standing behind him: Dash and Ridley.

She stared up at Dash for a moment, silver eyes meeting gold, and her instinct, as it had been lately, was to look away. But she forced herself to keep her gaze locked on him this time. He had spoken to her. He had made the effort. It was her turn.

She didn't respond to him, but she didn't hide the small smile that crept onto her face, and it wasn't long before he returned it.

She hadn't forgotten all the complications, hesitations, and hidden truths between them. She was sure he hadn't, either. It just didn't matter enough to stop.

"What are you two doing here?" she asked, this time focusing her attention toward Ridley, who she hadn't asked to be her date this time. She'd had a great time with him the last time, but her escapade on the roof with Dash hadn't exactly been fair to him. And she couldn't promise that the same thing wouldn't happen again. "Come to pregame with a bunch of underage students?"

Ridley and Dash both laughed, though she didn't miss the discomfort in Dash's laugh. *Probably for the best*, she mused. It *was* his job to keep them safe.

"Actually, I came here to let you know that I'm heading out on a run to Fiji," Ridley explained to her. "Just in case you had a crisis and wondered why you couldn't reach me."

The likelihood of that happening was high enough that she understood why he'd come, she had to admit. "A run? Like, picking up another recruit?"

"No, no," he said quickly. "We haven't had any new recruits since you— believe me, you'd know. Sometimes they send the security personnel to go pick up goods from Fiji. As you might have guessed, we have a bit of an under-the-radar world trade market going, and Fiji is our pickup point."

Quinn had never given it much thought, but it made sense. The clothes on her back, the alcohol they drank at parties, the ingredients in the food she ate, the movies she and Haley watched together —it all had to come from somewhere. There was probably a handful of people with the ability to conjure things up, but those types of abilities had their limitations. And while there were farmers and builders on the island, there was no way they supplied everything. Besides, what of Charlie's parents bringing their wealth from the real world back to the island? Wealth would mean nothing on the island unless there was some way to spend it.

Again, she wondered how their little island and its operations could be kept such a secret with so many gaping holes in its subtlety.

But she knew what response she would get from Ridley—the same one she had been getting from him and Dash for days. *There are things you don't know, and you're not ready to know.* So she let it go, wishing him safe travels, and he took his leave. Dash, to her surprise, did not.

"What about you?" she asked him. "You going to Fiji too?"

"No. But I won't be coming to the party, either. I came here to remind you all to be careful and to be safe tonight."

Booing erupted from all around them, but Quinn didn't listen to them, nor did she echo them. The look she had exchanged with him minutes ago had emboldened her, and suddenly she felt confident—powerful. Powerful enough to know that she could change his mind. Whether he knew it or not, he was going to the party.

"Really," she said, taking a step toward him. She reached out to touch his shirt—a crisp, black button-down that was more stylish than his normal ensemble. She latched two of her fingers between two of the buttons, locking eyes with him. "Nice shirt for a night in."

She kept hold of his shirt, staying tauntingly close to him. Neither of them blinked. Was she making the temperature in the room twice as hot, or was it her own skin?

"Laundry day," he said, though his tone was anything but dismissive. Whether he admitted it or not, she could see in his eyes that her strategy was working. "I've got work to catch up on. Evening run to go on. You know—the exciting things."

A grin played at the corners of her lips. He was toying with her. Daring her to beg him. Well, two could play at that game.

"I could think of a few more exciting things… But I understand." She released his shirt, bringing a finger up to her lips, tapping them and watching his eyes as she did so. He was staring right at her lips. She reached to twist her hair up on top of her head. She could feel his eyes on her neck now, her shoulders, her body. It would have been offensive if she hadn't led him to it so deliberately. She coyly turned her back to him, face still turned towards him. "Zip me up before you go?"

He took a step closer to her, resting one hand on the zipper. He hesitated for a split second. She held her breath, waiting.

He leaned down, ever so slightly, until his lips were at her ear.

He zipped the zipper so fast, he nearly broke it.

"I'll see you there," he whispered into her ear.

And he was gone.

She exhaled, realizing as she glanced around that everyone else had fallen to a dead silence and was staring at her with wide, intrigued eyes.

She blushed from ear to ear, running back into her room to finish getting ready.

. . .

Everyone continued to chat, dance, and goof around while getting ready for another hour or so. Quinn tried to focus on her friends, but she found it difficult to think about anything other than Dash's hands on her zipper. Slowly the crowd in the hallway filtered out until it was just her, Trent, Pence, Haley, and Charlie. Finally, Charlie pointed out that if they didn't leave soon, Drax would spend the rest of the night yelling at them.

They fell into step together, and Quinn tried to focus on the company at hand. Pence and Charlie looked great together—undoubtedly, they would be the handsomest couple in the room. Trent, as usual, looked dashing, and had the smug grin to match it.

"You two look incredible," he informed her and Haley. "Do you think they put the two prettiest girls on the island in a room together on purpose?"

Quinn rolled her eyes. Haley giggled. Quinn made a mental note to have a serious talk with Trent at some point. She knew exactly what he wanted, but Haley probably didn't. And even if she didn't do the best job of it, Quinn wanted to look out for Haley whenever possible.

It was already dark outside when they exited the dorms, moon shining steadily. *Perfect night to spend on a roof,* thought Quinn.

The penthouse was packed when they arrived—much more so than at Quinn's own party. It wasn't just members of the YA and their age group that were there. There were people Quinn didn't even recognize. Many of them were monsters, just like Drax.

A circle of people stood in the center of the penthouse, all of whom turned to cheer when they saw the fivesome enter. Included in the circle were Drax, Angel, Izzo, and Tommy. Trent, Pence, Haley, and Charlie headed straight for the circle, but Quinn hung back, scanning the room.

She didn't see Dash yet, which was no surprise. She assumed he'd made some subtle entrance in a shadowy corner of the room if he entered the real party at all. She might not even see him until she decided to go to the roof.

But she wasn't going to go up there just yet. She had to at least make some effort to socialize, if only for Drax.

Her eyes stopped scanning when they reached the unlikeliest target: Shade. She had to blink to make sure he was real; this was the last place she would have expected to see him.

But it was him, and he was alone—hunched over the bar at the far end of the room, looking down into an untouched, lime green drink.

She headed over to him, deciding that if nothing else, she would have to rescue him from that drink.

She walked slowly, not wanting to alarm him, and left one stool between them as she took her seat at the bar. He noticed her the moment she sat, she could tell. But he looked back down at his drink immediately.

"Hey, Quinn," the bartender said good-naturedly when he saw her. He reached under the bar and pulled out a pack of Parliaments, sliding them across the bar. "I stocked up on these for you after last time."

She beamed, accepting them gratefully. "Thanks, Hank. But I gotta ask you, man. Did you concoct this poisonous-looking substance my friend Shade has over here?"

Shade looked up, eyes wide and embarrassed. It was the first time Quinn had seen any sort of vulnerable emotion in him.

Hank, too, looked embarrassed. "My little sister came up with the drink menu," he explained. "Monster-themed drinks. She's a big fan of Drax."

Quinn followed his gaze over to a teenage girl, probably fifteen or so, who had made her way to the YA circle and was chatting with Drax. The girl looked almost normal from where Quinn was sitting, save for her long, striped tail.

"Might wanna warn her," Quinn said, turning back to Hank with a small grin. "I hear the guy plays for the other team."

He laughed. "She knows. She just looks up to him. It's rare for someone like us to have so many friends, to have a job outside of security. He's sort of a role model to her."

Quinn nodded. She loved hearing that Drax was a role model with this crowd; he was a much better one than she was. "So, what's the drink?" she asked, turning to face Shade, who was back to pretending not to notice her.

"It's called a Frankenstein," Hank said when he saw that Shade wasn't going to answer her. "I guess I should make him something else."

"I'll take the same whiskey I got last time. And let's try a nice mint mojito for my friend here."

Hank nodded and got to work on the drinks. Quinn stripped the wrapping off her pack of cigarettes, giving Shade the chance to start the conversation. To her surprise, he finally did.

"Why did you say that?" he asked her, pushing the green drink away from him. "Why did you call me your friend?"

His question made her sad. A lot of things about Shade made her sad. "Why not? We're both in the YA together. We stopped torturing each other in power tech and went for a milder approach, before Dash changed up the groups. Doesn't that mean we kind of like each other?"

He didn't look directly into her eyes; he looked somewhere down and to the left of them. His voice was shaky, but his words were direct. "I don't like any of you. Especially you. You put me in—"

"Immeasurable pain, I know, I know. Look, Shade, I'm sorry about that. At the time, I thought you were reading my mind—you know—forcing me to watch my best friend die. I mean, you *were* forcing me to watch my best friend die, you just didn't know it."

Hank slid their drinks to them wordlessly, sensing the tone shift in conversation. She gave him a visual thank-you before turning back to Shade.

"Why don't you like us?" she asked him, sensing that she wasn't going to get a response to her previous statement. She sipped her drink, waiting for him to drink his. He did not.

"You're bad people," he told her, looking down at the new drink. He stirred the straw, pushing the mint leaves around. "Monsters."

She stared at him, floored. What was *that* supposed to mean? Not everyone in the YA was visibly affected, which meant Shade considered all deviants to be monsters. "Wouldn't that mean you're a monster, too?"

He stood suddenly, expression darker than ever. He glared at her, finally looking into her eyes.

"Yes. I am a monster."

And he started to leave.

"Shade," she said, jumping out of her own chair. For the first time in several minutes, she became aware of the room around her. Dash was there, she realized, in the center of the room with the YA, watching her. Everyone was watching her. But none of that mattered in that moment.

There was something wrong with Shade, and she had no idea what to do about it.

She caught up to him, blocking his path and grabbing him by the arm, realizing the moment she saw his reaction that it was a bad idea. He wasn't good with touching. She released him, but stood firmly in his way.

It wasn't easy mustering up the courage to say what she wanted to say to him. Not when she was about to contradict everything she had tried so hard convincing everyone else she believed. But she had to.

"You're not a monster. Neither am I. Neither is Drax. Okay? We're different than them, so fear us. They call us these names because they don't understand. And we go along with them because we're too tired not to. But *we are not monsters*. We're people."

He hesitated, frozen still, and for a split second, she thought she may have actually gotten to him.

But then he left.

She stared after him for several seconds, unsure what to think. What had happened to Shade that made him think so little of himself and those like him? She was often the first to call herself a monster to outsiders, but it was different for her. She used the phrase with a sense of twisted pride—almost bragging. That wasn't the case with Shade. He used it with utter self-loathing.

It explained so much about him, and yet it opened the door to so many new questions. She felt sadder than ever for him.

"Hey," said a gentle voice from behind her. She didn't have to turn to know who it was. The way that one simple word instantly calmed her nerves, it could only be one person.

Of course, directly after her nerves were calmed by his voice, she turned around, saw his face, and lost her nerves all over again.

At least this discomfort, she was used to.

"You okay?" Dash asked her. "That looked... intense."

She nodded, finishing off her whiskey in one large gulp. "It was a lot easier hating Shade when I thought he was an asshole. Now I just..." She shook her head. She didn't even know what she thought any more.

"I know. Savannah says he's damaged beyond repair. We don't know what happened to him before he came here, but it was bad. And beyond that, his emotional issues... He needs more help than we can give him here, unfortunately."

She nodded, deep in thought. They had done horrible things to her out there in the real world—unforgivable things. But she wasn't the only one. She was starting to realize that maybe she hadn't gotten the worst of it.

"You look like you need another drink," he decided, clearly trying to lighten the mood. "I'll grab it. Why don't you go say hi to the group? They said they were waiting for you... Some sort of game?"

She groaned, having forgotten all about the game she had helped invent. He laughed, giving her a playful shove in their direction as he made his way to the bar to get their round of drinks. She trudged over to the rest of the group, mind spinning between thoughts of Shade and Dash.

"Well, look who it is," Drax said in amusement when she finally made it to the YA circle. "Thought maybe you'd replaced me with Shade there for a second."

Everyone harder than they should have at that, as if the idea of Quinn and Shade being friends was somehow unthinkable. Quinn tried to fake a laugh, as much as it hurt. She knew she shouldn't resent them for making fun of Shade; they didn't understand.

"Now that you've finally graced us with your presence," Angel said to Quinn, a twinge of amusement rather than the usual hostility to her tone, "we can get started. Drax, in honor of you, we have come up with a game that we think you'll enjoy. It's called strip story."

Drax raised his eyebrows, grinning. "I'm intrigued."

Angel began to rattle off the rules, but it wasn't long before Dash returned with their drinks, slipping directly next to her, rendering her unable to think about anything except the intense heat radiating between them. She drank her fresh whiskey a little faster than usual, hoping the fiery sensation from the drink would at least give her an excuse for the feeling.

"...and anyway, it was Quinn who came up with it," Angel was saying, "so I say she asks the first question. And picks the first victim."

Quinn grimaced. She didn't hate the idea of asking the first question, but it would inevitably flip on her, and the last thing she wanted was to tell these people a story of their choosing. Still, they had been waiting on her to start the game; she couldn't just leave without even attempting to participate.

She scanned the faces around her, considering her options. She had recently learned more about Tommy, Izzo, and Angel. She knew Pence and Charlie's stories fairly well, and though she still didn't know the specifics of Haley's history, she would never ask her closest friend such a personal question at a party. That left Trent. She had always considered him an open book, but what did she really know about him?

Besides, if anyone was going to ask her a throwaway return question that was easy for her to answer, or at least to lie about, it was him.

"Trent," she said, taking a sip of her drink. "You walk around like the world's your oyster. Like you've got it all dialed in and you're just here for the ride. Is that how it's always been for you?"

He held her gaze. His expression was hard to read. Hurt, slightly. Flattered, at the same time. She could see from the flashing behind those handsome eyes of his that it wasn't as simple as she had expected. She knew that if she had asked him in a different place, in a different context, she probably would have gotten a more honest answer. But she had a feeling she'd still get a bit of the truth.

"I was the coolest kid around," he said. "For years. After the event. Middle school. Even the beginning of high school. My ability was easy to hide, you know? Everyone just thought I worked out a lot. But I took it too far. Bragged too much. My parents tried to help me, told people they were crazy, I couldn't possibly be a deviant. I was everyone's best friend. But it didn't matter. A freak's a freak. They caught me and that was that."

"And then you came here, and you were the cool kid again."

Trent crossed his arms. Watched her closely. "Am I, though?"

She saw his point. If 'cool kids' existed here, they probably weren't Trent types. Her constant rejection of him probably didn't help, either. Was it possible that Trent's whole confidence act was just that—an act?

"Trent," Angel said, shaking Quinn from her line of thought. "Your turn. You can challenge Quinn back, or you can challenge someone else."

"I'll tell you what," Trent said, eyeing Quinn sharply. "I'll challenge you with the simplest question: If I were to ask you something as personal as what you just asked me, would you really tell me the truth?"

She could so easily lie, just as he was suggesting she would. But why bother? He had called her bluff, and left such an easy note for her to take her leave on.

"No. I would lie."

Everyone stared at her wordlessly.

"To most of you," she muttered, so quietly that she was pretty sure Dash was the only one who heard it. *Good,* she thought; he was the one it had been intended for. Their eyes met briefly, and suddenly she had no desire to be in that circle of people any more. She just wanted to be with him.

"Drax," she said, stepping forward to hug her friend. "Congratulations again. I think this is where I take my leave for now. You know, given that now everyone knows I'd cheat at the game anyway." She winked at him, and luckily, he only smiled back at her. She might be a terrible person, she reckoned, but at least those who were getting to know her weren't surprised by it any more.

Before anyone could boo her, and before Dash had too much time to think about what she had whispered, she headed for the roof.

It was bold, she knew. It was still early in the party, and in the brief time she *had* been at the party, she had probably pissed everyone off. But in that moment, all she cared about was him. It was rare for him to be in the state of mind that she wanted him to be in, but when he was, it electrified her.

Once she got to the roof, she pulled the pack of cigarettes out, contemplating it. It had been thoughtful of Hank to stock up like that. But did she really want one? If she knew she'd be alone up here—if it was about taking a break from people—sure. But she felt confident that Dash would join her. And if he was with her, she wasn't sure she needed the nicotine. He brought something different to the table.

She set the pack of cigarettes down on the edge of the railing, deciding to let the evening pan out a little more before partaking.

"Something wrong?" he asked as he climbed up. She turned to him, wondering what he meant, and grinned when she saw the two fresh whiskies in his hands.

"I'm referring to the pack of cigarettes you just put down," he explained, coming over to her and handing her the drink. She gulped down the remainder of her first drink before accepting it.

"Oh, that," she said, locking eyes with him. "I don't think I'll need them. I have a different sort of craving tonight."

Her words had exactly the effect she had wanted on him; she could tell the moment they escaped her lips.

"So, strip story," he said, flustered. "That was your invention?"

"People on this island have a lot of secrets. Thought maybe they just needed the right incentive to share."

"Even though you won't share with them."

"With *them*," she emphasized. "I think we both know I can't seem to avoid being honest with you."

He watched her. Satisfaction and intrigue sparked in his eyes. And that same vulnerability that she knew sparked in her own eyes whenever he was around. "So, you're not opposed to playing with me," he inferred carefully.

"I'm game if you are."

"Okay. Me first, then. A question for you."

She waited, breath held. She had known this was what she had signed up for—she had learned by now that the only way to drive their connection forward was with honesty and vulnerability—and yet, she still loathed it.

"You said you never fell in love," he told her. "I found that hard to believe. At the very least, someone must have fallen in love with you."

She considered this. Besides Kurt, who had loved her so much it got him killed, only a few others had truly fallen for her. It was easy to hook them, to manipulate them, but she drove most of them crazy with rage before they had the chance to really love her. But did she want to share this story with him? Was it worth folding so early?

She decided to give this one to him.

"There was a boy or two. I guess you could say they fell in love with me. Couldn't tell you why. I never really gave anyone any reason to."

It clearly wasn't enough for him. "Why not?"

She sighed. "Look, you never knew your dad. I knew mine. And he was there, crushing my chances of ever loving or trusting a man, long before any other man was. By the time the boys started coming around, that hope was long gone. Besides, I was on the run before I ever started dating. If I was with someone, chances were, I was using them. For a safe place to sleep, for protection, for whatever."

"And the boys? Were any of them using you?"

"Just about all of them, I'd imagine. But none of the boys I was with were ever really the problem. It was mainly the guys I *wasn't* with, if you know what I mean."

She could tell from his expression that he didn't fully understand the implications of her words. But he also seemed to understand that that she wanted to say nothing more on the matter. She didn't care to relive her experiences as a young, mostly powerless teenage girl, being beaten, shot at, and even violated by the men who hunted her. Besides, in her way, she didn't regret any of it happening. It had made her as strong as she was now.

"Okay," he said, easing up on the pressure. "Your turn."

She considered her first question carefully. Despite how personal her answer had gotten, his first question had been mostly harmless. She knew she needed to ease into her questions, not start with the ones she really wanted to know. She started with an easier one that paralleled his own question—one she was still curious about.

"You told me about the love of your life—the one I sort of remind you of but sort of also don't remind you of at all." She ignored his eye roll at this. "But you also said that was many years ago. Has there been no one since then? All these years on the island?"

He had seemed nervous when she first brought up his old girlfriend, but relaxed once he realized the simplicity of the question. He answered easily. "No, I can honestly say there hasn't been anyone."

She watched him, waiting for more, but she could see that there was no more. An *until now* would have been nice, she mused, but she knew they were both still being careful. A part of her, guilty as she felt for thinking it, was glad to hear he hadn't ever been in love with Angel. She wondered if he would accept a small follow-up question.

"It's just," she said, "the way Angel acts around me—the way she brings you up—it almost seems like there's some sort of history there."

His eyes seemed to grow sad at the mention of Angel. "Angel was truly a shell of a girl when she came here. Torn from her family. She was so young—eleven, maybe, and I was only seventeen and still crushed by what had happened with Charlotte. I wasn't teaching yet, but she made me want to. She came to me for advice, for help, for everything. Maybe I helped her too much, I couldn't really say. I know that she grew to feel differently towards me than I ever felt towards her. I think of her as a little sister. Someone I will always want to protect, but not love. Not like…" He trailed off.

Quinn didn't mind him stopping himself. They both had miles to go before they could truly say everything they felt—if that time ever came at all. She also understood what he was saying about Angel. It almost sounded like her relationship with Rory.

He chuckled slightly as he took another sip of his drink. "That should count as two questions. My turn. I've put together some of the pieces of what brought you to Siloh, but it still doesn't totally make sense to me. The stories say you went into Crowley Enterprises to steal money. You can't have known Crowley was the director of the DCA—it wasn't public knowledge; hadn't been since the last director got murdered by a deviant. It had to have been some kind of setup. But you don't strike me as an easy victim of a setup. There was a reason they didn't catch you sooner."

She stared at him for a few seconds, contemplating her answer. She couldn't tell him the story. Not that one. Not about Kurt. What could she do? She could either make up a story—which, she reminded herself, he would inevitably sense—or she could remove an article of clothing.

Without a word, she reached for the clip of her bra, snapped it off with one hand, and flipped it out of her dress with ease. She let the bra drop to the ground, grinning at his wide-eyed boyishness. But he regained composure quickly enough, joking, "I was almost disappointed you didn't answer. Until you did that."

She smirked. "Happy to help. Now, my turn. Where were you the night of the event?"

His expression became more serious, eyes searching hers. She knew why. He wanted to know why she was asking this question—whether she still believed he had been there with her.

"We had just left dinner," he told her. "Me, Reese, Savannah, Charlotte, and Ridley."

"Ridley? You knew him in the real world?"

"He was a close friend of Reese's back then. He lived in our neighborhood, a few doors down from us."

She couldn't recall ever seeing Reese and Ridley interact; it surprised her that they had been close friends.

"Anyway," he said, "I'm sorry to say, there isn't that much more to the story than that. Savannah had been meeting with a client and his family—she was a lawyer, back then. I don't even remember how the dinner went. I was really only paying attention to Charlotte. Don't even know what happened to the client and his family."

"And that's it? You stayed together and waited it out?"

He nodded, eyes sad. "16th and Mulberry was the intersection. Nowhere near a bank. I've thought it over many times since meeting you. Trying to imagine some scenario where your memory could be real. I just… can't think of one. I mean, hell, Quinn. I'd remember you."

She knew he meant to be flattering. She knew he was trying to be kind. But his words stung her. It was one of the most vivid memories she had, and it wasn't real.

"I'd like to know, though," he said. "Maybe that could be my next question…

I'd like to know how that night happened for you. What you thought I did for you."

It wasn't an easy memory, but given that it was basically a memory of him, she supposed she could share it. "I had just left my dad's. My mom had just died, and she left me with his address... I hadn't seen him in years. I went to him, tried to explain that I had nowhere else to go... He slammed the door in my face."

She kept her eyes cast downward. She knew the pitying expression he was undoubtedly watching her with all too well.

"I left his apartment and started walking, and I just kept walking, trying to find somewhere that didn't scare me. I made it to the front of this Bank of America building and just sort of camped out there. I remember thinking it was pretty, the way the lights were, and that the people in that area seemed nice, friendly. Like they wouldn't hurt me. So... I stayed there. I stayed there through the alarms, and the warnings, all of it. And in the thick of it, when I was being trampled by all of these panicked people, when I could barely see or even think straight any more... You came. You didn't say much. You looked exactly like you do now. You told me that I could trust you, and that you wouldn't leave me. And you stayed with me until I drifted out of consciousness."

She could see in his eyes that he was both mesmerized and completely lost. "It just doesn't make sense. I wouldn't have looked the way I do now. Even if I hadn't aged, I wouldn't have these eyes, wouldn't be—"

"—a pretty monster," she finished for him. "I know. Now that I know you, it doesn't make any sense. Must have just been some kind of strange dream. Some coping mechanism for what really happened."

He nodded. Eyes sad. Utterly silent.

She knew, from the honesty of that last answer, that she deserved a big question. She decided to ask the question she had wanted to ask to begin with.

"What happened to Charlotte?"

He ran a hand through his hair. He didn't look entirely surprised that this was her next question. In fact, he seemed emotionally ready to answer. "I'll tell you. But you might want to brace yourself, because if I'm not mistaken, I think we have a common enemy."

She waited, intrigued. Could he mean Crowley?

"After the event, Savannah was in denial for a long time. She wasn't affected, as I'm sure you know. And she refused to accept that we were. By the time she finally realized there was no escaping it, things were getting bad. I'm sure you remember… the widespread panic, the fear of deviants, the resistance fighting back. It scared her. I think more than anything it scared her that we might join the resistance. So she decided to do something about it. She met up with this man— one of her clients at the time. Told him that she had two boys she needed to shield from the world before it was too late. He told her he'd take care of us, he had a place to put us, a place to put everyone like us. And she trusted him. His name was Cole Crowley."

Quinn's spine went rigid. Savannah and Cole Crowley, allies? It had always been a fear of hers, yet like everything else about the island, it had never quite added up. Nothing Savannah did ever seemed to add up.

"Everyone trusted him," Dash continued. "Her. Reese. Ridley. Even me, to some extent. But not Charlotte. She knew what it meant for them to ship us off like that. It didn't matter to her that he promised Savannah she could be the leader of this new place, that she could run it however she liked. Charlotte knew."

Quinn watched him silently. It was hard for him to tell this story; she could see it in his eyes. She could see the love for Charlotte still lingering there. She didn't think she could blame him. Charlotte sounded like a strong, instinctively smart woman.

"Charlotte stayed, and we went. I would have stayed, if I could have. But I didn't have much of a say in the matter. We kept in touch. As the island became what it is to the outside world—as what we thought of as 'recruits' turned into what they thought of as 'prisoners'—she continued to write to me. Scared and desperate. Eventually she joined the resistance. Before long, she was its leader."

Its leader… The one deviant who had been more famous than the Siren.

"Blackout?" she whispered. "Charlotte… was Blackout?"

Dash nodded sadly. "It was strange. She was as powerful as you and me, but turning the world black, making her enemies blind, the way they described her… I don't remember her having those abilities. I only knew it was her from the letters she sent me. She loved the nickname. Never explained it to me, but loved it. She wore it like a badge of honor. Fearless."

Quinn swallowed. *Fearless...* the quality he had seen in both her and Charlotte. Blackout had always been Quinn's heroine, growing up. It was starting to make sense to her, why Dash had resented her so much upon meeting her. After all, that fearlessness had led to Blackout's infamous death—and the destruction of the entire resistance.

"Crowley wasn't the director of the DCA at the time," Dash continued. "But he wanted to be. And the previous director had been killed by a deviant in the resistance only days earlier. So, whatever political connections Crowley used to turn his island into a deviant prison, he used them again. Made some sort of deal. If he could kill Blackout and her associates..."

"...He'd become the new director."

He nodded silently.

"The way she died," Quinn said carefully. "They said she was in Canada when they found her—that she took down an entire US embassy before they got her. Killed hundreds of international diplomats. Triggered the formation of the UNCODA."

His eyes were dark. "Believe me, I remember."

"Well... Was it true?"

"What do you mean, was it true?"

"I mean, this is Cole Crowley we're talking about. He's insane, Dash. Beyond evil. I wouldn't put it past him to kill every last one of those people and frame her for it. Think about it. Cole Crowley, international savior."

She could tell from his expression that this thought had never even occurred to him. "I never wanted to believe it," he admitted. "That she would kill all those innocent people. I just... I thought the world had changed her."

"The world changed me," Quinn said softly. "But I never killed anyone."

A tear slid down his cheek. He didn't touch it or acknowledge it. Just seeing it, she felt a tear slide down her own. She wiped it quickly, annoyed with herself for shedding it at all.

Crowley really was their common enemy, she realized. If there was any man in the world who hated Crowley as much as she did, it had to be Dash.

She had more questions. So many more. Were Savannah and Crowley still allies? Was Crowley really okay with them all living in the conditions they were living in, or was it part of some kind of larger plan? What did Reese and Dash know of his plan?

But she already knew the answer she would receive—the same one he and Ridley had been giving her for weeks: *You'll know in good time.* She hated it, but she wasn't going to let it get to her in that moment. She was still getting personal answers out of him—answers to questions she had wondered since she met him. And for the first time in her life, she was enjoying giving someone else answers about herself.

She didn't wait for a question this time. She answered the one he had asked already.

"One of those poor boys who fell in love with me, despite me giving him absolutely no reason to do so… His name was Kurt. He was younger than me, and very innocent. Very kind. His father owned this simple little ice cream shop on the edge of the town we were living in at the time. I loved both of them like family. I stayed with them for longer than I stayed with anyone else when I was on the run. I probably would have stayed with them forever."

Dash watched her. She could see the realization in his eyes that he was finally going to get his answer.

"Cole Crowley," she continued, "offered to buy Kurt's father's ice cream shop—to keep him on but take over ownership. At the time, none of us knew who he was. We thought he was just some random, rich entrepreneur. Sure, we probably should have connected the dots—rich entrepreneur named Crowley, mega-corporation called Crowley Enterprises. But why would a billionaire want to buy an ice cream shop? The thought never even crossed our minds.

"Anyway, Crowley took Kurt's father out to a nice restaurant, flashed a bunch of papers in his face, got him drunk, and asked him to sign the papers. Told him he'd be receiving fifty thousand dollars, and would get to stay on as manager. Just fifty thousand. Nothing, to a man like Crowley. Everything, to a family like Kurt's. In the end, they never received a penny. The contract was faulty. Crowley turned the shop into a convenience store and kicked him out of it. There was nothing he could do about it."

Dash shook his head, confused. "I don't understand. Why would Crowley even bother? There's no way he became a billionaire conning small business owners out of their ice cream shops."

"Of course not. Once Kurt and I figured out who he was, we wondered the same thing. But more than anything, we just wanted that money back, so we devised a plan. It wouldn't be the first time we had committed a crime together. We had been keeping our little family afloat for months. It would be our highest-profile robbery, but I wasn't worried. I should have known, I guess. Should have trusted my gut—put the pieces together. But I didn't."

"Known what?" he asked, though she could tell from his voice that he already knew the answer.

"The real reason—the trap. The contract. The lies. Luring us there. He knew how much I loved that family—that I'd come and try to steal it back. And he was right. That was exactly what I did.

"He had a man with him—a man who had the ability to stop my compulsion from working. He called him Shield. When I saw that my compulsion wouldn't work, I was worried. But I had no idea how worried I should be. Not until they all turned their guns on Kurt."

"They killed him," he said softly. "Didn't they?"

"Oh, they killed him. But it was the *way* they killed him that keeps me up at night. We made a deal. My imprisonment for his life. I came willingly. Let them sedate me. Let them cuff me. And he was *still alive*." She shook her head, sickened by the memory. Feeling her own tears starting to fall. "It wasn't until I was seconds from blacking out completely that they killed him anyway. For no reason but to hurt me."

He seemed to be at a complete loss for words. The two of them stood there, watching each other, the weight of each other's stories sinking in. Two people who, twenty minutes earlier, had still barely known each other. Now, they knew close to everything.

Finally, he spoke. "I think we both want to kill the same man."

The light playfulness she had felt earlier in the evening was all but gone, replaced with something new—something heavier—something stronger. She found herself looking up at him with a new, impassioned hunger—the closest thing to a true craving she had felt yet.

She could see it in his eyes, too.

"I suppose you could put that bra back on," he said in a voice that clearly indicated he wanted her to do nothing of the sort. "Now that you've answered my question."

She took a step toward him, eyes serious, words playful.

"That," she said, "would be counterproductive."

And she kissed him.

. . .

When the two of them had kissed underwater, it had been a sensation unlike anything she had ever experienced. At the time, she imagined it was *because* they were underwater, combined with the fact that they both had emotionally charged abilities of every variety. But now, kissing him for the second time, she realized that it had nothing to do with the water. It did have to do with their abilities, but not the way she had initially thought.

It was almost like how she had felt when Rory had electrocuted her—like someone else's abilities were feeding her own—charging her up. It wasn't the effect of her own abilities she was feeling, but the effect of his on her. It felt electric; it felt fiery; it felt icy... it felt *everything*.

They kissed hungrily, desperately—so desperately, she didn't catch on for several seconds that they had disappeared from the roof altogether and were somehow now on a bed.

When she finally did notice, she found it such a welcome confusion, she continued to kiss him for several seconds, rolling on top of him and pinning him to the bed, ripping his shirt off, loving every second of it. But as her fingertips sunk into the soft, silk sheets, and the feeling of nighttime breeze abandoned her, she finally forced herself to pull away from him long enough to wonder...

Where the hell *was* she?

It was a bedroom; that much was clear. It was a nice one. Large. It had big, beautiful windows that overlooked…

The island.

She looked down at him, lost. They had teleported? They had teleported to somewhere else on the island?

His expression wasn't nearly as confused as hers; if anything, he looked amused. He reached out to touch her hair, lying contentedly on his back as she looked around. "Welcome to my room."

Her eyes widened as she turned back down to look at him. "You did this? You took us here?"

"Mostly by accident. Though I guess it tells you where my mind was going."

Well, obviously; she would have been offended if his mind hadn't gone there. But last she had checked, there was a big difference between thinking about a bedroom and magically being transported to it.

"You can *teleport*?" she demanded. "How did I not know this?"

He laughed. "It wasn't one of the questions you asked me. And anyway, as you can see, I'm not very good at it. Kind of happens whether I want it to or not sometimes."

She could hardly believe it. She loved her abilities, but she would trade every single one of them in a heartbeat for the ability to teleport. It was the ultimate freedom. No one would ever be able to catch her.

"But, if you could take us anywhere in the world," she asked, "why *here*? We could go anywhere, Dash. Do anything."

The amusement drained from his eyes. Suddenly, he looked sad. When he asked his question, she realized why. "Where would you have us go?"

She realized with a heavy heart that he was right. No matter where they went, they would always run the risk of being seen by a regular. Sure, there were quiet places with beautiful scenery, but there would always be a chance. And the moment word spread in the real world that the Siren was back….

She would never truly have her freedom, she realized. No matter how fast she could run, no matter how quickly she could disappear, they would always be chasing her. At least here, she was able to remain still.

But if she had to stay here, she had to know the truth. She had to know what other secrets about the island he and Ridley were keeping from her. He had told her many secrets that night, but he hadn't shared any of those.

"What is it you're still not telling me?" she asked him softly. "What are these 'things I still don't understand?'"

She had known going into the question that she might not get an answer, but his reaction still hurt. He sat up, looking down at his shredded shirt that just moments ago he would have laughed at. Now he seemed uncomfortable being shirtless around her. "I want to tell you everything, Quinn. If I could tell you everything right this second, I would. But there are so many factors besides me. I promise you'll know eventually. It's just—"

She shook her head, standing up, backing away from him, pulling the straps of her dress back on and covering herself up. She didn't want to be there any more. She had never seen Dash switch from hot to cold in the same interaction, but she could see it happening now. It was the worst possible time, but also the best possible time; she had been so close to making a huge mistake.

"Forget it," she said, refusing to look him in the eye. "Forget all this."

"Quinn," he said, starting to stand up, too—but she caught a glimpse of his eyes, and that was enough to send her flying to the door. There was no more hunger in his eyes, no more craving. He just looked sorry. And if there was one thing she couldn't stand, it was people feeling sorry for her.

. . .

She had no idea where she was as she exited his room into a large, open hallway. She had a feeling the entire floor might be his. She ran to the elevator, where she punched the 'G' button so hard, she nearly broke it. She watched the floors tick down—3—2—1—and flew out of the elevator, barely stopping to see what the lobby of the building looked like. When she did, she realized it was the same building they had been on the roof of. The tower. Dash lived on the floor below the penthouse.

Of all the buildings for him to live in—Charlie's parents'? Not something

149

belonging to the government, to Savannah? Was it possible he kept his distance from his mother as much as he could? Where did Reese live, then?

She glanced behind her toward the elevator, mind flashing. She *should* go back to the party, she thought. She should actually spend time with her real friends, make Drax feel loved, maybe even give Trent a chance. How could she feel so incredibly differently toward Trent than toward Dash? Seeing the honest side of Trent that night had been fascinating for her. The more she got to know him, the more she realized how similar he was to her. The façade of confidence toward the outside world; the hardened exterior of lies and winks and grins covering an interior soft as a baby's skin. Why couldn't she just desire him the same way he desired her? It would be so easy. So simple.

But she didn't want to go back to the party. She didn't want to see anyone else that night. She didn't even want to see her own bedroom.

She made her way to the waterfall. Some twisted, sad little part of her hoped he would sense that she was there, meet her there, apologize. Tell her all of the secrets he refused to tell her. But he didn't.

She forced herself to fall asleep.

9. DOMINOES

She woke up with the sun, greeted by a minor headache and a grumbling stomach. She made her way to her dorm quickly, stopping only to open the door to the lobby. Of course, when she did so, she saw Drax.

She had expected him to be wearing a smirk, perhaps, or to demand to know where she had spent her evening. But he didn't. In fact, he was surprisingly cordial to her.

"Good morning, Quinn," he said politely.

"Uh," she managed, stumbling through the door and coming over to the desk. "Hi, Drax. Sorry for not making more of an appearance last night. I know, I'm a shitty friend."

"You're not a shitty friend. Nothing to apologize for."

She stared at him, genuinely confused. What was wrong with him? He didn't seem mad, exactly, but he certainly didn't seem like his usual self. Was it about her? Or was it about something different?

As if on cue, the door opened behind her, and Drax's eyes shot over to it. She glanced backwards, body going rigid when she saw who it was.

Dash.

He seemed as surprised to see her as she was to see him. For a split second, he stared at her, an urge evident in his eyes—whether an urge to grab her, to kiss her, or just to *tell* her something, she wasn't sure. But it was only for a second, and then it was gone, and his gaze turned to Drax. He wasn't there for her at all, she realized.

"Come on," he said to Drax. "We're late."

Without a word, Drax gathered his things from behind the desk, nodded goodbye to Quinn, and followed Dash out of the door.

Quinn stood there, utterly perplexed.

. . .

She made her way up to her room after that. Haley was still asleep, so Quinn tiptoed to the shower as quietly as she could. By the time she got out of the shower, Haley was up and at her with dozens of questions. Quinn deflected all of them. If the night had gone differently, she might have been more willing to talk about it. But it hadn't, so she wasn't.

She met up with Rory again around lunchtime. They found a spot much deeper in the forest to practice, and Quinn taught her about having a strong force take up a small space. It was a lesson they spent several hours on, but Rory seemed healthier by the end of it.

Quinn spent the rest of her Sunday evening relaxing, watching more classic movies with Haley and Pence and deflecting questions from both of them about Dash. They didn't seem surprised; she had never been much of a sharer with any of them.

The next morning, they had English first. Quinn had almost finished the book Dash had given her. She loved it—and now she hated loving it. Her teacher, Simon, came over and talked to her for several minutes about the last few chapters she had read. She tried to engage with him the same way she had the last few times he'd asked her these kinds of questions, but she felt her answers changing. They were becoming resentful; angry. She could tell Simon was concerned, but he said nothing of it.

She had math next. Zerrick was one of her favorite teachers, but math remained one of her least favorite subjects. He constantly told her that she was learning at an impressive pace, but she never believed him. Not when the rest of the class stared at her the way they did as she thumbed through her elementary-level textbooks.

Zerrick came over to her that morning in good enough spirits, asking her to pull out her homework. She had it ready; she had done it before things had gone haywire that Saturday night. She pulled it out, trying to pretend everyone around her wasn't watching her as he began to go over it with her.

The only person in the classroom who *wasn't* watching her, she realized, was Drax. He hadn't even made it to English that morning. He had stumbled in late to math, and seemed completely distracted. What had he and Dash met about the day before? Had they met up again that morning? Since when had they even been friends?

"Quinn," Zerrick said, snapping her out of her trance. "Are you listening?"

"Sorry," she muttered, turning back to the homework she didn't care about. "Look, I understood the assignment. Okay? Can't you just give me another one?"

"I'm telling you, you didn't. You're doing the long division wrong. See here—you're supposed to multiply the number on top with—"

"*I get it*," she snapped, slamming her hand down on the table. If everyone hadn't been looking at her before, they certainly were now. "Who gives a shit how good I am at math, anyway? I'm stuck on this godforsaken island for the rest of my life, just like the rest of you, aren't I? When the hell am I going to need to do long division?"

Everyone else in the room had fallen completely silent. She didn't dare look at the other students; she had seen enough concerned expressions already. To her surprise, Zerrick didn't look concerned. He just looked angry.

"See me after class," he said, rising to his feet. He pulled a sheet of paper out of his binder, slapping it down on her desk. "This is tonight's homework."

• • •

She didn't see Zerrick after class. She shot out of the room before he had the chance to realize what she was doing. Next was power tech, and there was no way in hell she was going to that.

She contemplated her options as she left class. She could go back to her room, but odds were someone would come knocking, demanding to know why she wasn't in class. She could go to the waterfall, but she didn't want to be alone. Then again, who could she really spend time with? Ridley was in cahoots with Dash on the big secret, which crossed him off the list. Everyone in the YA was in power tech. Who did that leave?

She headed for Rory's room.

Rory's rubber-skinned roommate opened the door when she knocked. She was a cute girl with big, shiny eyes and a sad expression. She seemed to know the moment she saw Quinn that Quinn wasn't there for her. She headed back to her bed, leaving the door open for Quinn to step inside.

Rory stepped out of the bathroom a moment later, saving Quinn from a painfully awkward silence with the rubber girl. She gave Quinn a huge hug.

"I'm so happy to see you!" Rory squealed. "This weekend's practices made such a difference! Just ask Mallory. I haven't shocked her once!"

Quinn glanced over at Mallory, who gave a limp shrug.

"I'm glad to hear it, Rory," Quinn said, trying to feign enthusiasm. "Are you up for a little more practice?"

Rory's eyes widened—clearly, three times in three days was more than she had ever expected—but she nodded eagerly. "Of course! Lead the way."

Quinn led her back to the same place they had gone the day before, where no one had questioned them.

"So, first things first," she said to the girl. "You said your abilities have been cooperating better with all this practice, right?"

Rory frowned. "Well, yes—at least, my electric abilities have."

"You mean you have *other* abilities?"

Rory crossed her arms, not seeming sure how to form the right words. "I don't know… Nothing useful, that's for sure. I just keep getting these… flashes. Like everything's normal, and then suddenly I'm somewhere else, or with someone else. But just for a second. And then it's gone."

This was why Rory had looked so disheveled the last few days, Quinn realized. The overpowering strength of the girl's electric abilities probably hadn't helped, but this had to be the real root of the problem.

But how could Quinn help with what she didn't fully understand?

"When you see these things," Quinn asked, "do they seem like hallucinations? Like you're tired; sleep deprived? Or do they seem like something you're meant to be seeing—like a vision?"

"I can't say for sure, but I do sort of feel like I'm supposed to be seeing them."

The gravity of Rory's statement hit Quinn like a brick. Savannah had been looking for her seer in the wrong places.

"Rory," she said, voice suddenly dead-serious. "I need you to promise me something. Whatever you do, don't tell anyone else about these visions. Okay? Have you already?"

"No. I wanted to wait until I had someone I could trust—someone who was already working with me. I know Savannah's trying to find a seer."

Rory was even smarter than Quinn had thought.

"I don't really think that I *am* one," Rory added; "at least, not in the way she would want. But I know to keep it a secret."

Quinn nodded. "Good. Listen, Rory… as far as the visions go… I'm afraid there isn't much I can do to help you balance them. My best advice would be to do whatever you can to encourage the visions to last longer—to really see what it is they're trying to tell you. Maybe spend a little more time alone, where you won't be distracted, or maybe when you feel them coming on, excuse yourself and go to a private place?"

"There isn't ever much warning. But I'll try."

"Just be careful, okay? Above all else, be careful."

Quinn was pretty sure she wouldn't be able to live with herself if anything happened to Rory.

• • •

Quinn and Rory spent a good hour practicing Rory's electric abilities before calling it quits for the night. They made their way to the dining hall together, but Quinn took her food to go, sensing that the YA would be arriving from power tech any second. She made her way back to the dorms, deciding that if she could face anyone, it was Haley. But she didn't even make it through the front door, because Reese was there, waiting.

"Try to remember," he said when he saw her expression, "if it's good cop/bad cop we're playing, I'm the good one."

"Oh?" she asked him skeptically. "And which one is the bad cop—your brother or your mother?"

Reese chuckled. "I was referring to my brother, whose class you skipped. But I'm sure my mother would also have been the bad cop. Really, you should consider yourself lucky all around for getting me."

She didn't consider herself lucky. All she wanted was to be left alone by all three of them. But she supposed he really was her best option.

She thought back to the stories Dash had told her that night. Most of them hadn't had to do with Reese; they had been more incriminating toward Savannah. Then again, Reese had been the one to tell her stories about Dash and Savannah getting along, being partners, and so on—things that didn't remotely line up with Dash's stories. At the party, she had believed Dash. He had just seemed so genuine. But now she was back to wondering the same questions she had wondered for weeks.

"Why don't we go somewhere?" Reese suggested. "We could go on another flight, if you'd like. Or maybe go up to the top of the wall and talk."

She certainly didn't want to hang around there and wait for the entire YA to see her talking to the other brother; there were enough rumors spreading about her and Dash already. But she wasn't quite ready for another flight. That flight with Reese had been the closest thing to passion she had felt for him. And she'd had just about enough of Collins brothers' passion.

"We can go to the wall," she decided.

He nodded, reaching out his hands again, just as he had the last time. She accepted them, even more hesitant than she had been then, letting him hoist her into the air and up to the edge of the wall. There they took their seats, legs dangling just on the edge of freedom.

So much had happened since the last time Reese had taken her flying, she reminded herself. She had already changed her mind once after telling him she didn't want to leave. Why not now?

Then again, it was just as it had been during her and Dash's talk: where would she go? Freedom would never truly exist for her.

"I guess it wouldn't be good for you all," she said, glancing over at him. "Me leaving. The real world knowing people like us can escape from here."

"No, I suppose it wouldn't. Things might be forced to change around here if you did. Then again, sometimes I think things might be forced to change around here soon, anyway."

She raised her eyebrows, curious what he meant by that. Was it another vague comment followed by no explanation, as his brother always seemed to give? Or was he actually going somewhere with it?

"What do you mean?" she asked him carefully.

"I wish I knew, honestly. I don't know what Dash has been planning. I don't know whether he's got Savannah in on it or not. All I know is he seems to have others in on it with him."

His assessment of Dash's behavior mirrored her own. First Ridley, now Drax... It was almost like he was recruiting people to keep this little secret of his. Was it really possible Savannah was in on it, too?

"What could they be planning?" she asked him. "Some kind of uprising? Retaliation?"

"I guess, but against what? Against who? The way Dash runs his classes, the way my mother's known to be—it's almost like he's building a small army. Not to protect us, but to hurt them."

She assumed that by 'them' he meant everyone else. It was within the realm of possibility, she supposed. If Dash's story about Crowley had been true, he had every right to wish harm upon him, just as she did. But how did it line up with Savannah, who was supposedly Crowley's ally? Was she in on it? Double-crossing Crowley? Could she be double-crossing her own son? Or was Reese just wrong altogether?

"Look," Reese said. "It's no use, speculating on it. He won't tell either of us anything, and neither will she. If you ask me, I say we both just keep our heads high. If they do something stupid, we're here to make sure the rest of the island is protected from the aftermath. You with me?"

She thought of Rory, who reminded her so much of Kurt. She would do anything to protect Rory, just as she had sacrificed her freedom for Kurt. If Dash really was planning something that would endanger the rest of the island, she would do whatever it took to defend Rory and the rest of the innocents he left behind.

But *was* he? Or was Reese the one messing with her head?

"Bottom line," Reese said, "whatever Dash is doing, if Savannah's in on it and you turn against them—skip Dash's classes, meddle behind their backs—you're going to get in trouble. A different kind of trouble than you've known here. Savannah means business, Quinn."

"I'm not afraid of her."

"You should be."

Her mind flashed to Crowley. Him, she was scared of. If Savannah really had been in cahoots with him at any point, Quinn should be scared of her, too.

Scared, and angry.

"The two of you are enough to drive me insane," she groaned. "One of you is lying. One of you isn't. How am I supposed to know which is which?"

"Now *that* would be a nice ability, wouldn't it? Look, Quinn, I've kept nothing from you. You know that Dash is keeping something from you. And the lies? I mean, hell, even that book you've been carrying around is a lie. He tell you it's one of his favorites? That those are his writings in the margins?"

Her breath caught in her throat. That book meant so much to her. Those notes in the margins had been a huge part of what drew her to Dash. If they weren't really his—if that had really been a lie—

"Page 77," he said. *"For hope is the thing that saves us from ourselves.* I wrote that my second time reading it. Quinn, I never even gave that book to my brother. It disappeared from my bag a few months ago. He must have stolen it from me."

She remembered that scrawl. It had been one of the most personal notes in the margins she had read. She had almost asked Dash about it during their last meeting. What would he have said?

"Believe it or not, I love my brother," Reese said. "But he never wanted to come here. He never wanted to leave Charlotte, and he blames himself for what happened to her. He's been angry and resentful ever since. And Savannah's stopped at nothing to try to win his favor back. They're too far gone, Quinn. They can't be trusted."

"And you?" she asked, watching him closely.

"It may not be as exciting, but I'm an open book. I'm just like most of the others here. I was a normal guy, the event happened, and I became a monster."

"You mean a maker. You can fly."

"Splitting hairs like that doesn't change the facts, does it?" he asked sadly. "We're all monsters to them."

. . .

Quinn sat on Reese's information for several days, trying to decide what to make of it. If what he was saying was true, she had to be careful who she asked about it. The moment she started asking questions to the wrong person, she could get into trouble.

Then again... why should she care?

What did she have to lose at this point? Would Dash kill her? She dared him to try. Would his secret group, whoever they were, try to kill her? It was possible, but even if they did, what did she really have to live for these days? She was a prisoner, whether she was in chains or not. And sometimes she felt like she was getting farther and farther from any sort of answers.

She made up her mind to talk to Haley about it. Haley had been following her around with wide, concerned eyes all week, curious what had happened between her and Dash at the party and concerned by Quinn's more-negative-than-usual attitude. Quinn had initially shrugged her questions off entirely, not wanting to open up about Dash, Reese, or even Drax. But she decided it might be worth it. There were some puzzle pieces her friend might be able to help her put together, and she highly doubted that Haley of all people was in some kind of evil league with Dash.

"How long have you been on the island?" she asked Haley, deciding bluntness and honesty were her best options in finding direct answers.

"A long time. Eight years, I think. Almost as long as it's been around."

Quinn found that surprising. "You look so normal. How'd they catch you so quickly?"

"Like I mentioned, it was hard for me to control my abilities. Pence's parents tried to protect her, but mine weren't around to. They both died in the event. No one at the orphanage tried to protect me, even for an instant."

A wave of sadness washed over Quinn. Again, she was struck with the realization that she wasn't the only one that had a hard life before Siloh. It seemed that just about everyone had. They hadn't all been chased and hunted by the DCA for most of their lives, but they'd had their own demons—maybe worse demons than her own.

"Have you ever suspected more going on here?" she asked Haley. "Whether it's Dash training some sort of army, or Savannah's bizarre rules trying to control us a little too much?"

Haley glanced around as if debating whether it was safe to answer her there. Quinn found that odd. What was she worried about, their room being bugged?

"You have to be careful where you talk about these things," Haley said quietly. "But, yes, Quinn. I have wondered. Savannah has been known to approach certain people. Shortly before they join the YA—before they start attending power tech classes with Dash."

Approach them, how, she wondered? The way she had been approached about being a seer, or something else entirely? "Did she approach you?"

"She did. Not Charlie. Not Pence. I don't know about the others... When I brought it up to Charlie and Pence, they told me not to speak of it to anyone else. For my own sake."

Quinn couldn't help but feel both flattered and guilty that now Haley was trusting her with this information. At least someone was.

"What did she say to you?" Quinn asked her.

"She told me that as I became more powerful, people would start approaching me. People who wanted me to become a part of some sort of rebellion, or resistance. She said she didn't know who they were, but she knew that they were dangerous. She told me to come and tell her if they did. She said that one day, the conflict would come to the surface, and before it did, I should make sure I was on the right side of it."

Quinn could hardly believe her ears. Resistance? Like the movement Charlotte had led? Did that mean that Dash was a part of it? Or was he on his mother's side, protecting against people like…

People like who? Who was in this new resistance?

"What did Charlie and Pence say?" Quinn asked. "Exactly?"

"Not much. I wondered, too—whether they were a part of the resistance, or whether they worked for her. But, Quinn, they're good people. The more I got to know them, the more I knew I could trust them."

"But how could you trust someone you knew was keeping secrets from you? Did they ever say anything else to you about it?"

"They told me to never cross Savannah publicly and to never bring up the conversation to anyone again. Any time I tried to ask them more, they'd just say they couldn't say anything more. That there were things—"

"—you'd come to understand eventually," Quinn finished for her.

"It just doesn't matter to me like it does to you, Quinn. They're my friends. They have their secrets and I have mine. And that's okay with me."

In that moment, Quinn didn't care what was or wasn't okay with Haley. All she cared was that it wasn't just Ridley, Dash, and Drax that were in on the big secret. It was Charlie and Pence, too. And regardless of which side they were all on, it meant one thing: there was a new resistance.

There was probably a war coming.

• • •

Breakfast was always the hardest. She did a good job of dodging Dash at power tech, where she avoided him like the plague and continued to duel Haley in class. But ever since her last meeting with Reese, Dash seemed intent on sitting just close enough to her at breakfast that she could feel the intensity of his glares. As if nothing had changed since the day they had met.

Meanwhile, Charlie and Pence were still giving her the third degree on her evening with Dash, despite a week having passed since then.

"What is going on with the two of you?" Pence asked her. "First you disappear at the party together, then you ditch power tech, then rumors spread that you were out flying with Reese again, and Dash glares daggers at you every second you're in the same room together?"

"So what if I went flying with Reese? He's the head of law enforcement around here, isn't he?"

"It's not about the law, Quinn," Charlie said, eyeing her seriously. "It's about Dash and Reese. Spending time with Reese, hurting Dash like that—you don't know what kind of message that sends to everyone else here—or, frankly, what Reese is even capable of."

"Oh, really," she said, temper rising. It was becoming more and more apparent that whatever the big secret was, Charlie and Pence were in on it. If it *was* a resistance, shouldn't she be the first who should be asked to join? And if it wasn't— if Pence and Charlie and the rest of them were involved with Savannah's controlling, anti-rebellion fears—then she hated them for it. "Tell me, then, Charlie. What is he capable of?"

He glanced over at Pence, who slowly shook her head. He turned back to Quinn, eyes serious. "You don't need to know the details. You just need to know that you can't trust him—you don't know him like you think you do."

"I don't know *him*?" she demanded, slamming her hands on the table and unintentionally smashing the entire thing. Dishes shattered to the ground. She saw Dash stand, making a move to come over to them. She caught Haley out of the corner of her eye, warning him to stay back.

"Lately, I'm starting to think I think I know him better than I know the majority of you," Quinn snapped at Charlie. "Every goddamn person I've gotten close to since coming here is keeping something from me. Why is it that you're all so concerned who I talk to and who I don't, and yet none of you give a shit what I actually *know*?"

Out of the corner of her eye, she spotted someone rising from a table in the back, making his way to the door, watching her every step of the way. Almost like he had something to report. If she wasn't mistaken, it was Shade…

Who would Shade be reporting to?

"Quinn," Trent said, standing up and facing her. "Calm down. No one's keeping anything from you, okay? Charlie and Pence have been on this island a long time. They just have different experiences…"

But Quinn had had enough. Maybe Trent was telling a truth he thought he knew; maybe he wasn't. Regardless, everyone else seemed to be lying to her. And she'd had enough.

. . .

As the days passed, attending classes and pretending like everything was fine became harder and harder for Quinn. She was sick of embarrassing herself in class, sick of Haley and Trent being overly concerned for her, and sick of Drax avoiding her. More than anything, she was sick of having to be around Dash for an hour every day at power tech.

She felt herself checking out—not just out of class; not just out of power tech; out of everything. She spent her days in class staring out the window, thinking about Kurt, thinking about her mother, thinking about the few good memories she had to hang onto. She spent power tech letting Haley attack her without even bothering to attack back; of course, being Haley, this meant Haley's attacks also dwindled to virtually nothing.

"What is going on with you?" Haley finally asked her one day at power tech when Quinn took three thorn-related assaults in a row without so much lifting a finger in return. "You're barely checking in to classes. You're ignoring everything and everyone around you. Is this because of what I told you about Charlie and Pence? Because like I told you, whatever is going on, our friends are still trustworthy, Quinn—the YA, Dash—"

"Trustworthy?" Quinn nearly spat at her. "Haley, Dash isn't trustworthy. He's lying to me—has been for weeks now. Same with Ridley, and now Drax, Charlie and Pence. Who's next? You? Trent?"

Haley sighed. "Quinn, what Savannah told me… I'm sure it was just her own fear talking. Trying to keep us all in check. I'm sure Charlie and Pence were just looking out for me—trying to make sure I was safe. Even if there *was* more to it than that, it wouldn't mean they're out to get you or me. Who's putting these thoughts in your head? Is it Reese?"

Quinn knew she sounded crazy to someone who didn't already know, which gave her the sense that Haley really wasn't involved in whatever was going on. She appreciated that. But she also felt confident that she wasn't crazy. After all, they had all *admitted* it, to some extent. Maybe they couldn't say what they were involved in, but it was definitely something big.

The real question was, which side was everyone on?

"Look," she said to Haley. "I know not to trust Reese. I know not to trust Dash. I know not to trust anyone, just as I always have. So don't worry about me, okay, Haley? I'll be fine."

• • •

Dash wasn't wearing the same glare he had been wearing as of late when she came to power tech the next day. She was the last to arrive, and if she wasn't mistaken, she saw concern on his face, and possibly even relief when she arrived. Not that she cared. Any care she had for him was long gone.

He stood silently as the rest of the class chatted amongst themselves. Charlie and Pence tried to have a word with her—nothing serious; there was nothing serious they could actually *say* to her; they were just trying to lure some semblance of politeness out of her. *Good luck there*, she thought grimly, completely ignoring their comments and watching Dash with cold, expressionless eyes. Finally, Trent arrived. He approached Quinn, expression surprisingly supportive.

"You okay?" he asked her, offering her a small smile.

Quinn liked that smile. She liked his question, too, even if it meant Haley had been warning everyone in the YA that she was losing it. Trent's question felt like the only genuine thing she'd experienced in days—like he was the only one not lying to her.

"Am I ever?" she asked him jokingly, but he didn't get the chance to respond before Dash was speaking.

"Listen up, everyone." Quinn hated his voice. It was too perfect. "Here's today's assignments. Pence, Haley. Charlie, Tommy. Trent, Izzo—"

Quinn raised her hand, not really sure what she was doing, but deciding to wing it.

Dash ignored her, continuing with his list. "—Shade, Drax—"

Quinn cleared her throat, intentionally projecting it so loudly, not a person for two blocks would miss it.

Dash sighed, turning his gaze to her. "Yes, Quinn?"

"I'd like to work with Trent today. Please."

"That's nice, but that's not who I have you paired with. Last I checked, I'm the one who decides these things."

"I know you're used to calling all the shots around here. But that's not what *I* want. If you pair me with anyone else, I'll just send them into a nice, immeasurable pain again, so really, you'll be saving them all the headache. Literally."

He glared at her. "Then I'll just have to pair you with myself."

"You could. But given the romantic evening we had the other night that was abruptly cut short by the reminder of your never-ending lies and secrets, it might not exactly be appropriate."

The humming murmur that had been keeping the field abuzz instantly died. Everyone stared from her to him, utterly shocked. Trent, she noticed, was the only one who didn't seem completely bewildered. He responded with something between a laugh and a gasp.

She couldn't read Dash's expression, but she didn't really care. She was going to have the upper hand for once, no matter what the cost.

"For what it's worth," Trent offered cheerfully, "I'd *love* to work with Quinn."

"See?" Quinn asked Dash smugly. "Easy."

Dash held her gaze for another second. She couldn't quite decide if there was *nothing* in his gaze or *everything;* was it a combination of anger, sadness, love, and fear, or was it simply that he had stopped caring?

"Fine," he finally said. "You win."

Equal parts pleased and disgusted with herself, she took Trent's arm and pulled him off into the trees.

• • •

"I have to ask," Trent said when they reached their destination and turned to face each other. "Did you really choose me because you wanted to practice with me? Or was your real intent to make out in the woods?"

"How about this—you versus me. Only ability I'm allowed to use is my own super-strength. If you win, then we make out in the woods."

He watched her, utterly taken with her. It was a refreshing change, she decided. She'd had just about all she could take of both of the brothers. "And if you win?" he asked.

She glanced backwards, sensing that Dash, along with the rest of the class, was still watching her.

"We make out in the woods."

He smirked. "You're on."

And so they began.

Quinn didn't practice her super-strength often. Despite having accidentally broken a table earlier that day, she didn't normally find herself exceptionally strong. Sure, when she focused, she could lift objects as heavy as a car or truck without breaking a sweat. But generally, it was an ability that fell lower on her radar—behind compulsion, fire, and electricity.

She waited for him to make the first move, deciding to see what he had before unleashing her own abilities on him. She didn't doubt that he would go easy on her at first, but that would change quickly.

Sure enough, his first attack on her was simple. He grabbed her by the arms, forcing her back against a tree and pinning her to it. It was more sexy than painful, she mused. But, not quite ready to give in to the prize just yet, she shoved him right back, pushing him against a tree of his own.

"Not bad," he offered, grinning. "But I'm just getting warmed up."

He pushed her back off of him, this time grabbing her in a headlock, his face inches from hers, forcing her down toward the ground.

"This is fun," she whispered to him, breathing easily through the mediocre force of the headlock, "but I get this feeling you're too chickenshit to hit me."

And she twisted out of the headlock with ease, deciding it was time to throw the first punch.

He flinched at the punch but didn't stumble, watching her calculatedly. She could tell he was debating whether or not to hit her.

Naturally, she hit him again. Harder. And then again, until, finally, he *was* stumbling.

"Trust me," she told him, starting to enjoy herself, "this will be a whole lot more fun if you hit me back."

And he did. Lightly, at first. Barely enough for her to feel it. But then she caught his second punch, twisting his arm backwards and giving him a kick to match. That was when they noticed them—the eyes all around them, watching them. People were watching her kick his ass.

So, he fought back.

He could hit *hard,* she discovered as both of them began to increase their momentum. Hard and fast. Before long, they were both hitting so hard, they were getting knocked to the ground, breathing becoming choppy, blood collecting in their mouths and noses. The rest of the class had stopped everything they were doing at this point, all eyes on the two of them.

"This is about fifty percent for me," he told her after throwing a particularly nasty punch that sent her spinning and falling to her arms and knees, catching herself and jumping back up within seconds.

"Ten," she fired back. "Come on, Trent. At least get me to twenty."

His eyes lit up with the drive to meet her challenge, and before she knew it, he was on top of her, pinning her to the ground, hands on her arms.

She rolled on top of him easily, pinning him beneath her, but she could feel his energy rising and his strength growing. He pushed her off of him completely, sending her flying backwards onto her back and reclaiming his position on top of her.

She grinned up at him. "Now we're just acting horny."

"Fun as this is, if the same thing happens whether you win or I win…"

"Right," she said, flipping on top of him again, "but we have an audience, and it's very important for me to keep up appearances as the strongest one around."

He held her gaze, clearly loving every second of this interaction. "Fine. But if anyone asks, I just didn't want to hit a girl."

She laughed out loud. "Think you're too far gone there," she teased, but he was grabbing her and kissing her before she could say another word.

· · ·

It had felt good, kissing Trent, she decided as she left power tech. Dash had come and broken it up within a few minutes, the rest of the class just behind him, eyes wide, intrigued. Dash wasn't intrigued, of course. He simply shouted that class was dismissed and to get out of his sight. She wasn't sure she had ever seen him that angry, and it pleased her. At least, it should have.

It wasn't just about pissing off Dash. It was about kisses being simple again. With Dash, there was literally so much power behind their kisses, she had no choice but to lose herself. With Trent, they were what they were supposed to be: fun, but easy. She was able to stay in control.

Trent tried to follow her, but she dismissively told him she'd text him; she had things to do. She wanted to meet up with Rory again. Ever since learning that Rory might be a seer, her fear for the girl had tripled. If Savannah, or Dash, or any of them were to find out about it...

Quinn spotted Haley on the way back to the dorm, realizing Haley must have left class before her.

"Hey," Quinn shouted to Haley, catching up to her easily. "Haley. Hold up."

But Haley didn't stop, nor did she look Quinn in the eye. She kept her eyes cast downward, increasing her speed.

Quinn stared over at her, fearing the worst. "Not you, too."

Haley glared up at her for the first time. Quinn was shocked to see that there were tears in her eyes. "No, Quinn, I haven't joined your little made-up cult. I just can't believe you would do that to me."

"Do...?"

But Quinn trailed off when she realized what Haley was referring to: Trent. Quinn and Trent.

"Oh," Quinn managed, her voice becoming faint.

"Look," Haley said, coming to a stop and facing Quinn. "I know we never talked about it much. And I know you haven't really had a chance to figure out what friendship is. But, Quinn, that was a shitty thing to do. And not just to me. It wasn't fair to Trent, either."

Quinn knew Haley was right. She had used Trent to make Dash jealous, and in the process, she had hurt her closest friend—who, of course, was in love with Trent. What had she been thinking?

About yourself. Just as she always did.

"Haley," she said, shaking her head. "I'm sorry."

Haley nodded, eyes sad. "I know."

And she left.

• • •

Quinn's friendship with Haley had been one of the last things that mattered to her at Siloh; with that gone, her spirits sank lower than ever. Her relationship with Rory became just about the only thing that kept her going.

Rory's handle on her electric abilities got better and better by the day, though she still didn't quite seem to have a handle on her micro-visions. She explained to Quinn that though the advice had helped her focus, the visions were still only brief flashes, and didn't make any sense. Some of them, she explained, seemed to be from the past—distant memories she had almost forgotten.

Quinn wanted to give the girl better advice, to help her see things more clearly, but she wasn't sure how. For all of her influence over others' thoughts, she had never experienced anything more than a vague feeling about the future. Now and again, she thought she could sense which decision someone might make, or which action someone might take, but never anything like what Rory was experiencing— never a vision.

She told the girl to keep focusing, keep inviting the visions with an open mind, and most importantly, not tell a single other soul about it.

She and Rory were on their way back to the dorm when they passed Ridley. He wasn't after them this time; that much was clear. Still, when he saw them, his expression changed. He looked frustrated.

"Ridley," Quinn said, voice cold and distant.

"Quinn. Haven't seen much of you lately. Doing Dash's job again?"

"Dash refused to *do* his job when it came to Rory," Quinn snapped at him, hating the mere mention of Dash's name. She stood protectively in front of Rory, glaring at him. "And to be honest, I've had just about all I can take of the lot of you—Dash's little fan club."

"Dash's fan club?"

"Oh, don't act like you're not. Like you're not keeping secrets from me. Like you haven't been his cheerleader from day one. Thanks for the encouragement there, Ridley. You pushed me right into that mouse trap, didn't you?"

"Mouse trap? Quinn, I told you there were things you didn't know, not that we're all out to get you. Who's been poisoning your head with these ideas?"

"Well, let's see. Dash, for one, when he chose kicking me out of his bed over actually tell me the truth." She knew she shouldn't say so much in front of Rory, but she couldn't bring herself to care. "You and Drax, and now Pence and Charlie, for all taking his side and refusing to be honest with me, just like him. You know, you're all quick to point fingers at Reese and tell me he's turning me against you, but you've all been doing that all on your own."

Ridley shook his head, eyes thick with disappointment. "I'm sorry you feel that way," he told her. "I can see how you would be feeling alone right now, Quinn. But there is a lot more going on here than just you or Dash. If there wasn't, I'm sure it would be a very different story."

"Who cares about me and Dash? How about me and you? You were my first friend here, Ridley. And now I can't even get a straight answer from you."

He sighed. "This would all be so much easier if not for Reese."

"*What* would be?"

"Look, Quinn, there's only so much I can say, and I've said it. I'm sorry you're hurting. At this point the only advice I can give you is to make a choice who you trust, and to choose carefully. Everything else depends on it."

"I choose not to trust *anyone*, just as I always have."

He deflated, visibly defeated. "Then the next time you find yourself feeling isolated and alone, and you want to blame us, I suggest you remember those words."

She stared at him, speechless.

"You made your choice," he said, and walked away from them.

• • •

Quinn was surprised to learn that Rory remained on her side. If she had to choose between Dash and Reese, she told Quinn, she would choose Dash; then again, if she had had the kind of life Quinn had, she would probably know better than to choose anyone but herself.

"I swear," Quinn said to her as they parted ways, "sometimes I think your real ability is wisdom."

"Well, we know I've got more than one," Rory said, winking at her. "Could be."

And they took their leave of each other.

Quinn made her way back to the bedroom, but Haley was nowhere to be found. Quinn showered and changed for bed, hoping Haley would be there upon her return, but still she was gone. Quinn reached for her phone, wondering whether she should text Trent if only to avoid being alone, but decided against it. As Haley had said, the Trent situation wasn't fair to anyone.

She thought about what Ridley had said to her that night and well into the morning. *You made your choice.* She had chosen isolation. She had done it to herself.

The thing was, he wasn't wrong. The difference was, every other time in her life she had chosen isolation, it had been what she wanted. Now, it was driving her insane.

She was unable to focus on anything during math that next morning. Zerrick tried everything to get her to work with him, but it was useless. As much as she liked him, she hated school. She didn't belong. She didn't belong anywhere near there.

She tried to talk to Haley after class, but Haley avoided her like the plague, taking an intentionally longer route to their next class just to stay away from her.

Quinn tried not to overthink it, but she couldn't help it. Haley had been devastated by Quinn's behavior with Trent, but she had still been willing to talk that night. Avoidance wasn't her style. Avoidance meant something different.

Quinn decided to approach Trent.

She wasn't even sure why she did. It wasn't to flirt, and it wasn't to make anyone jealous. It wasn't to apologize, either. It was just that she felt so incredibly alone.

But to her dismay, he gave her the same treatment as Haley.

"I can't talk right now, Quinn," he said, avoiding her gaze and repelling away from her.

"Oh, come on. Trent, I'm sorry if yesterday meant something different to you than it did me. I was just having fun. I really—"

"It's not that," he said. He still avoided her gaze, but he seemed a little more willing to give her answers—almost like he felt bad for her. How was that possible? After she had wracked herself with guilt over him all day?

"I don't think we should hang out any more," Trent told her. "Things are changing here, Quinn. I need to grow up. I need to make some tough choices."

She could read between the same vague lines that had been drawn for her by about a dozen people in the past week.

Trent was in on it, too.

Haley, Trent, Ridley, Dash, Pence, Charlie, and Drax.

She tried to remind herself that this was why she didn't let herself trust people. But the truth was, she was hurting as if she had trusted them all along.

10. THE RESISTANCE

The week dragged on at a steady decline. Quinn's productivity in her classes became worse and worse. All of her teachers were worried about her, but their speeches made no difference. Haley was no longer willing to be her partner in power tech, for obvious reasons; Trent and the others, for less obvious reasons. Since Quinn still refused to work with Dash, that left her partnered with Shade.

He didn't look pleased with the pairing, but Quinn took it as a good sign that he hadn't flat-out refused like the others.

Their session started the same way they had left off several weeks earlier: Shade sent a mild, sight-based illusion her way. There was no Kurt in it, nothing aimed at alarming or upsetting her. Just standard practice.

But she wasn't in the mood for standard practice. She was in the mood for answers. And even though she felt fairly certain Shade wasn't involved with whatever Dash and the others were, she was starting to think just about everyone was on one side or the other. Just about everyone had answers.

She focused all of her energy on pushing the illusion away, the same way she had with the illusion of Kurt all those weeks ago. It hurt, stirring up those feelings again—forcing herself to remember the illusion of him in order to remember what it had taken to send the illusion away. But it worked, and it left her staring face-to-face at a bewildered Shade.

"Again?" he asked. "How is this possible?"

"Don't worry about it. Listen, Shade. Remember what I said to you at the party? That we're not monsters—that we're human?"

Shade nodded carefully.

"I stand by that statement. But I want to elaborate. We aren't monsters simply *because* we're deviants. Okay? We get to choose who we want to be."

He stared at her, confused.

"Some of us, though," she continued, "make the *wrong* choice. Choose the wrong friends. Become a part of something that might just turn us into monsters."

"I'm not friends with any of you."

"Yeah," she said, laughing shortly to herself. "I'm not exactly friends with any of them at the moment, either. But I have to ask you, Shade—do you have friends? *Other* friends, maybe? On the island?"

He looked away from her. He looked almost nervous, strangely enough—like she was the first person to ask him these questions in a very long time.

"Yes," he said quietly.

"Who?" she asked, taking a step toward him. She could sense that her desperation was triggering him, but she couldn't help herself. "Is it Savannah? Is it Reese? Is—"

But he shook his head, eyes frantic, looking everywhere but toward her. Before she knew what was happening, he was leaving. Running away from her, away from class.

Everyone looked over at her, no doubt assuming she had done something horrific to him again. No one even seemed surprised.

· · ·

Reese came to see her that weekend. He asked if she wanted to go on another flight, but she declined. She remained convinced that he was one of the few people not in on the secrets Dash and the others were keeping, but he could still be keeping secrets of his own. And if Ridley was right, her friendship with Reese might very well be what was keeping her old friends away.

Not that it was fair. Who were they to keep her away from anyone?

She told him to say what he had to say to her there, on level ground, and he did. He told her that everyone was worried about her. He told her that word had gotten back to Savannah that she had all but given up on her classes, and Savannah wasn't happy.

"Why do I care if she's happy?" Quinn asked him in annoyance. "Why does *she* care if *I* am?"

"Savannah makes mistakes. She has a very skewed view of the world. But the way she sees it, the classes, the island—it's all a gift. Something we should all be grateful for. And the moment we *stop* being grateful, we deserve punishment."

Quinn shuddered at the idea. There was something beyond corrupt about Savannah, and none of it seemed to match up in her mind with Dash's views. Could Reese's theory really be right—that Dash and Savannah were in on something together? Or was it something else entirely?

"I don't know what you want me to say," she said. "I'm not going to magically become smarter, Reese. I'm also not going to magically develop a great personality. Frankly, if she wants to try and punish me for that, I'd like to see her try."

"I really don't think you would," he told her, but raised his hands in surrender when he saw her expression. "I did my part. Do what you can. I wish you nothing but the best."

And he left.

She let his words sink in as she made her way to Rory's, preparing for an evening practice. First of all, why was Reese always the bearer of Savannah's warnings? Considering his claims that Dash was the one in cahoots with his mother, she sure did send Reese on her missions often. Secondly, why had he almost seemed to defend Savannah's view of the island being a gift?

"I'm glad you're here," Rory said when she answered the door. Her expression was grim. "We need to talk."

Both of them knew better than to speak openly in those halls. As far as Quinn was concerned, everyone besides Rory was the enemy until someone started telling her the truth. She'd be damned if she revealed anything to any of them in the meantime.

They made their way to their practice spot, deep to the south of the island, before Rory explained herself.

"I still haven't been able to see much. A snippit here, a snippit there. But what I have seen… It all involves Savannah. It's like my mind is trying to warn me about her. It's something serious."

"Serious, how?"

"Serious, like... some of the pictures, the flashes I've seen... They're of death, Quinn. Death, and fire, and Siloh destroyed. And then Savannah, and these other figures... watching us burn."

"These other figures... Could you make out any faces? Shade, maybe? Either of the brothers?"

She didn't care which brother at this point. She just wanted to know.

But Rory shook her head. "It's all so dark. Hazy. I could barely tell it's Savannah, it's just... she has such a specific look. The brothers, when they're in profile, dark like that... They look so similar. It could be either one."

Figures. Quinn wanted to punch something, but refrained. "Well, we've got two options, don't we? We investigate further—try to figure out what she's planning—try to save everyone else on this godforsaken island."

"Or?"

"Or, we run."

It was a clear favorite for her. What did she care what happened to the rest of the residents of Siloh? They clearly didn't care about her any more. The only one left for her to care about was Rory, and she would bring Rory with her.

Rory smiled sadly. "That's your thing, isn't it? It was the same with the boy I remind you of. You were able to tell yourself you didn't care about anyone else in the world. Anyone but him."

Quinn stared at her, shocked. "I never told you about Kurt."

"You didn't have to."

That was when Quinn knew it for sure: Rory was the real deal. Everything she was saying, everything she was seeing... It was all true. She was a seer.

"I'm not running," Rory told her. "Not yet."

"Fine," Quinn said, disappointed but not surprised. "Then I think we both know what to do next."

$$\bullet \ \bullet \ \bullet$$

She wanted so desperately to have the power of invisibility. It would make this so easy. To be like Tommy, to close her eyes and blend into whatever was behind her, seamlessly and completely... Tommy probably knew more than any of them. Tommy probably knew it all.

Tommy's probably in on it, too, she thought grimly.

What could she do to hide them, she wondered, if they were to go and spy on Savannah? It was late, but Savannah was known to work late—to stay in her room in the town hall, door closed, doing God knew what.

Her mind flashed to Izzo's ability. Could she turn into an animal, like Izzo? A bug, perhaps, and listen in that way? She had never accomplished such a thing before, but then, she had never had much incentive to.

"What if I come out of it?" Quinn asked as they discussed this option. "Run out of juice—change back into a human right there in her office?"

"First of all," Rory said, "you shouldn't be going all the way into her office. It's too dangerous. You should literally be a fly on the window. Or whichever insect has the best hearing. And second of all, I've got a plan for that. Electricity juices you up, right? Gives you energy? I'll keep sending you juice. It'll keep you bugged out." She giggled, pleased with her pun.

Quinn sighed. It was crazy. It was probably suicide.

But she was sick of being kept in the dark.

They had already made it close to the town hall, lurking in the shadows, whispering of their plan. All that was left was for her to change.

"Try and be a moth," Rory advised. "If I remember right from biology, they have the best hearing."

Quinn stared at Rory, both amused and strangely envious of her knowledge. Quinn couldn't even answer basic math questions, and this young girl knew which insect had the best sense of hearing?

"You are one special little girl," Quinn whispered in amazement. And she closed her eyes and changed into a moth.

She couldn't tell how she looked. She couldn't tell how well she had pulled it off. But from her new senses of smell, taste, sight, and hearing, and the fact that she had wings, she could tell it had worked enough. She was a flying insect.

She flew over to the exterior window of Savannah's office and watched.

Savannah was still there. She was on her cell phone. Pacing. Muttering things… hushed things. Her eyebrows were furrowed; her mouth was moving. But Quinn heard nothing.

She *could* hear, though, was the strange thing—she could hear well. Was it possible that Savannah had some sort of soundproofing—something to keep stray ears from listening, just as she was trying to do?

She wanted to get closer, but she knew it would be a disaster. She glanced behind her into the tree line. She could see Rory off in the distance, watching her. If only Quinn could crack the window with her telekinesis… Not as an insect, though; she'd have to change back into a human for that…

She sighed, frustrated. She started to fly away, but doubled back when she saw Savannah opening a small, sealed envelope. She squinted through the window, trying to make out what was inside it.

It was airline tickets, she realized. Airline tickets and passports.

Savannah looked up then, straight at the window. Her eyes were sharp, predatory. She seemed to sense that someone was watching her.

Quinn stayed dead still, her many legs resting carefully on the ledge. She could feel her power draining, and her heart began to pound. Had Rory been juicing her up? Was she going to? If she changed, here, now, with Savannah watching her…

But just as she thought it, she felt it: a small, but perfectly calculated pulse of electricity coming up at her from the ground. Just enough to re-energize her.

Savannah reached for the blinds to the window, snapping them closed. Quinn exhaled, flying back to Rory in the woods before changing back.

"Let's get back to our spot," Quinn said. "It's not safe here."

• • •

"I wasn't able to make out anything," Quinn told Rory when they reached their spot. "Her windows were soundproofed, somehow. I was about to give up completely when I saw her pull something out of an envelope—plane tickets. And passports. She's planning on going to the real world, Rory. And not alone."

Rory frowned, considering this. "You weren't able to make out any of it?"

"No… Like I said, it was soundproofed. But, Rory, the plane tickets mean something. She's not just taking an under-the-radar helicopter trip to Fiji, okay, she's got a passport, an identity, things none of us have had since we were in the real world. Things she could use to go *to* the real world. And not just her."

"It's just," Rory said, crossing her arms, "you're so powerful, normally. I'm finding it hard to believe that you couldn't hear what she was saying and I could."

Quinn's eyes bulged. She grabbed Rory by the shoulders. "*What*?"

"I should say, I couldn't hear her from where *I* was, but by listening in on what *you* were listening in on, putting myself inside your head, and juicing up both of us from back where I was staying, I was able to hear *through* you."

"I can't even begin to understand that," Quinn admitted, awestruck, "but I don't think I care at the moment. Rory, what did you hear?"

"We came in at the tail end of a conversation. The details, I could tell, they had already laid out. But she kept saying his name—Cole."

Quinn swallowed. Suddenly her throat was on fire.

"They were talking about an attack," Rory continued. "They didn't say when, or what, or even where. She kept talking about this group of people. 'The alliance.' Saying that she was almost done putting it together. That she had to get them out first—before the attack. Them, herself… and her son."

"Her son," Quinn repeated. "Singular."

Rory nodded.

Quinn groaned. She didn't have the energy to waste wondering which Collins brother Savannah meant. Not again. Besides, there were bigger things to worry about. "If she's trying to get people out, that means the attack will be here."

"I know. It's the visions I've been seeing. Siloh, burned. Everyone dead. But remember—we know that as long as Savannah is here, we're safe."

Quinn shook her head. This was all too much. Hadn't killing Kurt and Charlotte been enough for Crowley? Hadn't sending Quinn to Siloh, exiling her from the real world, been enough? Now he wanted to kill everyone on Siloh, save for the select few deviants who were useful to him and Savannah? This 'alliance?'

Who was in the alliance?

She kept trying to avoid it, but her mind kept coming back to the same question.

Which brother?

. . .

Quinn and Rory parted ways after that, not feeling safe anywhere near the town hall with the knowledge they had. Quinn made her swear not to repeat a word of what they had heard, not that she had any real fear that she would. Rory was a smart girl. She proved herself smarter with every passing day.

Haley was nowhere to be found when Quinn got back to her room, which was no surprise. For the first time since Haley had started avoiding her, Quinn was glad; she needed time to process everything she had just learned. She needed time to make a plan.

Again, it ultimately came down to the question she had asked Rory earlier. Did they protect Siloh, or did they run?

All of these people that were in on something—Dash, Haley, Trent, the gang—were they in the alliance? From what she gathered, the alliance was the *opposite* of the resistance. But was it possible that Savannah was trying to play Crowley somehow? That all of them were?

She knew Savannah's plan now, but she still didn't know nearly enough.

Still, she found herself unable to trust anyone but Rory. With that being the case, her only option was to run.

But she knew Rory, and she knew she wouldn't want to. Tomorrow's goal would be to convince Rory to leave with her. For now, she would sleep.

. . .

When she showed up to science class the next morning, she was in for a rude awakening: it wasn't the normal teacher, Lydia. It was Dash.

"Good morning," he said to the class. "Today, in place of your normal science class, we're going to be having a seminar. The topic: astrophysics and religion."

Quinn groaned out loud. She didn't even know what astrophysics were. She did not have the patience or the time for this.

"Something wrong, Quinn?" he asked, surprising her. Dash hadn't said a word to her in almost a week. He had more or less been acting like she didn't exist.

"Nope," she mumbled, not in the mood to pick a fight with him.

"Right." His gaze lingered on her for a moment before turning back to the rest of the class. "Now. Who knows what astrophysics is?"

Angel's hand shot up, followed by Pence's, Charlie's, and a handful of others.

"Pence," Dash said.

Quinn rolled her eyes. Figured, he'd choose one of his own.

"It's a branch of astronomy specific to physics and chemistry," Pence said. "Kind of... how things came to be, and remain to be."

Dash nodded. "Very good. And how about... religion?"

They all stared at him for a moment, thrown by how easy the question was. Finally, a few hands raised. Quinn didn't bother. She hadn't raised her hand once since arriving on the island; just because she finally knew the answer didn't mean she would bother trying.

But apparently the lack of her raised hand meant nothing to him, because he said, "Quinn?"

She glared at him. She wanted to ignore him altogether, but knowing what she knew about Savannah, she decided not to push it until she was ready to take her leave of Siloh. "It's where people who are too selfish to accept the idea of a world without them make up an afterlife in which they can live forever."

Everyone turned to look at her at that point. Some looked amused. Some looked sad. Dash was included in the latter.

"I take it you don't believe in the afterlife."

"Doesn't matter what I believe, does it? I'll turn into nothing, or I'll go to hell. I'll figure it out when I get there—or I won't."

"Interesting." He crossed his arms. "Who in this class believes in God?"

A startlingly low number of hands raised into the air. Angel, Quinn noticed with bitter irony, was not one of them; Drax, Haley, and Shade were the only ones who raised their hands.

"Drax," Dash said. "Would you care to tell Quinn how you feel about what she just said?"

Drax turned to face Quinn, looking her in the eye for the first time in weeks. "It makes me sad. I don't think you would go to hell, Quinn. I think you've made mistakes, but you're a good person. And I think you have plenty of time to turn your life around."

She laughed out loud.

"You think that's funny?" Dash challenged her.

She hated him. She really did. After all that had happened between them, for him to keep so many secrets from her—for him to know of her imminent demise— *all* of their imminent demises—and do nothing, say nothing… It disgusted her.

"I do, actually," she said, chest rising and falling rapidly. "I have a question for the class, if I may."

He spread his arms as if to say, *Why not?*

"How many of you feel that way?" she asked the class. "Like maybe you've made some mistakes, but you've got plenty of time to sort it all out?"

Most of the class raised their hands.

"Right," she said, rising to her feet. She knew it was a mistake, but at this point, she had so little to lose. A little justification before she went, a little satisfaction… And then, if she was lucky, she could get herself and Rory out of there before it was too late. "And what if I were to tell you all that you're going to die? Not in a few decades, not in a few years, but soon? Any day now?"

Most of them stared at her like she was insane. Those select few—the ones working with Dash—were looking at her with a different expression.

Fear.

"What's wrong, Dash?" she asked. "Am I saying too much? Revealing too many secrets? Or are you just mad that I finally figured it out?"

"Quinn," he said slowly, taking a step toward her. "Stop."

"The way I see it, if an island full of people is going to die, they have the right to know about it. But I guess that's the difference between you and me."

Dash wasn't ultimately the one who lunged for her. Trent was.

But it didn't matter. She was gone before any of them could touch her.

She'd always been good at running.

. . .

Her mind ran through a million different thoughts as she scrambled out of the classroom and sprinted out of the building. What had she done? Word was going to spread, and with it, panic. Students and residents alike would try to run, flee, or fight; it would become utter madness. All thanks to her.

And yet... *so what?* It was the truth. Didn't they all deserve to know? Hadn't *she?* Whatever Dash had or hadn't known, whatever he had or hadn't been in on, he had to have known of the imminent danger. It had to be the secret he had been keeping from her. And, frankly, how *could* he? How could any of them?

She knew she had to leave; she knew Savannah would be after her the moment she heard who had started all this. But she also knew she couldn't leave without Rory. She zipped through what little she knew of Rory's schedule in her mind, trying to piece it together... Where would the girl be? She could try her phone, but the odds of her answering it were slim...

It didn't matter, she learned; Rory was standing right outside of the exit to the building.

"Rory," Quinn gasped. "How—?"

"I don't know. I think we have some kind of mind link at this point. I heard your thoughts again... I sensed that you were looking for me... and I just sort of found you."

Quinn wanted to linger on that, whether to ask her questions or even just to mentally process the fact that someone could now read her mind, but she knew there wasn't time. She grabbed Rory by the arm. "We've got to go."

Quinn began her sprint again, a sprint that could hold its own against Charlie's. Rory kept up mostly by way of Quinn's strength, but she didn't seem to like it.

"Where are we going?" Rory demanded as they ran.

"To the river. We'll follow it downstream and dive under at the wall. I almost did it once before... I just got caught in the waterfall."

"We can't run away!" Rory insisted, digging in her heels and refusing to keep up. Quinn groaned, picking the girl up entirely and carrying her as she continued to run. "Quinn, these people are in trouble and they don't even know it."

"Oh, they know. I told them. And now my ass is on the line. I have to leave, Rory. And I can't leave you here to die."

Rory stared up at her, eyes suddenly big and childlike. Afraid. It reminded Quinn how young Rory was for the first time in a long time.

They had reached the river. They were downstream from the waterfall; there was nothing stopping them. Quinn stopped moving just long enough to look Rory in the eye.

"I know you don't want to go," she said softly. "I won't make you, Rory. But things are about to get very, very bad here. I can't leave you behind. Not unless you swear to me that's what you want."

Rory looked down at the water, considering her answer.

But she didn't get the chance.

"Quinn!"

Quinn and Rory looked up at the waterfall in shock as Dash crashed down it, into the river, and then straight up into the air. Quinn may have thought she was bad at flying, she mused, but he was *terrible*; he fell to the ground so hard that it shook.

She wanted to laugh. She wanted to make fun of him, to joke with him, even to ask if he was okay. All of the things that she couldn't do.

For all she knew, he was there to kill her.

She stepped directly in front of Rory. She glared at him, fingers balling up into fists. "We're leaving, Dash," she said, voice darker and lower than it had ever been with him before.

"You can't," he said, shaking his head, still sputtering water. "Quinn—"

But she didn't give him a chance to finish. She blasted him with the strongest burst of electricity that she had ever conjured. It was, she was certain, an ability that had been magnified because of her connection with Rory.

He went flying, slamming into the ground again, arms-first, cursing in pain. But he stood, coming back over to her. "You don't understand. If we could just—"

She blasted him again, this time with fire. She focused all of the flames of the hell she refused to believe in into that blast. She wanted to hurt him. She wanted to hurt every one of them who had been keeping this painful truth from her.

"Stop it!" Rory shouted at her, tugging at her sleeve, voice high-pitched and afraid. "Quinn, he just wants to talk to us!"

But it was no use. Quinn's mind had gone into a rage, and her powers along with it. All she cared about was getting out of there. She hit him with another wave—this time, of ice.

Rather, she tried.

Nothing happened.

Rory stood in front of her, facing her, chest heaving. Beads of sweat ran down her face. Behind her, Quinn could see Dash rising.

"We are going," Rory told Quinn, "to hear him out."

"Rory," Quinn said just as slowly. "Stop it."

"No. You let him speak, or you don't get your abilities back. Not as long as you have me with you."

Quinn was amazed—not only by Rory's power, but by her spunk. In fact, if the girl reminded her of anyone, it was of herself.

If Quinn wasn't mistaken, she read the same thought on Dash's face.

She sighed. "Fine."

Rory came back to stand next to Quinn, both of them turning to face Dash, who shakily found his footing.

"We don't have much time," he said. "I left Charlie with the class to try to salvage what was left of it. The island is going to split down the middle. The resistance and those who are putting their trust in Savannah."

"And you're saying you're not one of them?" Quinn asked him. "That you're not in the alliance?"

He blinked, confused. "The alliance?"

"Savannah's army," Rory explained to him. "The people she wants to save before she kills the rest of us. The ones she's convinced are *tame,* we expect."

Dash's eyes widened. This really did seem to be news to him. "I knew she was corrupt. I knew she was planning something. But I had no idea."

"Even if you didn't know about the alliance," Quinn said, "you've been hiding things from the beginning. Including things about the imminent destruction of the entire island—something I, along with everyone else, have the right to know about."

"I didn't *know* about it," Dash nearly shouted; "at least, not the way you two clearly do. Listen, Quinn. There's only one way to do this, since you clearly have retained that stubborn inability to trust anything anyone says."

Quinn waited.

"I'm standing in front of two seers. Between the two of you, there must be a way to ascertain whether someone is telling the truth. I need you to find that way. Because I'm going to tell you everything. And we don't have time for you to believe I'm lying any more."

She knew his plan made sense. She wanted to get to the bottom of the truth. She wanted to be honest. She was so sick of all the lies. But in that moment, lying was necessary; the truth would expose Rory. "We're not seers."

Dash rolled his eyes impatiently. "Call it what you like. You've been reading each other's minds for days. You found a way to get past Savannah's security. You *must* have a way to truth-tell—"

"I think we can do it," Rory said, glancing over at Quinn. "You look him in the eyes. Compel him. Make him tell the truth. I use my abilities to sense whether the compulsion is working. Then, together, we hear him out, and use our best judgment. It's not perfect, but I think we'll know. I think even if we can't trust anyone else, we can trust our own instincts, our own abilities."

Quinn hesitated. It wasn't a bad plan, but there was one problem. There was only one way for Quinn to compel Dash, and it was to be honest with him first.

"I can't," she said, taking a step back.

"Quinn," Dash said, taking a step forward. "Thirty seconds of vulnerability, and you'll know everything. We have to do this."

She knew he was right. She just hated it.

"Fine. I have never hated and loved someone as much as you. I wanted to trust you so badly that I think I actually did. And then I watched you not only lie to me, but turn everyone who mattered to me against me, picking and choosing favorites that you would let in on your precious little secret, and it drove me slowly more and more mad with rage until I snapped. I went to go see what she was planning on my own. And then I decided I truly hated you, because whichever side you were on, you *knew*, and you did *nothing,* and that, more than anything, proved to me that you couldn't be trusted at all."

He stared at her, devastated. Crushed.

She knew it had worked.

"Tell me the truth," she compelled him.

She could see before Rory said a word that she had him. His eyes were hers. She saw obedience, and she saw truth.

"I have never lied to you," he told her. "I never wanted to come to this island. I wanted to be with Charlotte. But Savannah told me to come here, and so I did. At that point, I was still obedient to her. I still trusted her.

"I told you that Charlotte was killed by Crowley, and that was true. What I left out was that Savannah was in on it, too. I could see in her eyes the fear she felt whenever I would receive a letter from Charlotte—whenever I would try to help her. She kept warning me, telling me that if I kept communicating with the resistance, I would be the next one on Crowley's list. I ignored her. I received a letter from Charlotte three days before she was killed, telling me that she was going to the US Embassy in Canada to try and get them to talk peace terms. That had to be how Crowley knew where to find her—how he had time to plan out the whole thing. Savannah read the letter and told him everything. She did it for my protection, but it didn't matter. Not to me."

"As it shouldn't have. But why keep this from me? Why tell me everything else, but not this?"

"I'll get to that. I promise."

She believed him, she decided, so she let him continue.

"Once the resistance died on the mainland, I decided to start one here on the island. Not necessarily to break out of here, or to do something drastic, but for our own protection. I didn't trust Savannah any more. I didn't know exactly what her end game was, or Crowley's. But I knew that she had it in her to kill. And that was enough for me to want nothing to do with her.

"Little did I know, the Siloh resistance had already begun. Shortly after

Charlotte's murder, Charlie's parents came to me. They told me that if I was truly ready to give up my mother, they would have me join them."

Charlie's parents—Dr. Donovan and her wealthy husband—were the leaders of the resistance? She certainly hadn't seen that one coming.

"I knew they were the real deal," he explained, "because they and Savannah had never gotten along. They came to Siloh with more money and power than she did—and, soon, more allies. Their roots moved here. Hers stayed out there. They were rivals from the beginning.

"I couldn't tell Savannah, of course. I had to convince her she could trust me. So I asked her to let me teach. The way she was having people teach, it was out of fear. The way the kids are still taught—telling people to hold back. I told her I wanted to teach them how to really *use* their abilities. For their own sakes.

"She agreed, on one condition: she wanted me reporting back to her, keeping her posted on everyone's abilities, whether we had any seers, that sort of thing. She wouldn't tell me everything, but I inferred that she was reporting back to someone. Whether it was the UNCODA or Crowley, I didn't know. But I knew she had to trust me, and I knew I couldn't endanger my students. So I fed her lies about my students—lies grounded just enough in the truth that she believed them. I protected those students at all costs. And I became a leader in the resistance."

"And Reese?" Quinn asked. "Where does Reese fit into all of this?"

"Reese has never been concerned with anyone but himself. I knew it all along, but the moment it was confirmed for me was when Ridley turned. We had all just recovered from the event—we hadn't even moved to Siloh yet—and Reese wrote him off entirely. His best friend. Wouldn't even look at him any more."

Quinn could hardly believe it; and yet, looking over at Rory, she could see that, to the best of their abilities, they both believed he was telling the truth.

"It wasn't just me and Charlie's parents," Dash said. "There were others. Adults, people you still don't know. People they trusted. They let me invite people, too, but slowly. Every existing member of the resistance had to approve each new member. For anyone in our movement to leak anything back to Savannah... It would be over for us. We knew at that point what kind of power she had. She'd had people killed. And she was planning something bigger.

"Ridley was my first recruit, and he was a tough one, but a valuable one. His position in security made things complicated, but also useful. He leaked information back to us quickly and truthfully—helped us gain intel that we hadn't had before. They loved him. Then, Charlie's parents wanted my opinion on Charlie and Pence. The two of them got together almost as soon as Pence came to Siloh, and Charlie's parents trusted both of them implicitly. But they knew how teenagers could be, and they knew how Savannah and Reese could get to them—manipulate them. They asked me to watch them; talk to them. Determine whether they were right for the resistance. I knew within months that they were. They were strong-hearted and independent, and it didn't hurt that Savannah distrusted Charlie's parents so much, she wouldn't even consider approaching their children. They were the first of the younger generation to join."

It made sense, she supposed. What Haley had told her about Savannah having come to her, but not Pence and Charlie, and for them to have warned Haley against telling anyone—they had probably already been in the resistance at that point.

"For years, they were the only teenagers in the resistance," Dash continued. "There were others I recommended heavily—Haley, in particular. But I wasn't the only one trying to get to them. Reese and Savannah were, too. Every time one of them met with Reese or Savannah, red flags were raised to the resistance. Haley was just... too kind. Some people mistook her kindness for weakness. As much as I believed her heart was in the right place, the others wouldn't risk it. They knew Savannah had approached her, and they feared that if she joined the resistance, she might in a moment of weakness or intimidation reveal too much to Savannah."

Quinn didn't typically have much faith in people, but even she knew Haley was tougher and smarter than that.

"And then you came here," he said. "You were the talk of the resistance, Quinn. Everyone wanted you, and yet everyone was afraid of you. They all thought you were both a powerful asset and a ticking time bomb."

Sounds about right, Quinn mused. Especially considering her latest stunt.

"And you?" she asked him. "What did you think?"

"At first, I wanted you nowhere near that group. I had seen all the havoc you'd wreaked on the real world. I thought you were reckless. I thought you were selfish.

I thought you were giving the world justification for fearing us and hating us."

His words hurt, but they didn't surprise her. She'd had her suspicions about why he had been so cold to her when he'd first met her, and she hadn't been far off.

"The world already hated us and feared us," she pointed out. "If they didn't, I would have led an entirely different life."

"I know. I was wrong."

She said nothing. But it helped.

"I learned early on that there was more to you than I had assumed, but Reese had you in the palm of his hands so quickly," he continued. "With his claws in you, none of us wanted to risk recruiting you. It was too dangerous.

"And then I got to know you, and I saw your heart. I knew that you had the exact same motives that I did—even down to Crowley himself."

She shuddered at the sound of his name, even now. She could sense Rory's breath held next to her, just as transfixed.

"I tried to convince them," he said. "I did. The closer I got to you, the harder it was to keep it from you. But every time I came close to convincing them, Reese would swoop in. It was all intentional, Quinn. I know it was. Reese and Savannah saw us getting close, and she sent him to intervene. To keep you away."

"But Savannah doesn't even know you're in the resistance," she said. "According to you."

"I wouldn't put anything past her. It's possible she knows everything. At the very least, she suspects. And she wouldn't leave a risk factor like you to chance."

"Makes sense," Quinn admitted. "But at the same time, she never tried to get me to join her, either. Not really. Not this 'alliance.' And Reese? He made up this twisted web of lies about how you and Savannah were in on something. Why would that be? What was their end game?"

"My guess is they wanted to keep you from joining *either* side. Reese wanted you to distrust me so that you wouldn't become his enemy, but he knew better than to expect you to willingly join a movement spearheaded by the man you hate the most—Crowley. As much of an asset as you could be to them, you'd always be more of a liability."

In a disturbing way, it made perfect sense.

"It was the day after Drax's party that we learned what Savannah was up to—at least, we got an idea of it," he continued. "Ridley went on a scout to the mainland to pick up a load of goods, and included in the load was some mail for her. On the helicopter back, he opened one of the envelopes. It was a letter from Crowley. It was coded, but we gathered what we could. It was a plan of attack."

She nodded. It was as she and Rory had gathered.

"Keep in mind, we didn't know as much as you do now. This 'alliance' you say she has created—her plan of saving them and killing the rest—it's news to me. We envisioned a battle, perhaps—her demanding surrender or death—but not such a cowardly plan. Not taking one group away and leaving the rest to die.

"Regardless, once we knew an attack was looming, we went into overdrive. Recruiting more quickly. Drax was the next of my students. He had just recovered from the incident with Haley, and we had all seen how bravely he forgave you and pushed you to make amends with Haley. We saw him realize that he was stronger than he thought, and we saw the bravery that came with that realization. When Charlie and I came to him with the invitation, he was thrilled. Said he wanted to do whatever he could to help.

"Haley and Trent, we approached next. Trent first, followed shortly by Haley. We had always seen them as a package. What happened with you and Trent that day concerned Charlie, Pence, and a few of the others. Myself, too, though for different reasons." Quinn tried not to blush. "They were worried that Trent's connection with you would threaten our secrecy, if you really were in cahoots with Reese. We almost didn't recruit him over it. But Pence decided it was safe. She said that when she asked Haley about it, Haley told her it was a fluke—that he meant nothing to you."

Quinn grimaced. *Thanks, Haley.*

"I can't say I wasn't relieved to hear it," he admitted, instantly lifting her spirits back up. "Anyway, Haley and Trent were next in. We still debated you. Every day. I fought to include you, Quinn. Even after you started hating me. So did Haley, and so did Ridley. We all saw the good in you. We just feared what they might be polluting your mind with."

She understood where he was coming from. She did. From the moment she had met Reese, she had been taken with him; it had to have shown to those who were looking. And she knew she had never been the most trustworthy of people.

But to *him?* To Dash, who she had more or less laid her heart out to?

It still hurt.

"Anyway," Dash said, "none of it really matters any more. After all these years of secrecy, of planning…. You've put it all out in the open. Now everyone is forced to choose sides. And we hope that within our side, there are no moles."

She swallowed. *Way to go, Quinn.*

"What can I do?" she finally asked.

He blinked. "What do you mean?"

"I mean, I *am* trustworthy, and I *do* want to help, and now that you have no other choice, I guess you're going to have to deal with that."

He sighed. "I guess I thought you might still run."

Rory glared at him. "She was running because she didn't think there was anyone left for her to trust. You've explained yourself and your reasons. She accepts them. Now, tell her how she can help."

He smiled slightly, which was good, since Quinn was busy fuming. Not only did the girl read her mind, but she spoke for her, too? She *was* spot-on, but still.

"Charlie and Pence stayed behind to convince the rest of the class to stay put until we returned," Dash explained. "If we're lucky, no one's left yet. The moment that classroom splits up, all hell will break loose—unless, by some miracle, none of them go to Savannah."

"I don't think that will happen," she told him, thinking back to her last conversation with Shade about his 'other friends' at Siloh. "Shade's in that class."

"I would like to think she hasn't gotten to him," he said sadly. "But I admit I was never able to."

"I think you never could because she already had. He strikes me as someone who's been lost for a very long time. It's almost impossible for him to connect, but any time I come close, I can sense that a part of him desperately wants to. Savannah probably saw that in him long before any of us. It's the kind of manipulation she probably used to form the entire alliance—whoever that might consist of."

"I think you're right," he agreed. "We can only hope he hasn't gone back to her yet."

She nodded silently.

"So, we go back," he said. "We put all our cards on the table. We give everyone the choice. Once the doors open, we choose a base—a building for all the members of the resistance to stay. We take shelter there—formulate a plan to fight back."

Quinn frowned. "And in the meantime, what? We await our fate from the outside world—this attack Crowley's been planning with her? Are we sure that's wisest? What if we just got everyone out who needs to get out? And if someone chooses to stay behind, so be it?"

"It's an option. I'm sure we'll consider every option. But here, we have the ability to protect ourselves and our homeland. Stand our ground. Fight back. Out there? Our enemies would be multiplied a million times over. Every country, every leader, every *person* would be afraid of us. We would be invading their lands."

She understood. Here, they were a contained threat—one only a tiny percentage of the real world knew about. Out there, it would be utter mayhem.

She nodded. "Let's get to work."

. . .

When they returned to the classroom, the first thing Quinn noticed was that it was quiet—too quiet. All eyes went straight to the three of them as they entered, no one uttering a sound. Charlie and Pence stood at the front of the room, the rest of the students in their seats.

The rest of the students except one, she realized: Shade was slumped on the floor, unconscious.

"We had to take him out before he put us all under illusions and fought his way right to Savannah," Charlie explained to Dash. "Trent took the liberty."

Trent smirked, sending Quinn a wink. *Great,* she thought sarcastically; *now he decides he can trust me again.*

She supposed they were all beyond secrets now.

Her heart went out to Shade. It had been easy for her to put the pieces together that he was in the alliance once she knew who was in the resistance, but it was hard for her to blame him. She wished there was something she could say or do to make him change his mind, but she had a feeling he was too far gone.

"And the rest of them?" Dash asked Charlie.

"No one fought us or tried to leave," Pence told him. "But no one's happy."

Scanning the faces of the students watching them, Quinn could see that Pence was right. "Well, no shit, they're not happy. I told them they were all going to die. And then we forced them all to sit here and do nothing for half an hour."

She could see a few grins from the classroom, but mostly it was glares.

"What now?" Angel demanded, finally piping up. "Is someone finally going to explain to us what the hell's going on? Or will I have to be the next to get knocked out because I have to go pee?"

"Shade didn't have to *pee,* Angel," Charlie said. "He was trying to report back to Savannah. To tell her what we know."

"And what *do* we know, exactly?" asked Tommy. "Can anyone explain to me why all this time we've been told to obey Savannah's rules at all costs, and now we're being told that if we try to go see her, we'll be murdered?"

"Not murdered," said Trent. "No one here is threatening to kill you. We just might incapacitate you. Briefly."

Dash cleared his throat in an attempt to take back the room. "Look, all of you will be given a choice. Everyone is going to leave this room alive. What Pence and Charlie were ensuring for us was that we all make our choices *before* leaving this room—having a full understanding of what it is we're making choices about. That way, we all have time to get where we need to be, safely."

Everyone fell silent. It was only stares.

"I'll start with what I know," Dash said, "then I'll let Quinn speak. What I know is that I, along with Charlie, Pence, Trent, Haley, and Drax, and others not in this room, am a member of the new resistance. It is a secret group that has existed for many years here on the island, created in the wake of the resistance that was destroyed on the mainland. We have always known of Savannah's corruption, and we met in secret, doing what we could to keep tabs on what she was up to and whether we here on the island were still truly safe."

"What do you mean, Savannah's corruption?" Izzo asked him. Her question was clear, but her voice was nervous. She was clearly afraid. "What did she do?"

"She is involved with a very dangerous man—the very man who was responsible for the destruction of the first resistance. His name is Cole Crowley, and he is the leader of the DCA. He has made it his mission to not only send all deviants from the real world to Siloh, but also to punish us in other ways... ways I think we are just beginning to understand."

"Basically," Trent said, helping him out, "he wants to kill us all."

"Why would Savannah agree to that?" Tommy asked. "She's got two sons who are deviants. You're trying to tell me she doesn't care about you?"

"My brother has been on her side all along. I know she'll protect him at all costs. I'm sure it's part of the deal with Crowley. As for me, I'm not sure what she would do. Savannah and I haven't truly trusted each other in a long time."

Quinn raised a hand awkwardly. Dash glanced over at her. "Yes?"

"Well," she said, "this might not be the best time to tell you this, but I can pretty much confirm for you that if she's planning on saving Reese, she's not planning on saving you."

He hesitated, confused. "How could you know that?"

"Well, when Rory and I heard her on the phone... it was '*son*' that she was ensuring protection for. Singular. Not '*sons.*'"

Dash held her gaze for a second, letting that settle in. Then he looked down. It seemed to hurt him more than she had expected. She supposed some small part of him must have been clinging to the idea that his mother still loved him.

Probably should have waited to tell him that, Quinn thought grimly.

"There you have it," Charlie said, swinging in like a true politician and using Quinn's mistake to his advantage. "More proof that Dash is on our side—not hers."

Angel rolled her eyes. "Let's be clear: none of this is proof. But please, continue. I'm fascinated."

And Dash did continue, changing the subject. "What Trent said—it's more complicated than Crowley wanting to kill all of us. Sure, he wants us dead, but he also sees us as valuable weapons. If Quinn, Rory, and I have put the pieces together correctly, we think he's having Savannah create an army for him. Those who she says are trustworthy become part of the alliance—a group that she and Crowley will protect, in exchange for their servitude and loyalty—or, as far as I'm concerned, slavery."

"So, we join the resistance, and probably die, or we join the alliance, and become slaves," Angel said, nodding. "I'm liking my options here."

"Let's get back to the attack," said Tommy. This was the most vocal Quinn had ever seen him. Then again, it *was* his life on the line.

"All the resistance was able to ascertain for sure was that Crowley has been in communications with Savannah regarding a plan of attack," Dash said. "We don't know when. We don't know where, though we assume it will be here on Siloh. Aside from the resistance, Quinn and Rory here did a little recon of their own."

He glanced over at Quinn, inviting her to speak. She bit her lip, suddenly feeling uncomfortable. "Right.... Basically, we know that she's got plane tickets and passports, and that she's trying to get herself, the alliance, and her son—that is, Reese—out of here before the attack. So, putting two and two together, when we see Savannah and everyone who isn't in the resistance leave the island, we know we're all doomed."

Angel watched Quinn carefully. "Why didn't you run?"

"Excuse me?"

"It was clearly what you were planning on doing when you left class earlier, and your boyfriend chased after you," Angel pointed out. Dash made a face like he considered objecting, but decided against it. "So, why didn't you? What could Dash possibly say to someone as selfish as you to convince you to stay here and protect your own kind?"

Quinn stared at her, utterly speechless. Because, of course, Angel was right.

It was Rory, to her surprise, who spoke up for her.

"It was never a question of whether or not Quinn was willing to protect you. She loves you all, whether she'd admit it or not. It was a question of why no one in the resistance *let* her. They shut her out for so long, she gave up. When Dash finally came and told her everything, that was enough for her. She just wanted the truth."

"Right," Tommy said, glaring at Dash. "So did we."

"I'm truly sorry," Dash said, "for keeping so many of you in the dark for so long. It wasn't my choice—I'm by no means the leader of this movement—but I'm still sorry. I just have to ask that you all understand our positions. If anyone in the resistance were to leak anything back to Savannah—if we were to make one single judgment error—it would all be over."

"And now?" Angel asked. "Now that we all know everything? You're still going to let Shade go—let *us* go, if we decide to side with Savannah?"

"Why *would* you?" Haley asked her. "Why would any of you even consider teaming up with the woman who is currently arranging a mass murder?"

"Because they don't think we'll be able to stop her," Drax answered her sadly. "And they hope that putting their trust in her will save them."

"It might save them for the time being," Dash said, "but not in the long run. Anyone who sides with Savannah is siding with Crowley—and working for Crowley is worse than selling your soul. He will ask you to do vile things, to hunt and kill your own kind, and the moment you try to resist, he will kill you. You'll wish you had stayed and fought—that's a promise."

Everyone remained silent, letting that sink in.

"And yes, Angel," he continued, "in response to your question—I *would* let them go. Shade, and anyone else who makes that choice. The secret is out now. It will get back to Savannah, if it hasn't already. If you still choose her—if you can live with the slavery and the half-life—then I invite you to do so. But those of you who want to stay, to defend our land, to defend our loved ones—you, I side with."

"And then just hope?" Angel asked. "Hope that you don't have a mole in your group? Hope that Savannah hasn't already gotten to one of us that you didn't trust so easily for your own resistance?"

"Yes," Dash said, looking her straight in the eyes. "That's exactly what I hope."

She fell silent.

Charlie cleared his throat. "We've established a base camp for the resistance. There's room for everyone to eat, sleep, practice, and plan as we form our alliances. When everyone here has made up their minds, we move out. Everyone who chooses to join the resistance will head for the tower—I believe everyone is familiar with it. Everyone who chooses to to join this 'alliance'—I believe you're all familiar with the town hall, as well. I'm sure that's where she will be expecting you."

Pence took a deep breath. "Any further questions?"

The class sat in silence, eyes wide. Afraid.

Izzo raised her hand. Dash nodded to her. "It's just," she said timidly, "what if... What if we don't want to choose?"

"I'm afraid it's not an option," Dash told her. "You could try to hide. We wouldn't chase you. But Savannah would find you. You could try to run—to jump the wall and go far away from here. But Reese would stop you. I have no doubt he'll be patrolling the skies until this is all over."

"Besides," Charlie said, "amidst all of this fear and confusion, I encourage you all to remember: this is our home. We fight to protect it. If any of us leave—particularly anyone who is known to have been brought here—it sends a message to the world that we aren't ready to send. We have enough on our plates already. For the world to fear this island more than they already do..." He shuddered. "Crowley is enough of an enemy for now. Let's not make it the entire world."

Izzo nodded sadly.

"Hands in the air," Dash announced, "if you have come to a decision."

One by one, every hand went into the air—that was, every hand but Shade's. Quinn had to admit, she was impressed by the knockout power of Trent's punch.

"Hands down," Dash said, and everyone lowered their hands. Quinn could see the fear in Dash's eyes before he gave his next order. "Hands in the air if you wish to go back to Savannah."

Eyes darted around. Everyone remained jittery, on edge. No one seemed certain.

But no one raised a hand.

Dash smiled. She could see the relief in his eyes, and yet the fear was still there. She knew that, in a way, this scared him more than the alternative. This was what he had been avoiding all along.

"Right," he said, nodding. "We make for the tower."

11. PLAN B

As they all exited the building, Quinn felt on edge, to say the least. Her biggest question was whether there would be an army awaiting them—and whether Reese would be in that army.

It was starting to settle in, how angry she was with him—how many questions she still had. How much he had lied to her. If her and Rory's truth detections had been accurate with Dash, just about everything Reese had ever told her was a lie. A part of her hoped he would be there—almost *dared* him to be.

But he wasn't. No one was. The island was quiet.

"Do you think they already know?" she asked Dash.

"Probably, though by no fault of Shade's. He is very powerful, but I feel pretty confident he's no seer. Charlie and Pence checked his phone when they knocked him out. He hadn't reported anything yet. If Savannah and Reese know about us, it's because of our own actions."

"Meaning?"

"While we were in the classroom, Charlie was communicating with his parents. They've been recruiting, all around the island. As quietly as possible, but someone was bound to take notice. Everything's gone into overdrive now. Ridley's been back the tower, setting everything up. Stationing people at all of the exits; preparing the living quarters; food; the whole nine yards."

Quinn smiled to herself. "He's pretty high up in the movement, isn't he?"

He nodded. "Things are different in the resistance. Where people like Savannah and Reese held him back in Siloh, not giving him the opportunities he deserved... We're not like that. We realize that trust is the most important thing at a time like this, and if there's one thing we all agree on, it's that we can trust Ridley."

"I know the feeling."

He watched her for a moment as they walked. She could tell there were things he wanted to say to her. There were things she wanted to say to him, too. But not there. Not in front of the entirety of the YA.

They reached the tower. At first, Quinn didn't see any obvious signs of security. But the moment Dash opened the door for her, she spotted two people standing guard: Hank, the monster she had met back at the bar, and a woman, beautiful, though not a pretty monster like Quinn and Dash. She had long, red hair, and fireballs emerged from her hands the moment she saw people stepping in.

"At ease, Roxy," Dash said calmly to her as he led the class into the lobby. "They're all with me."

Quinn watched the woman as her fireballs subsided and she smiled at Dash. Quinn couldn't help but feel a pang of rivalry. Roxy was closer to his age, and inevitably less of a head case than Quinn. Quinn wondered whether anything had happened between them since she and Dash had stopped speaking.

She groaned, frustrated by her own inner dialog, blushing when she realized everyone had heard her groan. Dash glanced back at her, confused. She pretended she didn't know why.

Dash led them to the elevator, which they piled into. He punched the button for the fourth floor—the penthouse where all the parties were thrown. As they passed the third floor, her mind flashed back to Dash's room—the room they had nearly made love in. She wondered whether they had repurposed it, too, or whether it remained private.

Somehow, she doubted she'd be receiving an invitation, either way.

The elevator doors opened to the fourth floor, and she was both impressed and saddened to see a complete 180 from the party room it had been before. The bar was completely gone, along with the tables, chairs, and party lights. Instead, there were dozens of neat little cots organized by rows, each with a dresser and desk boxing around it. Each like a tiny, wall-less room.

"How could they have done all of this?" she asked Dash in amazement. "So quickly?"

"We have a conjurer," he explained. "Whatever she draws, she creates. There are limits, of course. She can't draw food, she can't draw actions, she can't draw people. But when it comes to things like this, she's indispensable."

Quinn made a mental note to insist on being introduced to this artist of theirs.

"Okay, everyone," Dash said. "This is the new fourth floor. Choose a bed. Any bed. Respect each other's privacy as best you can here—I know it's not easy. Spare clothes are available in all of the dressers. Community-style bathrooms are located at each end. Once you are all settled in, report to the second floor, which has been made into a dining hall. There, we'll eat and await the rest of the resistance to report for a meeting. That will be at two o'clock sharp."

Everyone nodded wordlessly.

"Every floor of this building is considered safe, but I think we should all keep in mind that the most safety is in numbers. The second and fourth floors are the safest. The first floor is where we will be having new and improved power tech. Every day, ten AM sharp, starting tomorrow. It won't be just us anymore. It'll be everyone, of all ages.

"Finally, with the cat out of the bag, we're all going to have to do our part and step up when it comes to security. There is a board on this far wall—" he gestured to a giant whiteboard near the bathrooms "—with slots available to sign up for. Two per shift for now. Three-hour shifts. Round the clock. Any questions?"

"Yeah," said Angel. "What if we don't want to do that?"

Dash didn't seem surprised by her question. He answered her in the frankest way possible. "Then you know where the door is. And I wish you the best of luck."

Angel held Dash's gaze for a second before walking past him and toward the door. For a second, Quinn thought that was it—they had already lost their first member.

But Angel stopped at the whiteboard and wrote her name into one of the slots.

Quinn smiled to herself. Despite their differences, Quinn had never thought of Angel as a bad person. She was glad to see that she wasn't wrong.

"Right," Dash said. "Everyone get settled. I'll see you all soon. Second floor."

· · ·

Quinn watched her classmates scatter about, throwing bags and possessions onto various beds. She didn't choose a bed; she wouldn't be sleeping there. If she was lucky, she'd find someplace within the tower's four floors with a free couch for her to sleep on. If not, she'd sleep in a bathtub somewhere. But not here. Not like this.

Again, her mind flashed to Dash's bedroom. The thought of sleeping there—really, the thought of *not* sleeping there, but rather doing everything but sleep—was becoming just as intoxicating to her as it had been before everything had gone haywire. After all, Dash had been the honest one all along, hadn't he? As much as she hated to admit it, he'd had valid reasons for keeping her in the dark.

"Everything okay?" Rory asked her, walking up to her with wide eyes. "I saved you a bed."

Quinn tried to force a smile. "Thanks. I'm not sure I'm going to be able to get much sleeping done in here. But you'll be safe here."

Rory rolled her eyes. "This again? Quinn, you're just gonna have to accept you're not a lone wolf any more. I'm in your head and I'm there to stay. And I don't think I'm the only one."

Quinn could tell that Rory was referring to Dash, but she pretended she had no idea what she was talking about. "Go to the second floor. Save me a seat and a burger. I'll be right behind you, okay?"

Rory grinned. "Sure. Have fun on the third floor."

Quinn didn't want to know how Rory knew which floor Dash was on.

She made her way to the elevators, waiting for the first group to take off before getting her own, not wanting everyone to see which floor she was going to.

It was hard to retrace her footsteps, given the intoxicated state of mind she'd been in the last time she was there. But it was definitely the right floor. Long, ornate hallway, a few doors on her left, a bathroom on her right, and….

There it was, on the end. Even with her memory failing her, even with every door looking the same, there was something telling her it was his room. It was that sixth sense that had always made her question whether she really was a seer.

She hesitated before knocking, not at all sure what to say or do. A part of her wanted to grab him, kiss him, and never let go. A part of her wanted to ask him whether he'd already moved on. A part of her just wanted to say she was sorry.

She knocked, deciding to figure out the rest when she saw his face.

"Who is it?" he asked through the door. She knew he wouldn't normally ask, but given the circumstances, she couldn't blame him.

She considered joking. It would usually be her go-to in this situation. Pretend to be Savannah, Reese, or even the attractive new fire woman downstairs guarding the entrance. Just to get a laugh out of him. Just to make *herself* laugh, even.

But she didn't have the heart to. Not in that moment. So she said, with a certain degree of exhaustion, "It's me."

There was a hesitation on his end; she didn't miss it. But it was only a second, and then the door opened.

"Hi." He sounded tired.

"Hi." She swallowed, mouth suddenly feeling dry. "Can I come in?"

He hesitated again. He clearly didn't think it was a good idea. But he backed up, making way for her to step into his room.

It hurt her, looking around in that room. In a strange way, teleporting there, hitting those soft, silky sheets, being locked in an embrace with him—it had been the closest thing to paradise she'd experienced. A brief paradise, but still a paradise.

And then she had gone and ruined it.

"Look," she said. "I don't know why I'm here, exactly. I just... I guess I wanted to say that I'm sorry."

A glint of surprise sparked in his eyes. He hadn't expected this.

"I can see that it hurt you," she said, "me not trusting you completely, me not choosing you. The same way it hurt me that you didn't tell me everything."

"But you see the difference, don't you? At least, from my perspective? I *did* trust you, Quinn. I knew who you were. The only reason I didn't tell you everything was because of my loyalty to the resistance."

She understood. She had failed him, just as she always failed everyone.

"I know," she said. "So... I'm sorry."

He held her gaze for several seconds. She could see it, just beyond his eyes, trying to work its way to the surface. All of things he wanted to say. So much more.

She knew, at least on some level, that same desire was there for him, too—the desire to grab her and kiss her, to pick up where they had left off.

But he didn't do that.

"Reese," he said, "he's… he's not even capable of love. He's the closest thing we have on this island to an old-fashioned monster, which is the irony of all ironies, given how many 'monsters' we have." He sighed. "Look, Quinn. I know he played you. I know you were confused. But for you to see Reese, my snake of a brother, no differently than you saw me… It's just not something I can forget any time soon. I hope you can understand that."

There was so much she could say. She could tell him the lies Reese had told her about him. The things he'd made up. She could tell him so much.

But it didn't really matter, because he didn't want to hear it. He wanted to be left alone.

So she left.

• • •

She knew it was suicide. She knew it was not only dangerous, but that it would piss off all of the friends she had finally convinced to trust her again. She knew she would miss the first meeting the resistance had held since she joined. She knew all of this, but she did it anyway.

Reese had ruined her one shot at a good thing. Not just Dash, but Siloh, too. He was trying to take it all away from her. And he had played her for a fool.

She wasn't going to kill him. She knew that, in a situation so much bigger than any one person, a single death could mean an entire war. So, as much as she wanted to, she wouldn't.

But she certainly planned to rough him up a bit.

Hank and Roxy tried to stop her when she left the tower, but she laughed in their faces. Roxy's abilities were impressive—fire, after all, was one of Quinn's own favorites—but it was nothing when faced with someone powered by water, and Quinn was no beginner with water. She doused the girl's flames with ease, ducked past Hank, and headed back out to the island.

It wasn't hard to find Reese. She made her way toward the town hall, but she didn't have to walk far; she just had to look up. It was like Dash had said: he was patrolling the skies.

This might be trickier than I thought, she mused as she lifted up into the air. Flying had always been one of her weakest abilities; focusing all her energy into it, she wouldn't have much left to hurt him with when she faced him.

She could sense people gathering beneath her, shouting things, watching her, as she made her way up to him. She knew it had already begun. No doubt before long, someone would be firing bullets at her. But it wouldn't be the first time. She could deal with bullets.

She scanned the rest of her surroundings as she ascended. She didn't see any soldiers from the mainland, but she did see helicopters. Just far enough from the island to not pose an immediate threat… Just close enough to make it clear they were there. Waiting.

"Quinn," Reese said when she reached him, smiling calmly over at her. "What a nice surprise. Guess you were a better flyer than you let on."

"I think we both misled each other, if I'm not mistaken," she growled at him.

He chuckled. "Perhaps. It was just so easy, Quinn. You were so desperate *not* to trust my brother, you almost begged me to give you reasons not to."

She knew he was right; it was the reason Dash was having such a hard time forgiving her. But just because he was right didn't mean he was any less of an asshole, she decided, so she punched him in the face.

He took it surprisingly well, smirk never leaving his face, clutching the bruise without whimpering about it. "Not a bad hit, Quinn. We could still use you on our side. You know, if you prefer not being obliterated on judgment day."

"Judgment day?" She laughed out loud. "Please. I'm not scared of anything you or your mother tries to throw at us. She doesn't even have abilities, and *you?* You fly. It's pathetic."

His smirk faded; she was starting to hit the right spots. "When Siloh gets what's coming to it, it won't matter whose abilities are strong and whose aren't. No one will have a chance in hell."

Quinn's mind flashed with questions. She wanted to know what he meant by that. She wanted to know more about their plan.

But she knew he wouldn't answer any of those questions, and anyway, only one answer mattered to her in that moment.

"Was it even yours?" she asked him. "The book?"

"No, Quinn, you poor little thing. It was never mine."

"But the quote," she nearly whispered, looking at him with almost as much disdain as she had for Crowley. "You knew the quote. You knew the *page number.*"

"I had Shade look through it when he was in class with you. He put you under a mild illusion. Made sure you wouldn't notice. It was child's play. Too easy."

She floated closer to him, mind slowly entering a kind of rage, everything starting to boil. Thinking of the alliance manipulating Shade that way—using him to their advantage like a trained guinea pig—it disgusted her.

Her hand flew to his neck, and she wrapped her fingers around it, tightening her grip just enough to block his airwaves, but not quite enough to snap his neck.

"If I was back in the real world," she hissed at him, face inches from his, watching his asphyxiation with extreme pleasure, "with no one to protect, no one to care about…" She let go as suddenly as she'd grabbed him, ignoring his gasps and coughs as he struggled to stay airborne. "I'd kill you with my bare hands."

And she went back to the tower.

• • •

There was a new duo guarding the entrance when Quinn returned: Charlie and Pence.

"Oh, thank God," Pence breathed when she saw Quinn, exhaling audibly.

"What?" Quinn asked, not sure the 'thank God' was entirely necessary. She hadn't been gone for long. "Why aren't you two at the meeting?"

"We practically *wrote* the meeting," Charlie said. "Someone had to stand guard. And my parents had to be the faces of it. Why aren't *you* there? More importantly, why would you *do* that to us?"

"I just had to take care of something. What's the big deal?"

"Quinn," Pence said, shaking her head. "When Roxy told us what happened, we all thought you'd turned on us—gone to join Savannah. Or just fled."

Quinn frowned. It *had* looked bad, she supposed, her escaping out of the foyer, nearly taking out Roxy in the process, and missing the meeting.

"You need to go see Dash," Charlie told her. "He hasn't come out of his room since Roxy told him. He was supposed to be the keynote speaker at this meeting."

Quinn suddenly felt light-years worse. After all she had already put Dash through—after all they had put each *other* through—now she had done it to him again. How many times could the two of them question the other's trustworthiness before giving up completely?

But she wasn't ready to give up, and she wasn't ready to let him give up on her. So she headed for the elevators.

"Third floor," Pence told Quinn as she stepped in, and grinned slightly. "Though something tells me you already knew that."

Quinn grinned devilishly back at her friend as the elevator doors closed.

Her grin faded as she watched the floors tick by. By the time she got to Dash's floor, crossed the seemingly never-ending hallway, and wound up at his door, she had virtually no confidence left in her, nor any idea what she was doing.

It's going to be okay, she told herself as she knocked, *it's going to be o—*

"Go away," he shouted through the door.

She raised her eyebrows at the unfamiliar sound of his voice. Was it just her, or were his words slurred?

She knocked again.

"I'm not going to the fucking meeting," he shouted, "so back the fuck off."

"Well, that makes two of us," she called back, trying to feign confidence and aware that she was falling short. "Maybe we could think of something else to do."

There was a silence. Longer than it needed to be, and much heavier.

And then, footsteps. A surprisingly aggressive yank on the door.

He stared at her, eyes a strange mixture of confusion, wonder, and fierce anger.

She stared at him back, contemplating what to say next. There was a whole world of words and explanations and stories she could give him in that moment. But there was only one that kept coming back to her.

"He told me it was his book," she said, so softly it was almost a whisper. "He told me they were his words in the margins… he even quoted them to me. My favorite thing you wrote."

He held her gaze. Eyes flickering. Believing her.

"*For hope is the thing that saves us from ourselves,*" she said softly.

And finally, they were kissing. And finally, everything was going to be okay.

. . .

They couldn't disappear forever. They really couldn't even disappear for the amount of time they already had. There was about to be a mass genocide of their kind, after all.

But none of that seemed to matter to either of them as they lost themselves in each other. Nothing else seemed to matter at all.

However powerful, however wild, however incredible those first kisses had been, they were nothing compared to what came next. It was so far beyond anything either of them had ever experienced—more sensation, more exhilaration, more excitement than either of them had even known was possible. In fact, with any other two people in the world, it probably *wasn't* possible.

When it was over, they lay next to each other, staring up at the ceiling, chests heaving, arms and legs entwined. Simultaneously, they turned to face each other.

"Holy shit," she said, grin forming. "That's what I've been missing out on?"

"I think that's what *everyone's* been missing out on. Something tells me that was a first for the human race."

She smiled, shaking her head and turning back to the ceiling.

She couldn't remember feeling this happy in a very long time. It was strange, considering they were probably going to die any day now.

"You know," he said, "we should probably get back to that meeting. At least make an appearance. Let the rest of the resistance know you didn't jump ship."

She turned back to him, grin fading, eyes becoming serious. "Did you really believe it? That I'd left?"

"Did you really believe I stole the book?"

She understood his point. Had she believed it? Yes. Reese had provided facts;

her brain had accepted them. But had she accepted it, deep down? Not so readily.

"How about we both just believe each other from now on?" she suggested.

"Deal," he said, kissing her cheek and reaching for his shirt. "Let's start with you believing me when I say that if we don't get to that meeting soon, there will be hell to pay."

. . .

As it turned out, the meeting was filing out as they arrived. Dash was right: there was hell to pay.

Hell, in this case, came in the form of Charlie's parents—one of whom Quinn still hadn't met, and the other of whom she had only met in the medical wing.

"Dash Collins," Charlie's mother said the moment they entered, bee-lining over to him. "Where in the *hell* have you been? Half of this entire presentation was supposed to be—"

"I know," Dash interrupted. "I'm sorry, Evelyn. I was... working on getting Quinn back."

Evelyn—or, as Quinn knew her, Dr. Donovan—glared over at Quinn. "And what, may I ask, is your excuse for vacating the premises right before the meeting, and nearly taking out one of our guards in the process?"

"Jesus," Quinn said, unable to help herself; "that girl is *so* overdramatic." Then, seeing both of Charlie's parents' exasperated expressions, she added quickly, "I'm sorry! I'm sorry. I had to just go tell Reese Collins that I despise him and punch and strangle him a little bit. It was important."

Dash couldn't help but laugh. Evelyn, though, did not look happy—nor did her husband.

"You both missed the entire meeting," said Charlie's father. "We already formulated a plan for our next move. Seeing as neither of you were present, we left you out of the plan."

Dash's expression darkened. "Michael, Quinn and I are your most powerful options. Are you sure about this? What plan did you come up with?"

"You might be our most powerful options, but you're now our riskiest.

Tommy, Izzo, and Roxy will run the show. Diversion tactics and flying under the radar. They will find out when the attack will occur, and what it will entail. All the rest of us need to do is wait."

Dash looked like he wanted to argue his case further, but Quinn stopped him. "It's fine. Their job is to find out what the attack will be. Our job is to stop it."

Dash sighed, but nodded.

"I'm disappointed in both of you," Evelyn said, clucking her tongue. "This isn't the time for personal affairs. This is the time for unity. Get yourselves together. I'll see you tomorrow for power technique—ten AM sharp. Don't be late."

She and Michael took their leave.

Dash and Quinn turned to each other, both at a loss for words. But their silence was interrupted by Rory running toward them from the elevators.

"Guys!" Rory shouted, tugging at their sleeves. "Where *were* you? It was awful. They kicked me out of the meeting before it even started. They clearly have no idea what I can do—"

"Did you tell them?" Quinn asked her, alarmed. It would be one thing for Rory to tell a few trustworthy members of the resistance that she was a seer; it would be very different for her to announce it to a room full of people who had just joined the resistance that day.

"No," Rory said. "I wanted to, but I waited for you. Now what do I do?"

Quinn glanced at Dash, hoping he was thinking what she was thinking.

She wasn't disappointed.

"Come with us," he said, leading Rory back out, away from the meeting hall and the rest of the group. "We'll call it the resistance's plan B."

· · ·

The three of them brainstormed for several hours in Dash's room. Even after establishing the bond of trust that she finally had with Dash, it was still hard for Quinn to be so open about Rory's secret with him. But Rory wanted her to. She could sense it before the words even needed to be said.

Their clear and, frankly, only option was to use Rory's foresight, bolstered by whatever connection she had with Quinn, to predict exactly when and how the attack would occur.

"It's a great *idea* and all," Rory said, "but it's not that *simple*. I've never even really *had* a vision, let alone one that specific."

"Right," said Dash. "Which is why we have to really focus and hone in on juicing you both up with as much extra energy as possible. I don't think this is going to be a three-man operation. I think we're going to need more help."

Quinn nodded, following his logic. It meant telling a select few people the truth about Rory, but she knew it was worth it. "Haley and Trent would help us, I think. Haley's abilities would be useful—I'm not so sure about Trent's."

Dash considered this. "When you and Trent fought that day—you know, before you started kissing—" she glared at him; he dismissed it with an amused smile "—did it seem to energize you, or did you grow tired? Theoretically, if getting struck by the elements energizes you, so would fighting someone like Trent."

"A little of both. I think that aspect of it energized me, but the literal exertion of my own powers against him was de-energizing."

He nodded. "We could find a way to work it in right. We should talk to both of them. Who else?"

"Pence's water power would probably be a huge help. Charlie's speed, maybe. But with their parents feeling like they do about us, I'm not sure it's the best idea."

"You talk to Haley and Trent. I'll talk to Pence and Charlie. I'd like to get Ridley involved, too, in whatever way we can. Also—Zerrick will be of use to us."

Quinn raised her eyebrows. "Zerrick, as in, my math teacher?"

"Your math teacher, and a very skilled telekinetic."

Quinn was impressed. Zerrick had never displayed his abilities in class; she would have had much more respect for him. Besides, telekinesis was tough; it was something she hadn't remotely mastered.

"You talk to Zerrick," she said. "I'll talk to Ridley." She had been meaning to speak with Ridley since learning about the truth of the state of things on the island. He had, of course, been trying to tell her as much as he could all along.

"What about me?" Rory asked them. "What can I do?"

Dash knelt down to look at her eye-to-eye. "Stay here. I want you to meditate.

Have you ever meditated before?"

Rory shook her head, eyes wide.

Quinn watched Dash take the girl through the motions of meditation, impressed. She had never had the patience for it. But, watching Dash with Rory, it was clear that he did. It made her smile.

Once Rory felt satisfied with her instructions, Quinn and Dash headed upstairs to rally the troops.

• • •

"I'm sorry," Haley said, looking from Quinn to Trent and back. "You want us to double-cross the entire movement that we've only recently agreed to be involved with ourselves?"

Quinn sighed. "That's not what I'm saying. First of all, we all want the same thing. We're on the same team. We're just going about it a different way."

"Then why so secretive?" Trent asked, gesturing to the distance between the secluded corner of the room they were in and the other resistance members.

"Because they chose to put their faith in one plan, and we choose to put our faith another—one they don't exactly support. There's nothing wrong with that."

"And what, exactly, *is* your plan?" asked Haley. "Power up a twelve-year-old into having a vision when she's never had one before?"

"She's had snippits of visions before," Quinn said defensively. "And her psychic power has been evident to me for some time now. Look, I know she can do it, Haley. We just need help."

Haley and Trent glanced at each other, frowning.

'Who else is in on this?" Haley asked. "You, Dash? Who else?"

"Dash is going after Zerrick—don't ask me why," she added when she saw their surprised expressions. "And Charlie and Pence. I'm supposed to ask Ridley. Dash seems convinced he'll say yes."

Haley's expression changed notably. "Okay. I'm in."

Quinn raised her eyebrows, curious why hearing that Ridley was involved had given Haley the quick change of heart, but she decided to question it later. She glanced over at Trent. "You?"

"I'm in," he said, and glanced down at his watch. "But I've got guard duty in a few hours. Think you're gonna be able to convince Ridley pretty quickly?"

"Yeah, I'm sure," Quinn said, and frowned. "Guard duty. I guess I'm supposed to sign up for that, huh?"

"I signed you up," Haley said, grinning slightly. "With me. Middle of the night shift. We've got some catching up to do."

· · ·

Haley and Trent headed down to Dash's room to standby for the new group meeting, leaving Quinn to hunt down Ridley. Luckily, she didn't have much trouble finding him; he was on the second floor, lingering where the meeting had left off.

There weren't many others in the room; a few were scattered about, munching on snacks, but they weren't within earshot of Ridley, who was pacing back and forth, deep in thought.

Quinn approached him carefully. "Hey. Can we talk?"

Ridley glanced up at her, expression both surprised and relieved. "Yeah. It's good to see you. We were worried when we didn't see you at the meeting—and also, you know, when we didn't see you *before* the meeting."

"I guess my attendance hasn't been the best lately," she admitted.

"We had a feeling, with Dash gone too, that everything was okay. That, or that you both ran off together."

"Not really my style. If I go, I go solo."

"Or with a twelve-year-old in tow."

Quinn tried to laugh, but it felt forced. Did everyone know about her and Rory's relationship? What else did they know?

"I know she's special," Ridley said. "I've known for a while. No one else ever seems to. I was glad to see you help her, even if I was worried for your safety in doing so. You two seem to have a real connection."

"That's actually why I'm here," she said, trying to ignore her overprotective internal alarms going off at the thought of people knowing what Rory was capable of. "Dash and I have a plan—a much better plan, if you ask me, than the one Charlie's parents came up with."

"Good, because I'm not a fan of that one."

"Because you don't think it will work? Or because you don't trust them?"

"Both," he admitted. "What's your plan?"

She filled him in on plan B, realizing as she said it how weak of a plan it really was. But even then, she was sure it was better than the alternative.

"And we've got some others involved," she added, deciding to test a theory. "Dash is trying to get Zerrick. And there's Charlie, Pence, and Trent. And Haley."

He glanced up the moment he heard Haley's name, nodding. "I'm in."

Just like Haley.

Quinn considered asking him about Haley, just as she had considered asking Haley about him. But she knew that she and Haley would have the chance to talk that night at their post, and she also knew that the group had a lot of work to do.

So she led Ridley up to Dash's room, her half of plan B fulfilled.

• • •

Dash's half, she learned quickly, had been fulfilled as well; Charlie, Pence, and Zerrick were there waiting for them when they arrived, along with Haley and Trent.

"Well done," Dash said with a warm smile when she and Ridley entered. "So. How much does everyone know?"

"We all know everything," Haley said dismissively. "Not the least of which includes the idiocy of this plan. Powering up a twelve-year-old to have a psychic revelation about an evil self-proclaimed president and her DCA-director boss."

"Everyone in this room," Quinn said, against her better judgment, "I trust. I can't say the same about everyone the resistance sent to carry out plan A."

Silence hung in the air for a moment. Ridley beamed proudly at Quinn. He, after all, had begged her multiple times to choose the right side and trust who she could. She had finally made the right decision.

If only you all knew how hard it was, she thought. But she knew, at the very least, that Dash did. And that mattered most to her.

"It's not necessarily that they're untrustworthy," Trent pointed out. "I mean, we know them, for the most part."

"Right," Haley said, "except for Roxy. What's her deal?"

"She's fine," Dash said. "I've known her a long time."

Quinn had to remind herself not to be jealous. It didn't quite work.

"Anyway," Dash continued, seeming amused by Quinn's annoyed expression, "the bigger issue is that their plan won't work. Savannah is already done planning whatever she's planning. All that's left now is to wait for her and Reese to leave, and to prepare. That, or our plan. To find out a different way."

"To see the future," said Trent, voice thick with sarcasm.

"It wouldn't be the first time I've done it," Rory told him proudly.

Trent said nothing. Intrigue sparked behind his eyes.

"Okay," Pence said, straightening. "So, we do what, exactly? We attack Quinn, and somehow that powers her up, and she telepathically communicates with Rory?"

"More or less," Quinn admitted. "It's going to take time to figure out exactly what works best. I'm not even sure all of you *can* help. Ridley, in particular."

Ridley nodded. "I know. But I think it's good that I'm here. One of us needs to stay grounded and in touch with reality during this bizarre project."

Dash grinned.

"Let's start with whoever powers you up the most," Ridley suggested. "We start with them, and you begin focusing your abilities into Rory's mind. From there, the rest of us gradually take hold, offering you energy without being invasive."

Quinn's eyes traveled silently to Dash. There was no question.

He nodded silently, reaching out to offer her his hand.

The moment she took it, the energy in the room changed. It was like everything tripled in momentum—in brightness, color, and even in sound; a distinctive buzz filled the room. From the moment that energy hit her, she focused on one thing: transferring that energy to Rory.

"Rory," she could hear Ridley saying, though she tried to focus on nothing but her mental transference. "Close your eyes. I want you to think of nothing but the abilities flowing from Quinn to you."

Quinn knew, whether Ridley said it or not, that she should do the same.

The others began to touch her, to release their powers onto her. Water and wind washed over her, and she felt the speed of Charlie doing laps around her, of Trent pushing at her physically and Zerrick pushing at her with telekinetic force, but she kept her eyes closed and thought of nothing but Rory.

Rory...

Quinn knew that Rory could do it. She knew that Rory was strong—stronger than any of them. But they were pushing the girl too far, just as Quinn had pushed herself too far so many times before. Where had that landed Quinn? In the hospital. Unconscious. How could she let that happen to Rory? What if *worse* things happened to Rory?

She refocused her thoughts. She wouldn't force her abilities onto Rory; she would focus her abilities into having the premonition *for* her. Admittedly, she'd never had a premonition before; she'd had little more than fleeting feelings about the future. Admittedly, she probably wasn't a seer at all.

But if there was even the tiniest sliver of a chance that she was—that she could bear this weight for Rory—then she would take it.

Time passed—maybe minutes; maybe hours—and Quinn saw nothing. She couldn't tell whether Rory did or not.

Finally, the overwhelming power became too much for her, and she felt herself give in to it.

· · ·

When she woke up, she was in his bed again. She knew the feeling of those glorious sheets before she even opened her eyes. Not to mention, the soft, charged touch of his perfect hands.

"Quinn," he was whispering to her. "Please wake up. Please."

Her eyelids fluttered open as she looked around in confusion. Where were the rest of them? How long had it been? Where was Rory?

"Did it work?" she asked, sitting up.

He smiled softly, not letting go of her hand. "Not exactly. She did see things—

new things—more specific things. But we couldn't gather a time, or an exact plan, which was what we were really after."

"What did she see?" she asked, eyes settling on his. His eyes instantly calmed her, but her fear for the girl remained. "She's just a girl."

"I know. But she wants to be more."

Quinn understood. She had been the same way at Rory's age. She had to be.

"She saw death," he continued. "The same thing she had seen before, but more specific. Skeletons, almost entirely decimated. Rendered to ashes. The whole island, ruined."

"Yeah," Quinn said grimly, curling her legs up to her chest and resting her chin on her knees. "Well, we pretty much already knew that, didn't we?"

"There's more. She saw a mushroom cloud, Quinn. She said it was unmistakable. It'll be a nuclear attack."

That was new information. She shouldn't be shocked, she supposed; it would be too easy for deviants like her and Dash to deflect firebombs or grenades. Crowley and Savannah were smarter than that.

Still, she had imagined some sort of battle. Not the coward's approach.

Her mind wandered to the logistics—where the nuclear weapon would come from; how many leaders around the world would have to approve of the attack. It made her shudder, how much the rest of the world must still hate deviants.

"So that's it," she said quietly. "Their plan. Just to eradicate all of us in one, fell swoop. No soldiers needed."

"I know," he said, squeezing her hand. "It's disgusting. There aren't even three hundred of us, and that's including those in the alliance… a regular old bomb isn't good enough for them?"

"They want to fry us all until we disappear entirely," she muttered. "And our island right along with us."

"They know how strong we are. They fear that anything less than nuclear, we can handle."

"And what do you think? Can we handle nuclear?"

"None of us have nuclear-specific abilities. Nor do any of us have experience stopping such things. But between all of us, banding together, sort of like we did today… I have hope."

She nodded sadly, finding comfort in those golden eyes of his. Comfort, despite their impending doom. "You know, it's funny… I was always so ready to die. I knew it was inevitable. And now, here I am, at death's doorstep, and… For the first time, I'm not ready at all."

His eyes were sad, but he refused to give in to it. "Good," he said, reaching to touch her face. "Because I'm not ready to lose you."

• • •

They brought it up at dinner that night. Without any specifics, any real explanations of how they had been doing the digging they'd been doing, they revealed to the rest of the resistance that they thought the attack would be nuclear.

"That is a very serious prediction," Evelyn told Dash when he announced it to the room full of wide eyes and nervous faces. "Our preparations for the attack would change drastically if that were true. How can you be sure?"

"We can't reveal the identities of those who have shared this information with us," Dash said. "Not with the forced decisions of so many as of late. Not with the chance of moles existing among us. But I *can* tell you all that we do have a seer amongst us. And that person is confident that the attack will be nuclear."

Whispers and gasps erupted amongst the dining hall. Quinn tried to avoid the glances in her direction; most of them probably thought it was her who had seen the future. To her relief, no eyes seemed to be cast in Rory's direction.

"Very well," Evelyn said. "We continue our efforts with Tommy, Izzo, and Roxy. We still need to learn of an exact date and time to expect this attack. Meanwhile, we must form a plan of defense. Who here knows anything about defending against a nuclear attack?"

No hands raised.

"I know that it's impossible," Angel finally offered. "I know that the US government has spent trillions of dollars trying to figure out how to do it, and that we're kidding ourselves if we think we have anything they don't."

"Forgive me, but I think *you're* the one who's kidding yourself, Angel," said

Zerrick. "We're deviants. What they spend trillions on, we can do with our eyes closed. Besides—wouldn't it feel good? Showing them how easy it is for us?"

"I'm sure we would all agree that it would feel good, Zerrick," Evelyn said. "But Angel's question is one I believe many of us share: Is it really possible?"

"I think there's a chance," he said. "A slim chance, perhaps, but a chance. We use our abilities to make a shield—one that we project high enough in the sky that it destroys the bomb before it gets close enough to impact us."

Simon, the English teacher Quinn had never liked half as much as Dash, was the first to question this idea. "If we were able to completely destroy the bomb, we would—in theory—be able to keep it from going nuclear. But is that a chance we are willing to take? What if something goes wrong? What if it does go nuclear? A shield wouldn't be enough, even if we could project it upwards. The odds of us eliminating all of the fallout radiation would be miniscule."

"We would need more than a shield," Dash agreed. "In order to destroy the bomb before it reached us, and negate the effects of its detonation if anything went wrong…. We would need a blanket of energy so thick and so powerful that nothing could travel through it without being eradicated. Not even the fallout radiation."

Evelyn looked doubtful. "Not a single one of us has a shield ability. The only one in the world we know of who does, currently works for the DCA. And to my knowledge, none of us can create 'blankets of energy'—especially not one that happens to solve our radiation problem. What would you suggest?"

"I would suggest we band together," Dash said, rising to his feet. "Project everything we've got. Zerrick uses his telekinetic force to push the bomb up and out—up toward the sky, out toward the ocean. We implement Roxy's fire, Haley's gravitational forces, me and Quinn's elemental forces… We focus everything each of us has, a mile up in the air, spreading those abilities like a dome around our island. Protecting it. Focusing on nothing but destruction—way above us."

"I just want to be clear about something," Evelyn said, not backing down. "Radiation—bio-warfare—rolling the dice and taking our chances with things we don't fully understand—it's exactly how we got here. And we're the *lucky* ones. I don't think I need to remind anyone here how many people died in the event."

Everyone fell silent, letting Evelyn's words sink in. For a moment, it felt as if everyone in the room had lost hope.

Finally, someone spoke: Haley. Her voice was soft, shaky, but her words were confident. "I can do it."

All eyes turned to her.

"I've only tapped into the full force of my abilities once," she said. "It was when Quinn compelled me to. In that moment, I had a whole new sense of the world. My abilities weren't just limited to the earth itself... I could feel the wind. I could feel the elements. I could feel every wave on the spectrum. Each of them, independent of each other. And they... *obeyed* me. Now, I'm not saying I'm at a point where I could single-handedly deflect this bomb. My abilities aren't that finessed. But I think, with some of practice and Quinn compelling me to give it my all... I think I could transmute the fallout."

Everyone fell silent again, this time for the opposite reason: hope was returning to them. Quinn tried to ignore the tears prickling at her eyes; she was so proud of her friend, she could barely keep it together.

"It's not a bad idea," said Michael. "It's just... there's no guarantee. We can help Haley practice manipulating the elements, but there's no way for us to simulate the situation we'll be in—for her purposes or for the shield's. We'd have no idea whether it would work or not until it was too late."

"We could run," Tommy said, offering the same option Angel had suggested earlier. "I don't mean far, and I don't mean now. But once Izzo and I find out when it will happen, we could leave then—just far enough and just long enough to avoid getting hit. Then we'd come back. The real world wouldn't even know we left."

"It won't work," Angel said, shaking her head. "Believe me, I'd love for it to work; it was my idea first. But I went on a flight a few hours ago, just to see what it's like out there—how it's changed. Reese isn't the only one patrolling the skies. They've got helicopters surrounding us, just far enough to not pose an immediate threat, just close enough that they'd try and take us down if we moved to escape."

Quinn smiled to herself, impressed not only that Angel had the guts to sneak out, but also that she had the same thought process as Quinn about the helicopters. Not that it was anything to celebrate.

"It was never our best option, anyway," Dash pointed out. "There are too many other risk factors once we re-enter the real world. Here, we remain grounded. We fight defensively—not offensively."

Quinn could tell from the expressions of those around her that it was unanimous: this was their best shot.

. . .

The dinner meeting broke apart shortly thereafter, murmurs spreading amongst every member of the resistance. The plan B group met up briefly to touch base, but agreed to take a break for the evening. Rory and Quinn both needed rest.

Rory headed back for the fourth floor, deciding she was ready for a nap. Haley left with Ridley for an undisclosed location, promising Quinn that they'd catch up that night at their guard posts. One by one everyone else scattered until it was just Quinn and Dash, alone again.

"What do you think?" he asked her, eyes tired. "Do you think that between us, we can all stop a nuclear bomb?"

She held his gaze, thinking carefully about her answer. The old her—the Quinn she had been forced to be for most of her life—would have said no. That was the Quinn who had always erred on the pessimistic side; the Quinn who had refused to trust anyone; the Quinn who had almost gotten herself and everyone she cared about killed.

This Quinn, though, was different. This one actually had hope.

For hope is the thing that saves us from ourselves.

"I think we're going to have to."

12. THE MEMORY

Quinn spent the next few hours in Dash's room. They didn't make love again. They didn't delve deep into each other's pasts again. Instead, they just talked. About anything; about everything. About their favorite colors. Both blue. About their favorite bands. He had always loved Led Zeppelin. She had always loved Pink Floyd. Neither of them had ever cared for the Beatles. Then they put on the Beatles and closed their eyes and decided that they had both been wrong all along. They did like the Beatles, after all.

Finally, the time came for Quinn's guard duty, and Dash was having a hard time letting her go.

"Let me go with you," he urged. "It's the middle of the night. Who knows what could happen?"

"Savannah and Reese are still here. Angel's been checking. There's not going to be a nuclear attack—not tonight. Anything else, I can handle."

He held her gaze, hesitant.

"I'm starting to be able to trust for the first time," she told him. "But that doesn't mean I'm also now going to let other people fight my battles for me and protect me all the time. Come on, Dash. You know me better than that."

He smiled softly. "I guess you're right."

She smiled back, leaning forward to kiss him. "I'll see you soon," she whispered, and she left to go meet her friend.

• • •

It was strange down there, on the first floor of the tower, late at night. There were lights on in the lobby, but they were dim. As Quinn looked out through the glass doors toward the island, she noticed that there were no lights anywhere. Not even the usual street lamps. Savannah had turned them all off.

Haley hadn't made it there yet by the time Quinn got there. The two on patrol before them were Simon (Quinn's English teacher) and an older woman she didn't recognize. Quinn was starting to realize just how many people on the island she still didn't know.

"Quinn," Simon said good-naturedly when she arrived. "I'd heard you had the next shift. You get some sleep in before your shift?"

Quinn considered lying just to appease him, but she decided that the time for pleasing her teachers was over now that Savannah wasn't in charge. She could finally treat them like equals.

"No," she admitted, "but don't worry—I'll have good company. I'll stay awake."

Simon nodded. "Good. Quinn, this is Rita. She works at the library."

Quinn raised her eyebrows; she hadn't even known there *was* a library on the island. "Nice to meet you, Rita," she said politely. The woman looked very kind. She *looked* like a librarian, if that was possible. Soft-featured, petite. Older—one of the oldest people Quinn had met so far on the island.

"Nice to meet you, too, dear," Rita said warmly.

"Rita, why don't you head on up to bed?" Simon asked the woman kindly. "I'll wait with Quinn until Haley arrives."

Rita smiled gratefully and waved goodbye to both of them as she headed up the stairs.

"Wow," Quinn said, turning to face Simon. "They put *her* on patrol? Doesn't look like she could hurt a fly."

"No, and she probably wouldn't. Rita's ability is intelligence. You'd be surprised how much that can come in handy on patrol. Half the people who agreed to be in Savannah's 'alliance' could probably be talked out of it with enough wisdom."

Quinn didn't doubt it; she had a feeling even *she* could convince some of them, if she really tried.

Her thoughts flashed to Shade, whose mind she hadn't been able to change in the slightest, and she second-guessed herself.

"If she's so smart," she said, "one of us should ask her whether our nuclear shield plan will work."

"Believe me, I did."

"And?"

His face grew more serious. "She thinks it's risky. She thinks our chances of destroying the bomb aren't bad, but our chances of neutralizing the radioactive fallout if we fail are much slimmer. Everything Haley said made sense, but... It's a lot to put on the shoulders of one girl."

Quinn smiled softly to herself. How many times had that phrase been thrown at her growing up? How people had told her she wouldn't be able to survive on her own, wouldn't be able to outrun the DCA? Admittedly, she *had* eventually been caught. But she had lasted longer than any of them had ever predicted. She had proven them all wrong. And she knew Haley could, too.

"She can do it," she told Simon, not a doubt in her mind. "I know she can."

Haley reached them at that point, blushing deeply over her tardiness. She clearly still thought of Simon as her teacher, even if Quinn didn't. "Sorry, Simon," she said when she stepped into the lobby. "I totally lost track of time."

"All good," Simon told her. "It gave me the opportunity to have a very reassuring conversation with Quinn here."

Haley raised her eyebrows at Quinn, looking half amused, half confused. Simon took his leave.

"Don't worry about it," Quinn said, waving a hand. "We'll get back to the whole you-saving-the-world thing. What the hell is going on with you and Ridley?"

Haley's blush turned much more crimson. "Shit," she said, forcing Quinn to laugh out loud. She was fairly certain she had never heard Haley curse before. "Are we that obvious?"

"I could lie and tell you no, but who are we kidding? Who cares, anyway? We're all about to die. No time for secrecy."

"You would know. I'm pretty sure everyone and their mother knows about you and Dash by now."

Quinn chuckled. She couldn't care less what anyone thought about her at this point—not that she ever really had. "Me and Dash has been a long time coming. But you and Ridley? When did this happen? Wasn't it not so long ago you were ripping me a new one for making out with the other love of your life?"

Haley gave her a sarcastic look. "Whether I'm in love with him or not, Trent will always be my dear friend, and what you did was wrong on every level, Quinn."

Quinn sighed. She knew Haley was right.

"Anyway," Haley said, "you're right—it *was* recent. I just never really knew Ridley until you started bringing him around. That first party, when you went up to the rooftop and he was still down there, chatting with Drax and Angel, I started talking to him. Then, when I joined the resistance, I started talking to him more. About you, mainly. Me, him, and Dash, we were all so worried about you, and we were trying to figure out a solution when—"

"When I screwed everything up," Quinn finished for her. "By outing the whole operation."

"Yeah. But you know what? I think you did the right thing. That bomb could drop any day now. And we could still be holed up in secret, plotting without really accomplishing anything. Leaving everyone blissfully unaware of their options."

"That's right," Quinn said, sticking her chin up. "I'm a hero."

Haley laughed, but there was a heaviness in her eyes. "You're going to have to be," she said heavily. "We both are."

• • •

Quinn went back to Dash's room after her watch was over. She knew she was supposed to sleep on the fourth floor with all the other members of the resistance, but she couldn't bring herself to do it. She had lived alone for so long. Living with one person had been enough of a change for her, but this? Living with a hundred?

He was asleep when she reached his room, but he had left the door unlocked for her. She hesitated when she entered, wondering whether she should just curl up on the floor or in the bathtub, not wanting to invade his space more than she already had. But watching him sleep, she just wanted to be close to him. If they were all going to die, she might as well soak up her last remaining moments with him.

She only got a few hours in before his alarm went off, waking both of them up. She groaned, yanking her pillow over her head and kicking her feet in protest. He laughed out loud, pulling the pillow off her head and looking her in the eyes.

"I shouldn't be surprised you're not a morning person," he teased.

She glared at him, but he kissed her before she had the chance to object.

"Sorry for totally invading your personal space," she said when he pulled away from her, stepping out of bed to get dressed. "It's kind of a shock to my system, that whole community living thing they've got going on up there."

"You are welcome here," he told her, pulling on his pants and a t-shirt, "any time you like."

She tried not to beam too obviously.

"I'm going to grab some breakfast before power tech," he told her. "You want to join me?"

She considered, but she'd had quite enough of the dining hall for the time being. "That's okay. I'll catch up with you at power tech."

"I'll bring you a muffin," he said with a wink as he headed out.

She stayed there for a few minutes, taking it all in. How things had gone from so bad to so good, so quickly. How 'good' was quite a relative term, given their imminent demise.

She sighed, heading for the door herself. She'd shower when she was dead, she reckoned. For now, she'd go check on Rory.

• • •

She found her telepathic partner in the living quarters, the very place she had been trying so desperately to avoid. Rory was already glaring at her when she arrived.

"I get that you don't want to sleep here," Rory grumbled, "but you could at least offer to take me with you. I'm sure Dash has a couch or something up there."

Quinn chuckled. "I'll check with him. But we'd have to have some very strict rules involving socks on the door handle, or something."

Rory didn't seem to get the reference, which Quinn was fine with. She wouldn't really invoke a system like that on someone as innocent as Rory. More likely, she and Dash would probably just have to find some new private spots.

He does *have the ability to teleport,* she reminded herself smugly.

"You doing okay other than your resentment toward me?" Quinn asked the girl, looking her in the eyes to make sure there didn't seem to be any residual emotional effects from their work the day before. "Any bad dreams or anything?"

"I did see those images in my dreams last night, but nothing new."

"And you're okay? The images aren't getting to you?"

"I already knew we were all going to die. It's not exactly news."

Quinn didn't find this particularly comforting.

"Anyway," Rory said, "I'm fine. I'm looking forward to this power tech class. My old power tech teacher's with Savannah on the other side. It'll be nice to work with someone who encourages me to *use* my powers. You know—besides you."

"It'll be good for you," Quinn agreed. "Come on, then, squirt. Let's get going."

The first floor was already crowded by the time Quinn and Rory got there. Quinn spotted the majority of the YA over on one side of the room, packed tightly together, expressions wary. Ridley and Dash were there, too. Quinn grinned when she saw the muffin waiting for her in Dash's hand.

"I told you I wasn't hungry," she told him playfully as she snatched the muffin out of his outstretched palm.

"Clearly," Dash replied, watching her in amusement as she took a huge bite.

"Get a room," Trent grumbled, back to his old, jealous self. Quinn had a feeling this resentment had less to do with her and Dash and more to do with Haley's close proximity to Ridley.

"So, who's leading this thing today?" Quinn asked the others, scanning the room with interest. The divides seemed to be mostly by age. Other than Rory, most of the kids were standing near their parents on the opposite side of the room. Roxy, Hank, Simon, and Zerrick were toward the middle of the room, along with some of the teachers and Dash-aged deviants. A cluster of monsters lined the perimeter, with the older crowd sticking near the door.

"Who do you think?" Charlie answered, bitterness lining his voice. "My mom and dad."

Pence nudged him, chastising him for sounding so bitter. "Evelyn and Michael are the leaders of the resistance for a reason."

"Right," Quinn said, and rubbed her thumb across the tips of her first two fingers, the visual cue for cash money.

Charlie chuckled, but Pence looked annoyed. "It's not just that," she said. "They've been here for a long time. They've called Savannah's bullshit from the beginning. And they're the only ones who would have any idea what to do next if we actually pulled this off."

Quinn didn't have any strong feelings on the matter, so she decided to remain silent. Luckily, Evelyn and Michael stepped in at that point, and the silence spread.

"Welcome," Evelyn said to all of them. "I'm pleased to see we still have a full house. Now, I know that you all have taken different power tech courses, with very different kinds of trainers. Some have been one-on-one combat training. Some have been no combat training whatsoever. Today, we are going to do something different—something that has to do with our specific goal of creating shields."

Murmurs erupted, but they were silenced by Michael.

"Everyone in the room who has a physical ability that can both project out of them and do harm to others, come forward."

Quinn, Dash, Haley, Rory, and Pence all stepped forward. Glancing around, Quinn realized she didn't know many others with projectile abilities on the island. Of the twenty or thirty other people who had stepped forward, the only one she recognized by name was Roxy.

"Each of you," Michael continued, "one at a time, will be opposing the rest of us, head-on. You versus us. Whatever you choose to project at us, we must stop with a shield. A *group* shield."

Quinn was impressed not only by the exercise, but also by Charlie's parents for coming up with it.

"Pence," Evelyn said. "You first."

Pence nodded, coming to stand next to Evelyn, facing Quinn and the others. Quinn took a few steps back, glancing behind her as she watched the room transform. The half of the room surrounding Pence disappeared behind the line of

Quinn, Dash, Haley, and Rory, who remained at the front, facing Pence.

"Everyone on this half of the room," Michael said to their side. "Your goal is not to hurt Pence, but rather, to keep whatever she is attacking us with from ever hitting us. To create a shield."

Every set of eyes but Quinn's was rooted to Michael as he spoke. Quinn watched everyone else, an unfamiliar feeling washing over her. People all around the world had known who she was for years, but this was the first time in her life that she truly felt like she was experiencing history in the making. These people who had been exiled from the real world, restricted and confined in their freedoms and their territory, who had bowed their heads and accepted their fates for so long, were finally embracing their power. They were coming together; they were becoming something bigger. She could see in their eyes that they realized it, too.

"If you do not think your ability can help defend the group," Michael continued, "I encourage you to take the hand of someone who does. Band together. Transfer your energy and strength into that person… Even if only psychologically, we truly believe that this will make a difference."

It wasn't unlike plan B's strategy for sparking premonitions, Quinn realized. Their strategy had certainly had its flaws—Quinn passing out; Rory's premonitions remaining vague—but without it, they'd still be at square one.

"Pence," Evelyn said, stepping away from her and over to the populated half of the room. "Are you ready?"

Pence nodded.

"Are we ready?" Michael asked the rest of them.

They nodded.

"And," Michael said, "begin."

Almost instantaneously, a wall appeared in the middle of the room. It was a strange, beautiful sight to behold, made of everything from fire and lightning to ice and stone. It wasn't just made of tangible elements, though; it was made of *forces.* Wind, gravity, light, heat. All of it coming together at that exact point. The wall.

Quinn could see Pence, on the other side of the wall, squinting in determined focus as she attempted to launch a sharp jet stream of water out at them. Quinn knew from having seen Pence in action before that the stream was strong enough to impale someone if they weren't careful. But it had no effect on the wall. It disappeared on impact.

Finally, Pence gave up, and the wall disappeared. They all turned to look at each other, hope in their eyes.

"Good," Evelyn said. "Next."

. . .

They continued the exercise with everyone who had projectile abilities. A few of them—Quinn and Dash included—were able to break through the wall enough that the people on the other side felt minor effects. But none of them were successfully able to harm anyone on the other side. No one's powers remained fully intact.

"It might even be *easier* when it's the nuclear bomb," Rory pointed out to Quinn as the majority of the participants filed out of the training room. "It'll be a concrete object, not an element or force shooting out at us, so abilities like Zerrick's will come in handy more."

"Sure," Zerrick said, voice a mixture of amused and terrified, "but let's not all bank on my ability to steer a nuclear warhead against its trajectory."

Rory didn't look discouraged. "I'm just saying. I've got a good feeling."

Zerrick took his leave, but Evelyn and Michael requested that Haley and Quinn stay behind to practice Haley's special mission—which, of course, meant Dash, Ridley, and Rory stayed, as well.

This aspect of the training was harder for Quinn, who, beyond compelling Haley to 'give it her all,' felt she had nothing to offer.

The first time they tried it, they could all sense Haley's frustration; she was close, but it wasn't enough. So they tried what they had tried in the group training session—the same thing plan B was trying to perfect: energizing. Quinn took one of Haley's hands, and Ridley took the other; Rory and Dash completed the circle.

The effect was instantaneous. The Haley they all knew disappeared, replaced by a version of her that resembled a goddess more than a deviant. She floated into the air, dropping Quinn and Ridley's hands; her head tilted back; her eyes closed. Her entire body began to radiate a strange, luminescent shade of gold.

For a split second, all of the oxygen in the room seemed to disappear. The sunlight leaking through the room intensified until it was so bright that Quinn had to close her eyes in pain. The sound of the air conditioner crescendoed into a deafening, maddening buzz that drove them all to cover their ears.

It was like entering another dimension.

And, just like that, they were back to reality. Haley came crashing to the ground.

"Haley!" Ridley shouted, scrambling over to her. "Are you okay?"

Quinn and Dash moved behind Ridley. Quinn scanned her fallen friend's eyes as they opened. Haley's expression was unlike anything Quinn had ever seen. Serene; enlightened.

"Damn," Quinn said, weakly attempting to lighten the mood. "You look like you just discovered the meaning of life."

"Yeah," Rory said with a grin, "or some really good drugs."

Dash half-laughed, half-groaned, tousling Rory's hair. "You've been spending *way* too much time with Quinn."

"I haven't discovered the meaning of everything," Haley admitted, rising to her feet and giving Ridley's hand a squeeze. "But I know how to save us."

. . .

As comforted as they all were by Haley's progress, there was one thing her confident words hadn't accounted for. No matter how prepared Haley was—no matter how prepared they *all* were—they couldn't save themselves without knowing when the attack would take place.

Which, of course, left the ball back in Quinn's court.

"You need to stop putting so much pressure on yourself," Rory told her as they all sat in Dash's room later that day, trying to power up Rory as effectively as they had powered up Haley. "You know why it worked so well for Haley and not for us? Because you knew there was only so much you could do for her. You let her take the reins. You just helped."

Quinn wrinkled her nose. She hated how smart Rory was becoming, as helpful as it was. "What's your point?" she grumbled, even though she already knew.

"Her point is," Dash said, "let her do it. It's like you're trying to have the vision for her. Rory is the one who saw the nuclear vision, not you."

"Yeah, well, you're the one who keeps insisting I'm a seer, too," she muttered.

She knew he was right. They both were. It was just so hard for her to let go when it came to Rory. She didn't want the girl to have to see such awful things, to strain herself so much. She wanted to take some of the burden away.

She promised them she would try to back off, but it was no use. Just as before, they tried several times to force a premonition out of Rory, and before long, Quinn was back in Dash's bed, passed out again.

When she woke up, he had news for her.

"Plan A worked. The attack happens Friday."

• • •

Quinn let his words sink in. Judgment day, as Reese had called it. The day they would either face a mass extinction of their population (minus the alliance) or live to fight another day. *Another day,* and then start all over again…

She looked up at him, suddenly feeling very sad. She wasn't ready to die. She wasn't ready for him to die. Not so soon.

"Do you believe them?" she asked.

He considered this. His eyes were sad, too. When he finally spoke, it wasn't about Tommy, Izzo, and Roxy.

"When I was a kid, probably five or six, we lived in this tiny little apartment in Brooklyn. Land was already expensive there, though not like it is today. We had this landlord… Her name was Elena, I think. Sweet, old Hispanic widow. Had married an American man who died and left her with the building. Barely spoke English. Never cared if we paid rent late. Never harassed us about the noise we made or anything like that. So, my mom starts making more money, the years go by, and we move away. And then one day, I'm probably ten or eleven, she goes back to see Elena, and she makes her this offer. Says she wants to get into real estate. Offers to buy the whole building off her."

Quinn watched him, confused and intrigued by the story.

"So Elena says no, and Elena says no, and Savannah assures her that they'll be partners, that she can be as involved as she wants, that she'll get more than her fair share in the process. That she can finally retire one day."

This story was starting to sound too familiar... like the story of Kurt's father and Cole Crowley.

"So finally Elena agrees, and they sit down and start to go over paperwork. And Elena stares at the paperwork in disbelief, because the way it is worded, Elena is supposed to give Savannah the building for free.

"That's when Savannah explains that she knows about Elena's little sister— the illegal immigrant with two children. Next thing I know, we're the proud new owners of an apartment building. And we're no poorer. All Savannah had to do was threaten to have Elena's family deported. The poor woman signed in seconds."

Quinn shuddered. Crowley and Savannah really were two peas in a pod, she marveled.

"And it's not just that," he continued. "Savannah didn't even *keep* the apartments. The only reason she wanted them was because she'd caught wind that the neighborhood was gentrifying. She bulldozed the building immediately and now it's a Whole Foods."

"And Elena's family?"

"Still got deported."

Just like Kurt. Still killed.

"Elena left, too. I think Savannah ruined America for her. Look, I guess what I'm trying to say is... Savannah can convince you of anything with the right tactics, or the right threats, on her side. I believe Tommy, Izzo, and Roxy are all good people. But I also believe that she could poison them into thinking *we're* the bad people—that or, more simply, that none of us stand a chance against this nuke. She could poison them into thinking whatever she wanted."

"That's why you were so careful, isn't it? In who you let into the resistance. You knew how far she would go to get people on her side."

He nodded. "It is. But we would've had to come to this, anyway, wouldn't we? The attack's in three days. Everyone would have to make their choices now, if they hadn't already."

It helped, but not much.

• • •

Quinn decided to go see Tommy and Izzo when she left Dash's. She wasn't sure there was anything she could do, but she figured she could at least try. She knew she'd have better luck with them than with Roxy, the woman she'd probably scared half to death during her escape to confront Reese.

She found Tommy and Izzo in the living quarters, huddled together on one cot, whispering.

Not a good sign, she thought grimly.

"Hey," she said, ignoring the looks she received from those she passed as she approached Tommy and Izzo. Everyone seemed to know everyone else's business in that little building, which of course meant everyone knew that Quinn had staged her own version of the investigation Tommy and Izzo were involved in.

Tommy and Izzo both turned to look at her—too quickly.

"Hey," Tommy said guardedly, smiling politely. "What's up, Quinn?"

"I just wanted to touch base with you. About what you learned. Crazy, isn't it? This Friday, our imminent demise?"

Tommy smiled awkwardly; Izzo didn't even fake it.

"How did you say you pulled that off?" Quinn asked them. "Just curious."

"Maybe if you'd been at the meeting where we planned everything," Izzo pointed out, "you might already know."

Strange, Quinn thought. Izzo had always been so shy—so quiet. Where was this coming from?

"Right," Quinn said, trying to keep her voice even, "but I wasn't. So maybe you could fill me in."

"We don't owe you anything," Izzo snapped, surprising Quinn further. "You might have the majority of the group wrapped around your finger, but not us. From the day you got here, I knew you were trouble, Quinn. And you kept proving me right, over and over again. Why all these people trust you is beyond me, but I don't.

234

So I'm not going to tell you anything."

To be fair, the girl had a point: Quinn had done plenty in her time at Siloh to lead anyone to distrust her. If that was truly Izzo's motive for what she was saying, perhaps Quinn would be satisfied with that.

But she wasn't satisfied. There was something more. The hatred in Izzo's eyes—it wasn't hatred caused by the story she was telling. It was deeper—darker. It was a hatred someone had brainwashed her into feeling.

And why wasn't Tommy saying anything?

"Okay," Quinn said, taking a seat on the edge of the cot without being invited. "Touché. I don't blame you for not trusting me. Let me talk, instead of ask. Let me tell you this. I know Savannah. I know her, and I know her business partner, Cole Crowley. I watched him give the command to shoot an innocent, sixteen-year-old boy—my best friend—who had done absolutely nothing wrong. I know what they're both capable of: murder and deceit. I know that they both have experience conning people into believing that they're *not* evil—that they have reasons, motivations behind everything they do. But it's not true. They're pure evil."

She watched their eyes closely. Tommy's, she had a read on. They were nervous. Afraid. Her words were getting to him.

But Izzo...

"Come on, Tommy," she said, standing up and grabbing him by the arm. "We don't need this."

Quinn sighed, grabbing Tommy by her other arm and looking him in the eyes. "Tommy," she said, locking on, compulsion mode activating. "Talk to me."

Tommy's lips parted, and he was close—*so close*— to saying what he wanted to say. The truth.

But Izzo pulled him away, and Quinn was left knowing only one thing:

They were lying.

• • •

Night settled in, and with it came Quinn's fear and desperation; chiefly, the knowledge that she was running out of time.

Izzo and Tommy had said Friday, which, if they had really been lying, could only mean one thing: it was going to happen sooner.

Now that they knew she was onto them, sooner could be any second.

She couldn't pound on Dash's door quickly enough.

"Forget plan B," she said the moment he answered. "You, me, and Rory. She has to see it. It's the only way."

Dash shook his head, looking tired. "They've already figured it out. It's Friday."

"They're lying! You said it yourself—Savannah's more than capable of poisoning their minds. You should have seen the hatred in Izzo's eyes. Out of nowhere. And Tommy... I'm sure of it, Dash. Rory *has* to have that premonition."

"Then you're going to have to let her."

• • •

She wasn't sure why, exactly, the idea had come to her not to use the others from plan B. It wasn't that she didn't trust them. It wasn't that she thought they were *hurting* the cause.

It was just that, when it came down to it, her abilities had the same weakness Dash had pointed out shortly after meeting her: they were tied to her emotions. And as much as she cared for everyone in the YA, and even many outside of it, there were only two people on that island who she felt a deep, burning whirlwind of passion towards. One was romantic. One was... familial. Almost maternal.

Dash and Rory.

Besides, if she was going to successfully force herself to let Rory see the visions she didn't want her to see, she needed to focus. No distractions.

The first thing she would have to do, she decided as she closed her eyes and took their hands, was stop focusing on the future—stop focusing on having a premonition. As Rory and Dash had both pointed out, that was up to Rory.

There was one other thing she could think of to focus on that would draw enough emotion out of her to power up Rory: Kurt.

It was always hard, thinking about Kurt. But something new happened this time: her rage at the injustice of what had happened to him spread. It spread to thoughts all of the other injustices she had learned of since coming to Siloh. She thought of Charlotte, the heroine she had known as Blackout, a woman who had not only been murdered but had also been set up to look like a mass murderer. She thought of everyone in the original resistance, who had been slaughtered right alongside Charlotte. She thought every other person in the world who had been killed for absolutely nothing.

The more she focused, the more she attempted to think of nothing but them, the wearier she became. She was exhausted. Exhausted by all of the pain. Exhausted by all of the cruelty in the world. As the exhaustion set in, she found her mind flashing back to something different entirely: Dash.

Not Dash now, touching her hand, transferring his massive powers into her, but Dash *then,* years ago, when she had been nothing but a small child in a pink blanket. She wasn't even sure *why,* exactly; that Dash had nothing to do with the situation at hand. He wasn't even *real;* he was a made-up memory; he had nothing to do with anything.

Maybe it was because she was reaching the brink, she mused. Her exhaustion was draining her powers. She was about to lose consciousness, to give up, to wind up right where she had started, and then the fight would be over, and Savannah and Crowley would win. It was the same mindset that little girl had before the event. That she was going to die. And that was when Dash—or whatever alternate reality version of Dash had been with her that night—had come to her.

Her thoughts of that Dash, whatever the motivation, kept her going. She let Dash's power continue to flow through her and into Rory.

And then, abruptly, it all stopped. Rory pulled away from them, eyes huge, voice tiny.

"It happens tonight."

• • •

Their session had taken hours, as it turned out. Long enough for dinner and the evening meetings to pass, for everyone on the fourth floor to curl up and settle in for bed. Long enough for everyone who had been promised refuge in exchange for their betrayal of the resistance—the alliance—to escape.

They sprinted up to the fourth floor together.

"*Evelyn!*" Dash shouted as they barged inside. "*Michael!*"

Evelyn and Michael looked up at them from the conversation they had been having with their son, alarmed. Quinn could see it in their eyes. They knew what it was about.

"It's been foreseen," Quinn told them, using her abilities to project her voice loud enough for the entire floor to hear it. Those who had been asleep rose; those who hadn't fell silent. All eyes were on her.

"The attack," she said. "It happens tonight. Just before sunrise."

Charlie shook his head, looking to his parents, shocked, confused. "No," he said. "No… they said Friday. They heard Friday. We need more time to prepare."

"*Who* said Friday?" Dash demanded, looking earnestly around the room. "Izzo? Tommy? Roxy? Where are they now?"

Eyes everywhere flittered around the room, terrified to realize that he was right: they were nowhere to be found. They were already gone.

"But how could you have seen it?" Haley asked them, stepping forward from her own conversation with Ridley. "Just the three of you? We couldn't generate enough power for a premonition between nine of us."

Quinn wasn't concerned about anyone's hurt feelings over not being invited; she had bigger fish to fry. "It doesn't matter. It's been seen."

"By who?" asked someone else—someone Quinn didn't recognize. "Who is this alleged seer?"

"It doesn't—" Quinn started to say, but Rory cut her off.

"It's me. Okay?" Seeing Quinn's frightened expression, Rory said to her, "We don't have to worry about trust any more, Quinn. Anyone who's decided to betray us is long gone."

Quinn looked around the room, scanning the faces. It did seem to be thinner in population than it had been previous nights, she hated to admit.

"Angel," Evelyn said. "I need you to scout the rest of the island. If what they say is true, there will be no one left from the other side."

Angel stepped forward. Quinn was unsurprised, but pleased, to see that she was still there with them, rather than the alliance. "And if they're wrong? If they're still here and they try to kill me?"

"Angel," Quinn said, walking over to her. She looked her straight in the eyes. "I know we never really got along, but I would never, *ever* intentionally send you in harm's way. We're not wrong. I promise."

Angel watched her for a moment, eyes still distrusting. But she seemed to realize what everyone else did: that those who were left were all to be trusted.

She nodded and made for the window.

"Okay," Michael said, straightening. "Trent, come forward."

Silence. No movement.

Quinn looked around, eyes wide. Where was he? What could he possibly be doing that was more important than this?

"I'm sure he's in the bathroom," Haley said quickly. "Or... down on patrol, maybe."

Michael nodded carefully. "Haley, Ridley—go scout the rest of the tower. Round up everyone and send them here. Rita—do you have the master list?"

Rita, the older, hyper-intelligent woman Quinn had met recently, stepped forward. She pulled out a clipboard. "I do."

"Everyone," Michael said. "Form a line in front of Rita. Single-file. She will check you all in. We'll find out who we're missing. Positions around the island for the attack have been charted based on abilities. She will give you your positions as she checks you in. If Angel returns with confirmation that Savannah's people are gone... We have only a few hours left to save ourselves."

· · ·

The line formed. Quinn heard murmurs, whispers, from every direction. The biggest trend she noticed was how many people wanted to flee.

"We could just leave," the man in front of her was saying. "With Savannah gone, the wall would be unmanned. We could let ourselves out. Escape."

"We could," Dash said to him. "And even if we were able to brave the open water, we would still face the alliance, along with Crowley's soldiers, when we got anywhere near dry land. And, sure, maybe we could take them. But then we would face a worse fate when the rest of the world heard of our breakout."

"And we would beat them, too," said another woman. "They don't stand a chance against us. At least in the real world, we wouldn't be trapped on this island like pigs ripe for the slaughter."

"We won't die," Quinn promised them. "We won't."

Angel made it back before Haley and Ridley did. She and Quinn exchanged a look upon her arrival; Quinn barely listened when she shared the news with the rest of them. There was no one on the island but them.

Quinn had almost made it to the front of the line by then. From what she could see of Rita's marked-up roster, there were a lot of people missing.

Charlie, Michael, and Evelyn stood at the front of the line, watching Rita check people off, eyes wide, panicked.

"Has anyone seen Trent yet?" Quinn asked, snapping them out of their trances.

"No," Charlie said. "But there's obviously no need to worry. Haley and Ridley will be back with him. They'll be back with lots of people. You know how we all get cooped up in this building. People wander."

He seemed to be convincing himself more than her, and when she realized why, it hit her like a punch in the stomach: Pence wasn't there, either.

She turned to Dash, heart stopping. *Pence?* she mouthed.

He looked just as flabbergasted as her. "I don't know," he whispered.

Haley and Ridley arrived a few minutes later. They were alone.

· · ·

The final roll call for those left on the island totaled at 76.

105 had been in the tower before sunset.

Quinn tried to focus as Rita, Evelyn, and Michael tried to give them all their positions. She knew all hope wasn't lost. Sure, Pence, Trent, and Roxy had been some of their most powerful means of defense. Sure, the resistance had stood a better chance protecting themselves against nuclear warheads with them on their side. But hope wasn't lost. They could still beat this.

But it wasn't the lack of hope that was on her mind as she let it all sink in. It was Charlie's face.

Charlie's face, and Pence's betrayal.

Pence's... and Trent's.

She wasn't sure which hurt more. Trent's, in a way. She had kissed the guy. She had exchanged so many flirtations with him, so many jokes, so many interactions... They had been friends.

But in a way, she almost couldn't blame him. He had been rejected by her. Haley had finally moved on. He had never been included to begin with. Always the cool guy back in the real world; always rejected here at Siloh. It was just like she had discovered at Drax's party when she had asked him about his history. *"And then you came here,"* she had said, *"and you were the cool kid again."*

"Am I, though?" he had asked her.

She had thought, hearing him say that, that he was no different from her. She had thought he put up a tough shell to cover his vulnerabilities. But maybe it was more than that. Maybe his soft side had been hardened, too.

And then there was Pence...

Charlie and Pence had been together for years before Quinn arrived. They were some of the first members of the resistance. They had trusted each other implicitly. Everyone else had trusted them implicitly. If there were any two people she could have pointed to and said there was no chance in hell they were double-crossing the resistance, it would have been them.

But that wasn't even the worst part. The worst part was that Pence had been double-crossing *him.*

Quinn had barely known Dash a fraction of the time Charlie and Pence had known each other. They'd fought with and resented each other for half of that time. They'd only really been *together* for a few days. If Charlie had been wrong about Pence after all that time, how could Quinn possibly be right about Dash?

He was whispering things to her. Touching her face. Telling her everything was going to be okay. But she wouldn't let herself listen to him. She couldn't believe anything that was happening, but above all, she couldn't believe him.

Not with so many people betraying their loved ones.

She knew, on some level, that it wasn't fair. She knew he had given her no real reason to doubt him. But they were on their deathbeds, and logic had gone out the window, and she was left with what she was always left with. Instinct.

Their positions for the shield were at opposite ends of the island. The most powerful had to spread out.

She rode next to him in the elevator. Walked next to him all the way to the parting point. Him, Haley, Ridley, and Rory. She held the girl's hand. Closed her eyes. Pretended, for the briefest of moments, that that hand was Kurt's.

And then they reached the parting point, and it was time for them to send Haley into the air.

Haley turned to Quinn, eyes heavy. She seemed to sense every emotion that Quinn was feeling. Quinn wondered whether it was a new ability stemming from her goddess mode, but decided that it was probably just what best friends did.

"You're a hero, you crazy girl," Haley said softly to Quinn, and she pulled her into a tight, fearless hug. "Now let's save our island."

A tear trickled down Quinn's cheek as she pulled back, looked Haley in the eye, and whispered, "Give it your all."

And then Haley kissed Ridley, and then Rory and Dash squeezed Haley's hand, and then she was gone. Glowing golden. Floating up into the sky.

It was time for the rest of them to say goodbye.

Quinn's exchange with Ridley was short—simple. He seemed to understand that she was all but lost; he didn't even try to hug her. He simply put his hands on her shoulders, looked straight into her soul, and smiled.

In that moment, Quinn noticed things about Ridley that she had never noticed before. She noticed the faint, intricate markings that were etched into his scales, just a shade lighter than the scales themselves—almost like art. She noticed the long, slender arch of his neck, so much more graceful than a mere regular's. She noticed the way his body almost seemed to glow every time he inhaled, and darken every time he exhaled.

He was beautiful, she thought to herself as she whispered goodbye to him. To see someone like him and be afraid… to see someone like him and dismiss him as a monster…

The world was an ugly place.

It was Rory's turn.

She was thankful that words weren't needed between the two of them, because she was sure that if she parted her lips to speak, she would only cry. She knelt down on one knee, looking into Rory's big, blue eyes—those eyes that were so much like Kurt's. But she didn't see Kurt in that moment. She just saw the girl that she had grown to care for more than life itself.

Let's be real, Rory said in her head, *you were never a huge fan of life itself. Just keep focusing on saving me.*

Quinn laughed out loud, but there was a sob mixed into her laugh, and she buried her head into the girl's hair, closing her eyes and thinking of nothing but that smell, nothing but that voice in her head.

And then Rory pulled away, and she was gone, and Ridley was gone.

And all that was left was Quinn and Dash.

He tried to kiss her goodbye. He tried to say more things to her. Tried to convey all of the feelings that she knew she was still feeling, too. But she didn't hear any of it. She couldn't.

She only heard three words: "I love you."

But those words only sent her away faster.

• • •

Her position in the perimeter was in between two people that she had come to care very much about—two people that she loved all the more for staying despite being virtually powerless. Angel and Drax.

Both of them were mostly silent as they stood on either side of her, a few yards apart, just far enough to have to raise their voices to be heard but not far enough to leave anyone feeling alone. That was the purpose of them being there, she supposed. Not just what Michael had said about 'transference of energy,' but also to remind those around them that they weren't alone.

The minutes ticked by slowly. The plan, as Evelyn and Michael had laid out before their departure, was to take formation, but not to produce the shield until exactly five o'clock. If Rory's vision had been precise, that would give them an hour of leeway before the sun began to rise, without draining their energy completely.

Finally, when five o'clock was upon them, she allowed herself to speak at full volume for the first time since she had learned of Pence and Trent's betrayal.

"I know they said to keep a few meters apart," she said to them, "but do you think you two could come a little closer?"

Angel and Drax both came to her side, and for what felt like the first time in her life, Quinn outstretched her hands to her friends.

If she was going to save this island, she was going to need help.

• • •

It was a thing to behold, that shield. Truly, it was.

Everyone was precise on the timing—almost instantaneous. The moment that second hand clicked into place, she went for it. Fire. Water. Ice. Stone. Abilities she didn't even know she had. Abilities she didn't understand.

She threw them all up into the sky.

And she wasn't alone.

It was a brilliant thing, full of light. Not unlike the walls they had casted that day at power tech, and yet so much more. It lit up the night with fire and lightning and rain; it emitted heat; it emitted cold; it emitted everything. It truly did look as if nothing could to get in its way.

But looks could be deceiving, she reminded herself. There were no guarantees. The shimmering, terrifying, magnificent shield up above her could very well be the last thing she would ever see.

She closed her eyes. Inhaled. Exhaled. But no matter how hard she tried to push it away, the same thought kept coming back to her.

The shield wasn't the last thing she wanted to see.

He was.

. . .

She wasn't sure how long it had been. She wasn't sure whether the bomb had already come, whether it had gone, or whether it was in the middle of its detonation. She wasn't sure what was going on at all. All she knew was that when she opened her eyes, Angel and Drax were on either side of her, passed out, energies drained— no doubt by her. *Transference of energy.* Michael had been right. The shield was still up above her.

She sat there, still as a statue, legs curled up to her chest, alone again, afraid.

And that was when he she heard it. The voice.

"Hey."

Her eyes widened, and she knew to turn and look, to do the logical thing, and yet she was paralyzed, stuck in some strange, alternate universe, some déjà vu, some *memory,* because she knew that voice, she knew that word, she knew this situation…

"Hey," the voice said again. It was his voice. Dash's. Soft, mystical… Unlike any other voice she had ever heard.

"Please don't be afraid of me."

It was him. Him, the man from that night, the man that had protected her when she was just a child… Dash.

"You can trust me," he whispered, and he held out his hand.

A tear streamed down her cheek as she put it all together. She could almost hear Rory's voice in her head, smirking. *Told you you're a seer.*

Because, of course, she had foreseen this.

And as the bright light came and swallowed them up, and everything turned to darkness, at least she was not alone.

13. SAVE SILOH

As it turned out, they didn't all die.

In fact, none of them did.

They kept the shield up for hours—probably far longer than they actually needed to. Slowly, piece by piece, it began to unravel. Person by person, they each collapsed, exhausted, until finally there was nothing left of the shield.

But there was nothing left of the bomb, either. Or the fallout.

When Quinn finally woke up, she was still in the grass on the edge of the perimeter, back to the wall. Angel was still on one side of her, and Drax was on the other. And Dash...

Well, he was right under her.

She couldn't help but grin when she rolled off of him, watching his sleeping face with a mixture of love and amusement.

His eyelids fluttered open as if he knew he was being watched; when he saw her, he smiled.

"What are you laughing at?" he asked her.

Her grin faded, and what was left was something more.

"I wasn't crazy," she told him softly. "Thinking I'd seen you that day. The event. I *did* see you. It was my first premonition. My first... *anything*."

He stared at her, processing. "You're saying... during the event... you had a premonition? Of what just happened?"

"Word for word. Exactly the words you said to me. Exactly the way you look right now. Down to the outfit. Even that bright white light I saw... It was Haley. Haley in her goddess mode."

He shook his head, eyes full of wonder. "That's incredible."

"I know. If that's not the universe trying to convince me you're my soul mate, I don't know what is."

"Get a room," Drax said from next to them as he came to, stretching and yawning. "Which, apparently, we still have. Nice to see our home hasn't been completely obliterated."

"Not even a little," Angel said from their other side, rising to her feet. "Do you think everyone's okay?"

They all rose to their feet, making their way to the center of the island to report back to the tower. But they stopped outside of the building, knowing that there really wasn't any reason to hide out there any more. Savannah was gone. Everyone who wanted to hurt them was gone.

For now.

The others filtered in slowly. Some stayed unconscious longer than others. Quinn counted silently in her head as people approached them. *35... 36...*

She stopped short when she saw number 37.

It was Pence.

Before she knew what she was doing, Quinn was attacking her.

"*What did you do?*" she shouted at her old friend, knocking into her at lightning speed and pinning her to the ground. Her hands grew hot as coals as she seared burns into Pence's wrists. She could feel Pence trying to put out the flames with her own abilities, but it was no use.

"Stop!" Pence shrieked, writhing beneath her. "Quinn, I came back! I came back before the attack! There are witnesses!"

"*Why did you leave in the first place?*" Quinn demanded, not letting up. She couldn't help it. After all the progress Quinn had made on the island learning to trust people again, Pence had made her question everything. She couldn't let it slide. She just couldn't.

"Quinn!" Charlie shouted, running up to her and knocking her off Pence and onto the ground. If not for his speed and the element of surprise, it wouldn't have worked, but it did. "Stop it!"

"Why?" Quinn asked him, shoving him off her. "Why should I forgive her for what she did to you—to all of us? Are you trying to tell me she didn't run away?"

"I did run away," Pence said, raising her hands in the air in surrender. Quinn tried not to look at the severe burns she had given the girl. "I did. And I'm sorry. I just... My family's still out there, Quinn. They don't even know whether I'm alive or dead. For them to hear about all of us dying in a nuclear attack, on the six o'clock news—to never see me or talk to me again? I couldn't bear it."

Angel stepped into the mix at that point, surprising both Pence and Quinn.

"My family's still out there, too," she told Pence. "I'm sure lots of people here still have family out there. I'm sure none of them know whether we're okay or not. But *this* is my family now, Pence. Has been for years. And as much as I can't stand a lot of them, I'd never betray them."

Pence swallowed. "I know. And that's why I came back."

"Are you sure?" Quinn asked darkly. "Are you sure you weren't *sent* back? The word got in Savannah's ear that we weren't all going to die, and she sent you to report back?"

"No," Pence said desperately. "It was never about going to Savannah or the alliance. I never even let them see me. Compel me to tell the truth, Quinn. Use Rory. Use whatever you can. You have to believe me. *No.*"

Quinn sighed. She could probably compel her to tell the truth. She could probably ask Rory to help. But at this point, she was starting to trust her own telepathic abilities. She was starting to trust that she knew when someone was lying.

And Pence wasn't lying.

More than anything, it was a relief. It made her happy. It made her feel like she might be able to let herself trust Dash again.

But it still annoyed her.

"Fine," she said, turning her back on the girl. "But don't expect me to like you any more."

"That's quite enough," Evelyn said, stepping forward. "We have reached our count. I am happy to say we lost no one during the attack. In fact, we even *gained* someone." She smiled over at Pence, who she had clearly already forgiven for running away. Quinn rolled her eyes.

"What do you all think about reclaiming our old dining hall?" Michael suggested.

Ridley nodded, eyes bright. "I think it's time we reclaim our whole island."

• • •

They all headed to the dining hall for the meeting about what to do next. As usual, Evelyn and Michael took the floor first. The YA—what was left of them—along with Ridley, Rory, and Zerrick, sat in the front row. Quinn could tell that just like her, they were all about ready for their voices to be heard.

"We have won this battle," Evelyn announced to all of them, "but not the war. We must now decide what to do next."

Quinn raised her hand immediately. Evelyn glared down at her, clearly not finished with her speech, but she let Quinn speak.

"I just wanted to point out that you have some people in your midst who have proven pretty spot-on about seeing the future," Quinn said. "So maybe, you know, you could trust us a little more this time around."

"Very good," Evelyn said, clearly annoyed; "but have you had a vision yet? About what comes next?"

Quinn crossed her arms. "No. I'm just saying."

Pence raised her hand next. "I was only in the real world for a few hours, but there were some things I learned there. Things that could be useful."

"You made it to the real world," Quinn asked doubtfully, "without Savannah or the alliance seeing you?"

"The alliance and the DCA guarded nearly the entire path to Fiji, like you all predicted. But they were all airborne or in boats. It was easy for me to make the whole trip underwater, undetected."

Quinn nodded, satisfied with this answer.

"Once I made it to Fiji, I saw Savannah, Reese, and several of the others camped out at this little cottage right on the coast. Plotting their next move. I waited for them to fall asleep and snuck into the cottage to use Savannah's computer. I got on to the internet there and tried to track down my family—get an idea of how hard it would be to get home. On the internet, I learned about this deviant rights movement that's emerged since Quinn was captured. It's called Save the Siren."

Quinn choked on her own breath, eyes widening. "*What*?"

Dash laughed out loud.

"I'm serious," Pence said. "Turns out you had this, like, mega fan base of regulars back there who were rooting for you—hoping you wouldn't get caught, then fighting for your rights once you were. They've used you as an example and are pushing this whole movement to free not only you, but all of us."

"Wouldn't we have heard of this movement?" Rory asked, frowning. "We have the same TV channels as them. We have the same internet access as them."

"Actually," Rita told Rory, "that's not entirely true. While we do have access to their cable channels, the censored internet access Savannah and Crowley allowed us to have was… minimal, at best. 'For our protection,' Savannah always said. Shouldn't be hard for me to undo."

"Save the Siren never made it to the live news," Pence explained to Rory. "Dangerous publicity, I guess. But the online movement is huge."

"That's a nice story," Michael said to her, "but I don't really see how—"

"What I'm saying is," Pence said impatiently, "the world is already thinking of us in terms of human rights. They're still scared of us, but they're thinking of us. What we have to do now is lead our own internet movement. We call it… I don't know… 'We're Not the Monsters.' We show them what life's really like here—tell them that we just want peace—tell them someone tried to nuke us. Make versions with subtitles in every language… Accessible to the entire world."

Evelyn and Michael glanced at each other, considering this.

"I think it's a decent idea," Quinn admitted. "Not quite as violent as I'd like, but I guess it's about time the world figured out what's really going on here. And we could expose Savannah and Crowley for the monsters they really are."

"We should appeal directly to world leaders if we are going to do this at all," Angel said. "The UNCODA were always more on our side than the DCA—they're more likely to listen. Releasing some public, online statement, directed at no one in particular… It's going to be disregarded by the people who really make the decisions."

"You're both right," Drax said. "We *should* appeal to the UNCODA. But we should also appeal to the public. Chances are, the UNCODA will just ignore us if all we do is make a private plea to them. They hate conflict—it's the same reason they told the DCA to stop killing deviants. But if we do both, the UNCODA will have no choice but to respond, because the public will be watching them."

Dash nodded. "Drax is right. It's the best shot we've got."

"Very well," Evelyn said. "With Savannah gone, we should be able to lift the restrictions she kept over the internet. Rita—I'm sure you could help me with that."

"I've got a camcorder," volunteered Simon, the English teacher. "It's not the best, but it's probably better than a cell phone."

"We'll need some sort of script," Michael said. "And a face. Someone to speak to the camera, to tell our story to the world."

"Quinn," Rory said automatically. "Obviously. Pence just said there's a whole movement to save her. She's by far the most famous of all of us. And she's the most familiar to them, since she was there the longest."

Quinn shook her head immediately. "No. I might have some fans out there, but the majority of the public was scared shitless of me. The last thing we want is to make them afraid of us."

"Quinn's right," Dash said. "And as much as I hate to say it, it shouldn't be anyone visibly affected. Not right away. We need to appeal to their emotional sides—show them someone relatable. Someone they could love."

"Haley," Ridley said, standing up. "She's perfect. She's soft-spoken. Smart. Attractive. Young enough that she can't properly be feared, but old enough that she won't be considered naïve."

Everyone seemed to like this idea. Quinn grinned as she watched Haley's soft brown skin turn crimson.

"I agree," Pence said, "but I have to point out something: If we put a kid in there, too, our emotional appeal skyrockets."

Quinn stiffened, knowing what came next. "Not Rory."

Rory turned to Quinn, eyes immediately narrowing. "Excuse me?"

"Quinn," Dash said, turning to look at her. "It's not a bad idea. They'll fall in love with her. They'll be furious at the thought of someone trying to kill her."

"She's just a *child*! She'd become a target!"

"If she did," Evelyn told Quinn, "we'd protect her. But the point is that she *isn't* a target. The point is that no one in their right mind would consider her one."

Quinn understood her point. But she also understood what they did not: how many people out there weren't in their right minds.

• • •

The meeting broke up shortly after that. Pence and Charlie, it was decided, were to direct the video. Rita and Simon would be in charge of the technical aspects of it, including lifting the internet filters and blocks. Rory and Haley, of course, would star in it. They insisted that the rest of the YA, plus Dash and Ridley, be heavily involved in the content creation.

But there was something Quinn wanted to do first.

"We need to have another premonition," she told them as the majority of the room filed out, leaving just their group to plan. "I like this video idea—I think it's the best we've got—but we still need to know what they're planning. What if they're faster? What if they're planning on trying again?"

"I doubt they're planning on trying *that* one again," Dash said; "it's not exactly an inexpensive strategy. But you're right. If we can, we should."

"How did you end up doing it last time?" Charlie asked Rory. "None of us were there."

"It was just me, Quinn, and Dash," Rory told him. "And it wasn't easy. But that was before."

Quinn sighed, knowing what was coming.

"Before what?" Pence asked.

"Before Quinn realized she's a seer, too."

"How do you even know that?" Quinn asked, rolling her eyes. But she already knew the answer. Their two minds were practically one by now.

"So, you're saying it might be easier now," Ridley said. "Like, what, you just hold hands and close your eyes and wham, vision?"

Quinn glanced at Rory, shrugging. "Worth a shot, isn't it?"

Rory extended her hand, and Quinn took it.

Wham.

Gunshots.

Not just gunshots. Fireballs. Illusions. Invisible attacks. The abilities of those who had betrayed them—the alliance—fighting alongside an army of regulars.

Quinn searched for anything in the vision, any indications of when this attack would be, of how long they had to prepare. Finally, she realized it: she was herself in the vision. It was like a lucid dream. She could act however she wanted.

She pulled out her phone and looked at the date.

One week.

• • •

"We add it to the video," Charlie said when Quinn and Rory told them what they had seen. "We say, guess what, world? You tried nuking us, and when that didn't work, you sent soldiers in. We know it's coming and we're telling you, *no.*"

Quinn rolled her eyes. "Like that'll work."

"We could redirect the video toward Cole and Savannah," Pence offered. "Tell them we know they're coming. Tell them we want to talk to them. Face-to-face. No weapons, no threats. Work it all out."

"Work it out?" Quinn laughed out loud. "Pence, they don't even know the meaning of the words."

"We force them to," Pence pushed. "We set up a live stream. We record them from the moment they land here. If they go straight into attack mode, the public knows. If either of them wimps out and doesn't show, the public knows. Basically, if they do anything but have a peaceful meeting with us to arrange terms of peace and freedom, the public knows."

"I think we're taking a step backwards," Angel said. "Our plan was to direct this at the UNCODA, not the DCA. Crowley's DCA. American. We already know all the Americans want us dead."

"The UNCODA will still see it," Dash told her. "Everyone will. But think about the timing. If we direct it toward the UNCODA, even if we finish and upload it in a few days, we'll never get a proper response by the time the attack comes.

Not from anyone that matters. Then we get attacked, and our attackers blame us, and the UNCODA decides we are too violent to work with. We lose our one opportunity."

Angel sighed. She seemed to understand his point.

"Well," Pence said, "I guess that settles that. Let's get shooting."

• • •

High, wide shot. Swooping over the beautiful scenery of the island, revealing its buildings, its river, its horse farm, its woods. Courtesy of Angel and her wings.

Cut to: Haley and Rory.

"Hello," Haley says, smiling a calm, serene smile. "My name is Haley Mylar."

"And I'm Rory Malone."

"This is our home."

Cut to: Pence and Charlie, flirting in the courtyard. Charlie zips over to Pence, knocking into her playfully and bending down to kiss her. She laugh-shrieks, squirting him with a gentle douse of water.

Haley: "You know this place as Devil's Island. You think it's a prison, where we are confined to cells, locked away, never to be thought of again. But it's not."

Rory: "We know this place as Siloh. And, by the way, you couldn't lock us away if you tried. Seriously."

Haley smiles. "What Rory means to say is"— we cut to Angel, flying high over the wall, yet not yet leaving—"we have stayed here, on this island, where you put us, for years, even though most of us have the abilities necessary to escape, because we respect your wishes. We don't want to harm you. We don't want to scare you. We've been mostly happy here."

Cut to: kids about Rory's age, one with feathery, fluffy skin and birdlike eyes, yet still quite obviously innocent; the other teleporting around her friend in two-foot bursts. They are playing.

Rory: "But last night, a very evil man named Cole Crowley, who you all for some strange reason put in charge of the Deviant Collection Agency, dropped a

254

nuclear bomb on our home."

Haley: "Don't worry. We're fine."

"It's just, you see, I have the ability to see the future. I saved us all by foreseeing that a bomb was going to be dropped, which is how we were able to— very easily—put up a shield and protect ourselves. Now I foresee that Mr. Crowley is going to send an army of people here to kill us. Look, guys, we don't want to fight you. We don't want to hurt you. We've only ever used our abilities to defend ourselves. But if you don't stop trying to kill us, we might have to fight back."

"To be clear, isn't a threat. This is a request, directed at Mr. Crowley."

Cut to: footage of Cole Crowley giving a speech at a shareholder's meeting. Face to name.

Rory: "Right, but also directed toward the public, because we don't trust Mr. Crowley as far as we could throw him. Which, by the way, is really far."

Cut to: a monster in his thirties with gigantic arms pitching a baseball across the entire island.

Haley: "Mr. Crowley, come to Siloh. We will be live-streaming your arrival. We will show the world that we don't intend to harm anyone. Never have. But we do want to talk. We need to talk."

"Yeah. You need to stop trying to kill us."

· · ·

"I don't know," Quinn said, shaking her head. "The tone is cute and playful, but the situation is serious. People's lives are on the line."

It had been three days since they had decided to make the video. After extensive planning, shooting, and editing, they had finally settled on the version they screened in the dining hall for the entire resistance. As always, everyone had an opinion.

"We do clearly state that a nuclear bomb was dropped on us," Haley pointed out. "Sure, it's a little gimmicky, but only enough to make us relatable. If we went any darker, we'd be isolating ourselves from them. They have to like us."

"I don't know, either," said Dash. "Rory gets a little wild there talking about her visions and how she saved us all. I'm wondering whether we've lost cute twelve-year-old Rory to psychic demon child Rory."

"I am totally still cute!" Rory objected.

"Cute, yes," Quinn said, growing queasy at the memory of Rory's lines in the video. "Insane, also. Rory, you're telling the entire world that you're the most powerful of all of us. You're making yourself a target for every foreign government official, every bureau, every—"

"She's also making herself a star," said Pence. "The public's going to love her, just like they loved you. And after everything we've told them about Crowley trying to kill us… They're going to be looking out for us. They're not going to let anything happen to Rory without a fight."

"Yeah," Quinn said grumpily, "well, neither are we."

Dash smiled softly, putting an arm around Quinn. "Don't worry," he whispered to her. "This is good."

"So, what do we do now?" Haley asked, turning to glance at Rita and Simon. "We just… hit 'post?'"

Simon nodded. "Rita designed the website. We were actually all fans of 'We're Not the Real Monsters,' but we decided it was more of a subheading. We decided to name the movement, and the website, 'Save Siloh.'"

Quinn nodded. It was a much better alternative.

"We will also be uploading to Facebook, YouTube, Twitter, and a handful of other websites I've never heard of," Rita explained. "Along with anonymous submissions to every legitimate government website, newspaper, and media outlet I could find. We're adding hashtags and links to the Save the Siren campaign along with all smaller human rights campaigns fighting for the cause. At the very least, this should be seen by a few hundred thousand. At the most…"

"Everyone," Simon finished for her.

"More or less."

"So that's it, then?" Quinn asked. "We think this will work?"

Pence gave a weak, simple shrug. "It has to."

· · ·

It did.

It reached a hundred thousand views in minutes. A hundred thousand shares within hours. A million views by lunch. By the time the sun set, twenty million.

Plus, a phone call from Cole Crowley.

It was for Quinn, of course.

They were back in Haley and Quinn's old dorm room when he called. She switched to speaker phone before answering, allowing Haley, Ridley, Dash, and their recording device to listen in.

"Ah," he said when she answered. She shuddered at the sound of his voice, a voice she hadn't heard since the day she lost Kurt. She fought as hard as she could to remain calm. "Miss Harper. So refreshing to hear your voice again."

"Really? 'Cause I thought maybe the nuclear bomb you dropped on me was some kind of indication that you weren't my biggest fan."

"On the contrary, I was always a fan of yours, Quinn. I had high hopes that you would join the alliance—escape that rotten place and come to work for me."

"I'd rather die."

"Clearly."

She wasn't sure she could continue this conversation much longer without unintentionally starting a very hot, very large fire. "What do you want, Crowley? Does this call mean you'll meet with us?"

"That's not what this phone call is about, specifically." He seemed to sense that he was being recorded. "I'll be releasing a public video directed toward you tomorrow—learned from the best, you know."

She gripped the phone tighter. God, how she loathed him.

"No, Quinn, this phone call is me telling you how much trouble you've caused for me. And me reminding you how bad things can get for people who cause me trouble."

Her throat was dry. Her face was hot. She looked up at Dash, who clearly sensed all of the rage she was feeling. His comforting gaze was the only thing keeping her together.

"However much trouble I caused you," she hissed at Crowley, "it's not enough. Death wouldn't be enough for you, you sick fuck. Immeasurable pain for the rest of your life wouldn't be enough."

Dash squeezed her hand, his face pained. It was incredible to her, the thought of someone else loving her so much that he felt her pain as if it was his own. It was a feeling she had almost forgotten since losing Kurt. She wished she could express to him in that moment how much it meant to her. She doubted he had any idea.

But Crowley's words snapped her out of her lovesick thoughts and back into her harsh reality.

"I'll see you next week, Quinn. Do take care. You'll need it."

• • •

They discussed releasing the recording of Quinn and Crowley's conversation to the public, but decided against it. It wasn't incriminating enough; besides, Quinn's threats about death and immeasurable pain wouldn't exactly help their cause.

They spent the next week training in a way Quinn was more familiar with: one-on-one combat. The only difference: guns were involved.

Tranquilizer guns, but still.

The biggest rule the resistance had agreed upon was that they would kill as few people as possible. They would be armed with fast-acting tranquilizer guns only. Of course, many of the members of the resistance—Quinn and Dash included—would have no need for guns; their abilities would do the trick. But for people like Ridley, Drax, and Angel, not having one was not an option.

Using tranquilizers for practice, Quinn decided, worked in her favor. Real gunshots did just about nothing to her. They caused her pain, certainly. They weren't fun. But her skin always forced them out with ease and healed right up. Strong enough tranquilizers actually managed to sedate her—if only briefly.

For the most part, she was good at dodging them. Drax, she learned quickly, was a terrible shot. Hank wasn't great. But Ridley and Angel were both impressive marksmen, and before long, she was on the verge of passing out from all of the sedatives flowing through her.

"The training is going well," Michael announced to all of them a few evenings later at the dinner meeting. "We're pleased with everyone's progress and have high hopes and confidence for what the future holds. Of course, to some extent, this is all precautionary. Our videos have been streamed and shared all over the world by millions upon millions of people. Crowley put out a response video that was weak, to say the least. Tried to convince everyone we had been threatening the world with some kind of mass, organized destruction. Said the attack had been a 'necessary evil' but that he is now ready to try diplomacy for the sake of the world's safety. Load of BS, clearly. They're saying his approval rating is in the toilet. None of his shareholders knew that he was the director of the DCA; many of them are livid. The stocks for his company are plummeting. Everyone will be watching what he does next. It would be idiotic of him to still try to attack us."

"You don't know him," Quinn warned. "I wouldn't be so sure."

"He *is* an idiot, in some ways," Dash told them. "But he's a genius in others. He'll have something planned. Something none of us would have thought of."

"Which is why we need to get into the specifics," Evelyn said. "Plan A and plan B. Plan A: All goes according to plan. Crowley does not attack. What then? What, exactly, do we ask for?"

"To be left alone," Hank suggested.

"That's not enough," Ridley told him. "We ask to be left alone, we're right where we started. We must ask to be *free*. To be independent. To be granted rights, the ability to write our own laws. To be able to travel, to trade."

"Maybe we could become a U.S. territory?" suggested Drax.

Boo's and screams erupted throughout the hall.

"You've got to be kidding me," Angel said to him, disagreeing with her best friend for one of the first times ever. "A U.S. territory? After all our country has done to us? Why would we *want* that?"

"Because we could demand things that way," Charlie said, understanding where Drax was going with it. "Reparations, for the way we were treated by them. Stipends of goods shipped to us for x-amount of years until we get on our feet. Money. Tax breaks. Their attention and protection, were we to be attacked by foreign countries. They'd have to at least consider it, if we asked. We're all Americans. Hell, most of us are native New Yorkers."

"No," Quinn said, standing up. "I'm sorry, but no. Charlie, Drax—everything you're both saying makes sense. It does. But you don't understand. Even if Crowley submits for now—even if he plays the game—he will *never* let us be free. Crowley *owns* this island. Okay? And he's an American, and as far as we know, this is American soil. As long as that's the case, he will think he owns us. He will continue to manipulate us and destroy us from the inside out."

Everyone fell silent, absorbing the significance of what she was saying.

"No matter what happens when Crowley gets here," she said, "no matter what he says… we *must* demand independent sovereignty. And if he says no, we take it to the UNCODA. Not the DCA. Not America. The world."

The silence remained. Drax's eyes were wide. He almost seemed ashamed of his suggestion.

"We vote," Michael said. "All those in favor of requesting to be a U.S. territory."

To her amazement, not a single person raised a hand.

"Very well," Michael said. "Independent sovereignty it is. My next question is this: How many of you would want to leave Siloh altogether? To move back to America, or another country entirely?"

More people than Quinn would have expected raised their hands. She realized she didn't even know the answer she herself should give.

"We will add that option in," Evelyn said.

Haley raised her hand, not waiting to be called on before speaking. "What do these conditions have to do with Cole Crowley? He's in charge of the DCA, not the United States Congress. He doesn't speak for the United States or the world."

"You're right," Dash told her, "and you're wrong. Crowley is America's authority on all things having to do with this island. Not to mention, as Quinn said, he *owns* the island. Politicians know of him. Law enforcement knows of him. They've all chosen to let him handle it, to run the DCA, simply so they could wash their hands of it."

"But even if he agrees to our terms," Rory asked, "will they?"

Dash smiled sadly at her. "It'll at least get them to pay attention."

She nodded quietly.

"Very well," Evelyn said, straightening. "This gives us a better feel for what terms of peace we should set. Now, for the terms of war, should it come to that."

And the battle strategy began.

. . .

Live stream. Handheld.

Open on a close-up: Quinn Harper. The Siren.

"Yeah, I know, you've all been wondering what happened to me," Quinn tells the camera. "Well, they kept me away for that first video. Didn't want me to scare you all. But seeing as I'm what you could call our friend Mr. Crowley's prime objective, we figured you'd see me sooner or later. Might as well be now."

Camera pans to: Dash Collins.

"And him. Crowley wants him, too. Pretty, isn't he?"

Camera makes a quick U-turn to reveal its wielder: Pence. She rolls her eyes.

"Mr. Crowley should be arriving any minute," Quinn says. The camera pans back to her. "Now, I need to make one thing very clear to anyone who may be watching: we don't want trouble. We just want to talk to Mr. Crowley. So if this live stream cuts off for any reason, or if you see him attacking any of us—"

. . .

"Stop," Rita shouted from her spot at a laptop nearby. "Stop!"

Quinn looked over at Rita, confused. "What?"

"We're not broadcasting any more. Something's wrong."

Quinn glanced out to the east, scanning the skies. Was Crowley landing? Was he close enough in range that he could already tamper with their signals?

Sure enough, she spotted his helicopter on the horizon. And behind it... Countless others.

It could just be precautionary, she tried to tell herself. *A security measure... just in case something were to go wrong.*

But she knew she couldn't kid herself. It was an army.

"We should still record this," Pence said, keeping the camera up. "He might be able to stop us from live streaming, but he can't stop us from filming altogether."

"Not unless he breaks our camera," Charlie pointed out. "Let me take it. We'll need you more than me if a fight comes. Besides, I can run from anyone who tries to tamper with it."

Pence nodded, handing the camera over to Charlie. She glanced back at Quinn, eyes full of concern. "Is this it? Is it going to be a battle?"

Quinn hesitated, but she knew the answer. It had been clear in his voice during the phone call. It was clear from the army of helicopters behind his. The answer was yes.

She didn't end up having to answer; Evelyn did it for her.

"It's going to be a fight."

"We could put up a shield again," Angel said, running up to them. "Cast it out at them... Keep them from making it to the island."

"We can't," Evelyn said somberly. "That shield was a hostile mixture of elements designed to incinerate anything that touched it. We'd kill dozens of them before they even figured out what it was."

"Well, then we should start firing at them," Angel urged. "Not to kill them— just to bang them up. Scare them. Maybe they'd turn away."

Evelyn glared at her, gesturing to the camera, which was still rolling. "Even if we think they're going to attack us, you know we can't throw the first stone, Angel. We need to prove to the rest of the world that we're not the problem. That we're the *victims*."

Angel sighed. It was clear that she knew Evelyn was right, as much as she hated to admit it.

"We won't always be the victims," Quinn said softly to Angel, offering her the most encouraging smile she could muster. She could feel Charlie panning the camera over toward her, but she ignored it. This wasn't about the camera. It was about the fact that despite their rivalry, despite any issues Quinn had ever had with Angel, Angel had stayed on the right side of things. She hadn't betrayed her friends, and she hadn't buckled out of fear when things got tough. If she needed support, Quinn would offer it willingly. "We're showing the world who we are. Who we *really* are—not who they've twisted us to become. I'm not worried about how it will go with Crowley today. I know that we'll win. And I know that we're good, and that we're right. And soon, the rest of the world will, too."

Angel nodded, offering Quinn a small smile in return. "I know." She took a deep breath. "I know."

Dash took Quinn's hand, squeezing it gently.

But none of them had any more time to linger on the plan, because Crowley's helicopter was landing.

With no regard for who stands below it, Quinn mused grimly as she watched people scatter beneath its shadow.

Crowley stepped out first, gesturing to the pilot to kill the engine to reduce the noise as he headed straight for Quinn and Dash.

"Ah," he said, extending his arms as if coming over to hug them. "My two favorite monsters."

Quinn snorted. "You took down our live stream. There's no need for pleasantries."

"Those weren't pleasantries," Dash told her, glaring at Crowley. "We're not monsters."

"Oh, but you are. You accepted that, Quinn, for so long. Didn't you? You acted accordingly with your nature. Why try to change that now? The world has already seen the real you. Why try to pretend?"

"I was what the world forced me to be, in order to survive," she snarled at him. "I never had a chance to figure out who I really was. Not until I came here."

"Right. This 'godforsaken' place that I allowed you all to live and prosper in. And what was the thanks I got? Secret allegiances? 'The resistance?'"

"You weren't 'allowing' us to do anything," Haley said, stepping forward. She may have never met Crowley before that day, but Quinn could tell from her tone that she hated him already. "You put up with our limited freedom so that Savannah could build an obedient little army for you, all the while gathering secrets and intel on the rest of us so that you could slaughter us when it best suited you."

"That is preposterous," he said, smug gaze suggesting that she was spot-on.

The other helicopters were landing. Quinn saw figures in the distance coming over to them. Most, she didn't recognize. Some, she did. Shade, Tommy, and...

Trent.

She had to look away the moment she saw him. His eyes were sad, but it didn't help.

"Quite an army you brought," Dash said to Crowley. "You know—considering you're here to talk terms of peace."

Crowley chuckled. "Mr. Collins, you are quite possibly even stupider than your dead girlfriend."

Quinn saw it coming a mile before it happened, and she didn't blame him in the slightest: Dash was going for the punch.

But she stopped him—for one, because she was the only one who could; and for another, because they were still recording everything, and they couldn't be the ones to throw the first punches. No matter how hard they were provoked.

"Save it, Crowley," she hissed. "There's nothing you can say that will surprise us. We all know you murdered Blackout in cold blood. We all know you framed her at the embassy. We all know you murdered my best friend after promising you'd let him go. We all know you're a sick, twisted shell of a man. But we're not going to throw the first punch. We're going to prove to the world that *we wanted peace.* And you were the one who attacked us. Again."

"Won't matter, anyway." He gestured to his soldiers to come into formation. "We will win, we will destroy the video, and that, as they say, will be that."

. . .

Quinn, Dash, Ridley, and everyone else in the group that was bulletproof stood front and center when the shooting started. They absorbed the bullets for everyone else. Zerrick stood just behind them, telekinetically forcing guns away from their wielders; Charlie zipped through the thick of it, simultaneously recording the whole thing while removing as many guns as he could safely do.

The hardest part for Quinn was not being able to unleash her abilities onto them. They were recording the battle, which meant the more violent she was, the more the real world would fear her. And besides that, she didn't want to kill anyone.

Well, she corrected herself, *except one person.*

From the moment the shooting began, three people circled around Crowley, protecting him. One was Shade, which didn't worry Quinn, who had long since mastered overcoming his illusions. *Thank you, power tech,* she thought; *thank you, Dash.* The second was Shield. Back at Crowley Enterprises, when she'd relied on her compulsion, Shield had scared her—him, and the threats that had been made against Kurt. But Kurt was gone, and she didn't have to rely on her compulsion any more. She had support; she had friends. Powerful friends.

The third person protecting Crowley, Quinn didn't recognize. He was a regular, she decided as she watched him shoot his gun. He was nothing.

She wanted to embrace her instincts—attack Crowley, then and there.

She *could,* she was convinced. No one protecting him was strong enough to beat her. She could kill him.

But just before she could make her move, she heard a scream. Rory's scream.

Suddenly, Crowley didn't matter. Nothing mattered but that little girl. She turned her back on Crowley and ran to find her friend.

• • •

As it turned out, Reese had Rory in the air.

She could hear him through her link with Rory. He was shouting at her. Threatening her. "*You're making a mistake! They'll kill you if you don't join us!*"

"Oh, will they?" Quinn asked him, flying up next to him, snatching Rory back from him before he had the chance to stop her.

He glared at her. "Quinn. Annoying as ever, I see."

"I'd say I've thought a lot about you," she told him. "About what you did to me. All the lies you told me. But I haven't. I'm in love with your brother, and for the first time in my life, I'm happy. And really I haven't thought of you at all."

She could see the rage and envy in his eyes at her words, but he tried to hide it. "I'm glad you're happy, Quinn. In your final hour."

She laughed, genuinely unafraid. "How could you possibly think this is it? I could kill every last one of you right now with my bare hands."

"Right. But you won't. Which is why we'll win."

She floated closer to him, struggling not only with keeping up the flight but also with having to carry Rory. But the moment she thought it, she felt Rory feeding her more energy, keeping her strong.

"You're right about one thing," she told him. "I won't kill you. You wouldn't be worth the sweat... Not that I'd even have to break one. But we *will* win. Because as easy as it would be for me to kill you, it's even easier for me to do this."

For the second time in a matter of weeks, she punched him. It was harder this time—so hard, he didn't manage to stay airborne. She watched with a calm smile as he slammed back down to the earth. She watched Hank and Ridley tie him up and take him to the basement of the tower. The new prison.

• • •

When she touched back down, she tried to convince Rory to go back to the tower and stay hidden.

Of course, she failed.

"We don't have time to have this argument," Rory snapped at her. "Look behind me. Angel and Drax are fighting Shade and Tommy. They're going to lose. We have to help."

Quinn glanced behind Rory, raising her eyebrows when she realized the girl was right. Shade had abandoned his post at Crowley's side, probably after seeing that Quinn had steered clear of him. But Angel and Drax didn't seem to be holding up well against the illusions and invisibility.

"Try and get inside Shade's head," Quinn told Rory as they ran over to their friends. "Stop him from projecting those illusions. I'll worry about the rest."

But when she reached them, she realized someone else had gotten there first: Trent.

She stopped dead in her tracks when she saw him. He looked exactly the same on the outside—cool, calm, collected—and yet, there was something in his eyes, which looked straight over at her...

He looked unbelievably sad.

Well, she thought, *he should.*

And she slammed him to the ground.

It was strange, she thought as she did so, engaging him in the same sort of fight she had back then in class—the day she had kissed him. Strange that back then, the stakes had been so low, and here, today, they were everything.

But as she hit him, repeatedly, fiercely, she realized something: he wasn't hitting her back.

He's not fighting us, Rory told her in her head. Quinn stopped hitting him, body keeping him pinned to the ground, looking back over at Rory, whose expression was calm and collected.

He's protecting us, Rory told her.

Quinn stared down at Trent, eyes wide, confused. "Is that true?" she whispered to him, even though of course he had no idea what she was referring to.

Somehow, he nodded, anyway. Eyes sad, but honest. "I'm so sorry, Quinn. The moment I left, I wanted to come back. I just thought I'd be more useful this way."

She could hesitate. She could decide she didn't trust him, that she should knock him out, anyway, have the boys take him to the prison.

But she was tired of that. She was tired of not trusting people. With Trent back on her side, that meant no one she had truly cared about had betrayed her, after all.

She stood, reaching a hand out to help him to his feet.

But not in time.

Bang.

Invisible man. Visible gun. Visible bullet. Only one person had seen it coming: Drax. He dove in front of Angel so quickly, one might have thought he had borrowed Charlie's speed, if only for that instant.

The bullet hit him square in the chest. Angel's scream was loud enough to freeze every person on the island, if only for that instant.

"*I'll kill you!*" Angel screamed at Tommy, who of course she couldn't see, launching for the direction the shot had come from; the gun had already been dropped to the ground. Quinn stared from the fallen Drax to Angel and back, frozen. She wanted to go to her friend, to comfort him, to tell him everything was going to be okay, even if it wasn't—but it shouldn't be her. It should be Angel.

"Angel," Quinn said, reaching out to stop her. Angel writhed away from her, screaming profanities toward a Tommy that she still couldn't see. Tears streamed down her face. Quinn knew those tears well: they were tears of anger. In that moment, Angel wanted vengeance more than love.

It was a mistake Quinn had made that she wouldn't let Angel make, too.

"Angel," she said again. "Drax needs you. Let me take care of Tommy."

Angel turned to look at Quinn. Her soft, blue eyes looked bottomless in that moment—like a well of sadness that could swallow her up. It broke Quinn's heart. She knew how Angel felt all too well.

But Drax wasn't gone yet.

"He needs you," Quinn whispered.

Swallowing her pride and anger, Angel nodded and went to her fallen friend.

Quinn turned to face the direction the shot had come from, narrowing her eyebrows. She glanced over at Trent, who seemed to be waiting for her cue.

"Take care of Shade," she told him. "Don't worry about the illusions—he can't get you with Rory here. And, Trent?"

Trent waited, listening. She could tell Shade was listening, too. It was her intention.

"Don't hurt him, okay? I don't blame him. For any of this."

Trent nodded, making his way over to Shade with confidence and bravery, leaving Quinn to face her invisible nemesis.

She didn't have the power to see Tommy when he was invisible. But if she were able to reveal him some other way...

As if on cue, Haley appeared, sprinting over to them.

"I heard Angel's scream." Her eyes fell to Drax, and her hand flew to her mouth, instantly devastated. "Oh, my God."

"There's no time," Quinn said, grabbing her by the arm. "You're Earth powered. Do you think you could conjure up oil?"

"Yeah," she stammered, eyes still on Drax, "I think I could—but where?"

"Everywhere," Quinn said, not letting go of Haley's arm. "Everywhere you can't see someone."

It would have worked with just the oil; Quinn knew that. But in that moment, filled with rage and ferocity toward Tommy for what he had done to both Drax and Angel, she couldn't stop herself. She didn't want to kill him, but she wanted to hurt him—to punish him. So as Haley conjured the oil, Quinn conjured the flames.

Within seconds, she found him: the invisible man, up in flames. Screaming.

She pounced, not subduing the flames until she had him flat on the ground with his hands behind his back. Within seconds, Ridley and Hank were there with the cuffs, injecting him with enough liquid sedatives to tranquilize a small horse.

It still wasn't satisfying. It still wasn't enough. Drax was going to die, and Tommy wasn't going to pay for it, and that wasn't enough for Quinn.

But just as she had told Angel, she knew what had to matter more to her more than revenge: getting to say goodbye. So she turned away from the charred body being dragged away and made her way toward her friend.

Angel was a mess—not that Quinn could blame her. She was sobbing, begging him to hold on, to stay with her. Telling him he was the most important person in her life. The only person who had ever truly understood her.

"Don't be afraid," he said softly, reaching up to touch her cheek. "I'm going to go be with my family now, Angel. Yours is still here. I want you to promise me that you won't give up. Not until you find them again."

"You are my family," Angel whispered.

The tears were streaming down all of their cheeks now, Haley and Quinn included. Angel seemed to see in Drax's eyes that it wasn't enough, that he had to know that she was going to be okay—that she was going to find her real family when he left her.

"I promise," she choked out.

Drax smiled, taking Angel's hand and kissing it. Sensing that Angel had said all she could manage to say to him, Quinn knelt beside her, looking down at Drax, taking his other hand. She couldn't let him go without one last goodbye. "I'm sorry we let them get you."

"Ironic, isn't it? I can take a tree, but I'm still not bulletproof."

She tried to laugh, but it came out more of a sob.

"I don't regret it," he whispered to both of them. "Angel, I'd die for you a thousand times over. And Quinn... If not for you, I probably wouldn't have even been out here, fighting, risking my life for the people I love. It took me so long to realize that I was strong. But once you showed that to me... It changed my world."

"Yeah," she muttered, hating herself, "it got you killed."

"No. It saved Angel."

• • •

She wanted to be there with him until the end, to hold his hand and never let go. But Angel was there with him, and she knew that she had a more important mission: Crowley.

She had to kill him.

He was responsible for all of it. Drax's death. Tommy's betrayal. All the other deaths, all of this war...

She tried to focus on the plan as she made her way back to him. *Knock them out. Knock them unconscious, get them to Ridley and Hank, get them to the prison.*

But she couldn't focus on knocking people out. She couldn't focus on anything, really, except Cole Crowley and how much she wanted to kill him.

Dash wasn't far from her now. He was face-to-face with a few tough-looking monsters who were firing assault rifles at him. He was handling it surprisingly well. Still, he repeatedly glanced back at her, watching her approach Crowley and his people, knowing—*he must know*—what she had to do.

He didn't try to stop her.

"Tell me why," she said to Crowley when she reached him, giving his right-hand man, Shield, a nice, hard kick in the chest. She took pleasure in that kick. The man had been partially responsible for Kurt's death; he was lucky she didn't do what she really wanted to do to him. "Tell me why you did it."

"Did what?" Crowley asked with a smirk. "Killed Charlotte? Killed Kurt? Nuked the island?"

"All of it. What did any of us ever do to you, Crowley? Why hate us so much?"

"I wouldn't take it so personally. It's not personal. It's simple. You're all monsters. Monsters should be exterminated."

She glared at him, reaching out to grab him by throat. Instantly, a whole new wave of bullets and projectiles shot out at her, Crowley's army rushing to his defense. Shield jumped at her, hitting her, scratching her, yanking at her. But he couldn't stop her. Even if he could negate her physical abilities, it wouldn't matter. She was stronger than Crowley to begin with.

"Kurt wasn't a monster," she told Crowley. "Why should he deserve our fate?"

"You're right," Crowley hissed, voice barely escaping her chokehold. "He didn't deserve it. Had he chosen any other friend—any other partner—he would have lived."

It wasn't news to her. It was something she had thought about many times.

And yet, hearing it said out loud, it made her heart ache.

"It was your fault," he said. "Don't you know that?"

It wasn't entirely intentional, her grip tightening around his neck, snapping his bones, piercing his airways. Killing him instantly. It wasn't even a fully conscious decision.

But had she given herself the time to think about it, she wouldn't have done things differently.

At least, not until she saw who collapsed to her feet when she let them go, crumpled and limp—someone who wasn't Crowley at all.

Izzo.

14. LIE AFTER LIE

The battle continued on. The world kept spinning around her. One by one, every soldier and every deviant who had betrayed them was knocked out, tied up, and taken away. None of them were killed. Not a single person.

Except for Izzo.

Quinn stood there, staring down at the ruined body, for what felt like hours. She could hear Rory's voice in her head, telling her it wasn't her fault, telling her Izzo had to have known what she was getting herself into, that the girl had probably had some kind of death wish all along. She could hear Dash's voice out loud. He was trying to hold her. Comfort her. Tell her the same things Rory was telling her. Tell her things about Crowley that she already knew. How he was a coward. How he was twisted. How they would show the world that he hadn't even been man enough to come fight his own battle.

"Will we?" she whispered when he told her that. She looked over at him, tears in her eyes. "That's why he sent her, isn't it? To make me kill her. To show the world they couldn't trust me."

He sighed, taking her into an embrace so tight, she could feel the love radiating out of him—like he never wanted to let her go—like he wanted to protect her from everything that was happening.

But he couldn't. She had just committed her first murder.

• • •

"We edit it out of the video. We have no other choice."

It was later that evening. Quinn was still numb. If it was up to her, she would have stayed there, staring down at the dead body of the girl she had once made decorations with and attended class with, the girl she had killed with her bare hands. But they had taken the body away, and they had taken her to the dining hall, the damned dining hall where they always had to meet about something and talk about something, because it was never, ever over.

Evelyn was the one speaking, which was no surprise to Quinn.

"Time is of the essence. Whatever we release has to be quick. The entire world is looking to us, waiting to see what happened when our live stream went dark."

"The camera wasn't on Quinn and Crowley—er, Izzo—when it happened," Charlie pointed out. "I didn't record the actual... strangling. By the time I panned over to Quinn, Izzo was already down. It's clear that it's the girl who was posing to be Crowley. Maybe people assume she's just been knocked unconscious."

"The second half of the video," Michael reminded him, "will be panning through the prison, proving to everyone watching that the alliance survived—that we didn't kill them. What if someone out there is looking for Izzo? What if people ask questions and don't see her in the faces of the survivors? Do we really say that we killed no one, and then apologize later if someone finds out?"

"Her family is still alive," Pence said, frowning. "It's a long shot, them looking for her—they turned her in to the DCA, all those years ago—but there is a chance."

"We can't hide it," Quinn said. "We won't."

All eyes turned to her. She was surprised by the confusion in them; she thought the choice was obvious.

"We tell people that I went rogue," she said. "It's the only card we have over Crowley. He wants us to hide this. He knew I'd go rogue, I'd kill Izzo, he'd point it out, he'd demand to see her. When we weren't able to show her to the world, the world would decide that we were liars and couldn't be trusted. It was a brilliant plan, really. It can't come to fruition. We can't let it. We tell the full, honest story. I apologize, and I say I'm ready to face the consequences. We show me, down there, locked up."

Dash shook his head. "It wouldn't be painting a fair picture. You're not a murderer. Half of them already think you are. To tell them that you—"

"I *am* a murderer. That's what I did. I murdered someone. Someone I went to school with. Someone I ate lunch with. Someone who had a family, somewhere out there. And if it's all right with all of you, I'd like to fucking own up to it, okay?"

Dash fell silent. So did the others.

"Very well," Evelyn finally said. "Let's begin."

• • •

Close-up on: Haley.

Her eyes are sad. Her hair is unkempt. Her clothes are worn and frayed. She speaks with a heaviness she did not have in the previous video.

"It's me again. I'm here to explain what happened when the live feed cut off. Or should I say—when Cole Crowley's people had it cut off."

Wider two-shot on Haley and Rory.

Rory: "We could explain everything. But what's the point? We got it all on video. So instead, we'll show you."

Cue entire battle video sequence, starting with Quinn, Dash, and Crowley's conversation: "Ah, my two favorite monsters"—including, but not limited to, "We will win, and we will destroy the video, and that, as they say, will be that."

Quinn and Reese's fight. The fight between Tommy, Shade, Drax, and Angel. Countless other fights, ones Quinn hadn't even known were happening… And yet, other than Drax, no deaths from either side.

Not until the camera pans down to Izzo's body.

The camera doesn't linger long on it. Not long enough to know for sure. The camera pulls back out and records the final stretch of the battle. A dozen or so soldiers load back into their helicopters and fly away. The rest are dragged down to the prison. Evelyn and Michael take their place at the center of the battlefield and instruct everyone to make way to the dining hall.

The screen cuts to black for a moment. When we open again, we are back on Haley.

"In just a second, we will cut away from this and over to our prison, where my friend Charlie will walk through our entire prison basement and show you all

that everyone is alive. That we took no lives... except one."

Cut to: Quinn. Close-up. Locked in a jail cell. The camera is behind the bars.

"Hello again," Quinn says. "I know you must all have a lot of questions. Did I kill that girl? What happened to Cole Crowley? Didn't I swear that I didn't want to hurt anyone?

"The truth is, from the beginning, I wanted to hurt Cole Crowley. From the moment he killed my best friend, Kurt Rhodes—who, by the way, was not a deviant, and posed no threat to any of you—I had made it my mission to kill him. I told this to no one here on the island. They had no reason to think I should behave that way in battle. So, please, don't let my mistakes speak for the rest of them.

"That being said, Cole Crowley was the only one I wanted to hurt. The girl you see in the video—her name is Izzo Jones. She was a classmate of mine. I would have never killed her knowing that it was her. She was posing as Crowley—using her shapeshifting abilities to protect him. Despite our requests that he come meet with us and talk terms of peace, he didn't. He sent us an army and an imposter.

"I killed her. And I'm sorry for that. I will stay here, in this jail cell, on this island, for as long as you all think I deserve to. Maybe you will decide I should stay here forever. I wouldn't blame you. I don't think I belong there with you any more. But these people... They do belong there. And they should be welcome there. Even after having a nuke dropped on them, even after having bullets fired at them... Even when one of their own was killed... They haven't hurt anyone."

She falls silent for a moment, eyes cast downward. The camera lingers on her face. Her expression is hard to read. Dark. Solemn. Finally, she looks up at the camera one last time and says, "I'm so sorry."

And we cut to black.

Finally, we re-open on Haley and Rory. Their message is simple.

Haley: "We are not threatening the people in our prison. We won't kill them. We won't hurt them. We will give them back to you, no matter what you decide. Send us the helicopters, we'll load them up."

Rory: "But, when you do, send someone to reason with us. Not Crowley. Not an army. Someone who can actually help us—the way we keep trying to help you."

"This isn't a threat," Haley says again, and something in her eyes changes.

"Let's keep it that way."

. . .

Quinn didn't see the video. She didn't ask to, and she didn't want to. She didn't want to do anything except sit in that cell and hate herself.

She had been put in a cell down the hall from the others—the alliance and the Crowley soldiers—but she was still close enough to them that she could hear them jeering at her. Most of them called her names she had heard before—'death singer;' 'she-devil'—but some had worse taunts for her. She tried to block them all out. The only one that really got to her was the man who proudly told her was one of the men who had opened fire on Kurt. That one got to her. That one almost had her killing all over again.

But for the most part, she drowned it all out, sitting on the cold, stone floor, hating herself. The image of Izzo's cold, dead face lingering in her mind.

Dash came and checked on her. Told her it was absurd that she was forcing herself to stay down there with the alliance. Told her that no one blamed her for what she had done, not even out in the real world. That they all wanted her back.

"You said you'd only stay here if it was what they wanted," he urged her, eyes hopeful, full of love despite the horrible thing she had done. She didn't know why. She wouldn't blame him if he couldn't love her any more. "They don't want it, Quinn. 'Save the Siren' says you did what you had to do. They're all calling for Crowley's head, too."

She didn't care what 'Save the Siren' thought. They were an online movement full of people who considered themselves brave for having controversial opinions while hiding behind their computer screens. Just like the rest of the world.

"We need your help," he tried when he saw that his first argument wasn't working. "The video's everywhere, and the people are rising up, but the diplomats still aren't reaching out to us. Rory wants to try for another premonition. To see what we should do next. But she can't do it without you."

"I shouldn't be involved with the resistance any more," she told him, eyes cold, ashamed. "I shouldn't be allowed to."

"Quinn, this is a *war*. You did what you had to do. Can't you see that?"

"I didn't, though. I did what he wanted me to do."

And she turned away from him.

• • •

Another day or two went by. They wouldn't stop checking on her—not just Dash, but the others, too. They brought her the food she had always ordered the most, offered her blankets, pillows. She accepted none of it. She couldn't even think about food. She could barely make herself drink water.

Finally, on the evening of the second day, when Dash was summoned upstairs to help with the responses to the public's questions, someone new came downstairs—someone Quinn hadn't seen since the battle. Someone who looked almost as rough as she did.

Angel.

"You look terrible," Angel informed Quinn, taking a seat in front of her, inches on the other side of the bars from her.

"You, too." Quinn had intended for it to come out cold and distant, like everything else she had said as of late, but she caught an unintentional sort of dry humor in her own words.

Angel didn't miss it, but she didn't seem amused. "You're torturing Dash. As if you haven't hurt the poor guy enough already. All he wants to do is help you."

"You sure you want to convince me to come back?" Quinn snapped. "Maybe if I stay down here long enough, you could finally get who you've always wanted."

Angel chuckled, not seeming offended in the slightest. "Quinn, you could rot down here for thirty years and that man would still love you. You think I don't see it? All of us do. It's why I've hated you for so long."

Quinn said nothing. She already felt guilty enough; had Angel really come to make her feel worse?

"I'm not here because of him," Angel said, straightening. "Not really. I'm here because of Drax. Because of what he would say if he saw you here like this."

Quinn looked down, eyes dark, at the memory of her fallen friend. "Drax is dead," she said coldly.

"You think I don't know that? I know he's dead, you stupid little girl. I was *there.* And if not for you, I would have killed Tommy for it."

Quinn swallowed, starting to sense where Angel was going with this.

"And if I had—if I watched him kill my best friend, and then murdered him for it—would you have told me that I should lock myself away, torture myself, torture everyone who loved me?"

Quinn shook her head. "It's not the same."

"It's *exactly* the same. Look, Quinn, I'm not saying it's excusable. We weren't supposed to kill anyone. We're supposed to be better than them. But this is a *war.* I would have been justified in killing Tommy, just as you and Dash would have both been justified in killing Crowley. There was no way for anyone to know that was Izzo. No one even knew she had that ability. No one knew that *anyone* did."

Quinn sighed, tugging at her hair. She knew Angel was right. She knew Dash was right. She just wished they could understand why she deserved to be punished. All her life, she had hated men like Crowley for what they did to innocents like Kurt. As twisted as Izzo had become, Quinn had still thought of her as that naïve young girl she had met in class those many months ago. And she had killed her. She was no different than the men she had always hated.

Angel seemed to sense what Quinn was thinking. "Those men, Quinn—they kill for no reason. No reason but themselves. They aren't avenging anyone. They aren't carrying out any justice. You can't compare yourself to them."

Quinn remained silent, but the words hit her in the right places.

Angel rose to her feet, reaching into her bag and pulling out a keychain full of cell keys. She thumbed to the one for Quinn's cell, unlocking it without waiting to be told she could.

"Just come out," she told Quinn. "We've both done enough to hurt the people who love us. It's time to start making things better."

. . .

It was hard, stepping back out onto that island. She wasn't ready to go back to the dining hall, or the tower, or any of those old gathering spots. Not with all of those people knowing what she had done.

She made for the place on the island where she had always felt the most comfortable. The waterfall.

Of course, when she got there, he was there.

He looked up at her, eyes wide, surprised, and yet so completely elated, she couldn't help but smile. He jumped up, running over to her and grabbing her in the tightest embrace she'd ever felt.

She smiled to herself as she let him hold her, breathing in his perfect smell and thinking of nothing but how much he amazed her. Never had she felt so loved. Not by Kurt. Not by anyone.

"I'm sorry," she said softly as he pulled away from her, looking her right in the eyes. "I'm sorry I keep hurting you. You keep proving to me how good you are, and I just... I keep..."

"Stop," he said, reaching out to touch her face. The spark she felt on impact only reminded her of how good things were between the two of them—so much better than she deserved. "You're hurting *yourself,* and yes, that hurts me. But don't worry about me. You're here, and you're alive, and that's all that matters to me."

"It should matter. It should matter to you that I'm a killer. How can it not?"

He took a step away from her, gesturing to the river behind her, where they had once played that silly game of I Never. "Do you not remember? Do you not remember treading water with me and telling me that you wanted to kill a man? Do you not remember me saying that I did, too?"

She sighed. "I remember."

"Quinn, if it hadn't been you, it would have been me. Or Haley, or Ridley, or any number of the many other people that evil man has hurt along the way. None of us could have known it wasn't him. And none of us blame you."

She sighed, looking into those perfect eyes of his. A thought occurred to her as she scanned the bright, golden embers in his eyes: It didn't overpower her any more. The fear. The distrust. The hatred.

It wasn't that she was a different person now. Everything she had been through before she came to Siloh had shaped who she was, and that wasn't going anywhere.

But Siloh had shaped who she became from that point forward. And that was someone who had control over that fear, that distrust, that hatred.

Someone who could love.

"I love you," she said softly.

He smiled. "I know."

. . .

The next premonition was different than the others: it was completely unprovoked. It came to Quinn and Rory, simultaneously, in the middle of dinner. Quinn, who could only assume this was a sign of their abilities strengthening, didn't have time to linger on it; the premonition was a big one.

They were going to meet with the UNCODA at the United Nations headquarters in New York, she learned. In one week.

She let the bitter irony of that full-circle geographical journey sink in as she delved deeper into the vision, Rory by her side.

Crowley was there—that was the first thing she noticed. He was on the stand, speaking. His wrists were cuffed, but he looked clean, groomed—not like he had spent the last few weeks in prison, but rather, like the cuffs were all for show.

Savannah was seated on the stage behind him, also in cuffs, either next in line to speak or already having spoken. Haley and Ridley on the opposite side of the stage. Neither of them were cuffed, but judging from the heavily armed guards on either side of them, they had their own version of cuffs.

On one side of the auditorium were the leaders of the UNCODA—the United Nations Council of Deviant Affairs. The UN's most powerful division.

Quinn thought back to what he had said to her that day in his office. *"Kill you? Six years ago, I probably would have. But things are different now. Regulations, limitations. Your own country might be okay with me killing you, but the UNCODA would never let me hear the end of it."*

She knew better than to have much hope. They might be the only group powerful enough to keep Crowley's madness in check, but they had still assisted in the international capture of deviants for years, turning blind eyes to the conditions of the prison they knew as Devil's Island.

Not that that's such a bad thing, she reminded herself; if they *had* paid more attention, Siloh probably would have been turned into what Devil's Island was supposed to be all along.

On the other side of the room were the deviants. Not just one of them. Not just Charlie's parents, not just Rory, not just Dash. *All* of them.

They weren't handcuffed either, she noticed. Like Haley and Ridley, they were surrounded by armed guards; she could see the same glowing vials of sedatives that had knocked her out in Crowley's office. Still, thinking back to that day on the helicopter when she couldn't break free of her handcuffs even at full strength, she decided she preferred guards over handcuffs.

In the middle of the auditorium were the families. Another surprise, Quinn marveled, that civilians would be invited to a summit like this; then again, given the giant cameras in every corner of the room, Quinn assumed the entire movement had garnered so much pro-deviant press and distrust for the government, the public had insisted on the same live streaming that the deviants themselves had provided.

She wasn't sure how she knew, exactly, that they were family members. It wasn't as if her own father was in the crowd. It had something to do with her channeling Rory's feelings within the vision. She realized, as she watched two, young, brown-haired people that Rory was focusing on, that she had never asked Rory about her family. She had always assumed that the girl, who had been little more than an infant during the event, had lost her parents that night.

Rory recognized them, though. Quinn could tell. And from the elation Quinn could feel swirling around the girl's head, she was happy to see them.

Quinn tried to push away the strange, territorial feeling that was creeping its way in, focusing instead on Crowley's words. She knew that whatever he was going to say at this meeting was the key to this premonition.

"...lie, after lie, after lie," he was saying. "She manipulated me... She manipulated the people of Siloh... She manipulated her own *sons*."

Quinn realized, looking at the shocked and furious expression on Savannah's face, that he wasn't talking about Quinn, nor any of the deviants, but Savannah—his own partner. *This* was his strategy?

It was strangely brilliant; the resistance had garnered too much attention from the outside world, too much support. Savannah was already the bad guy in their story. If she was the bad guy in Crowley's, too...

"Nuclear warfare was never my intent. The peace the people of Siloh enjoyed for so long—the goodness, the good health—that was all my doing. You all entrusted me with keeping the world protected from these people, but I knew the only way to do so was to keep these people happy. Savannah was *supposed* to be my outlet for that. Little did I know, she was stirring up a movement of her own— creating an army of people she trusted—planning on taking over the world with them. Plotting to kill those who refused to follow her."

"But were *you* not the one, Mr. Crowley," asked the woman who was questioning him, a sharply-dressed, fast-talking woman with a British accent, "who came to us requesting permission to deploy the weapon? Were you not the one who deployed the weapon against our wishes after we denied your request?"

Everyone in the audience stirred at that one, even the men behind Crowley who Quinn inferred were FBI and US government. *This* was interesting, she thought. The UNCODA had told Crowley not to nuke the island... And he had somehow convinced the U.S. government to let him, anyway?

Wouldn't be the first time the States had gone against the wishes of the United Nations, she supposed. But things were different now. The UNCODA funded the majority of the DCA's expenses; the American government itself was nearly bankrupt. Why would they take such a risk? Was it possible they were in on it— that they wanted access to the deviant army Crowley was creating?

"I did press on," Crowley admitted, "for the sake of public safety. I was told when I was charged with the command of the Deviant Collection Agency that I was to use whatever means necessary to keep the people safe from these monsters. I believed that was what I was doing."

"A quick sidebar, if I may," the questioner said. "Could the director of the FBI, Mr. Mark Weber, please step forward?"

Crowley stepped to the side as another man stepped forward. From the look of him, he was just as slimy as Crowley himself.

"Mr. Weber," the questioner said. "Were you not aware, when Mr. Crowley came to you, that his request had already been denied by the UNCODA?"

"I was aware. But the affairs of deviants are Mr. Crowley's jurisdiction, not mine. When he came to me and told me that a coalition of deviants was planning on taking over the world, and that a nuclear attack was the only solution we had, I believed him. It was my mistake, director. But an understandable one, I think. How was I to know that the man we entrusted with deviant affairs would be so mistaken about the state of those affairs?"

"Perhaps," the questioner—*director,* Quinn corrected herself mentally; could this woman be the director of the UNCODA?—said bitterly, "in the case of nuclear warfare, we owe it to ourselves to do more than 'take someone's word for it.'"

Crowley forced his way back to the podium, eyes hungry, desperate. "Please, director. It's not his fault. It's not *mine.* These creatures are poisonous—they find ways to get into your mind and change the way you think. The woman I had entrusted to report the *truth* back to me, the woman who was to warn me if there was any risk of safety for the outside world—she manipulated me. She told me that there was a resistance forming that wanted to take over the world—and *that* was true—but she told me that those people were the ones she would leave behind. She promised me that those she was removing from the island—they were the good ones. The ones who didn't want to hurt anyone. They were the ones we would send back to the island, once the attack was over. The rest, she told me, we had to destroy. For the sake of public safety."

Quinn shook her head. Now Crowley was trying to convince them that Savannah had some kind of mind control over him?

"And you just... trusted her," the director said. "Staked the lives of hundreds on that trust."

"I had no choice. She made me fall in love with her."

Savannah looked like she was going to scream; everyone on Quinn's side of the audience looked like they were right there with her. But Crowley wasn't finished.

"I knew it would be hard for you all to believe. But none of you understand what it's like when one of them tries to get inside your head—when they force you to love them. I ask you to call upon the people who followed Savannah. The group that has come to be known as the alliance. Ask them. Ask them what she promised them. Ask them whether they intended to take over the world. Ask them whether or not I knew about it."

And there, Quinn realized, was the sick, incredible genius of it all. Crowley had taken the same group of people he had been able to manipulate before, through Savannah, and turned them against her. He knew they were weak. He knew he could control them.

He was going to get off the hook.

She wasn't going to let him.

• • •

They had a handful of other premonitions after that—shorter ones. Visions of Crowley walking out a free man, Savannah being imprisoned, the alliance being sent back into exile, the resistance being set free. It was something, she supposed as she watched her friends board airplanes and go on their ways. Their movement had still been enough to convince the world that they were no threat—the majority of them, at least.

But as she continued to watch, she realized that it wouldn't be enough for Crowley. He would keep using their weaknesses to his advantage. He would set them up. Mount them as threats again. Make the world fear them. Send them all back to Siloh, one by one. Turn it into a prison again.

It wasn't enough, she decided as she came out of the premonition. Their initial freedom wasn't enough.

They were going to have to stop Crowley.

• • •

"I never thought I'd say this, but I almost feel bad for my mother."

They were gathered in Dash's room, the same old group it had been so many weeks before—Haley, Ridley, Dash, Quinn, Trent, Pence, and Charlie—along with one new recruit—Angel. For the life of her, Quinn couldn't figure out why they hadn't been inviting her and Drax to these things all along. Both of them had more than proven themselves in that last battle—one with his own life.

She might still have a love-hate relationship with Angel, but she had come to admire her nonetheless.

"Here's the good news," Charlie said. "All of those people Crowley's planning on convincing to work for him again—they're in our basement right now. And he's not. He's going to talk to them somewhere between now and that meeting—which means we have the chance to get to them first."

Quinn grimaced. "I have nothing to say to those people. And as we already know, we can't trust them. What good would it do talking to them?"

"You could compel them," Angel suggested. "Make them say whatever we want at the summit. No matter how convincing Crowley is, they'd be forced to obey you."

"No," Quinn said, shaking her head. "It would be clear that they were being compelled. They wouldn't be fluent—wouldn't make sound and logical sense when they were called to the stands. My compulsion isn't that specific. I can't control every word they utter, days in advance."

"Besides the fact," Dash added pointedly, "that it would be wrong."

"Yeah," Quinn said, grinning slightly at him. "That, too."

Angel rolled her eyes. "Fine. What, then? We threaten them? Scare them? Seems to be the only thing that works with them, doesn't it?"

"Fear, yes," Trent said. "But we won't need to threaten anyone. We just need to bend the truth a little. They all know Quinn has premonitions, right? So, we tell them we've seen what Crowley will ask them to do—and where it lands them. And that aspect of it, we embellish a bit."

"Where *does* it land them?" Pence asked him. "In our version of the truth."

"Wherever we want. Maybe the people at the summit don't believe them, and they're imprisoned for lying. Maybe they're killed for treason. Maybe—"

"Crowley kills them anyway," Quinn interrupted. "Despite them doing exactly as he asked. It might not be what really happens, but it's happened before. Hell, it's what he's doing to Savannah now. Anyone with half a brain would believe it."

"What's our counter-offer?" Ridley asked the group. "Do as Crowley asks, get killed. Tell the truth, as we ask, and…?"

"What, 'live' isn't enough?" Angel asked sourly.

"We let them return to the island," Rory said. "Which is what happened in the vision, anyway, so it's probably bound to happen in real life. In both sides of the story, they were still the bad guys. And the leaders of the summit still let them return to the island. It may have been an exile, but it was better than an execution."

Quinn nodded. "It's the closest thing we can give them to an honest promise. But if they do return to the island—free—it's going to have to be different than it was. We're going to have to talk to them. *Really* talk to them. Make sure that they're not going to betray us again."

Ridley nodded. "We'll need to start off with security measures, if they're going to join us here. Guard shifts. Monitoring devices. We'll phase it out, of course… I think the majority of them are good people who just need people like Crowley and Savannah to leave them be. But we should still be careful."

"So, it's settled," Dash said. "Now, who volunteers to have this conversation with them?"

• • •

Quinn didn't want to go anywhere near the dungeons again. She didn't think she was the best person to convince these people to ignore Crowley. Without her compulsion, she had never been all that compelling.

But there was one person she wanted to speak to—one person she should never have given up on in the first place.

Shade.

Trent and Charlie came with her. They would speak to the others—Tommy, in particular, who neither Quinn nor Angel trusted themselves around. Trent, Quinn noticed, seemed to have overcome all of his fears and doubts since returning to Siloh; he was full of good ideas to help the cause.

Trent and Charlie were both in agreement not to let any members of the alliance out of their cells, but Quinn decided to break that rule. It didn't feel right, reasoning with Shade when he was behind bars. So she headed for his cell, key in hand, and unlocked it. Just like that.

He stared at the open cell door, eyes wide. Confused.

"I don't want you to leave," she said to him. "Not yet. I just want to show you that I'm not your enemy. That we need to talk."

Shade lifted a hand, pushing the door open carefully. He took one step, then another, until he was in the hallway with her.

"I know you're not my enemy," he finally said. "You told Trent not to hurt me."

She nodded. *Good choice, past Quinn.* "Do you want to go somewhere? The dining hall, maybe? Your old room?"

He shook his head. "I know that I deserve to be down here. Why don't you just tell me what you want to know?"

She bit her lip, thinking back on her own words to her friends when she had refused to leave that place. It was strange, how much she suddenly felt she had in common with Shade.

"There's going to be a summit," she told him. "Sort of like a trial. To see what happens to all of us. And before that summit, Crowley's going to try to tell you more lies. He's going to try to convince you to turn against Savannah."

"I know."

Her eyes widened. How could he possibly know that?

"I knew when you killed him," he explained, "and he turned into Izzo. Well, I guess I knew before that. Years and years. He did a lot of bad things. But Izzo was different. She was good... She was just lost. She was so scared. She came to him because she didn't want to die, and he killed her."

Quinn could barely keep up with him. She had never heard him speak so much at one time. Everything he was saying about Izzo made sense. But what did he mean by 'years and years?'

"Shade... how long have you been working for Crowley?"

"He found me after the event. He wanted children whose parents died in the event... he only found a few of us, and I was the strongest."

She watched him, frozen.

"He made me think that he loved me. For a year, I thought I was so lucky. My own parents never knew how to talk to me. I was sad that they were dead, but... Mr. Crowley was different. He made me feel like I was a part of something. Not a family but... something else. Something special.

"Then, when the resistance formed... He made me hate them. Told me that they were going to get everyone like me killed. And when he felt like I hated them enough, he sent me to them. Told me to join them, only... to report back to him."

Quinn could hardly believe it. Shade would have been the same age Quinn had been—ten, eleven at the most, at this point. She had never even considered joining the resistance back then; she had been struggling just to stay alive.

"Remember the woman that they called Blackout?" he asked her.

She nodded.

"It wasn't her that made the blackouts. She took me under her wing, you see. Always kept me close so that I wouldn't get hurt. It was me who caused the blackouts. They just assumed it was her."

Quinn's heart was starting to pound. She remembered Dash's words as he had thought back on Charlotte's nickname... *"I don't even remember her having those abilities."*

"Anyway," Shade said, "none of it matters now... It's just, I think I finally realized someone needs to stop him. And I think I can tell you how."

Quinn realized she was finally going to learn the truth—the truth that she and Dash had already suspected. The truth about Charlotte's death, and the destruction of the original resistance.

"We were in Canada. Hiding out. The UNCODA didn't exist yet, you see, and we were safer outside of America. All the deviants were doing it—not just us. While we were in Canada, Charlotte said she wanted to visit the U.S. embassy. She still wanted to talk to the Americans, you see. She wanted to talk peace. She said they wouldn't hurt her there. I told Crowley about her plan, and that was when he came up with his own: to kill everybody in and around the embassy. Make it look like she did it."

Quinn shuddered. It as she had suspected: Charlotte had been framed. But *why?* Why kill all those innocent people, just to get a few deviants?

"He was obsessed," he said, as if reading her mind. "I wasn't enough for him.

Shield wasn't enough for him. He wanted an army. He thought he could get that army by becoming the director of the DCA. He had killed the last director, framed it on a deviant. But it wasn't enough. They appointed an interim director and told him that they couldn't hire him because he was a CEO, not a government official. He didn't have the credentials. They said if he wanted it, he had to prove himself.

"He knew that the FBI wanted to get the rest of the world in on it. To force the UN to help fund and power the hunt. An international DCA. He knew the only way to do it was to make an international disaster happen."

"But even if it worked, he couldn't take the credit for something like that," she said, confused. "He'd be known as a mass murderer."

"That's why he pinned it on Charlotte. But he and his men were there in seconds. He knew that if he killed them all, after what they had just done, he'd be a hero. He also knew that something like the UNCODA would be formed. An establishment designed to help with the hunt—if only so that Americans would stop killing deviants on foreign soil."

"And it worked," she breathed, shaking her head. "They were satisfied... He was appointed."

Shade nodded. "And his identity was kept secret. The way they thought the previous director had been killed, they said the position was too unsafe to be released as public knowledge."

It all made sense. But how was she going to prove any of it?

"Even if you were willing to say all this on the stand," she said, "we'd have no way to prove it, would we? How do we get him?"

"That's just it. In order to make it look like deviants killed all those people, Crowley ordered a special chemical—a poisonous gas, designed by an old friend of his from his military days. A gas that didn't appear man-made."

"But this friend would never admit to anything, would he?"

Shade leaned forward. "I know how you feel about your compulsion, but in this case, it's the clear solution. All you have to do is make him tell the truth. When he describes how he made the poison, where he got the materials—it'll be clear that you couldn't possibly have put all that in his head. You would have had no way of knowing it. It will be clear that, compulsion or not, the weapon came from him."

• • •

Quinn shared Shade's story with the others as soon as she left the dungeon—first with Dash, in private, then with the entire resistance. It was hard, watching Dash's face as she described the intricacies of how Crowley had murdered his first love. But she knew that, in a way, it helped. It was confirmation, after all that time, that Charlotte had been framed—that she hadn't killed anyone. It also proved that her death wasn't Dash's fault, nor was it Savannah's; Crowley had learned of the embassy visit from Shade, not from Dash and Charlotte's letters.

Charlie and Pence were given the mission to find and capture Crowley's weapon-maker. Dash didn't like the idea of the capture any more than he liked the idea of Quinn compelling him, but he seemed to understand.

"I still wish we had more," said Ridley the next morning as they watched the helicopters roll in. "We dug up this dirt on Crowley from six years ago that, if they buy it, should be enough to convince them. But what if they don't buy it? Do we have proof of his crimes today?"

Quinn watched the helicopters, feeling hopeful despite Ridley's words. Everything had fallen into place. She, Charlie, and Trent had gotten to the members of the alliance in time; they would be flown off to Crowley, who would try to get to them, too. They would let him think he succeeded. But he would be wrong.

"They've already seen the proof," Dash reminded Ridley, his eyes also on the horizon. "It's all in the video."

"But we need proof that it wasn't all Savannah," Ridley said. "I mean, sure, we've got him on video saying things—things that, if he reached, could still align with the story he's planning on using. But we need a piece of evidence that proves the two of them conspired *together*—not to protect the world from some made-up threat, but to commit the mass murder of innocent people."

"That's why we talked to the alliance," Angel reminded him. "They're our proof."

"Crowley is a powerful man," Quinn admitted, starting to see Ridley's point. "With friends in very high places. The words of twenty deviants won't mean half as much as his own. Not to them. Ridley's right—more evidence couldn't hurt."

"It's not a bad idea," Angel agreed. "If we can swing it, provide one more piece of evidence that he was in on the attack, those friends in high places of his aren't going to want anything to do with him. Fear of association."

"What about that letter?" Dash asked Ridley. "The one with the battle plan. It was pretty heavily coded, but I'm sure there are experts who could read it better than we could."

"It's not a bad idea, but that letter could be anywhere. I sealed it back up after reading it and delivered it to Savannah, as I was supposed to."

"Well," Angel pointed out, "last time Savannah left Siloh, she was pretty damn sure the whole place was going to be decimated by a nuclear warhead. It's possible she left it behind, thinking she wouldn't have to worry about the cover-up."

"Worth a shot," Ridley agreed. "I'll check the town hall. Dash, why don't you check her living quarters? Quinn, maybe you try Reese's?"

Quinn grimaced at the thought. "Fine, but only so I can graffiti 'ass wipe' onto the wall of his bedroom."

Dash chuckled, kissing the top of her head. "Come on, grumpy. We've got work to do."

. . .

Those who hadn't been given assignments stayed to meet the helicopters and guide their passengers down to the dungeons, where they were to collect their soldiers. Quinn wanted to be involved, just in case something went wrong, but Rory pointed out that she should go along with the promise she had made in her video: that she would remain locked up until she was given permission by the public to leave.

Knowing that Rory was right, Quinn made her way back down to her cell, watching through the bars as the soldiers and the alliance were loaded up.

To Quinn's surprise, one of the new visitors approached her cell. It was the woman from her premonition, she realized—the director of the UNCODA.

"Miss Harper," the woman said as she strode over to her. She stuck a hand between the bars of her cell. "My name is Lauren Wilson. I'm the director of the

UNCODA."

Quinn shook the woman's hand cautiously, watching her with rapt attention.

"This cell," Lauren said, taken a step back to eye Quinn's cage. "It's a bit of a formality, isn't it? Why don't we go ahead and let you out of here?"

And with that, she surfaced a key—one Quinn imagined Dash or Ridley had given her.

"Wait," Quinn said, hesitating. "I don't… I don't want to be let out unless it's what the people want."

"Well," Lauren said, looking amused, "short of holding a worldwide election over the issue, I can assure you that the people seem to be on your side, Miss Harper. And as the international director of deviant affairs, I grant you my permission."

Quinn sighed, gesturing for the woman to unlock the cell. She supposed that was about all she could ask for.

"I'm not here to apologize for anything," Lauren informed Quinn; "not yet, at least. I have a feeling that, within good time, plenty of apologies will be made on your behalf."

Quinn waited.

"All I came to tell you is that you, along with everyone on this island, are invited to a summit that will determine your fate—and the fate of the man you have so publicly led a campaign against."

Quinn nodded. Crowley.

Lauren offered her a tiny smile. "But you already knew that, didn't you?"

• • •

It was bizarre for Quinn, seeing Reese's bedroom. She had never been before, and would certainly never go there again. It was nothing like Dash's. It was nothing like she would have expected, either.

Which, frankly, shouldn't have surprised her. He had never been what she thought he was; that much was obvious.

It was almost like Crowley's office had been—monochromatic, lifeless—but everything was black instead of white. It wasn't rich and grand like she was sure Savannah's room must be; it was a little smaller than Dash's room, with simple, dark, linoleum floors. Thick, black curtains covered the windows, as if he were blocking out the sun for a daytime nap. *Strange,* the thought; for a man whose ability had been flight, she would have thought he wouldn't mind the sun.

What was it about Reese? Why was he so hateful? So manipulative? Savannah, she could understand, in a way. Savannah was a regular—one whose sons were both turned into what she believed were monsters. Savannah had been faced with the same choice so many other parents had: turn in her children to the DCA, or find an alternative. In a way, her alternative had been much less cruel; it was the aftermath of that alternative that had driven her to cruelty.

But Reese... She shuddered, remembering what Dash had told her about how Reese had treated Ridley once he became a monster. And she knew how much Reese must hate Dash, to do everything he had done to both of them. Where did his hatred stem from, she wondered? It must be a self-loathing—a loathing of all deviants. That must have been how he had told himself he could get away with such cruelties. *They're just monsters. Just like me.*

She sighed as she began to tear apart his room.

She didn't think the letter would be in his room—not really. Sure, it was possible he'd have seen the letter, or even delivered it to her, but why would he hold on to it? They would have either burned it or taken it with them. Still, she had agreed to check, so here she was.

She found nothing for a long time. Nothing in the desk; nothing under the mattress; nothing anywhere she herself would have hidden something.

But it's not you who hid it, she reminded herself. As she had learned, she and Reese thought nothing alike.

She tried to focus herself on Reese's mindset—where she would hide something if she were him.

She glanced up at the ceiling. High ceilings.

She launched up into the air, scanning the walls, the surfaces of the higher dressers and cabinets. Nothing. She had just about given up when she saw it: the air vent in the corner of the room.

It should have been easy for her break into, that vent. The fact that it was almost difficult made her even more confident that this was his hiding place.

When she finally got it open, she saw a letter. It wasn't the one they had been looking for, but it would get the job done all the same—if not better.

Reese,

You have had plenty of time to find your seer. Your collection of deviants for the alliance thus far is disappointing, to say the least. With the Siren there now, and your brother's influence on her overshadowing your own, we are running out of time. I have sent Savannah the plan. I leave you with one month to gather the final members of the alliance, and I suggest you keep the Siren and any members of the resistance in check until then. You had better be right that she isn't a seer.
Cole

• • •

"It proves everything," Dash said, reading over it. They were all together again—not just the small group that Quinn trusted, but the entirety of the resistance. They were having their final meeting, discussing not only the evidence that Quinn had found, but also the plan for the summit, which they had all been invited to. Even Quinn the murderer.

"Did we know they were looking for a seer all that time?" Pence asked, taking the letter from Dash and scanning the words. She and Charlie had returned just before Quinn found the letter, Crowley's weapon-maker in tow. "Is that the only reason we weren't all killed sooner?"

It wasn't exactly news to Quinn, who had understood from early on how much Savannah wanted a seer. Still, if it was really the only thing that had kept them all alive for as long as they had been, it surprised her, too.

Not to mention, apparently her existence on the island had only made him want to drop the nuke faster.

"We have proof that the plan of attack came from Cole, and that it was sent to Savannah," Evelyn said. "We have proof that Cole knew the difference between the resistance and the alliance—that he wasn't being conveniently led to believe the opposite."

"And we have proof that Reese was a key player," Quinn added cheerfully. "However much time Savannah and Crowley get, let's make sure Reese gets some, too."

Dash tried to hide his grin as Evelyn rolled her eyes.

"This summit is about discovering the truth, and revealing that truth to the people," Evelyn scolded Quinn. "No one is going to be sentenced to jail time at the summit. How the United States chooses to punish Cole Crowley is up to them."

"Right," Quinn said, unable to resist, "but if we get our way, how Reese and Savannah are punished *won't* be up to them. Right? Maybe it'll be up to us."

Evelyn sighed, clearly not interested in arguing the topic.

"I think we have everything we need," Michael told them all. "Good work, everyone. Now it's all in the hands of the most important people in the world."

"Right," Quinn whispered to Dash. "We're screwed."

15. THE SUMMIT

It was just as it had looked in the vision. Just as huge; just as packed. Just as many cameras. She was greeted by everything from summit ushers to crazed fans with signs reading how much they loved her. Cameras were everywhere. If everything went according to plan, even if the UNCODA didn't grant them every freedom they asked for, even if they didn't lock Crowley away, the world would still know.

It wouldn't be enough, but it would be something.

Quinn held Dash's hand as they walked, mainly because she knew she would need support when she saw what she hadn't yet warned him about: Rory's family.

Rory, of course, had her other hand. But the moment she saw them, she let go.

Dash glanced over at Rory, confused, as the girl broke away from the single-file line they were walking in and ran into the audience. Security guards perked up, watching her closely with narrowed eyebrows. But Rory was already famous by then; no one was going to hurt her without good reason.

Sure enough, Rory stopped right in front of them—the two people Quinn had seen in their vision. Rory's parents. And she said, in that sweet little voice that had slowly captured Quinn's heart over her time on the island, "Hi. I'm Rory."

The tears in her parents' eyes, the elation and joy at finally seeing their daughter again after all that time, brought tears to Quinn's own eyes. And when she looked up at Dash and saw the sympathy in his expression, she knew that she wasn't just crying tears of joy.

"It's a good thing," he whispered to her, wrapping his arm around her shoulders and kissing the side of her forehead. He gently coaxed her into walking again as they made their way to their seats. She kept the seat next to her open, knowing that Rory would be expected to sit with the rest of the resistance, if only for that one last time.

"I know," she whispered back, eyes still on the girl, who was being embraced by her parents in hugs and kisses. "For her."

Dash said nothing, squeezing her hand and focusing toward the front of the auditorium as Savannah, Crowley, Haley, and Ridley took their places on stage.

A few minutes passed. Rory left her parents, running over to Dash and Quinn with big, wide, excited eyes. She jumped up into the chair next to Quinn, taking her other hand.

"They're perfect," she whispered to Quinn. "They're even better than I remembered."

Quinn smiled in spite of her thick throat and heavy heart. "It's obvious how much they love you," she told the girl, squeezing her hand. "I'm so happy for you."

Dash squeezed her other hand. Lauren Wilson stepped onto the stage, and everyone in the great auditorium fell silent.

"We are all gathered here today," Lauren said, "to hear the testimonies of the parties involved in the events that occurred on the island formerly known as Devil's Island—now known as Siloh—where the deviants of the New York Event were sent into exile following their collection."

Boo's and jeers erupted from the audience, the same human rights activists that had been on their side for weeks now. People who had a problem with phrases like 'collected' when it came to human beings. *If you could call us that,* Quinn thought grimly.

"Our witnesses today are seated behind me from left to right in the following order: Cole Crowley, C.E.O. of Crowley Enterprises and director of the Deviant Collection Agency; Savannah Collins, officially titled Assistant Director of the Deviant Collection Agency, unofficially titled the 'President' of Siloh'—until recently—and finally, Haley Mylar and Ridley Jeffries, the deviants chosen by the movement known as 'the resistance' to represent them in their plea for Siloh's world recognition as a sovereign state—one that is protected by the UNCODA."

Quinn raised her eyebrows. Quite a mouthful.

"The official statement of the UNCODA is as such: Six years ago, directly following the deviant terrorist attack in Ottawa, the Federal Bureau of Investigation—an American bureau—declared Cole Crowley president of the Deviant Collection Agency. He was charged with the responsibility of all matters related to the safety and security of civilians known as 'regulars' in relation to the deviant community. Simultaneously, the UNCODA was formed. We agreed to assist the United States in the collection of any deviants who had fled the United States, and to help fund their efforts to do so domestically. It was our belief that it was a necessary measure to keep the rest of the world safe from what we considered their mistake. In exchange for our help, we required, in no uncertain terms, that the DCA were not to kill any more deviants—that all deviants were to be exiled to the facility known as Devil's Island.

"When Mr. Crowley came to us for permission to deploy a nuclear warhead into Devil's Island, his request was denied. He tried to convince us, insisting that a group of lethal individuals there was plotting to, in his words, 'take over the world,' and that a nuclear strike was the only option he had. He claimed that he would safely remove all deviants not involved in said plot before unleashing the weapon. Despite all of this, I reiterate to all who are listening: his request was denied."

Lauren paused, letting her words sink in to the millions of people watching.

"With what we assume was approval from the United States government," Lauren continued, "the strike commenced. Upon the release of several videos recorded by those left on the island who survived the attack, we learned that the issue was more complicated than Mr. Crowley had let on. We requested a meeting with him immediately. Our request was ignored. Within days, the second attack on Siloh occurred."

Quinn was almost starting to like Lauren, despite the fact that she had been the one in charge of collecting deviants around the world for six years. Almost.

Savannah was the first to be called to the stand. Quinn wondered why her and Rory's premonition had jumped ahead of this speech, but she wasn't concerned. Their premonitions had proved themselves by now. It was probably just because Savannah wasn't going to say anything worth worrying about ahead of time.

Interestingly, though Savannah didn't say anything that caused the resistance's movement any trouble, she did bring a few new things to the table.

"I am finished lying," Savannah said to the world, "and I am finished working with men like Mr. Crowley. I know that I made a terrible mistake. Nothing I did is forgivable, and I accept whatever punishment I am given. I would just like to explain my side of things from the beginning... To tell you all what kind of man you have entrusted with a huge budget, a small army, and—at least in the case of the Americans—permission to kill.

"I knew Mr. Crowley before the event. I was his lawyer. I could get into all of the scandals he was involved in back then, all of the terrible things he had me do for him, but I won't. Even now, not having practiced law in a decade, I am bound to the same attorney-client privilege I was back then. Honor is important to me... I doubt many of you believe me, but it is.

"When the event occurred, both of my sons were affected, along with my younger son's girlfriend and our neighborhood friend, Ridley, who is sitting behind me at this very moment."

Ridley gave a strange, awkward wave; Quinn tried not to giggle. She could tell from Dash's stiffness next to her that he was in no mood to laugh. He wanted to hear this story. He wanted to hear how it had all began.

"Initially, I didn't understand what it all meant. I knew that one of my sons—Dash—was visibly affected. I knew that he had become incredibly beautiful... So beautiful, I feared for him. I knew that Ridley had been visibly affected, too, in a different way. I feared for him, too. But I didn't understand, yet, what the world would turn them into. To me, they were the same children they had been before the event. The same children I was responsible for.

"But then, rather quickly, the name 'deviant' came along, and the word was like poison, and everyone who looked different or who made something happen that wasn't supposed to happen was swept off into the prisons, and everyone else was so afraid, they didn't fight back. And the resistance began, and the thought of my children dying for the cause scared me even more than the thought of my children being arrested. I wanted to protect them. So I came to Mr. Crowley. He had more money than anyone else I knew. He had ties high up in the government, even then. I knew that if anyone could help me, he could.

"He smiled at me, and he told me that he was glad I had come to him. He told me that he had already bought an island—one so far on the outskirts of the world, the horrors happening in our country couldn't touch it. He told me that he was already reaching out to his friends—many of whom are in this room today—telling them about his island, that he would offer it up, for free, to be a different kind of prison—one that could actually hold these people—one that could keep them far away. It wouldn't really be a prison, of course. He knew that, and I knew that. If we're being honest, I think everyone knew that. But as far as you all were concerned, out of sight, out of mind. None of you wanted anything to do with the deviants, and here was a man offering to pay for a solution."

So far, her story pretty much lined up with the stories Dash had told her. Still, she could sense that more was coming—more details—details that, she only hoped, would incriminate Crowley farther.

"His friends agreed, and I agreed, and I moved there willingly with my sons and Ridley. My son's girlfriend refused to join us. She didn't trust Crowley... She was smart. Not long after we moved there, I began to realize how hard it was going to be. There were a few abandoned buildings there, places for us to sleep, and we had come with enough food and supplies for a while... but not forever. I reached out to Mr. Crowley and asked him what his plan was. How were we going to eat? How were we going to live? Had he thought any of this through?

"He told me that I had two options. I could continue to live in an isolated paradise. He would continue to send me 'recruits,' and we would find the means to take care of ourselves on our own. Catch fish, he told me. Pick fruits. Cross your fingers and hope for the best.

"Option two, he would appoint me the assistant director of the DCA and the unofficial 'president' of Siloh. He would ship me any goods I might need, even send me teachers and workers to train the deviants on the island to build and grow and work. In exchange, I was to turn the inhabitants of the island into an army. A group of people who would fight for him when the time came. A group of tamed, obedient soldiers. Preferably, a group that contained a seer."

Murmurs erupted in the room, but Dash remained completely silent. His eyes were riveted to his mother. He had not heard this story before. Quinn hadn't, either. She couldn't imagine what must be running through his mind at that moment.

"It wasn't that simple, of course. I knew that immediately. My younger son, Dash, was still in contact with his girlfriend back on the mainland. She was quickly becoming the leader of the entire resistance—you all would know her as Blackout. I knew I could never convince Dash to work for a man like Mr. Crowley. So I didn't even try.

"I counter-offered Mr. Crowley. I knew we were all going to starve if I did nothing. I knew I would be giving not only my sons, but so many others, a life not worth living. I knew I had to give him something. So I told him that I would select the best army I could for him. I told him I would pinpoint the weak ones, the desperate ones, the ones who lacked the morality and character that people like Dash had. And I did. I began to form the alliance. Not long after, my son began to form the island's own resistance."

From Dash, not a word. Not a blink. Quinn was pretty sure he wasn't breathing.

"It took years, but the more I got to know what kind of man Mr. Crowley truly was, the more I realized what he was inevitably going to do with everyone who didn't join the alliance. I knew he would kill them. I knew he wouldn't think twice about it. I tried to think of ways around it. I tried to think of things I could do. I could get Reese out—the son I knew would be obedient—and I could get the alliance out. And what could I do for Dash? I could pray for him. Or... I could do something I hadn't done in a very long time.

"You see, I wasn't visibly affected in the event, but I was affected. I kept it a secret from Mr. Crowley. I kept it a secret from everyone. I knew that it would be a thousand times easier for me to protect my sons if the world thought I was a regular. And of all the abilities I could have had, mine was the easiest to hide. It wasn't a physical power, you see."

Quinn stared at her in awe, heart nearly stopping.

Savannah was a seer.

"I had only seen the future a handful of times. I hadn't practiced. I had virtually ignored the ability altogether. I had no idea whether my plan would work or not. But I couldn't get the resistance out, which meant I had one alternative: I had to help them survive the attack. I assumed that their seer was Quinn Harper, though I

301

had never been able to prove it—I think a part of me had always tried not to. I knew what Mr. Crowley would do to her if he knew. The same thing he would do to me. So, I closed my eyes and focused on nothing but sending Quinn that premonition— the premonition I kept having—the premonition of the nuclear attack."

Dash finally looked over at her, eyes wide, confused. "She's lying," he whispered. "She must be lying."

"It didn't work at first," Savannah continued. "Quinn didn't fully accept herself as a seer yet. When I finally got into her head enough to dig, I realized that the child—Rory—was a seer, too. They were most powerful when they joined forces. I focused on sending the premonition to both of them. For several days, I could still only get flashes across to them. Quinn was trying too hard to protect Rory. It wasn't until the final hour that she finally gave in and let Rory see what I was trying to show them."

Quinn's mind raced as she watched Savannah. Everything the woman was saying was so spot-on, it was hard not to believe her. She squinted, searching the woman for any signs of the psychic connection that she and Rory shared. Was it possible she would be able to telepathically communicate with Savannah, too?

And there it was. The words continued to escape Savannah's lips, but different words poured into Quinn and Rory's heads. Words projected right at them.

I don't ask for your forgiveness, she told them. *I just want Dash to be happy.*

"It's true," she whispered to Dash, a tear running down her cheek again, this time a truly happy tear. After all this time, after Dash had thought his mother had abandoned him altogether, she had saved his life.

"If you recall," Savannah pointed out, "I was nowhere near the second attack. I did everything I could to warn Mr. Crowley not to attack. But I also knew, even then, that the resistance would win. Not because I foresaw it, but because I knew them. I had seen them fight. None of us are a match for them, you see. We should consider ourselves lucky they *don't* want to take over the world. We would lose."

She cleared her throat, considering saying more. Her final words were limited.

"I think that is all. Just know that I am sorry. And to my sons… Know that I love you both. Whatever happens."

Utter silence as she took her seat. No applause. Nothing.

Crowley rose without being invited to the stand. Quinn could see nothing but rage on his face. He was a ruined man. Maybe they hadn't even needed to do all of the extra digging, she reckoned. Maybe Savannah's story had been enough all along.

His speech was more or less the same. He came in with a booming laugh, telling them all that Savannah was a crazy liar, that she was not a deviant, that she was simply a master manipulator. He told them that he had agreed to get her the goods and the teachers from the beginning, that he had been in love with her from the beginning, that the only reason the alliance existed was because she planned on taking over the world with them. Unbeknownst to him.

It was nothing they weren't prepared for.

"I knew it would be hard for you all to believe," Crowley said, just as he had in the premonition. "I'm a smart man when it comes to everything but love. So, I ask you to call upon the people who followed Savannah. Ask them. Ask them what she promised them. Ask them whether they intended to take over the world. Ask them whether or not I knew about it."

One by one, each member of the alliance was called to the stand. One by one, they each denied Crowley's story. Quinn didn't feel great about the lie Charlie and Trent had told them—that Crowley would kill them all when he got away—but considering they had all left their friends to die in a nuclear attack, she refused to let herself feel too guilty.

Reese, she noticed, was nowhere to be found. Not that Charlie and Trent had even tried convincing him. Of all the members of the alliance, he was without a doubt the most far gone.

Shade was the last to speak against Crowley, and he did what Quinn had counted on him to do: after denying Crowley's story, he introduced his own.

The story of Charlotte's death.

He told it slowly, but emphatically—the same way he had told it to her. He wasn't careful with his words, wasn't sensitive to the pain or shock that he would be inflicting on so many people in the room. But it didn't matter. He didn't need to be.

When he was finished telling his story, over the scoffs and shouts of an infuriated Crowley, Shade asked the weapon-maker to come forward.

Quinn scanned the audience, eyebrows narrowed. She had compelled the man just before they traveled to the summit, then again just after they had landed. *You are to ride with us to the summit and act like our guest,* she had told him. *When Shade calls you to the stand, you are to tell the truth—the whole truth—nothing but the truth—about the weapon you made for Cole Crowley.*

And he did.

It wasn't obvious, by any means, that he had been compelled. For all anyone in that room knew, he was just a little different—not unlike Shade.

Crowley, of course, jumped to the podium the moment the man was finished speaking.

"She's compelled him! Can't you see it in his eyes? Can't you remember what the Siren is capable of? She's compelled him to say—"

Haley rose, eyes calm, expression certain. She stepped up to the podium without being asked, and began to speak.

"If I may," she said, not waiting for permission. She addressed Lauren directly. "Director, even if Quinn were able to compel such a specific action out of this man, she wouldn't be able to make up a story like this. She wouldn't know how to build a weapon like this—what materials he should say that he had purchased. This knowledge is coming from him because he experienced it. He made this weapon. For Crowley. He is speaking the truth."

"Lies," Crowley shouted; "all lies!"

Ridley stood at this point, walking up to join them at the stand. "We had a feeling it wouldn't be enough. That you'd need time to research the story—to speak amongst yourselves—come to a certain conclusion."

Haley smiled calmly, surfacing something from her pocket: the letter.

Crowley froze.

"Mr. Crowley," Lauren said. "Please take your seat. Miss Mylar, Mr. Jeffries, please continue."

For a moment, Crowley didn't move. He stood there, petrified, unwilling to let his enemies divulge any more of his secrets. But then the security officers rose, hands moving toward their weapons, and seeing that, he left the stand.

"This is a letter," Haley said to the audience, "that we found stowed away in an air vent near the ceiling of Reese Collins'—that is, Savannah's older son's—room."

And Haley read them all the letter.

When she was finished, Crowley went right back to the buffoonish laughing and yelling. He demanded that it was a forged letter, that anybody could forge a letter, that it wasn't even his handwriting. Lauren kicked him off the stage again at that point, calling to the stand a secretary of the UNCODA who had personally handled documents involving Crowley's handwriting and signature. The secretary affirmed that both were his.

• • •

A recess was called, at which point both Savannah and Crowley were put into handcuffs and escorted away from the stage. Most of the room emptied out into the lobby of the building, eager to stretch their legs and discuss the chain of events that was unfolding. Lauren and the UNCODA officials disappeared to a private conference room. Rory ran off to see her parents again, as did several others in their section, Pence included. But not Quinn and Dash. They stayed there, glued to their chairs, both dazed.

"You're sure?" Dash asked her. "Sure that she's telling the truth?"

"I don't know, Dash," she admitted, stress bubbling to the surface at the sheer thought of what he must be going through. "I'm sure she's a seer. I could hear her voice in my head as she was giving that speech. Rory could, too. But whether she put that premonition in our heads to save us?" She sighed. "What she said lined up with what I went through with Rory. Once we had the first premonition, I think we were able to have the second on our own... Then, the one of the summit, it came out of nowhere. I'm tempted to say she sent us that one, too. To stop Crowley."

"Her story... It made sense, didn't it? In a strange sort of way."

"It did. I think it made sense to all of them, too." She gestured to the mostly-empty auditorium. "That's why Crowley was so afraid."

"Do you think they'll let her off the hook?"

Quinn considered this. Savannah may have been manipulated into doing most of the things she had done, but she had still done them. She could have said no—could have found alternatives. Could have warned someone in the real world that an entire island was going to be attacked for the wrong reasons. Besides, there had never been any guarantee that, even with the premonition, they would live. They had all been uncertain; she must have, too.

"I don't know," she finally said. "As much as I hate to say this, Dash, I don't forgive her. It helps, and I'm happy that you know she still loves you. But she could have done more. And I think they might know that, too."

He nodded, putting his head in his hands, clearly exhausted. "I know. But it does help."

. . .

The recess lasted over two hours. When the UNCODA officials re-emerged from the private conference room, everyone in the lobby was called back to the auditorium, and Lauren took the stand again.

"I want to be clear: the island we have come to know as Siloh does not belong to the UNCODA. It belongs to Cole Crowley, and falls under the jurisdiction of the United States government. Therefore, it is not within the power of the UNCODA to grant Siloh independent sovereignty."

A murmur broke out amongst the audience. Quinn stared up at Dash, eyes wide. It made sense, what Lauren was saying. Still… what was the point of all this, if that was the case?

"As for the crimes that Mr. Crowley and Ms. Collins committed," Lauren continued, "along with the group of both deviants and regulars that we have come to know as the 'alliance…' It is not within our power to sentence them for their crimes."

This was rapidly becoming the most frustrating speech Quinn had ever heard.

"However, we are an international organization, and these are international crimes. And for reasons I feel confident that the entire world will understand, we are unwilling to continue to sit idly by as these atrocities continue to be committed."

Quinn took Dash's hand, breath held.

"So now," Lauren said, turning toward the men behind her, and then back to face the cameras, "I address the United States of America. And I suggest you listen closely. I have here a document that we at the UNCODA have been sitting on for some time. It is, in most honest terms, a threat. A threat to you."

Quinn watched in amazement as Lauren surfaced a thick, professionally bound document, holding it up for the audience to see.

"Signed by the leaders of 37 countries across six continents, this document assures you that, if you do not agree to the terms laid out for you by these nations, the financial assistance we have all been lending you for the past ten years—the assistance that has kept you afloat during the worst economic depression your country has ever faced—will no longer be offered. In fact, 21 of the 37 countries even specify that, should the United States not comply, they will cease *all* trade with the United States."

Quinn glanced over at Crowley and Weber, who both looked terrified. She wondered whether the United States had sent any other representatives; clearly the rest of the world had.

Sure enough, a new person rose from the stage side of the podium. Quinn didn't recognize the man, which didn't mean much.

"I've got to brush up on my American political figures," Dash whispered to her, "but I think that's the Secretary of State."

The man made his way to the podium, expression serious and—in Quinn's opinion—quite boring.

"Director Wilson," he said. "I'm afraid that the necessary representatives to make such decisions on behalf of the United States are not with us in this room today."

"Oh, I'm well aware, Mr. Davis." She glanced pointedly around the room, gesturing to the hundreds of representatives from around the world. "Interesting, isn't it? Presidents, prime ministers, chancellors, from around the world—all here to discuss an American-originated conflict. And barely any Americans."

The man said nothing.

"We will have to trust you, Secretary Davis, to relay our terms to your

307

officials. You, and these cameras."

And without further ado, Lauren rattled off the UNCODA's terms.

"First, the United States is to incarcerate Cole Crowley—without bail—and try him for his crimes against his country and the world. No less than five representatives of the UNCODA are to attend this trial. Should a verdict be reached that those representatives feel does not properly reflect the findings of the trial, the case will be taken to the International Court of Justice, and the United States will waive all sentencing rights.

"Second, the United States is to exercise eminent domain upon Mr. Crowley and purchase from him the island known as Siloh. The United States will then, with the full support of the United Nations, grant independent sovereignty to Siloh, relinquishing all jurisdiction over them.

"Finally, regarding Savannah Collins and the deviant members of the group known as 'the alliance,' it is the view of the UNCODA that their sentencing should fall into the hands of Siloh, rather than the United States government, once Siloh is granted its sovereignty."

Quinn glanced over at Dash. His expression was hard to read, but she had a feeling he liked that stipulation. She had to admit, it felt a lot better imagining the alliance's punishment being in her friends' hands than in men like Crowley and Weber's.

"And now I ask," Lauren said, turning to glance back at Haley and Ridley, "before we send Secretary Davis back to the United States officials with his terms: is there anything the people of Siloh would like me to add or alter?"

Haley and Ridley glanced at each other. Quinn could tell from Haley's expression that there was something she wanted to add. Ridley nodded encouragingly at Haley, who carefully rose and made her way to the podium.

"Thank you, Director. We… we would like the DCA to be disbanded, leaving the universal authority over deviant affairs to the UNCODA. We'd like to put a deviant in the council, as well. Two, if possible."

Lauren smiled. "Very well. Secretary Davis, added to the terms: no more Deviant Collection Agency. And as for my fellow UNCODA councilmen and women… Please meet Haley Mylar and Ridley Jeffries. They'll be joining us."

16. SIREN'S SONG

A year had passed since the summit, and much had changed on the island. It was a sovereign state, for one, with no remaining ties to the United States. For another, the wall was gone.

But there was a third change, Quinn thought to herself as she stared down at Drax's headstone. One that, to her, mattered more than any of that. It was the loss of her friends. Drax... and Rory.

Rory wasn't dead, of course. Quite the opposite, as a matter of fact. She had come back to the island briefly, as they all had, to wait and see what would happen. But it hadn't taken long for the United States to agree to every term the UNCODA had laid out for them. They were humiliated—ruined. They wanted nothing more to do with deviants for a very long time.

Once Siloh was granted its independence and Crowley was sentenced to life without parole, Rory had gone straight home—back to her parents. She had said her goodbyes to Quinn, loaded up the helicopter, and never looked back.

She had thanked Quinn, of course, for all she had done for her. Her parents had thanked Quinn, too. They seemed like stand-up people. Veterinarians; animal lovers. Owned their own practice. It should have helped, but it didn't.

She had thought, watching that sweet girl step onto that helicopter, that she would hear from her constantly. She had thought that their mental connection was so strong, the thousands of miles between them wouldn't matter. She had thought she could never truly lose Rory.

But here she was, months later, and she hadn't heard that eager little voice in her head even once.

Pence and Charlie were gone, too. They had left quickly to go see Pence's family. They had received offers to stay and work in the new hurricane that was Siloh's government. Their help would certainly have been valuable. But they were both done with politics for a while, Pence explained. They were ready to just live.

Haley and Ridley were, more or less, the leaders now; Haley had been elected President of Siloh, and Ridley Vice President. It was a lot to juggle, on top of their positions as councilmen at the UNCODA, which had been renamed the UCDPM—the United Council for Deviant Protection and Monitoring. It was hard for them, from what Quinn could tell, being in charge of monitoring their own people as much as they were in charge of protecting them. But it was necessary. One slip-up—one crime committed, even a set-up—all of this freedom could disappear in an instant. Quinn knew it as well as the rest of them. They had their freedom, but they had to be careful.

As for Charlie's parents, they were still involved. They stayed on the island. Evelyn expanded the hospital, preparing for the flood of journalists and travelers that would be coming in once the island got on its feet. Michael was appointed by Haley as the island's Secretary of Commerce, using his influence and experience in the real world to help them build a new, self-sustaining economy based on more than just 'allowances' and 'wages' from government-assigned jobs. He also helped set up systems and programs to train deviants to expand their skill sets—almost like college.

And then there was Quinn and Dash. They had talked about leaving. Having the option to do so was certainly a welcome change. But it was the same as it ever was for them—nothing and no one to go back to. And, as hard as it was for her to admit, Quinn had come to love Siloh. It was the one place since her mother's little trailer in New Jersey that she had ever called home—the place she had learned to love and trust. So they stayed, and Haley encouraged Dash to keep his old job in power tech, and for Quinn to join him.

"We fired Rory's old teacher," Haley had explained to Quinn with a grin. "You know—the one who never let them actually use their abilities? And then went and joined the alliance? We're in need of a replacement."

Quinn had accepted, on the condition that no one was forced to take power tech—nor were they forced to attend classes. *No more forcing anything,* Haley had promised her. *Never again.*

And there she sat, staring down at Drax's headstone, telling him about her life. Telling him that she missed him. Telling him that she missed Rory. Telling him that she never knew happiness could be so sad.

"I don't think it's happiness that's sad," Angel said from behind her, startling her so much she jumped. "I think it's just life."

Quinn shifted slightly to her left, leaving an open spot for Angel to come kneel beside her. Quinn and Angel had encountered each other several times at Drax's grave. Angel was probably the only person who spent more time there than Quinn.

Angel set a white rose down on his headstone, balancing it on top of the dozens of white roses she had left before it. She was nothing if not consistent.

"You promised him, Angel," Quinn said, looking into the eyes of the girl who had never quite been her friend, but had nevertheless earned her respect. "You promised him you would go see your family."

Angel looked down at the headstone, wings swaying slightly with the wind. This wasn't the first time they had had this conversation. Quinn already knew she wasn't going to get much of a response.

"Did you know my name's not really Angel?" Angel asked her, turning to face her again. "I mean—I'm sure you must know that. What are the chances my parents would name the infant version of me after the monstrosity I would become eight years later?"

"You're no monstrosity," Quinn told her friend, staring at her thick, feathery wings in awe. "I don't think I've ever seen anything as beautiful as your wings."

"Beautiful, sure," Angel said, waving a hand. "But a monstrosity, still. I'm sure you could understand that."

Quinn did understand—she always had. A pretty monster was still a monster.

"What was your name?" she asked Angel. "Before."

"It was Jennifer. Jenny, for short. God, I hated that name. So common. So normal. Exactly the way my parents wanted me to be. Imagine their disappointment when I became who I am now."

"But your parents didn't ship you away," Quinn said, hugging her legs to her chest. "Did they?"

"No; not really. They tried to protect me as best they could. Which wasn't very well. When the DCA came and took me away…" She shook her head. "It was relief I saw in their eyes. I know it was."

Quinn wanted to say that she knew it wasn't true. She wanted to say that she was sure Angel's parents had loved her, that they must not have felt that way. But after all the cruelty and all the heartlessness she had seen in the world, she knew better than to assume any such thing again.

"Did you and Drax change your names together?" Quinn asked. "At the same time?"

Angel nodded. "He was here first, but he went by his real name for that time. Stuart. Can you believe that?" She laughed a strange, crazed sort of laugh. "Stuart."

Quinn *could* believe that; Drax had told her, once before. But Angel wasn't looking for an answer. She wasn't looking for anything.

"When I met him, and he asked me what my name was, I said, 'Jenny. But I'm working on a better one.' And he said, 'I'm Stuart. And I've got one for you if you've got one for me.' Maybe that's why both of our new names are a little silly, you know, a little obvious. But I wouldn't trade it for anything now. I wouldn't go back to being Jenny. Not when he gave me Angel." She turned back to the headstone. "That's why I can't leave. I have to stay his Angel."

. . .

The days passed slowly now, and in a way, Quinn enjoyed it. Her life had always moved so quickly; now that it was a good one, a peaceful one, she didn't mind it slowing down.

She was in the river, taking an afternoon swim, when Dash came to her with the news. His eyes were bright, excited—more excited than she had seen them in months. Just as her heart ached for Rory, she knew his had been ached for his mother, who had locked herself in the dungeons upon being sent to Siloh. It wasn't even that he *missed* her, Quinn had discerned. It was more that he wanted to know the truth, and Savannah hadn't spoken to him since giving that speech to the world.

"The helicopters are landing," Dash shouted to her as he ran over to her, reaching his hands into the water to help pull her out. "It's Trent. He found some."

The 'some' he was referring to were recruits—new recruits. Shortly after the summit, Ridley had pointed out to Haley and the others that there was now a chance that new deviants might reveal themselves—deviants who had always been afraid to reveal themselves before. Most of them had doubted that there was anyone left, but Trent had fought for the opportunity to go off in search of them. He said that he couldn't think of a better way to redeem himself than by helping those who lived in fear come and find safety in Siloh.

Quinn let Dash pull her out of the water, shaking the water off and pulling on some dry clothes before following him over toward the town hall. Haley and Ridley were both there when they arrived, hands held, looking up at the helicopters with as much wonder on their faces as on Dash's.

"There's three of them," Haley told Quinn, smiling from ear to ear. "Three helicopters… Fifteen new recruits. Trent found all of them. Reached out to these refugee camps in Canada, France, and England. Found them hiding out there. Convinced them to give Siloh a chance."

"*Fifteen*?" Quinn asked in utter disbelief. "In less than a year? How many do you think are still out there?"

"Dozens," Ridley said, "if not more. Hundreds, even. We never knew, officially, how many were affected in the event. There was no written record. We just assumed from the dwindling of the recruits that we had gotten all of them."

Haley smiled over at Quinn. "Just think. All the people you and Dash will get to help. People who never had the opportunity to embrace their abilities until now."

The helicopters landed. Trent was the first to step out, followed by five terrified-looking recruits. To her amazement, two were monsters—*visibly affected,* she caught herself. How was that even possible? How had they shielded themselves for so long?

Trent proceeded with the introductions as the helicopters took back off. Quinn shook the recruits' hands, sizing them up as she did so. The oldest was a frail, sweet-looking man who had to be at least in his seventies; the youngest was a boy no older than eleven.

313

Haley began her speech at that point, promising them that they would be safe at Siloh, that their freedom would be protected, that they never had to feel like outsiders again. Watching their faces as Haley spoke brought tears to Quinn's eyes. Trent saw this, smiled slightly, and leaned down to whisper in her ear.

"She's incredible, isn't she? Worst mistake I ever made was not loving her back when I had the chance."

"Yeah," Quinn whispered back, grinning slightly. "That, and going for me."

Trent laughed good-naturedly before stepping back over to the group. Quinn glanced over at Dash, who had been approached by one of the new recruits. The recruit was asking Dash about Savannah.

"It was so strange," the man was saying, "the story she gave at that summit. We all watched it together and wondered whether it was true, or whether she was just lying to save her own skin."

"Yeah," Dash said, so quietly she could tell he was trying to make sure she didn't hear him, so grimly she could tell his heart hurt with the answer. "I wonder the same thing every day."

. . .

It wasn't easy for Quinn, going back down into those dungeons. As far as she was concerned, she still belonged down there herself. She had been forgiven far too easily for what she had done to Izzo. Sometimes she still thought of locking herself back up.

It was different with the DCA and the alliance gone. No one jeered at her when she stepped down into the basement. No one said a word. In fact, Savannah didn't even look up until Quinn sat down right in front of her, right across the bars, the same as Angel had when Quinn locked herself up.

"Hello, Quinn. Nice of you to visit me."

Savannah had always looked so proper, so put together. Down here, face free of makeup, hair a tangled mess, she looked like a different person. In a strange way, Quinn thought she looked better. Not as beautiful, perhaps, but certainly more real.

Without saying a word, Quinn reached into her pocket, pulled out the key to

Savannah's jail cell, and unlocked it. She cracked open the door, remaining seated.

"Kind of you to rescue me," Savannah said in a lightly sarcastic tone, "but I'm sure you know that I'm not going anywhere."

Quinn stared at her, just as confused by Savannah's true intentions as she had once been by both Dash and Reese's. "He's confused. How could you not know that? How could you not want to help him understand? If your story was true?"

Savannah smiled sadly. "Quinn, I lied to my son his entire life. I did terrible things both for him and for myself. I was no hero. What I said may have been true, but I could never help him understand the things I've done. No one could. There's no justification for them."

"Even if there's not, you could at least tell him that you love him."

"And I will, one day. Once I've paid my penance down here. Once I've proven to him that I'm capable of more than just the words."

Quinn sighed, running a hand through her hair. In a way, everything Savannah was saying made sense to her. After all, it wasn't long ago that she had been in the same position as Savannah, with Angel on the other side of the bars.

But understanding how Savannah felt didn't help Dash.

"No one's seen Reese in months," Quinn said, deciding to change the subject. "He wasn't at the summit. He hasn't come back to Siloh."

"I know. I helped him escape. Before the summit."

Quinn groaned, disgusted all over again. "He's such a coward. You both are."

"I know that. I've always known it. You see, Quinn, you can't choose your children. You can only choose to protect them. I always knew that Dash would be okay. He was so much stronger than either of us. And that left Reese. And it left me doing what I had to do."

Quinn shook her head. "You didn't have to do the things you did. I can't accept that."

"Wouldn't you have done the same? For Rory? If it came to that?"

It was such an impossible question to ask. Rory was *good;* she was nothing but good; Quinn would have never had to do anything to protect her from her own demons. But she did see Savannah's point. She would have stopped at nothing to protect Rory; how was Savannah's situation any different?

"I would do anything for Rory," Quinn told her. "And if you'd do the same for Dash, all it takes is one simple thing. Go to him."

• • •

As it turned out, Savannah *did* go to Dash. Quinn wasn't there for the conversation; in fact, she was utterly shocked when Dash told her that it had happened.

"Do you think she was telling the truth?" Quinn asked him. "Do you believe her?"

He swallowed, considering his words carefully. "I think I do. I don't know that it's enough. It helps—really, it does. But the story I told you, about her and the landlord—all the new stories, about the things she did for Crowley, whether they were out of fear or not—they're still there. They're still her."

Quinn nodded. "She's weak. You always knew that. We both did. I guess the thing I'm just starting to understand is that there's a certain weakness that comes with parenting—a weakness when it comes to caring for your own children. A weakness that's almost a strength in and of itself."

He gazed at her in that way that only he ever had—that way that she loved to see him look at her—like she was the only person like her in the world, the only person for him. "Thank you," he said softly. "Not just for your words… but for going to her. She told me it was you that convinced her to see me."

She smiled softly. "It hasn't been easy for either of us. Me without Rory, you without Savannah. I figured at least one of our situations was resolvable."

"I wish I could bring you Rory. I wish I could do more for you. But we know she's happy, and we know she loves you. There is one thing I can do for you, though. If you'll let me."

She cocked her head to the side, curious.

"Follow me."

As they began to walk, she thought he was leading her to the waterfall. They went deep into the island, past the buildings, new and old. But they didn't go all the way to the waterfall. Instead, they took a turn she had never taken before: toward the horse stable.

She glanced over at Dash, confused, as he led her toward one of the fenced-in paddocks. Inside of the paddock, galloping from fence to fence, was a horse she had never seen before. It was a jet-black beast, utterly breathtaking. From the moment she saw it, she couldn't take her eyes off it.

Standing along the fence line were two people Quinn didn't recognize. Cowboys, from the looks of them. One was tall, middle-aged, with a plaid shirt, a cowboy hat, and a belt with a big, bronze buckle. The other was a boy—his son, most likely. The age of Rory... the big, blue eyes and soft, blond hair of Kurt. Just looking at the boy hurt her heart.

"Mr. Crowe," Dash said to the man, extending a hand. "Thank you for coming. Travel safely?"

"*We* sure did," the man said with a chuckle, shaking Dash's hand. He had a thick accent Quinn couldn't quite place. "*Her*, on the other hand..."

All eyes went back to the horse, who was still galloping as fiercely and wildly as ever. Quinn couldn't imagine trying to ship a beast like that. They probably had to sedate her. *Just like me,* she thought.

"Quinn," Dash said, turning back to look at her. "This is John Crowe. And this is his son, John Jr. They have a horse farm in New Zealand where they breed and train horses for the racing circuit."

Quinn looked from John to John Jr., clueless as to where this was going.

"This horse," Dash continued, "is a filly—a young female. She's just two years old. She was fast—one of the fastest John had—but they couldn't control her. " He grinned slightly. "She didn't want to be tamed."

Quinn was starting to put it all together, but she still could barely believe her ears. Dash had bought her a horse?

"It was this or the glue factory," John told her, voice regretful but pragmatic. It was his career; she understood that. He had to make a living. "We always try to find 'em homes, but it's hard. She's a lucky one. Most of the duds aren't so fortunate."

So, he hadn't *bought* her a horse, though she was sure the travel bill hadn't been cheap. Still, he'd rescued one, which was even more shocking to her. It wasn't that she didn't appreciate it; she did. But where was this coming from? Was this filly supposed to be some kind of replacement in her heart for Rory?

"What on Earth made you think of doing this?" she asked Dash, shaking her head. "Of all things?"

"I think it was her name that got him," John told her, smiling a charming, Southern gentleman sort of smile.

"Her name?"

"Siren's Song."

Quinn felt the tears pricking at her eyes. She used to be so good at holding back tears. Her entire life. Now it felt like every day was a thunderstorm.

It was just so *kind,* so incredible, that she had someone in her life who loved her so much, he would do this for her. It didn't even make sense. It was a crazy idea. But he had heard the horse's name, he had heard the situation, he had known how lonely Quinn was—he had just *known.*

He had been right.

"You guys weren't afraid to come here?" she asked John and John Jr., wiping a tear from her cheek and reaching out to hold Dash's hand. He squeezed hers tightly. "To come to Siloh?"

"You kidding?" John asked. He put a hand on his son's shoulder. "Junior, you tell her."

The boy smiled shyly up at Quinn, and those blue eyes killed her, but she forced herself to smile back at him. "I begged Daddy to let me come here," he told her. "All of my friends wanna come, too."

"Haley's been working on the paperwork," Dash told Quinn. "The logistics. But there's thousands of people trying to come and see this place. Some want to offer us their support. Some want to see us in action. Some just want to see the unbelievable story for themselves."

She had known that Siloh had been preparing for civilian visits. She had known that the photographers, videographers, newscasters, and journalists would be upon them soon. Maybe the adventurers—the daredevils. But this? Families; children? It blew her mind that they weren't afraid. They didn't think of it as an island full of monsters. At least, not dangerous ones.

"Well, we've got some cleaning up to do," John told them, "and then I believe a Mr. Trent Taylor was going to show us around the island before we take our leave. It was a pleasure meeting both of you, though. You're a mighty fine couple."

He tipped his hat to both of them, and John Jr. did the same, leaving Quinn to stare up at Dash in awe.

"I don't know anything about horses," she told him, shaking her head.

"You didn't know anything about kids, either. And you did a beautiful job with the one that found her way to you."

· · ·

She didn't have any interest in riding the filly. She didn't have any interest in keeping her locked up. In fact, when Dash headed back inside and she stared out at the crazed creature, she made up her mind to open the gate entirely.

She might not be a horse trainer, but she understood what it was like to be treated the way that horse had been treated. And she knew all that horse really wanted was to be free.

So, she opened the gate and let her run free. She wouldn't go far; she couldn't. The wall might be gone, but the ocean still surrounded them. No one on the island would dare hurt something belonging to Quinn or Dash; they all had far too much respect for both of them.

Whatever work Quinn did with that horse, whatever trust she built with her, it wasn't going to be done in a cage. It couldn't.

As the filly dove past her, out of the paddock and into the woods of the island, Quinn reached out ever so slightly. Just to touch her. Just for a second.

As her fingertips touched the thick, black fur of the creature, all of her thoughts were of Rory. Of the hole in her heart that she wasn't sure she could ever fill.

And that was when she heard her. For the first time in months. For the first time in far, far too long.

It's a good thing my parents are vets, Rory said in Quinn's head. *She ever gets sick, I think we could find some time in our schedule to come help.*

It was so good to hear Rory's voice, so overwhelmingly perfect, that Quinn actually fell to her knees. She clutched her chest, sure something was about to fly

319

out of it.

Rory.

I know. It's been too long. I think about you all the time, Quinn. But I think for us to talk to each other, when we're this far away, we have to be thinking about each other at the same time. In the same moment.

Quinn wondered whether that was true. She doubted it. She felt like she spent just about every second thinking about Rory.

I feel the same way. But neither of us does. Not really. We get to live life now. We get to be real people for the first time.

Quinn wanted to say more. She wanted to tell the girl how much she missed her. She wanted to ask her whether her parents were good to her, whether they were deserving. She wanted to ask about school, and friends, and anything and everything.

But she didn't get the chance. Because for the first time in months, she was having a premonition.

• • •

It was Angel.

She was in a dorm room, by the looks of it. She had shared the room with Izzo once, if Quinn recalled properly, which meant she'd had it to herself for quite some time.

She was staring at herself in the full-length mirror. Her eyes were sad—sadder than Quinn had ever seen them. They were full of self-loathing—of hatred—but more than anything, of that sadness.

There was something in her hand. Quinn squinted, trying to make out what is was. Reminding herself that her premonitions were lucid, she took a few steps forward.

And that was when she saw it.

It was a knife.

Quinn screamed for her to stop when Angel took the knife to her wings, but Angel couldn't hear her. *It's just a premonition,* Rory assured her, *it's not real, not yet—*

But she couldn't stop screaming. Not as the bright, scarlet blood trickled its way down those pure, white feathers. Not as Angel's perfect wings fell to the floor.

• • •

She sprinted to the dormitories faster than she'd ever run before, probably faster than even Charlie could run. She heard Rory's voice in her head, promising her everything was going to be okay, saying all sorts of things, and as glorious as it was to hear her sweet friend's voice in her head again, she tuned it all out. All she could see was that blood on those wings.

"Angel!" she screamed as she sprinted up the stairs. Doors along the dorm hallway opened. Faces popped out. Confused faces. Some she recognized, some she didn't. She ignored all of them.

Finally, she made it to Angel's room. She tried the knob; it was locked; she turned it past the lock so sharply, it tore the door apart. She kicked through the remnants of the door, tripping her way into the room.

Angel looked up, into the mirror, into Quinn's reflection. The same eyes Quinn had seen in the vision. The same blood on the knife... the same blood on the wings.

But the wings hadn't fell to the ground yet. She hadn't finished.

Quinn ripped the knife from Angel's hand, took the girl into her arms, and carried her over to the hospital.

• • •

Between Evelyn's skills in the medical field and Rita's ability to intellectually tackle the unfamiliar, they were able to save both of Angel's wings. There was no guarantee that they would work as well as they once had, Evelyn explained, and there would be a long period of rehabilitation before Angel would get to use them again. But she felt confident that they would still work.

They had put Angel under heavy sedation to perform the surgery, but Quinn sat at her side for hours as the sedatives wore off. As she sat, more and more people came to join her. Haley came, and Trent, and Ridley. Dash came as soon as he heard, demanding to know why Quinn hadn't told him sooner. But he wasn't mad. Not really. Not as much as he was proud.

When Angel's eyes finally opened, the first emotion Quinn recognized was confusion. Confusion as to why so many people were in her hospital room.

But she didn't mention that confusion. Instead she met Quinn's eyes and said softly, "I had to fulfill my promise. I couldn't lie to Drax."

Quinn shook her head, anger bubbling to the surface, not anger toward Angel but anger toward Angel's parents. Anger toward the world that made Angel think she had to mutilate herself to fit into it.

"I refuse to accept it," she told Angel. "I knew Drax. Not as well as you, but I knew him. I refuse to accept that he would have wanted to you to go back to your parents—not if he knew who they really were. Not if he knew what they would want you to do to yourself."

"He didn't know. I was always hopeful with him. He made me hopeful. Not like you. You remind me who they really are."

Quinn cast her eyes downward at that, hurt but not surprised. She could feel Dash's eyes on her, full of the pity that she hated so much. She may have become a more hopeful person since coming to Siloh, but she had never been delusional. She had encountered hundreds of people like Angel's parents during her time on the run. She knew the type well.

"I'm sorry I pushed you to see them," Quinn said. "If I had known... Look, it doesn't matter, Angel. Just forget about them. Think about Drax. He wouldn't want you to do this... you must know that."

"I know that. But he's dead, Quinn. He was my family, and he's dead. I only have one family left, and they're only my family if I do this."

"They're not your only family. *We're* your family."

Angel laughed a thick, dry, sad laugh. Quinn knew what that meant. Even if they were her family, they were nothing compared to Drax.

"Angel," Quinn said, stubborn, insistent. "We're not Drax. We don't love you the same way he loved you, and you don't love us the same way you loved him.

But we still love you. Even when we *hate* you we love you. Any one of us would fight for you. Any one of us would give our lives for you. And whether you'd admit it or not, I know you feel the same way about us."

• • •

Angel decided to stay. She wasn't happy about it. She wasn't happy about much of anything those days. But she took Drax's old job at the front desk of the dormitories, and she snapped snarky responses every time a new, doe-eyed recruit asked her questions, and she smiled out of the corner of her eye at Quinn every time she walked by. And she flew again. And that was as close to happy as Quinn could ask her to be.

Quinn and Rory made the mutual decision to focus their thoughts on each other at the same time every day, no matter what they were doing, no matter who they were with. They would only talk for five minutes. One day, they would visit each other. For now, a daily conversation would be enough.

Quinn and Dash were content. They weren't as fiery and passionate as they had once been. She wasn't as intent on revenge and rebellion; he wasn't as intent on judgment and caution. People around them came and went, and the two of them stayed where they knew they would remain content. Siloh.

One day, as the two of them took a swim by their waterfall, Quinn decided that maybe she could handle just a little bit more. Maybe it was time for her to reach out and take the options she finally had. Maybe it was time for her to see the world the way it was meant to be seen for the very first time.

"So, I hear you have this really badass ability," she told him, wrapping her arms around his neck and curling her legs around his back, light as a feather in the water. "Something about teleportation?"

He grinned, placing his own hands around her waist and spinning her around him ever so slightly. "I'm a little rough around the edges, but I could certainly use the practice. I think the better question is—where would you have us go?"

It was the same question he had asked her in his bedroom, so long ago. Before they had learned all of each other's truths; before they had fought all of each other's battles. Before they had braved the storms together.

Back then, the answer had been nowhere. Back then, the answer had torn them apart.

She leaned forward, inches from his face, smile in her eyes, smile on her face. Behind him, off in the distance, she saw Siren's Song playing in the river. Content.

She kissed him. It was light, it was simple, but it was strong. It was who she was now.

"Anywhere."

94588788R00198

Made in the USA
Columbia, SC
26 April 2018